Praise for the *Henrietta and Inspector Howard* series

A Promise Given

"Cox's eye for historical detail remains sharp... A pleasant, escapist diversion."

—*Kirkus Reviews*

"Fans of Henrietta and Inspector Howard will delight in Michelle Cox's latest novel. Romantic and atmospheric, *A Promise Given* offers an intriguing glimpse into 1930s Chicago, by weaving in authentic period details and exploring the social tensions of the day. The unlikely pairing of the Howards—two characters from very different worlds—provides a tender love story."

—Susanna Calkins, award-winning author of
the Lucy Campion Historical Mysteries

"The mix of sleuthing and aristocratic life pairs well with Rhys Bowen's Royal Spyness series."

—*Booklist*

"*A Promise Given* is a well-told story which had me immersed and wanting more. Well done!"

—Windy City Reviews

A Ring of Truth:

"An engaging and effective romp rich with historical details."

—*Kirkus Reviews*

"There's a lot to love about the bloodhound couple at the center of this cozy mystery."

—*Foreword Reviews*

"Set in the 1930s, this romantic mystery combines the teetering elegance of *Downton Abbey* and the staid traditions of *Pride and Prejudice* with a bit of spunk and determination that suggest Jacqueline Winspear's Maisie Dobbs."

—*Booklist*

"The second book of this mystery series is laced with fiery romance so delicious every reader will struggle to put it down. If you devoured *Pride and Prejudice*, this love story will get your heart beating just as fast."

—*Redbook*, "20 Books By Women You Must Read This Spring"

"Henrietta and Inspector Howard make a charming odd couple in A Ring of Truth, mixing mystery and romance in a fizzy 1930s cocktail."

—Hallie Ephron, *New York Times* best-selling author of *Night Night, Sleep Tight*

A Girl Like You:

"Michelle Cox masterfully recreates 1930s Chicago, bringing to life its diverse neighborhoods and eclectic residents, as well as its seedy side. Henrietta and Inspector Howard are the best pair of sleuths I've come across in ages—Cox makes us care not just about the case, but about her characters. A fantastic start to what is sure to be a long-running series."

—Tasha Alexander, *New York Times* best-selling author of *The Adventuress*

"Fans of spunky, historical heroines will love Henrietta Von Harmon."

—*Booklist* starred review

"Flavored with 1930s slang and fashion, this first volume in what one hopes will be a long series is absorbing. Henrietta and Clive are a sexy, endearing, and downright fun pair of sleuths. Readers will not see the final twist coming."

—*Library Journal* starred review

A Promise
Given

A Promise Given

A HENRIETTA AND INSPECTOR HOWARD NOVEL

BOOK 3

MICHELLE COX

SHE WRITES PRESS

Published 2018
Printed in the United States of America
ISBN: 978-1-63152-373-1 pbk
ISBN: 978-1-63152-374-8 ebk
Library of Congress Control Number: 2017955637

For information, address:
She Writes Press
1563 Solano Ave #546
Berkeley, CA 94707

She Writes Press is a division of SparkPoint Studio, LLC.

To my parents, Walter and Susan Bonnet.
Yours may not have been the perfect marriage, but it
taught me much about unconditional love.

Chapter 1

Henrietta paused to look at the photograph in the cheap, gilded frame one more time. It was a picture of Helen Schuyler and her husband, Neils, and their baby daughter, Daphne, taken what must have been years ago. Even as Henrietta sat staring at the people in the photograph, it was still hard for her to believe that they were all tragically gone now. Gingerly she ran her finger along the frame, an overwhelming sadness coming over her once again at the realization that nothing more remained of this little family except the few possessions among which she currently sat.

Helen, the Howards' elderly, retired cook, had died in the hospital, never having recovered from Jack Fletcher's brutal attack nearly three months ago, and the cottage had stood empty over the summer until Henrietta had recently volunteered to clean it out. Mrs. Howard had initially declared Henrietta's odd proposal to be out of the question, that the servants would do it eventually, but Henrietta had practically begged, saying that she needed an occupation separate from the wedding plans and that, anyway, she wanted to. Henrietta had never said it out loud, and she knew that it wasn't really true, but she could not help feeling at times that she was somehow responsible for what had happened to Helen.

Despite Henrietta's pleading, Mrs. Howard had sniffed at her suggestion, saying that Henrietta had precious little free time for anything *but* to attend to the wedding plans, still slightly irritated by Henrietta and Clive's decision to marry quickly. In the end, however, after a quiet word in private from Clive, she had acquiesced. Henrietta had eagerly set about her new task, then, earlier this week, but even now, on Friday, she was still not finished. The problem was not that there were so very many items to be sorted, but rather that she was perpetually getting distracted. It was unlike her, but then again, she had a lot on her mind.

Henrietta shook herself and, looking at the photograph once again, hesitated before having to put it into either the box set aside for rubbish to be burned by Mr. McCreanney, or into one of the other boxes of items slated to be given to Sacred Heart's collection for the poor. Neither seemed an appropriate choice, so after a few more moments of deliberation, Henrietta resolutely slipped the small frame into the pocket of her apron. It was the least she could do for poor Helen to honor not only *her* memory but that of the daughter to whom she had been so delusionally devoted, despite the fact that Daphne herself had died over twenty years before. Henrietta wasn't sure what she was going to do with the photograph, but she would think of something.

She sighed as she opened another drawer of the dresser in the tiny bedroom, trying to determine what could still be of use to the poor. She held up an old-fashioned petticoat and wondered if anyone would still want such a thing. Finally deciding that someone with even mediocre sewing skills could make it into something else more useful if desperate enough, she carefully placed it in the Sacred Heart box. She scooped up the remaining petticoats and other undergarments and put them into the same box as well and then gave in to the urge to sit down again on Helen's lumpy bed. She stared out the open window to the lake beyond, the unassuming lace curtain permanently aloft on the gentle breeze that blew in, and reflected that not too long ago she herself had been nearly that desperate.

She anxiously hoped that Elsie and Ma were adjusting to their new place with all of the kids. She had helped them to get settled on moving day, of course, but the servants had done most of the real work. In truth, she actually *was* needed at Highbury for the myriad of things to be done for the wedding, so Ma and Elsie had had to do most of the unpacking themselves with the help of the permanent staff that now resided with them, which consisted, really, of only five persons, namely, a cook, a housekeeper, one maid, one nanny, and one man servant who doubled as the butler and the chauffeur. Ma, of course, had at first fought tooth and nail against such an arrangement, but, in the end, the fight had just gone out of her and she had given in.

Henrietta drew in a sharp breath as she remembered the day Ma had finally been reunited with her long-lost family, the Exleys. Not long after the engagement party at which Ma had failed to appear, the Exleys had lost little time in seeking out Martha on their own terms. As much as John and Agatha Exley were bosom friends with the Howards, old Mr. Exley Sr. decided that this was a family affair and was loath to use Antonia Howard as a go-between any longer. He had sent a direct letter to his daughter, but Ma had merely crumpled it, unread, and thrown it into the fire, or so Henrietta had learned via a whispered telephone call from Elsie made from the booth at the back of Kresge's. Henrietta had then received her own letter from her grandfather, requesting her help in his reunion with his only daughter. Henrietta, knowing that nothing would induce Ma to come to Lake Forest where the Exleys resided, had, after much thought, dutifully written to her grandfather and suggested a time when he might condescend to visit them at their shabby apartment in Logan Square.

There was nothing else for it. Something had to be done, Henrietta had realized. It was bad enough that Ma had not come to the engagement party, but it would be inexcusable for her not to attend her oldest daughter's wedding. Besides, now that they knew of Ma's whereabouts, Henrietta was certain the Exleys would not rest until they were reunited with her, so it was best, she reasoned, to get it over with.

Henrietta had accordingly gone home a few days before Mr. Exley Sr.'s expected visit to surreptitiously prepare, having chosen to not inform Ma of his coming until the very morning of the momentous event. When Henrietta *did* finally reveal the secret of Mr. Exley's imminent arrival, Ma was livid, of course, and screamed at both Henrietta and Elsie—as if she were also in on it—before she finally threw a plate against the wall, shattering it, and had then dissolved into tears. Elsie had abandoned her task of dusting and went to tend to her, while Henrietta had picked up the broken pieces of the smashed plate and continued to methodically scrub down the apartment and each of her siblings as well. She sent Eddie out to Schneider's to buy some decent tea and biscuits, with actual money rather than having to put it on their long charge bill, as they had had to do in the past. Clive had given Henrietta money to pay off their debts and to sustain them until a more formal arrangement could be agreed upon. Ma had predictably refused to have anything to do with the extra cash, so Henrietta had entrusted it to Elsie for the days when she had to be away at Highbury, which, as it was turning out, was most of the time.

And so, with just about an hour left before Mr. Exley was due to arrive, Henrietta made Herbert and Jimmy scrub the landing outside their front door, to no real avail, really, but it made Henrietta feel better to have it done. Eugene, meanwhile, had spent the morning out somewhere and, having only returned just before Mr. Exley's arrival, was informed of his auspicious relative's imminent visit as he lazily climbed the stairs, Jimmy shouting out the exciting news from his knees as he scrubbed. Not sharing Jimmy's excitement at the prospect of meeting their rich old grandfather—having already met him, for one thing, at Henrietta's engagement party—Eugene merely scowled and grumbled to Henrietta that she could have let a fellow know before now.

"Where's Ma?" he had asked, irritated. Henrietta nodded toward the bedroom where Ma had locked herself away about an hour before. Eugene took a step toward the bedroom but then hesitated and instead stalked off to the other one, slamming the door behind him, causing Henrietta and Elsie to look wearily at each other from across the room.

"You might help, you know!" shouted Henrietta, but no response was forthcoming. She had merely sighed, then, and kept scrubbing, guiltily knowing that Eugene's days were indeed numbered. She hoped the plan that her grandfather had concocted and which Clive had agreed to was not a mistake . . .

When Henrietta had received Elsie's letter shortly after the engagement party, informing her that she had found two golden, jewel-encrusted eggs shoved under the mattress in the boys' room, she had gone straight to Clive and told him, shamefully placing the letter in his hands to read. It was obvious that Eugene had stolen the two missing Fabergé eggs, which also called into question the truthfulness of his story regarding the planted candlesticks at the St. Sylvester rectory. Clive had finally pinned Fr. Finnegan down but had not gotten the hoped-for confession from him about framing Eugene, as Eugene had earlier claimed. Clive's intuition, however, had told him that both of them were lying somehow, but it wasn't officially his case and there wasn't much he could do now. He had tried consulting with O'Conner, the detective assigned to the case, but O'Connor had not been interested in Clive's help or his theories, as it turned out, himself upset that he had been ordered to step down on what seemed like an open-and-shut case. O'Connor was naturally of the opinion that a conviction would have looked good on his record, but the chief had called in a favor with a church dignitary for Clive and had disappointingly—for O'Connor, anyway—gotten the charges dropped.

"Clive, I'm so sorry," Henrietta said after finding him in the study and handing him Elsie's letter that fateful afternoon.

Clive quickly skimmed the letter and walked to the large windows running along one wall. From this vantage point he could see the vast expanse of Lake Michigan to which the grounds of Highbury abutted. "This puts me in a very awkward position, Henrietta," he said in a tight voice, looking out at the lake.

"Yes, I know. I'm sorry," Henrietta repeated, sensing that she should remain standing where she was rather than go to him. "What . . . what should we do?" She had forced herself to say "we" rather than "I," tentatively suggesting that the problem was now both of theirs.

"Damn him!" Clive said in a sudden burst of emotion. "He's determined to make a mess of it. How could he be so stupid?" He paused and exhaled deeply. "Leave it with me for now. But don't say anything to Eugene. Don't let on that you know anything. I'll let Father know."

"Must you?" Henrietta asked, her face burning with shame.

Clive raised his eyebrow. "I'm afraid so, Henrietta. Father's threatening to call the police this time, and we don't need the local nitwits crawling over the place, searching for something that isn't here."

"But what if Eugene sells them in the meantime . . . or loses them or something?"

"He won't. He didn't take them for that reason, if I've pegged him correctly. And anyway, he's smart enough to eventually realize that if he does sell them, they will be traced back to him."

"Why take them, then?" Henrietta asked, puzzled, as she looked up into his eyes.

Clive didn't answer at first, but merely looked at her and sighed. "I'm afraid Eugene might be one of those who steals for the thrill of stealing. Something about him. Just a guess, though," he muttered, stiffly handing her back the letter.

Before Clive could reason out the best course of action regarding Eugene, however, having only told his father the briefest of the facts regarding the Fabergé eggs, saying that he would handle their recovery, the problem was brought to a head by an unexpected visit to Highbury by Oldrich Exley himself.

Mr. Exley was shown into the library, where he had remained closeted with Clive and his father for the better part of an evening while they discussed what was to be done with the wayward Martha and her brood. Clive had explained that he had promised Henrietta that he would provide for her family and he still held to this promise, but Exley, it seemed, was having none of it. He requested, no, *demanded*, of both Clive and Alcott, that they agree that he, Oldrich Exley, be solely responsible for their welfare from here on out. He had already consulted with his lawyers, apparently, and had set the wheels in motion, so, really, he had said, his gout causing him to shift uncomfortably as he sat in one of the leather wingback chairs near the fireplace, there was no more need of discussion. He had it quite in hand, as it were. He explained that he was taking a house for them in Palmer Square, nothing too ostentatious, of course, but something reasonably respectable for his daughter and his grandchildren, an address suitable for him to occasionally call in for tea without risk of embarrassment. It was one of the smaller residences on the Square, he admitted with a slight wave of his hand, with apparently three floors and a small carriage house and a formal garden out back, or so his agent had led him to believe, not having set eyes upon it himself. Naturally, he would employ a small staff adequate to the keeping of the house and to whatever needs they might have, which he assumed would be minimal, having just come from a life of poverty and as most of the children, he pointed out, would be away at boarding school, anyway. He planned to send them to the establishment to which he had sent his own sons, Philips Exeter, in New Hampshire.

Upon hearing this, Clive silently groaned, but he let Mr. Exley continue laying out his plan, knowing full well that Mrs. Von Harmon would be irate, considering how she had already reacted to Clive's attempt to give them even small petty cash with which to buy staples. She would never agree to this, and yet, what choice did she have now? Clive wondered. Having finally found her, Clive doubted that much would stand in old Exley's way. He knew by reputation that Exley could be ruthless.

Clive watched as Mr. Exley drew out a piece of paper from his inner jacket pocket, unfolding it carefully and adjusting his spectacles.

The three oldest boys—Eugene, Herbert, and Edward—he read from his notes, would be sent away to be properly educated, whilst James, Donald, and Doris, he added, again adjusting his wire-rim glasses slightly, would be enrolled at St. Sylvester's until they were old enough to be sent away as well. At six, James was technically already old enough to attend Phillips, but Mr. Exley assumed he was academically behind and would need at least a year to catch up.

The girl, Elsie, was a different conundrum, he had gone on. At seventeen she should be just coming out, after her sister's wedding, of course. It was too late now for her education, Mr. Exley feared, and she was too old to have a governess. Better to employ a lady's companion to subtly educate her on the finer points of being a lady of society, he had decided.

Clive marveled at how much thought Exley had put into this plan without having even seen his daughter for over twenty years and how he casually assumed his dictations would be unquestioningly followed. As much as he was not overly fond of Mrs. Von Harmon at this point in his courtship with Henrietta, a glimmer of understanding occurred to Clive as to why the young Martha may have run away so many years ago. He quickly realized that there was not much he could do to alter the last twenty years of Exley family history, but, still, he felt he owed it to his future wife to at least try to suggest caution to Mr. Exley, knowing that Henrietta, not to mention Mrs. Von Harmon, would vehemently oppose this plan, at least in the beginning.

"Do you think it wise, Mr. Exley?" Clive finally put in carefully. "With respect, sir, all of these changes might be too much just at the beginning."

"Do you think me a fool, Clive?" Mr. Exley snapped, as if talking to a schoolboy. "I'm well aware of the delicateness of the situation. The move to a decent dwelling must be done as soon as possible, of course, but the rest of the plan can evolve over time. I'm merely outlining the grand scheme so as you can be assured that every aspect of their livelihood will be provided for. I should have done this years ago. It is to my shame that I have so grossly neglected my duty," he said bitterly. "But Martha was ever a stubborn one, as was Charity," he said, referring obviously to his late wife, but with no apparent trace of emotion. "However, I will not be thwarted in it this time. I mean to atone for the past whichever way I can." He paused to take a drink of the scotch Alcott had poured out for all of them when they had first sat down.

Clive, for his part, however, remained unconvinced.

"Damned generous, I'd say," Alcott acknowledged from where he sat opposite Exley, seemingly disquieted by the odd silence that had now crept into the room along with a descending air of gloom. He held up his glass now to Exley. "Damned generous."

"Yes, Mr. Exley, it is exceedingly generous," Clive added, "but, perhaps, as I am marrying into the Von Harmons, they should be *my* financial responsibility, at least in part, anyway." He cast a glance at his father, but Mr. Howard kept his face expressionless as he sat carefully eyeing Mr. Exley.

"Henrietta, yes, but the rest of them, no. Martha is my daughter, and the rest of them are my grandchildren. They are my responsibility from here on out." He looked at Clive sideways, then. "Unless you're suggesting you should be granted a dowry."

"Certainly not!" Clive exclaimed. "I am offended at the suggestion, sir," Clive added tightly.

"I sincerely beg your pardon," Mr. Exley said with a faint smile. "However, I want all of the cards to be on the table, and I only wish to have this rather awkward conversation once."

"I accept your apology, sir . . . and your arrangements," Clive said stiffly, "though I cannot speak for the Von Harmons. I would caution you, again, with all due respect, sir, to move slowly in these matters. Mrs. Von Harmon is very . . ." he paused, trying to think of the right word.

"Difficult?" Mr. Exley supplied.

Clive inclined his head in agreement.

"Understood," Mr. Exley said gruffly.

"There is just one thing, however," Clive added, "which I feel I must relate at this juncture." He paused, looking at his father. "I'm not sure Philips is the place for Eugene."

"And why would that be?" Mr. Exley asked with narrowed eyes, as if already defensive of his new grandson.

Clive then proceeded to explain Eugene's mishaps, leaving out, of course, what Eugene had told him at the police station about Fr. Finnegan's advances and his suspicion of Eugene's homosexuality, focusing instead on his more overt misdemeanors.

"I'm sorry, Howard," Mr. Exley said gravely to Alcott when Clive was finished, looking at the ground briefly as he did so. "A bad egg, it would seem. Must take after the father. I thought there was something a bit shifty about him when I met him last week at the party. I'll pay for any damages, of course."

"Not to worry, old boy," Alcott said gingerly. "Schoolboy pranks, let's put it down to, shall we? Anyway, Clive assures me he can recover the eggs. No harm done."

"But there *was* some harm done, Father," Clive put in. "Or could have been, anyway. Something has to be done with this boy."

"Agreed, Clive," put in Mr. Exley before Alcott could answer. "He'll have to go to Fishburne or maybe Valley Forge. They'll straighten him out or break him in the process."

"By Jove, that's a bit drastic, wouldn't you say?" Alcott sputtered. "What do you think, Clive?"

Clive quickly ran the suggestion through his mind and actually thought it a good idea, all things considered. A military academy would go far in keeping him in line more than Philips. Maybe all Eugene needed was discipline; he had, after all, lost his father at a young age. Perhaps it would be the making of him. The army had certainly cleansed himself of any of the spoiled selfishness he had once had as the only son of Highbury. Perhaps it would be good for Eugene as well. Henrietta, he knew, would be upset by this course of action, not to mention Mrs. Von Harmon, but the alternative would be jail. Clive had seen this type before. He had given him a chance after the candlestick affair because he was Henrietta's brother, but he did not appreciate being taken advantage of a second time and had quietly decided to turn him over to the authorities. Otherwise, there might never be an end to Eugene's grasping attempts to get more, especially now that his sister was to soon marry into the Howard wealth. Mr. Exley's proposal was not a bad one, and, frankly, Clive was relieved to be rid of this responsibility.

"It's not an unreasonable suggestion," Clive countered, filling up his glass with more scotch, "given the circumstances." He surreptitiously looked over at his father, who subtly responded with the quick rise of his right eyebrow.

"What do you think of Mr. Exley's plans as a whole, Father? Do you object to any of it?" Clive asked, looking directly at Alcott now for any hint of hesitation. He assumed there wouldn't be, as Mr. Exley's various arrangements relieved the Howards of not only the problem of Eugene, but also the looming financial burden of providing for the Von Harmons, which Clive and his father had not yet had a chance to discuss. As jarring as Mr. Exley's designs might be to the Von Harmons, Clive was relatively certain that they would raise no objections from his father.

"Yes, Howard, any objections?" Mr. Exley reiterated.

"None at all, Exley, if you're determined," Alcott said agreeably.

"Fine. I'll have the papers drawn up," Mr. Exley said, clearly gratified with the way things were proceeding.

"When do you plan to tell them all?" Clive asked Mr. Exley, worriedly rubbing his forehead with his thumb and forefinger.

"I shall write to Martha directly to request a meeting with her, long overdue, I might add, during which I will inform them of their future," Mr. Exley said, standing up now with the aid of his cane, apparently seeing no reason to extend the visit now that he had gotten what he came for. "I shan't take up any more of your time. Thank you for seeing me," he said stiffly. "I'll keep you abreast of any developments," he muttered, as Alcott walked with him to the main hall, leaving Clive alone to muse over the proposal.

—

Clive knew that Mr. Exley assumed that he would keep silent regarding his designs for the Von Harmons. He also knew that Mr. Exley's expectation was that if Clive *did* choose to confide in someone at some point, that someone would most certainly *not* be his betrothed. Men of that generation, Clive knew, frowned upon discussing business matters, even ones of a personal nature—depending upon how compromising they were—with the opposite sex. Clive took seriously, however, his promise given to Henrietta, after the whole wretched Jack Fletcher affair, to be forthright in all things, and, therefore, not long after Mr. Exley's visit, he accordingly sought her company on the terrace at Highbury. It had become something of a routine for them when Clive was at home at Highbury to retreat there in the evenings after Alcott and Antonia had gone to bed. The terrace was now an oasis of sorts in which they often caught a cool breeze coming in off the lake after the blistering heat of the day and during which they delighted in discovering each other more. For his part, Clive was beginning to enjoy having someone to talk intimately with at the end of a long day, something he had not done in many years. And there was something a bit thrilling to talk in the cover of darkness lit only by the dazzling array of summer stars overhead and the ancient lanterns attached to the back of the house, prompting confidences more than any of the beautifully ornate rooms inside the house itself ever could have done, and lending itself as well to lingering kisses and soft caresses.

The night Clive chose to tell Henrietta about her grandfather's scheme, it was a particularly fine evening, with an exceptionally cool breeze playing about them and gently lifting Henrietta's skirt hem just a bit, as she leaned against the wrought iron running along the top of the stone wall and tried to make sense of what Clive was saying.

"Oh, Clive!" she had said morosely. "Ma will never agree to any of this! I can't imagine what she's going to say," she groaned. "How dare he think he has the right to dictate what will happen to all the kids and where Ma should live!" she said.

"It's not as if he's sending them to the workhouse, darling," Clive said, trying to play it lightly. "Don't you think it's a good thing for them to have a decent place to live? To not have to work so hard? It's what I would have liked to have provided as well," he said, caressing her cheek. "Out of love for you."

"But that's not *his* motivation," Henrietta said petulantly.

"That we don't know, but, you are right, I suspect it does have rather more to do with pride."

"And why send the kids away? It's cruel. It will kill her, Clive!"

Clive deliberated. "It does seem hard," he said, slowly. "I'm grateful my parents did not see the benefit of boarding school. But Philips is probably the best school in the country—and the most expensive. Surely you can see the advantage for them."

Clive watched as Henrietta looked up at the massive house looming behind them, presumably pondering his words.

"I've been giving this some careful thought, Henrietta," Clive continued, "and I think that perhaps your mother is suffering from a bad case of nerves. Depression, if you will. Perhaps a respite from the children is just what she needs. From what you've told me, she hasn't exactly been . . . well, engaged, shall we say . . . with them for quite some time. Since you're father, really. It's been on you and Elsie for far too long . . ."

"But to send them away? It seems so harsh. Even if it would somehow benefit *her*, how are the children to feel? It's not their fault, and yet they're the ones who will pay the dearest price."

"You can't be certain of that," Clive said quietly. "It can't be very nice for them as it is. You know that, don't you?"

A flicker of what might have been guilt crossed Henrietta's face. "At least they have Elsie," she countered.

"But for how long?"

Henrietta sighed and wrapped her arms around herself. "But they've never even been away from home before," she persisted. "Why can't they go to a good school here?"

Clive put his strong, warm arm around her and was surprised

to find that she was shivering. "The Exleys are a very proud family, Henrietta. All Exley men go to Philips. I'm afraid it will be very difficult to sway your grandfather once his mind's made up."

"Well, it's difficult to sway Ma, too. And, anyway, they're Von Harmons, not Exleys," she said with what sounded like a hint of bitterness.

"Listen, darling," Clive said gently. "Perhaps it's not so bleak. I advised Exley to proceed slowly with this. His plan is not to send them away until after Christmas so that they will begin with the spring term. Perhaps in that time we can persuade him otherwise."

"Oh, Clive! Do you promise?" she asked, looking up at him now, hopeful.

"I promise to *try*," he emphasized. "Except where Eugene is concerned, of course. That must be done immediately. Even if Father didn't press charges, I would have advised him to. I want you to know that," he said slowly, looking at her steadily so that she clearly understood. "I'm fairly certain Eugene would do it again somewhere else, and then he won't get off so easily. He's been lucky so far, but I see it ending rather badly for him if his current course is not drastically altered in some way. Military school may be the making of him. All may not yet be lost."

Henrietta sighed again, knowing there was no rebuttal for this; he was right. In truth, she had become a bit frightened of Eugene's apparent amorality. If he dared to steal from the Howards, even after Clive had given them money and promised Eugene a job, what would he do next? His sense of entitlement was abhorrent to her, and his unpredictability unnerved her. She felt she was walking a tenuous line as it was in this new world, and she didn't need Eugene acting as an unknown variable. She knew Ma would fume and fret something terrible—she winced now at the thought of what Ma would say when she found out—but Henrietta had to admit the wisdom of Clive's words. She felt guilty that a part of her would be glad to have Eugene out of the way. It was a fair solution, she reasoned, all things taken into account, and she hoped, truly, that Eugene might still make something of himself. "I suppose you're right," she said reluctantly.

"The first thing will be getting them moved. We'll worry about the rest of it later."

"Ah, yes, the house." Henrietta smiled at this part of Mr. Exley's preposterous plan. "On Palmer Square? Really, Clive! That's a bit excessive, don't you agree?" Palmer Square proper was a long oval-shaped park that was surrounded by the summer mansions of Chicago's wealthy. Potter Palmer himself as well as the Fields, the Schwinns, and the Adlers, among others, owned houses there. "Couldn't you have done something? Explained?"

"Oldrich Exley seems a man not to be trifled with, Henrietta. There are limits to what even I—or Father, for that matter—can do, you know. He seems as stubborn as her." The exasperated look he gave her then somehow made her laugh despite the seriousness of the situation.

Clive smiled, then, too. "I'm led to believe it's very modest, actually—for Palmer Square," he said, gesturing with his pipe.

"Oh, Clive, I'm not sure," Henrietta said, sobering suddenly.

"Come on, let's go in. It's late," Clive said tenderly, kissing the top of her head. "It will look brighter in the morning. It always does, somehow."

As disturbing as Clive's revelation had been, Henrietta was grateful that he had shared it with her and had decided that the best course of action would be to not tell any of them at home about their proposed future until Mr. Exley himself appeared. She had briefly considered telling Elsie, but Elsie wore her heart on her sleeve, and Henrietta knew she would have a hard time hiding her feelings around Ma if she knew what was coming. Clive had generously offered to be in attendance when Mr. Exley descended upon them, and, as much as Henrietta would have welcomed his strong presence, she had declined, knowing it would make it worse with Ma.

Henrietta had eventually got Ma to unlock the bedroom door that

morning and had removed her Sunday dress, a plain black affair with
a belted waist, out of the armoire for her. She had offered to do her
hair, then, trying not to glance nervously at the clock, but Ma had
only glared at her in response. Her face looked blotchy, as if she may
have been crying.

"Why have you done this, Henrietta?"

"I haven't done anything, Ma," Henrietta said tiredly, as if they had
had this argument too many times before.

"Why couldn't you have found someone from the neighborhood?
Why'd you have to go sniffing for something better than you?" Ma
said as she obediently put on the dress over her dingy slip. She turned
then for Henrietta to fasten her buttons up the back, and it took all of
Henrietta's resolve not to retort, not blurt out that she was every bit
as good as Clive, that they were indeed equals.

"You could have had any man around here," Ma said, turning back
around slowly with a scowl that resembled one of Eugene's best. She
sat heavily on the bed now, the springs creaking, and reached underneath for her scuffed black oxfords while Henrietta wearily folded
her arms in front of her and sighed. "Why couldn't you have gone for
Ludmilla's son, Jacek?" Ma continued. "He was always keen enough.
Or even that Tommy Coghlin? I've seen him hangin' about in the
street more than he had reason to. Then of course there was Stan,
a perfectly decent boy, but oh, no! You won't have him, will you?
Luckily he's latched on to Elsie now. He hasn't completely gotten
away! You'll regret that one, girl," she said scornfully, shaking her
finger at her now.

Henrietta resisted the urge to roll her eyes. As if Stan were a better
catch than Clive! "I didn't plan it this way, Ma. It just happened. Just
like it did for you and Pa."

Ma's eyes blazed at her at the mention of her father. "Don't speak
of him!" she hissed.

"It's not my fault that you haven't spoken to your family in almost
twenty years!" Henrietta said, unable to hold in her anger any longer.
"That was all your own doing! If it wasn't for your stupid pride, we

wouldn't have had to live like this all these years," she said, gesturing widely.

"How dare you!" Ma shouted, standing up now and slapping Henrietta briskly across the face.

Stunned, Henrietta took a step back, cradling her cheek and staring at Ma in disbelief, her anger fanning. "Well, it's true, isn't it?" Henrietta burst out. This time she would not back down! "You even said so yourself. That you refused to go back, even after Grandfather tried to reconcile with you, but you . . ."

"Oh, yes! I could have gone back," Ma shouted, "if I agreed to give up both you and Les. Remember that part?"

Henrietta was silent.

"Maybe I *should* have given you over to them, for all the good it's done," Ma went on bitterly. "Here you are running back to them with open arms as if none of it mattered. Well, good luck to you and good riddance! You'll see what you're getting yourself into, but then it will be too late. It's not all fancy balls and china, you know!"

Henrietta could not believe her mother had stooped to this level. "You're just being plain old mean now, Ma!" she said hotly. "You . . . you're jealous, aren't you? You don't want me to be happy because you're not. But nothing can ever make you happy!"

"Happy?" Ma said with almost an incredulous laugh. "What's happiness got to do with it, you stupid girl? And even if it was somehow important, your chances of happiness with that lot are slim to none. And before you give me some malarkey about Clive being different, just you watch. All men are the same—they only want you on your back. Either getting a baby put in you or pushing one out."

"Ma!"

"Your father was no different, you know," she said bitingly, as if she couldn't stop the tirade that had now erupted from some deep place of hurt within her. "After me all the time, he was, even when I was already carryin' a baby. Didn't make no difference to him."

Henrietta stopped short as she absorbed her mother's latest blow, her heart beating fast. She didn't want to hear this. Childishly, she

was tempted to put her hands over her ears, but a morbid part of her
was curious, too.

"He forced himself on me. More than once," Ma said, looking away
now. "Didn't know that, did you?" she said, turning her piercing gaze
back to her. "Now what do you think of your precious father? All
these years making him out to be some sort of saint in your mind.
Well, he was no saint . . . especially after he'd been drinking. This is
as much his doing as mine. One baby we could have handled, maybe
two or three, but not the lot of you! I didn't want you all, but what
could I do? No, this is all *his* fault, this is."

Henrietta's mind was in turmoil as she tried to steady herself
from Ma's volley of words, which stung her more than the physical
slap had just a few moments before. Was this what Ma had meant all
these years about everything being her father's fault? But forcing her?
That couldn't be true, could it? She thought she might be sick.

"He's here!" they heard Jimmy shout from the other room where
he was perched in the bare front window. "Ooh! Eugene! Come see
his car!"

"The sooner you know what you're getting into, the better," Ma
went on, apparently unfazed by Jimmy's announcement. "Mark my
words. And the upper classes are no different; might be even worse.
Spread your legs and be quiet; don't struggle. That's my wedding
advice for you; take it or leave it," she said as she opened the bedroom door just as a knock was heard on the front one.

Henrietta stood for a few minutes alone in the bedroom trying to
collect herself and steady her nerves. She became aware that her legs
were slightly shaking. And to think she had been feeling sorry for Ma
up until this point, having to humiliatingly face her father after all of
this time, to have nothing really to show for the headstrong choices
she had made all those years ago except for this ragged bunch of
children surrounding her. But these better feelings had left her now.
Ma was about to get her comeuppance, and Henrietta couldn't help
but feel a little glad.

—

In the end, the reunion between estranged father and daughter was rather short. Excepting his driver, of course, who obediently waited in the car, Mr. Exley came alone and stepped authoritatively into the apartment once the door had been opened to him. He formally greeted Henrietta, Elsie, and Eugene (who had at the last moment slunk out of the bedroom), having previously met the three of them at the engagement party, and then condescended to be introduced to his five other grandchildren by a rather apprehensive Henrietta. Finally, his eyes rested on Ma, who had positioned herself near the fireplace with posture as straight as her rounded shoulders would now permit and with a face of stone. Henrietta thought she saw a wave of something cross Mr. Exley's face—Anger? Pity? Compassion? On Ma's face, however, she saw nothing.

"Martha," he said, coming toward her, one arm awkwardly stretched out. When she did not make a move to return his proposed half-embrace, however, Mr. Exley quickly dropped his arm and instead deposited a formal, brief kiss on her cheek.

"Hello, Father," she said, and it struck Henrietta how strange it sounded. "Come to see me brought low, is this what this is?"

"Now, now, Martha, this is not the way to begin, surely?" His voice was falsely sweet.

"Still correcting me?" she asked, her gaze steely.

He ignored her and instead looked around the room now from where he stood, making no attempt to disguise the fact that he was sizing up their pitiful situation, his repulsion evident. "May I sit down?" he finally asked coldly as he glanced at the worn sofa.

"As you wish," Martha said, stiffly following suit as she lowered herself down into the armchair across from him.

Mr. Exley sat down gingerly, as if to prevent dirtying his pressed trousers, and expectantly held out his walking stick toward the row of kids standing along the wall in their Sunday best, hair wetted down, anxiously peering at their new grandfather. Eddie hurriedly stepped from among them and took the stick, Mr. Exley observing him only momentarily.

"Would you like some tea, grandfather?" Elsie asked hesitantly, standing near Ma's armchair. "It's British—proper stuff . . ."

"No, I think not. I shan't be staying long."

"Oh," she replied disappointedly.

Only Henrietta sat down beside him on the sofa.

"I must congratulate you on Henrietta's match to the Howard boy," Mr. Exley said to Ma now. "You must be very proud."

"We were just discussing it before you came in," Ma said evenly, and Henrietta felt her face grow warm again, still feeling the sting of the slap, or imagining anyway that she did.

"We were so sorry to have missed you at the Howards' gathering. Henrietta here informed us you weren't well. I trust you are much better?"

"You know why I wasn't there, Father. That is not my world any longer. Why don't you say what you've come to say? There's always a point. Time is money; isn't that what you were ever fond of saying?" Ma's speech seemed to have altered as she addressed him, as if she remembered how she had once spoke in a different lifetime, and Henrietta watched her, amazed.

Mr. Exley studied her for a moment. "You haven't changed a bit, Martha. Still the same."

"Thank you, Father. Coming from you that's quite a compliment."

"Look, Martha. Let's start again. I'm here to try to smooth things over."

"You took your time."

"If you must know, there were many times I wished to resolve our differences. I even took to driving past your dwelling for a stretch of time until your mother discovered my actions, and that was the end of that. Soon after, you moved, I was informed, and I lost track of you."

"I'm sure you could have found me if you wanted to. Sent one of your agents to ferret me out of the woodwork, as it were."

"Yes, I considered that, but I thought maybe your anonymity might be for the best. You seemed to prefer it that way, anyway."

"I did. Yes."

"Your mother died."

"Yes, I read it in the paper."

"My God, Martha! You're cold!" he said, shifting slightly.

"I had an excellent teacher."

He paused for a moment before beginning again. "Your churlishness does you no credit, Martha. Fate, it seems, will have her way, however, and has seen fit to recross our paths, as it were, for better or worse," he said, gesturing toward Henrietta, who had remained very still during their disagreeable tête-à-tête. "It's no use keeping up this facade any longer, Martha. It simply won't do."

"So we'll put up a different one, is that it?"

"This is an unsuitable living arrangement considering you have a daughter in society now."

"I had nothing to do with that."

"I'm surely not suggesting otherwise, believe me, except to say that you have raised a well-mannered, and, might I add, beautiful, young lady. My compliments to you, Martha, on that score, at least."

When Ma did not respond, he continued, unflinching in his tone. "I have taken the liberty of discussing your livelihood with the Howards, who were perfectly willing to support all of you, I will say that here. As generous as that offer is, it is unacceptable to me. If anyone should be responsible for your welfare, it should be me."

"Like you've done all along, you mean?"

"That was your choice—and your mother's—not mine. As it is now, however, I cannot have my granddaughter marry into the Howards and have the lot of you become their responsibility, or, worse, to be seen living in poverty."

"So it really has more to do, as usual, with saving face, doesn't it, Father? You've not changed, either, it would seem."

"Call it what you will, Martha; the result will be the same. This is becoming tedious, so I will get to the point. I have taken a house for you in Palmer Square, where you will take up residency immediately."

There were excited, whispered gasps from along the wall, and

Elsie looked nervously at Henrietta for confirmation, who gave her the slightest nod.

"There is a small staff already in place, which should be suitable to your needs. If you find yourself wanting, however, I shall of course supply more."

"And if I refuse?"

Mr. Exley chuckled lightly. "Why, then, your other choice is to come and live with me at your brother Gerard's."

"You can't force me to move!" Ma said, angrily.

"True enough. But I can take the children to live with me in Lake Forest. I've already discussed it with Gerard, and he's more than obliging. Of course they'll always be seen as the poor cousins, but that's to be expected."

"They will be, anyway, no matter how fine the house on the Square."

"Not quite the same, though, is it?"

"You can't take my children away from me!" Ma said, Henrietta noting a trace of worry in her voice for the first time.

Mr. Exley looked around him with disgust. "I wouldn't be so sure. There seems quite a lot here that would qualify as neglect, don't you think?" he added with a slight curl of his lip.

"You wouldn't dare!"

"Don't try me, my dear. You've seen how that works out. And I should mention that if they come to live with me, I could not in all fairness impose upon Gerard's good nature indefinitely. It would of course then only be temporary until a place at Philips could be arranged," Mr. Exley said with almost forced casualness, resting two pointed fingers under his chin.

Henrietta made a move to speak—this isn't how Clive had presented the plan! Boarding school was already an understood part of the arrangement, but she saw that her grandfather was using it now as a way to convince Ma to move. She was shocked by his underhandedness, but at the same time she understood that something clever would have to be done to get Ma to budge. Moving, she had finally admitted to herself, would be a good thing for them . . . But, still, she felt uncomfortable that her grandfather was then, if not out-right lying, certainly holding back part of the truth. And what would happen, Henrietta thought uneasily, when Ma found out that they were to be shipped off to boarding school anyway? She would be furious, of course, and would accuse Henrietta of knowing about it all along, which was true. Henrietta tentatively opened her mouth to protest, but she then remembered her promise to Clive to remain silent, so she bit her lip instead, watching Ma's face for her reaction. It didn't take long to see that Ma had been beaten, though she was trying to retain her previous stoicism.

"Very well," Ma said matter-of-factly. "We will move, but do not think for one moment that we will be entering society to be paraded around according to your whims."

"I shouldn't worry about that, Martha. At least where you're concerned, anyway. I rather think your society days have passed you by, don't you? Except for the Howard wedding, that is. I trust you will be in attendance for that, suitably arrayed, of course?" he said, his eyes observing her old, black dress.

Ma glared at him with what seemed to Henrietta to be pure hatred.

"And as for the children, there may be some societal obligations, to be sure, but we will come to those all in good time. Once Henrietta, here, is married," he smiled briefly at her, "we must find a suitable match for Elsie."

"Oh, but grandfather, I . . ." Elsie tried to interrupt.

"We will discuss it some other time, my dear," he said, looking at her briefly before turning back to face Ma.

Ma continued to stare at him before she spoke again. "Do not expect for one minute that I am grateful."

"I wouldn't dream of it, Martha. That would be entirely out of character."

"Don't be like that, Ma," said Eugene, finally, a sly grin creeping across his face from where he had been standing behind Ma. "Seems our ship has come in with *Grandfather*," he said, almost distastefully.

Mr. Exley glanced up at him now, coolly, as if observing him for the first time. "Ah, yes, Eugene. I was coming to that. Been rather a naughty boy, as I understand."

Eugene's previous smug look faded and was replaced by one of faint concern.

"I have a different plan for you altogether which you might as well know about at once," Mr. Exley continued briskly. "I've enrolled you at Fishburne Military Academy in Virginia, where you will proceed to in one week's time. Consider yourself lucky to have gotten a place. I had to pull considerable strings."

A gasp went around the room, and Ma stood up slowly, leaning on the arm of the chair as she did. "You can't do that!"

"Oh, yes, I can, my dear," Mr. Exley said calmly, remaining in his seat.

"You can't make me go there!" Eugene whined, an angry scowl on his face now.

"I can, and I will. The arrangements have already been made, so there is no point to this unseemly belligerence."

"Ma! Don't send me away!" Eugene begged, turning to face Ma.

Ma's face flushed red as she took a step closer to her father, preparing to unleash her fury on him.

Before she could do so, however, Mr. Exley calmly held up his hand to stop her. "Before you even begin, Martha, I've quite made up my mind. He can either go to Fishburne or to jail, and don't think I won't do it."

"You can't do this! He's not a thief! Those charges were dropped!"

"Be that as it may, I understand it was not because his innocence was proven; it was merely the result of a connection of the Howards to whom I am now inconveniently indebted. And I have been embarrassingly informed of yet another incident of theft, which can, I am told, be proven very quickly."

"You can't mean Eugene!" Ma said incredulously. "He's hardly left his room since . . . since he was released!" she went on, though this wasn't actually true.

"I don't know what you're talking about!" Eugene said testily.

"Silence!" Mr. Exley shouted, causing everyone in the room to jump. A timorous hush fell over the room except for the sound of Doris wriggling behind Donny. "Lying is a sin for which I have no mercy, much less patience," he said steadily. "And you, sir," he said, looking directly at Eugene, "have severely tried my patience. Henrietta," he said, still not taking his eyes off Eugene, "would you be so kind as to oblige me?"

Eugene tore his eyes from Mr. Exley and gave Henrietta one last despairing look before she made her way stiffly to the bedroom and returned carrying a ragged, black sock. In front of the silent, watching group, she reached her hand inside and drew out two beautiful, golden Fabergé eggs covered with brilliant stones.

Ma gasped, and Elsie, her face burning, looked at the corner floorboards. It took only a moment before Ma regained her self-possession and stalked over to where Eugene stood, his own cheeks aflame now, and slapped him, hard, across the face. "How dare you!" she hissed. "Where did you get these?"

Eugene looked at her with searing anger before casting his gaze downward, not even giving her the pleasure of rubbing his cheek, which must have surely been in pain, judging from the bright red hue that had resulted from Ma's hand.

"They were taken from Highbury, it would seem, at Henrietta and Clive's engagement party, the Howard butler reports. Is this not correct, Henrietta?"

"Yes, Grandfather," Henrietta said quietly, handing them to him now, privately concerned that Ma had resorted to two slaps in one day.

"The Howards, understandably, are quite upset, and it was Alcott's intention to call the police before Clive intervened. He was kind enough to bring the matter to my attention before any legal action was taken. So," he said, standing up slowly, "there is nothing more to be said." He took a step toward Eugene, who was looking at him now with sullen fear. "I understand that there has been no one to take you in hand, but those days are very much over for you,

I'm afraid. You will report to Fishburne in one week's time." He pointed a somewhat crooked forefinger at him and looked at him with disgust. "You will not disgrace me again, boy. Fishburne will make a man of you, make no mistake about that, but take care as to what sort of man you will become. I've been made a fool of one too many times," he said, looking at Martha now. "I'll not endure another. Either make something of yourself at Fishburne, or you'll be swiftly hauled off to jail, or, if that's not to your liking, I own several mines where you will be sent to labor. And as your mother can tell you, I generally get my way in most matters, so don't try me. After all, look where it has gotten her."

"Don't speak about my mother that way," Eugene said angrily, scowling up at him now like a cornered dog.

"I'll do as I like, and don't you forget it," he said, tapping his finger, hard, on Eugene's chest. He turned away then and walked toward the door.

"I'll take my leave now," he said. "Have you anything else to say to me, Martha? My agent, Bernstein, will be in touch with all the arrangements."

"Even after all these years, I still haven't really escaped, have I?" she said rancorously, barely above a whisper.

"No, I suppose not, my dear. I trust your adventure was worth it, however," he said, looking around disparagingly. "Goodbye then, children," he said, giving them a last glance and then finally descending the stairs.

Ma's face crumpled then, and she silently retreated to the bedroom to lie down, giving in to a rare fit of tears, while Elsie made a move toward the kitchen to make her some of the expensive tea that Mr. Exley hadn't even partaken of. Eugene crossed the room as well, giving both Henrietta and Elsie a vile look as he did so.

"Thanks very much," he said viciously, stopping in front of Henrietta. "Your own brother? Why couldn't you let it alone, Hen? You think you're so much better than us now, don't you? Now I'm to be in the fucking army while you're the lady of the manor!"

"Eugene! Don't swear!" Elsie chided him.

"You're no better!" he said, turning his vengeance on Elsie now. "You were obviously in on it. How else would Henrietta have known they were there?"

"How dare you steal from the Howards, Gene!" Henrietta said angrily. "Clive was going to get you a good job! Why? Why do you have to be this way? He already helped you once, and this is how you repay him?"

"How dare you defend him over me!" he flung back. "Did you see how many gold trinkets they have lying around? They wouldn't miss one or two. It's not fair! We're starving, and they have gold bits of shit lying around everywhere. You should be thanking me, actually, for trying to help out the family instead of working in some factory for Clive making him more money."

"You ungrateful wretch!" Henrietta shouted. "Stealing is never the answer, Eugene! Especially from my *fiancé's parents*! How could you be so stupid?"

"Oh, my! I'm so very sorry to have ruined your precious image, Hen! Isn't this what this is really about? You must take after grandfather."

"How dare you! You don't even deserve to be in the army. You *should* be in jail. Pa would be ashamed of you."

"Do you think I care? He was a fucking coward."

"Eugene!" Elsie exclaimed.

Eugene stalked toward the door and paused before going out, looking at both Elsie and Henrietta and then the rest of them still huddled against the wall. "You can all just go to hell!" he said and walked soundlessly out the door.

No one said anything for a moment until Jimmy made a little movement forward, having taken his scrap of blanket from his pocket and put it up to his nose for comfort, a babyish habit he still clung to. "Are we really going to move, Hen?" he had asked, looking up at her with his big brown eyes.

—

Henrietta heard a noise then and was startled out of her thoughts. Surprised, she looked around and realized that she was still sitting on Helen's bed in the little cottage. She had been daydreaming again! What was wrong with her these days?

"Who is it?" she asked nervously, as she hurriedly stood up. She made her way across the little bedroom, assuming it was one of the servants and feeling ashamed that she had gotten so little accomplished. Her apprehension faded instantly, however, when she caught sight of none other than Clive leaning against the doorframe, his arms crossed casually in front of him.

"Clive!" she exclaimed. "You're back early!" A happy wave of excitement passed over her as she went to him. She had missed him this week while he wrapped up his job on the force in the city. She was used to him spending his weeks there, still trying to finish, once and for all, his position as detective inspector while she spent her time mostly at Highbury with his parents, only occasionally going home to the new house on Palmer Square, where she felt decidedly like a visitor. The wedding, in just over two weeks' time, would soon be upon them.

"Billings told me I'd find you here," he said as he wrapped his arms around her waist and kissed her. "Still mucking about down here? I thought you'd have finished by now."

Henrietta loosened his tie for him, a look she much preferred, but one they were only allowed when alone together, which wasn't often. "How was it?" she asked solicitously, knowing that he hadn't really wanted to give up his role as a detective inspector.

Clive arched his eyebrow. "The boys gave me a bit of a farewell party, just a little one, as most of them are still on duty. Very touching, however. The chief gave a very moving speech, for him anyway, given how sentimental he usually is," he said sarcastically. "Still, I was touched, really. Said some damned nice things."

"Such as?"

"Well, let's see. That I'm a first-rate detective," he said, ticking off the chief's comments on his fingers, "that I'll be missed, that I'm dashingly handsome, those types of things. But also that a certain woman is very lucky to get me, and I'm under strict orders to make her happy. So here I am," he said mischievously, kissing her again, longer this time as he drew her nearer to him, putting his hands on the small of her back. "How convenient that we're alone."

"Clive!" she said, pulling back.

Their willingness to be more intimate had ebbed and flowed between them over their short courtship. When she had first come to Highbury, Henrietta had been the more eager, it had seemed, sometimes teasing him, and even offering herself to Clive one night at his apartment in the city, but Clive, after his behavior in the park the night he had proposed, had kept an honorable distance and had resisted any of Henrietta's overtures, charming though they might have been. Now, however, as the wedding drew close and the prospect of the wedding night in particular loomed large, they had once again shifted roles. Clive's resolve was loosening while Henrietta was becoming more reticent and shy. Unfortunately she could not help dwelling on what her mother had confided to her about her father, and about men in general. Surely Clive would not be a brute, she reasoned, but she had indeed seen a violent side to him. Where she had once looked forward to her wedding night with Clive, having already felt on fire at times as he had kissed and sometimes touched her over the summer, she was now oddly nervous and even a bit afraid. Surely he would be gentle and patient, wouldn't he?

She smiled at him now. "Why don't I make us some tea?" she said, disengaging herself from his arms.

"Here?" he said, amused, folding his arms back across his chest and leaning again against the doorframe.

"Why not?" she said, making her way to the old-fashioned stove now. "I love this little place."

"Don't you have anything stronger?" Clive asked.

"I'm afraid not, you naughty thing," she teased. "And anyway, I think you're already a bit intoxicated."

"You can tell?" he asked, grinning now as he sat down at the old table, opposite to where she hovered in front of the stove, so that he could watch her.

"Yes, so some tea will do you good before you have to face your mother at dinner," she said, reaching for some mugs off the side hutch.

"You have a point," he said wearily, looking around the cottage. "Are you almost finished with all of this rubbish? You didn't really have to do this, you know. Or are you just trying to hide from Mother?" He grinned across at her.

She couldn't help but smile. "Maybe a little." She began pouring the boiling water into the teapot. "There's not too much left to do, I suppose. But what will become of the cottage, Clive?"

"Oh, I don't know. Father hasn't said. Probably board it up until it's needed. Either for when Mary retires, or perhaps Virgil and Edna might want it if they end up getting married."

"I see," she said, putting the cozy over the pot and coming around to where Clive sat. "Well, as a matter of fact, I had an idea . . ." she said hesitantly, looking down at him now. Clive reached for her hand, and when she slipped hers into his, he pulled her onto his lap.

"Clive!" she said, laughing a bit.

"Tell me your idea. I was having a hard time hearing you up there."

Henrietta paused, looking into his eyes. "Let's us live here," she said quietly.

"Here?" Clive laughed. "Don't be ridiculous!"

"I'm not being ridiculous, Clive! Please? Just for a little while," she went on hurriedly before he could say no. "Just until you have to take over Highbury. Or maybe not even that long . . . maybe just the first year. Please," she said earnestly.

The urgency in her voice caught his attention. "But why, darling?" he said softly now. "This is little more than a hovel. It isn't really fitting to what we both agreed to be. I thought you'd accepted your role at Highbury. Don't tell me we have to go through all this again."

"No, Clive. I . . . I have. Honestly. We can still be fully part of Highbury, entertaining and all of the duties, but . . . this could be *our* place. Somewhere just for the two of us. I . . . I want to take care of you," she said, putting her hand to his cheek, a gesture he had come to love, "not let it up to the servants. I . . . I want to learn to be your wife *here*. Just the two of us."

Clive let out a deep breath. "But Mother's had men altering the east wing for us for weeks now. She will not be amused that she's had a whole apartment done up for us simply so that we could live in this antiquated cottage."

"Well . . . we . . . sometimes we could stay there, too, I suppose."

"Henrietta, this is madness," he said, not unkindly, but suddenly seeming very tired.

"Please, Clive," she said, staring into his eyes.

He sighed. "Let me think about it," he said, somewhat unhappily and tried to smile—but it was unconvincing.

Timidly she leaned forward and kissed him. She retreated just a sliver then, and he paused to stare at her partially open lips and kissed her again, harder this time, breathing deeply.

Eventually she forced herself to pull back and rubbed the stubble on his cheek. "You won't hurt me, will you, Clive?" she asked, her voice barely audible.

"Hurt you?" he said, baffled, sitting up a bit straighter now. "Of course not, darling," he said, looking at her carefully. "But do you really need to ask me that?" he asked softly.

She longed to tell him her fears of the wedding night and what might be expected of her, sexually, as a wife, as her mother had alluded to. And what about the Howards? What did they expect of her? Unfortunately, she could not get Helen's revelation about the Howards' desperate need of an heir out of her mind. That she would be surely "kept busy" as a result, as Helen had put it. And what of Clive? she wondered. He had ever been gentle with her, but she had on more than one occasion felt his tense passion just under the surface, and likewise she had a hard time forgetting the image of him shattering Neptune's nose with his fist and the blood that had subsequently gushed forth. It made her feel sick even still. In her heart she did not doubt Clive's love for her, but she could not deny the nagging suggestion that her being very young with many childbearing years ahead of her was a definite bonus for the Howards. She had become more and more preoccupied with these thoughts as the wedding drew near, and then—miraculously almost—it had come to her one night that if she and Clive were to perhaps be somewhere outside of the confines of Highbury, somewhere like this isolated cottage, for example, they might thereby escape any expectations, any unpleasantness, as it were . . .

She struggled to find a way to explain all of these scattered thoughts to him, but it was difficult for her to figure them out herself. "I . . . nothing," she said finally, meeting his eyes momentarily before looking down at his hand that now grasped hers.

Gently Clive lifted her chin with the knuckle of his forefinger. "Henrietta, if you are referring to our wedding night, or *any* night thereafter, for that matter, I will *never* hurt you," he said quietly. She felt her face grow instantly red; he could ever read her mind. "I promise. We'll go slow, as slow as you want. I only want to please you," he said tenderly, the longing in his voice clear.

Though she was extremely embarrassed by the turn of the conversation, she searched his eyes nonetheless and found them, as always, sincere.

"Something has changed, however, which I would wish to know. I've been sensing it lately, anyway, and these questions would confirm it. I rather thought you enjoyed my attentions, desired them, even," he said tacitly.

Henrietta blushed again and looked away.

"What has changed, darling? Has someone said something to frighten you? Surely not Julia? Hers is a very different sort of marriage. An unfortunate one," he put in grimly.

Henrietta stood up now and brushed down her apron. "No," she said, "not Julia," mentally noting, though, that Julia might be a good person to confide in regarding such matters. "It was my mother, actually."

Clive sighed. "Of course it was," he said, languidly crossing his legs now and propping his head with his fist, his elbow casually resting on the table. "Henrietta, no doubt . . ."

There was a knock and a cough, then, which made Henrietta jump. Clive, however, did not even turn around.

"Yes, Billings?" he asked tiredly, still looking across at Henrietta as he said it.

"Forgive me, sir. But Madam wishes me to remind you that you are all dining at the Exleys' tonight and that Fritz will be bringing the car around in one hour's time."

Clive exhaled tiredly. "All right, Billings. We'll be there directly."

"Very good, sir," he said with a bow and promptly disappeared.

With a tired smile, Clive stood up. "Duty calls," he said wearily.

Henrietta came from around the table, unpinning her apron as she did so. Carefully she placed it on the thick, rustic planks of the table, but not before reaching inside the pocket to retrieve Helen's photograph.

"What's this?" Clive asked when he saw it.

Silently, Henrietta held it up for him to see.

He smiled sadly. "You were fond of her, weren't you?"

"I was, yes."

"You're a sentimentalist, wanting to keep this."

"Something should be kept, don't you think? To mark that she lived a life, however sad."

"How do you know it was sad?" Clive asked pointedly.

Henrietta shrugged and gave him a small smile. "True enough. Perhaps just a part of it was sad."

He took her hand, then, and led her out of the cottage. "As for the other matter, let's discuss it later," Clive said as they slowly began walking up to the house. "Perhaps on the terrace," he said, looking sideways at her. Henrietta returned his smile but, embarrassed now, secretly hoped that they would not.

Chapter 2

S everal hours later, Henrietta found herself seated in the formal dining room of the Exleys' mansion in Lake Forest. Mrs. Howard had advised her on what to wear and now looked on with apparent approval at the effect created by the indigo Jean Patou gown of silk crepe with a pleated bodice and matching evening gloves. The dress was pulled tight across Henrietta's waist but flounced out near the bottom, and the strand of creamy pearls that settled nicely in the deep cut of the bodice completed the remarkable illusion that she had been born to this life.

Though John and Agatha were perhaps the Howards' closest friends, Alcott and Antonia had rarely been invited to the mansion in Lake Forest belonging to the oldest Exley brother, Gerard, and his wife, Dorothy. Oldrich lived here with them, too, and Antonia had mentioned several times this week that she was looking forward to watching just who really ran the Exley roost, both the father and the son having equal reputations of ruthlessness. Of the third brother, Archibald, who resided in New York, Antonia knew little, she had said, except what she heard now and then from John and Agatha.

It was therefore revealing to observe that both Gerard and Dorothy commandeered the ends of the table, while Mr. Exley Sr. was seated at the midpoint of the table, forming a triangle between them. The rest of the seats were occupied by John and Agatha, of course, as well as Julia and Randolph, who had been obligingly invited as well, as it was to be considered a "family" dinner party.

It struck Henrietta as being exceptionally strange that during this dinner between the two families, the people that were supposed to be representing *her* family were still basically strangers to her and that the family she was marrying into seemed more like her actual family after having stayed with them for most of the summer. To Julia, especially, she had become rather close. Ma and Elsie had been invited tonight, of course, but Ma, as usual, had declined, and Elsie had stayed back to be with her, not wanting to come on her own. Everything seemed so mixed up and out of order.

Since the engagement party, Henrietta had not seen her Exley aunts and uncles, and, indeed, she had only seen her grandfather on two more occasions. Once, of course, had been the terrible day when he had descended upon them to be reunited, horribly, with Ma, and the other had been several weeks after that when he had invited just Henrietta for tea and a "proper chat" at the Lake Forest house. After the episode with Ma, she had been reluctant to go, not a little afraid of Mr. Exley Sr., if truth be told, but Antonia had insisted, saying that Mr. Exley very rarely entertained and pointing out the obvious, that she could not very well ignore her grandfather forever. Though she knew Mrs. Howard was right, Henrietta thought it rather unfair that Ma had somehow gotten away with avoiding the lord of the family all these years while she was not to be allowed that same luxury.

As it turned out, Martha had been the main subject of Henrietta's conversation with her grandfather. Upon arrival at the Lake Forest mansion, she had been shown into the drawing room and seated opposite Mr. Exley, who, in the morning light, seemed more frail than she had previously noticed. Mr. Exley was eager, it seemed, to want to set the record straight with Henrietta as to what exactly had happened between Martha and themselves, meaning he and his wife, Charity, of course, at least from his perspective. Henrietta found this curious and wondered why her opinion of him would matter in the slightest. Still, she dutifully listened as he proceeded to explain in his strong, determined voice what had happened between him and Ma all those years ago, noting, as he himself poured the tea, that his hand was a bit palsied. He was indeed a strange paradox—his body weak and failing and yet his mind and his will still as unbending as steel.

Mr. Exley had begun by saying that he and his wife, Charity, had been delighted when their fourth and last child, who had come much later in life, had been a girl, but, much to their dismay, Martha had proved to be a rather difficult child from the very beginning, given to tantrums and fits of melancholy. They went through a steady string of nannies with her, which they found alarming considering they had always managed to keep the same nanny throughout the years for their three other children, despite the fact that they were boys and were more than occasionally given to mischief. Martha's temper and disposition did not improve with age, much to their disappointment, and it was eventually decided that she should be sent away to a Swiss finishing school to try to reform her enough to marry well. Rather than improve her, however, her experience in Switzerland seemed to make her all the more surly, and when she did return home, she often lashed out at her mother in particular, who had nearly, at that point, all but washed her hands of the troubled girl. They had even begun, Mr. Exley said quietly, as he gripped the cane in front of him, to question her sanity, though naturally they did not openly discuss it. Instead, they began searching for a husband for her in earnest, but no young, or even older, man seemed willing to take on the sullen Exley girl who had neither beauty nor charm to recommend her, merely money.

And then, Mr. Exley continued, out of nowhere, just as they were deliberating what to do next with her, Martha informed them that she was with child by the butcher's delivery boy. Here Mr. Exley had stopped in his recounting of the story to rub his chin.

Henrietta likewise shifted uncomfortably and tried her best to meet his eyes.

Mr. Exley had gone on then, admitting that he and his wife were infuriated and beside themselves by what had seemed to be Martha's almost cavalier announcement. They quickly began to make arrangements for her to go live in New York with one of Oldrich's sisters, insisting that the baby be given up for adoption, much to Martha's protests. "You must understand, my dear, we thought it for the best," he said, looking directly at Henrietta now.

Henrietta tried to respond with some sort of polite smile but found that indeed she could not.

Mr. Exley had explained, then, how Martha had disappeared not long after, and had been eventually traced to a boarding house where she was living with her new husband, one Leslie Von Harmon, having married him just days before at the county clerk's office. Her mother was understandably distraught, Mr. Exley went on, having spent so much time and money to see her well placed. "All of our efforts had come down to this sordid state of affairs," he had said with deep regret in his voice. "Surely you can understand our disappointment, nay, angst, do you not?" he asked Henrietta.

Henrietta, remembering Ma's version of this story, was not so sure she did and remained silent.

Mr. Exley let out a deep breath. "I may have forgiven her, you know," he said. "I always did have a soft spot for her, but Charity was resolute. She shunned Martha from that moment on and refused to forgive what she saw as Martha's ultimate betrayal. To her dying day, she never spoke her name again and told each of the boys that if they ever spoke to her or sought her out, they would be cut off from the will.

"For my part, I had Martha followed from time to time by my agent, Bernstein, and I even wrote her a number of letters, begging her to give up Von Harmon and return to us. Predictably, I never received a reply. As it turned out, Charity eventually learned of my actions and promptly put an end to them. By then, however, I was beginning to give up hope anyway and was more than ready to abandon Martha of my own accord, my own bitter disappointment prevailing as well. I, too, began to harden my heart to Martha, convincing myself that she deserved everything she got and told myself from that point onward that she was dead to me. I know it sounds preposterous, but I think I half believed it." Mr. Exley, who had been speaking into the empty fireplace, paused at this point and looked up at Henrietta now and managed a weary smile. "Who would have known, though, that the child Martha was carrying would have eventually made her way back to us through a marriage into the Howards? Simply extraordinary."

Henrietta, not knowing what to say, took a sip of her tea, which had since grown cool. Mr. Exley's somewhat pained expression turned to one of appreciation as he continued to look at Henrietta. "Yes, my dear," he murmured. "Well done. Well done, indeed," he said, leaving the previous conversation hanging in the background. "The Howard boy is quite a catch, their blood running blue, as it were."

Henrietta looked worried. "Blue? What do you mean?"

Mr. Exley mistook her confusion for pretense. "Don't play the innocent with me, my dear," he said with a knowing sort of smile. "I'm sure it was the very first thing Clive Howard told you."

Henrietta swallowed nervously at what her grandfather might possibly be referring to.

"You must know that the Howards are part of the English aristoc-racy. Alcott's brother is Lord Linley. Surely you knew that, did you not? Alcott, of course, is the second son, so not in line for the title, but aristocratic, nonetheless, of course, hence my referring to him as 'blue.' I sometimes forget that your education was so lacking."

Henrietta felt her chest tighten slightly at the revelation of yet another secret. Of course Clive had neglected to mention this. It was becoming expected with him now. He had told her that he had spent part of his summers with his father's relatives in England, but he had failed to mention that they were lords or dukes or whatever they were called. At that moment, however, she was determined that her grandfather not know of this breach in confidence. "Yes, of course," she said, demurely. "Yes, he told me that a long time ago," she fibbed as she looked up at him. Something in his expression, however, told her that he suspected the truth.

"Not to say that you're not a catch as well, my dear," Mr. Exley put in now, causing Henrietta to look away again. "You're wonderfully beautiful and graceful, I'll give you that, and you *are* an Exley," he smiled at her proudly, "which holds its own weight, to be sure."

"I'm also a Von Harmon," Henrietta ventured tentatively. "My . . . my father said that the Von Harmons were once a great family back in France, or maybe it was Germany; I'm not sure."

"Nonsense, my dear," he said almost with a laugh. "I've never heard of them. Just fairy tales, I'm sure." He smiled at her condescendingly. "An Exley is quite good enough, even for the Howards. And by the look of you, you'll do your duty. Especially if you at all take after Martha. Who would have believed that she could birth ten children? No," he almost chuckled, "it's obvious what the Howards have in mind, and we don't mind obliging them one bit, do we, my dear?"

Henrietta had a pretty good idea what he was referring to, but she again chose not to respond.

The tea had ended shortly after, with Fritz, having been gratefully reinstated as the Howard chauffer after the Jack Fletcher affair, bringing the car around to take her back to Highbury. Mr. Exley stood to kiss her hand before she left. She was not entirely sure how she felt about him, even now. He was definitely a man of extreme authority, not to be trifled with, a cunning old fox that could be domineering and even cruel, Henrietta had decided. But perhaps he was not entirely bad, she tried to convince herself, thinking of how, at least initially, he had tried to win Martha back and how, once upon a time, anyway, he had wanted to forgive her.

She was still trying to figure him out, however, and warily watched him, seated across from her now at the dinner table as the conversation around her naturally turned to the subject of the upcoming wedding.

"Yes," Uncle John was saying. "It *is* rather unfortunate that poor Eugene will not be there, but at least we got to meet him at the party," he said deferentially to Mrs. Howard, who was seated to his left. He obviously did not know, or, rather, perhaps pretended not to know, about the thefts.

Mrs. Howard smiled falsely but did not verbally respond.

Eugene had been in residence at Fishburne for nearly three months now, and he would consequently not be attending the wedding, as only the death of a parent, not the mere wedding of a sibling, constituted an acceptable reason to be granted leave to return home before the scheduled Christmas break. Henrietta had had to admit that she had breathed a sigh of relief when she heard the news from Mr. Exley Sr. earlier in the evening that Eugene would not be in attendance. Eugene had not written to them once since his exile, though Mr. Exley apparently received periodic reports on his progress from his commanding officers.

"How are the wedding plans coming along, Henrietta?" Aunt Agatha asked, charitably changing the subject.

All eyes turned to Henrietta now, and her stomach clenched in distress. "Fine, thank you, Aunt Agatha," she answered, her eyes darting to Mrs. Howard for confirmation, who seemed, on her part, to be mentally willing Henrietta to perform well.

Agatha continued to look at her as if expecting more information, so Henrietta carefully set her soupspoon down while she thought up something suitable to say.

"We've only a few fittings left, I believe, and we've finalized the menu now," she said, looking again at Mrs. Howard. "I couldn't have done it all without Antonia's help . . . and Julia's, of course," she said, looking down the table at her future sister-in-law, who flashed her a smile of encouragement.

"Have you the final numbers, Antonia?" Agatha asked, turning her attention back to Mrs. Howard.

"Two hundred and sixty-two, I believe," Antonia answered, as she delicately wiped the corner of her mouth with her napkin.

There it was again. That number. Henrietta felt a wave of nausea pass over her. How did any one family know over two hundred people? She looked across to Clive, who had been seated kitty-corner to her, and he gave her a reassuring wink. At least she had him, she thought, trying to calm herself down. He seemed untouched by all of these trappings, and at this moment she loved him just for that. He had become her rock in the swirl of the wedding euphoria that had descended upon Highbury in the last few months.

"Will Lord Linley attend?" Dorothy, Gerard's wife, asked primly from where she sat next to Clive, her curiosity unmistakable despite the emotionless mask her face always wore.

"I'm afraid not," Antonia answered indifferently and managed a pleasant smile, despite the defeat in her answer. "Not with parliament in session just now. Isn't that right, Alcott?"

"What? What? Yes, quite so. Quite so," Alcott agreed, despite the fact that Montague Howard, Lord Linley, had only minimally attended his parliamentary duties these last few years.

"They're to give a reception for Clive and Henrietta at Castle Linley when they stop there on their honeymoon," Antonia went on.

Henrietta felt yet another wave of nausea upon hearing "Castle Linley" again. Since her tea in the summer with her grandfather, Henrietta had of course asked Clive about his uncle being a lord, to which he had reluctantly, letting out a deep breath, replied in the affirmative, though in an offhand sort of way . . .

"It's really not what you're thinking, darling. Not quite as impressive as it sounds. *Honestly*," he had said, picking up on one of her favorite sayings in an attempt to soften the confession and forcing out an odd little laugh as he did so.

When Henrietta merely looked at him dubiously, his face had become more serious. "You'll see when we get there. Not quite as grand as it once was, I'm afraid. The war hit those massive estates hard; most of them are rambling old giants now, filled with more ghosts than people."

"That's hardly comforting, Clive! I don't know which is worse."

They had been sitting down by the boathouse on the dock when she had questioned him, her feet scandalously naked and dipped

into the cold Lake Michigan water. She splashed a tiny bit of water at
him now with her toe. When she had taken off her shoes and rolled
down her stockings to put her feet in, Clive had been visibly shocked,
watching her with an arched eyebrow. "That's quite risqué, Miss Von
Harmon," he had said thickly, clearing his throat. "Hardly suitable as
the mistress of Highbury."

"All the more reason to do it now before it becomes official," she
said with a mischievous grin. "Come join me," she suggested, holding her hand up to him. He hesitated at first, glancing reactively
toward the house before bending to untie his laces and strip off his
shiny brown brogues and socks.

"Billings is sure to turn up at any moment," he said wryly.

"Better enjoy it while you can, then," she responded, and they had
both laughed.

"Have I told you that I love you?" he asked, as he eased himself
down beside her and put his feet in next to hers.

"Not yet today," she responded, leaning against him and at that
moment forgetting altogether the question of Castle Linley as he
brushed a finger along her jawline and bent to kiss her neck.

But now, as part of the dinner conversation at the Exleys', the reference to the Howards' aristocratic connection was making her uneasy
all over again as no one present seemed inclined to refer to Castle
Linley as a ghost-filled rambling barn of a place, as Clive had tried
to imply, but rather as the impressive family seat she feared in her
imaginings.

"Sounds positively divine. Where are you going exactly, Clive?"
Agatha asked him.

"Four days after the wedding, we sail on the *Queen Mary* for
Liverpool and then travel on to Castle Linley. We'll spend the major-
ity of our time there before travelling down to London. From there
we go to Paris and then Venice.

"Lovely," Julia put in. "I'm sure Uncle Montague and Aunt Margaret
will be delighted to have you."

"It's a pity you won't be there for the Season," Aunt Dorothy said in a deep nasal voice. "This wedding was ill-timed is all I can say. More thought should have been put to attending the Season," she added with a disgruntled sniff.

"But people don't go in for all those sorts of things these days, do they?" Julia tried to add helpfully. "Especially since the war." Henrietta couldn't help notice the resulting glare Julia's two comments had earned from her husband.

"There will always be a Season," Dorothy quipped, "war or no war."

"I'm sure the Howards have the wedding plans well in hand," Mr. Exley Sr. said abruptly, casting a warning look at his daughter-in-law Dorothy. She, in turn, did not say anything further but made sure he saw her scowl.

Two footmen appeared then and began clearing the table in preparation for the next course, during which the discussion moved in a different direction yet again.

"Perhaps you might tell us who will make up the wedding party," Aunt Dorothy asked Henrietta somewhat coldly as the servants were putting the main course in front of them now.

Henrietta cleared her throat and willed herself not to look at Mrs. Howard yet again in an obvious grasp for encouragement. "My sister, Elsie, is to be the maid of honor, of course," Henrietta began, "and Julia has agreed to be my bridesmaid," she said, sending a smile down the table to Julia, who returned it wholeheartedly. "Randolph is to be a groomsman, of course, and Clive has asked his commanding officer, Major Barnes-Smith, to be his best man."

"How nice!" Aunt Agatha twittered. "You'll make a lovely party."

"And your mother will be well enough to attend?" Dorothy asked archly.

"I'm quite sure, yes," Henrietta said, forcing herself to smile politely. "I'm hopeful, anyway. Thank you for asking after her," she answered, with just a slight toss of her hair.

"And with your poor father gone and your brother not being able to attend," Aunt Dorothy continued, "have you given any thought as to who's to walk you down the aisle?"

Mr. Exley Sr. gave a cough. "Naturally that duty would fall to me, of course," he said in an aggravated voice, glowering again at Dorothy; the two seemed always at odds. "And a very pleasant one it will be to execute," he said, now bestowing a look of what could almost be called benevolence upon Henrietta.

Henrietta stiffened a bit and nervously glanced at Clive. "Well, actually, grandfather, I . . . I've . . ."

"*We've*," Clive put in with quiet resolve, and Henrietta felt a fresh surge of love for him yet again and gave him a grateful smile before turning her gaze back to her grandfather.

"We've already asked Mr. Hennessey, my . . . my old friend . . . to give me away. I'm sorry . . . I didn't realize."

"No matter, my child, you'll just have to tell him that the plans have altered," Mr. Exley said, cutting into the thin, flaky pastry of his beef Wellington. "I'm sure he won't mind once you explain."

Henrietta's heart was racing, though no one else at the table seemed disturbed in any way and had indeed turned their attention to the food now placed in front of them. While it did actually make sense that her grandfather, as her most senior male relative, should give her away, how could she just rip that honor from Mr. Hennessey? He would be utterly crushed, given how moved he had been when she had asked him, if she told him now that he was not needed. Besides, it wasn't just *his* feelings she was worried about. She wanted him there; needed him, actually. He had become a pseudo father to her, depending on him over the years, and Clive had even asked him for her hand in marriage. Of course he should be the one to walk her down the aisle and give her to Clive! He had always been there for her, as had Mrs. Hennessey, when her own mother and father had been woefully absent. And yet she understood what the expectation was in this enchanted land in which she now dwelt, with its lords and castles and the London Season looming. She saw that it would be so much more fitting, so much more a satisfying closure to the circle if Oldrich Exley gave his granddaughter in marriage to the Howards after he had been denied that pleasure, that social passage, with his own daughter. It would somehow wash all the sins of the past away, and besides, Mr. Exley in tails at the church would cut a decidedly more elegant picture than the rotund Mr. Hennessey puffing up the aisle with her and most assuredly blubbering the whole time. But that very image made her breath catch in her throat, and suddenly Henrietta felt in danger of crying herself. These last few months had been filled with so much pressure, so much expectation, and she had allowed herself to be led in everything.

She had given in to everything Mrs. Howard and Julia had wanted for the wedding—the dress, the menu, the flowers, the orchestra, the church, the guest list, the society-page interviews and photos, the honeymoon plans. All of these capitulations, plus the guilt she sometimes still felt about abandoning Ma and the kids, even though they were now amply provided for, as well as the knowledge that the boys were to be soon sent away, weighed very heavily on her at times.

Not surprising, then, something cracked inside of her now as she sat at the Exley dinner table being told that she also was expected to give up Mr. Hennessey, too. She decided at this moment that she would have a say in at least one decision regarding her own wedding, and this was going to be it. It seemed a trivial thing to take a stand with, but she grasped on to it tightly as the only thing left to her.

"No, grandfather," she said quietly, causing all eyes to turn toward her in surprise. Her gaze as she said it was on her plate, but she looked across at him now. "I've asked Mr. Hennessey," she said slowly, "and I'll not change it now. He . . . he has been very good to me, and I won't ask him to step down."

"You can't be serious," Mr. Exley said with a smile, as if she had just uttered a charming quip, but when he saw the resoluteness in her face, any trace of amusement on his vanished. "That's ridiculous," he said calmly. "In the extreme."

"Perhaps Mr. Exley is right, dear," Mrs. Howard said eagerly, never liking the idea of Mr. Hennessey's involvement in the first place. "It would be infinitely more appropriate for your grandfather to escort you."

From the other end of the table, Randolph snickered.

"Mr. Hennessey," Clive chimed in now, deliberately putting down his fork, but not without first shooting Randolph a scornful look, "is an honorable man, one whom I deeply respect and to whom, consequently, I went to ask for Henrietta's hand, which is no small matter. In that way, he is the natural choice for who should take that final walk with her from her old life to her new. He was her protector when no one else was and has ever been a friend and father to her. He is infinitely appropriate, and we *will* have him, and would do so even if his only merit was merely being a whim of my future wife," Clive said in a firm, commanding tone that beckoned no arguments.

"He's right, Antonia," Alcott put in. "It's done now; leave it."

Oldrich Exley, however, was not about to let it drop so easily. "That's a very charming sentiment, young man, but you will find greater forces than that in the world, social standing being one of them, as you should very well know."

"Come now, Father," Gerard put in sternly, as if chastising a child, causing Henrietta, like Antonia, to wonder who was really the authority here. Why, for example, had Mr. Exley Sr. come to live with Gerard and Dorothy rather than the other way around? "You've said yourself that the Howards have the wedding well in hand," Gerard was saying. "Perhaps it would be best to leave it with them."

Mr. Exley Sr. inclined his head ever so slightly. "Very well. I'll not stand in the way of my granddaughter's wishes." He looked across at her now and attempted, badly, to disguise his fury with a polite smile, but Henrietta, with a sinking heart, felt she may have just made an enemy. "I will say, I'm very disappointed," he said curtly. "Very disappointed, indeed."

Gerard turned his attention now to Clive. "Will you see any shooting in Derbyshire while you're there?" he asked, smoothly attempting to steer the conversation in another direction.

The dialogue turned then to more benign topics until dessert was finally over and they eventually stood up, the ladies retiring to the drawing room while the men remained to discuss politics, most of them bored by the wedding plans that had dominated most of the dinner discourse. Henrietta badly wanted to go to Clive and kiss his cheek before she left the room with the women, but she knew it would be regarded as highly improper, so she settled for sending him a grateful look, which she hoped conveyed the depth of her love. And Clive, watching her go, indeed caught and understood it and responded in kind.

Chapter 3

With the big day nearly upon them now, it was decided that Henrietta would return to the house in Palmer Square for the remaining days leading up to the wedding. Tradition held that the wedding should have been conducted at St. Sylvester, as it was, after all, Henrietta's home parish, but it had been agreed upon by all parties, even Ma, that that was out of the question considering Eugene's unfortunate experience with Fr. Finnegan, though only Henrietta and Clive knew the whole of the story. Instead, the wedding was set to be held at Sacred Heart in Winnetka, the Howards' parish, with the full pomp and circumstance that would be expected with the son of such a prestigious house.

Shortly after this had been decided, Clive and Henrietta had had, of course, to go and meet with the pastor of Sacred Heart, a Fr. Michaels, who, after a call from Mrs. Howard and very probably a large donation to the St. Vincent DePaul Society, was willing to waive the usual six-month waiting period once he was convinced that there was no extenuating circumstance that required haste, as in, for example, the expected "premature" arrival of a child upon the scene.

Henrietta had been dreadfully nervous to meet with the priest, though she wasn't sure why, but she was immediately put at her ease upon their arrival at the rectory after Fr. Michaels made a joke about his cat asleep again on his favorite chair, as he led them through to his tiny office. He was a surprisingly young priest, with very bright blue eyes, and he had a kind, patient manner to him as he engaged them in a casual exchange of pleasantries and then listened with genuine interest to each of their stories. He carefully went through the rite of marriage, then, stopping every so often to ask questions and to explain what the Church required of married couples. When he finished, he gently closed the worn book before him and, clearing his throat a bit, asked them both if they felt they could honestly commit their lives to one another, considering a few of the more obvious obstacles he saw before them, namely the vast difference in their economic backgrounds and, might he add, age. Clive had taken Henrietta's hand as he looked at her sitting beside him on the stiff, wooden chairs and said that indeed he could. Henrietta, too, had said she could, her heart clenching as she looked into his hazel eyes, despite the presence of Fr. Michael just across the desk from them. She wondered how many times a heart could melt and be reformed, only to be melted all over again.

Fr. Michaels had declared, then, with a glad smile, that he saw no reason for them not to enter into a marriage and had given them his blessing. Both Clive and Henrietta had broken into a smile as well, as if they had passed some sort of test. That, of course, was not true, but they both felt confirmed somehow in their decision, knowing that most of their family members, in actuality, whether they said it out loud or not, still did not approve.

Julia, however, was not one of them, and before Henrietta returned to the city, she insisted on taking her to lunch at The Laurel in Winnetka in lieu of a shower, which Aunt Agatha had been pressing for. Mrs. Howard had skillfully managed to dissuade Agatha, however, saying that there wasn't time, really, for all of the aunts and relatives on the East Coast to come in, seeing as they would have to come in again so soon for the actual wedding, and that a big turnout for the wedding itself was infinitely more preferable. Agatha had had to agree with this wisdom, but she regretted a missed opportunity to be more involved with her new niece and offered to help with any of the wedding plans almost every time she spoke to Antonia. Aunt Dorothy, on the other hand, had retained a chilly distance.

Antonia was acutely aware of the delicate situation she found herself in, oddly playing, at times, the role of both the mother of the groom *and* the bride, seeking to tuck Henrietta's embarrassing immediate family out of sight (remembering with shame Elsie's appearance at the engagement party in a wool suit, for heaven's sake), but finding this exceedingly difficult considering that, in the larger sense, they were, after all, Exleys. It was a strange conundrum to be in, but having begun the wedding plans, she was hesitant to give them up. Not wanting to commit a social faux pas in overstepping her bounds as merely the mother of the groom, however, she had gracefully relinquished certain small duties to Agatha, such as arranging for the wedding cake and the favors and ordering the programs for the church, but she had managed to keep control of most of the details herself, explaining that she did not want Henrietta to feel too over-whelmed by too many people too quickly. Agatha, clearly being the more submissive of the two friends, had reluctantly agreed. Both women were silently conscious of the fact that they were interlopers of a sort, as Henrietta's mother should have been in charge of all of the planning for her daughter's big day herself.

Antonia had uncomfortably approached Henrietta early on about her mother's potential role, especially concerning the wed-ding dress at least, but Henrietta had given Antonia to believe that Ma would not be much help, and Antonia in that moment had genuinely felt sorry for Henrietta, having come to like her more and more, especially after her rather marvelous performance at the engagement party. She had proved that she had talent and that she was moldable, and Antonia was beginning to likewise see something of the spark that so attracted Clive. And in this way, she began to feel protective of her and also for this reason did not relish handing her over to the Exleys just yet, despite her and Alcott's personal regard for John and Agatha.

Etiquette demanded, however, that Antonia at least *attempt* to involve Martha, so she had written to her on lavender-scented stationary just after the formal engagement had been listed in the society pages of the *Tribune*, in which she invited Martha to tea to discuss the wedding, but she had had no reply. She had not really expected one, but at least now she could proceed with little, if any, feelings of guilt, and had chosen Julia to be her faithful ally instead.

Julia could indeed be relied upon, despite the fact that as a girl she had flirted with—and, on more than one occasion, had seemed shockingly close to—abandoning the strict confines of the narrow society in which they both moved, but she had been ultimately made to see reason before it was too late. Julia, always headstrong and vocal in her opinions, had become decidedly less so since her marriage to Randolph Cunningham. Mrs. Howard again congratulated herself on their union, convinced that it was the calming influence of Randolph who had had a hand in taming the otherwise willful Julia. The marriage had been good for her, Antonia often noted with satisfaction, though Julia was decidedly less . . . what was the word? . . . carefree? . . . than she had once been, but that was natural, wasn't it? Antonia reasoned. After all, Julia was a wife and a mother now, and there was no place for her old girlish exuberance. No, Julia, for all her rebellious speeches over the years, could now be relied upon to follow the rules and had proved herself immeasurably useful on a number of occasions, this ridiculously rushed wedding of Clive's being a prime example. And, besides, though she didn't like to admit it out loud, it gave Antonia a chance to see her daughter and her grandsons more often, the three of them spending much more time at Highbury this summer than Julia's very busy social calendar normally allowed for.

The luncheon had been Antonia's idea, but Julia had readily accepted this last assignment, wanting a chance, anyway, to give Henrietta a small gift and to offer, she had said, whatever last-minute advice might be needed. They had just been served dessert, and Julia chose this moment to hand Henrietta the beautifully wrapped box from Francesca's, a most discriminating boutique downtown that had been previously unknown, of course, to Henrietta, but which, after living with the Howards for the last few months, had now become a quite familiar establishment.

"Oh, Julia! You shouldn't have gotten me a gift!" Henrietta said, though she was, in truth, delighted.

Gifts had been pouring into the house for the new couple over the last month, the display of which on a massive table in the morning room was under the special jurisdiction of Billings. Henrietta had never heard of opening gifts before an event, much less displaying them, and had likewise been utterly unprepared for the amount of china, silver, and crystal that had already begun to overflow onto side tables and even onto the floor now. It scared her, actually, as she had no idea what to do with half of these new possessions or where to put them, causing the old doubts about her worthiness to someday be mistress of Highbury to hover close. She had also been utterly unprepared for the thank-yous that had to be written for each gift on brand-new stationary embossed with her and Clive's future initials. For a half an hour each morning, she and Mrs. Howard dutifully sat down together in the morning room to work on them before Julia arrived for the day and other wedding tasks then took over. As it happened, before she had left for lunch this morning, Billings had quite been at his wits' end and was considering moving the whole display to the much larger dining room, though he would of course need Mrs. Howard's permission for so drastic a motion.

But Henrietta had not received any personal gifts as yet, besides, of course, the emerald-and-diamond engagement ring, the family heirloom that Clive had presented her with at the Burgess Club, as well as the family pearls he had given her on the night of the engagement party. She looked excitedly at the gift and gave Julia a grateful smile. "I should be giving *you* a gift for all the work you've done," Henrietta said, and Julia pooh-poohed her with a wave of her hand.

Henrietta carefully opened the box, then, and drew out a long white silk dressing gown complete with a white faux fur and feathery collar and matching slippers.

"I know Mother's prepared your trousseau for you, but I thought you might like to have something special for the honeymoon," she said with a sly smile.

"Julia! It's beautiful," Henrietta exclaimed, though she blushed slightly at the garment's obvious purpose. "Thank you," she said sincerely.

"Not to worry, my dear. As your faithful bridesmaid—or matron, I should say—it is my duty to see you well prepared for your wedding night, even if the groom *is* my brother!" she laughed gaily.

Henrietta never stopped marveling at Julia's obsequious good humor. She had had much time to observe Julia over the last few months, with her being at Highbury so often of late, and she found Julia to always be very light and gay, always up for a laugh. Likewise she seemed to adore her two boys, Randolph and Howard, though Henrietta noticed they spent most of their time in the care of their nanny, who was brought along on each occasion to tag after them. It was only when Julia's husband, Randolph Sr., was around that she became just a bit more subdued and even on edge, though she hid it well, Henrietta had noticed. They seemed to make no pretense about the fact that theirs was a loveless relationship, and Henrietta remembered Clive's words to her that their marriage was unfortunate. Henrietta had often wondered why they had gotten married in the first place; surely there had been love between them once upon a time? She had often been tempted to ask Julia about it, but it never seemed the right moment.

As she carefully placed the robe back in the box and set it to the side, Henrietta wondered if this might be her only chance to ask Julia about her marriage, now that they were blessedly away from the servants or Mrs. Howard or any other number of people that always seemed to be coming or going at the estate. Henrietta found it odd that in a place as large as Highbury, there seemed to be a definite lack of privacy, and it added to her anxiety. Would she ever be truly alone with Clive? she often wondered and pushed away the thoughts of the cottage that had again popped up in her mind.

"What . . . what was your wedding like, Julia?" Henrietta asked, deciding to go about it this way.

"Oh, the usual society wedding. Yours is small by comparison!" she laughed.

"No! Honestly?" Henrietta answered, still unsettled about the numbers that had confirmed.

"Yes, I think the final count for us was over four hundred. Very intimate!" she drawled.

"Was it at the Winnetka Yacht Club, as well?"

"Of course, darling. Except mine was in spring, so the flowers were entirely different. No one's had a fall wedding for ages!" she said, finishing up her tea. "Several people think you're expecting, you know," Julia grinned at her from behind the rim of her teacup.

"Expecting!" Henrietta said, blushing very red now. "How dare they! It isn't true!"

"Oh, don't worry, darling. I know that, but the biddies need something to gossip about. You'll soon prove them wrong," Julia laughed, though Henrietta found it hard to join in despite the fact that Julia's laugh was usually quite contagious.

"Had you . . . had you known Randolph long?" Henrietta asked, reaching for her own cup now.

"Not really," Julia smiled thinly. "I met him at my coming-out ball. I danced with him at one point. He seemed rather dashing at the time."

Henrietta waited for her to continue, but she did not. "Did you like him right away, or . . . did you . . ."

"You're trying to ask, I think, how I ended up marrying a man such as Randolph, am I right?" she asked, her smile sadder now. "No doubt you've observed our less-than-loving ways."

"Well . . . yes," Henrietta faltered.

"It was Mother's idea that he call for tea shortly after my coming-out ball," Julia explained rather matter-of-factly, as if she had been over this, maybe even just to herself, a thousand times before. "He seemed polite, elegant even, more refined somehow than all the other young men I'd met in the past. I was in danger of becoming a loose woman, you see," Julia laughed. "I was a flapper, you see, and given to drinking and smoking with a rather fast set."

Henrietta's eyes widened. Julia seemed to be the model of decorum now.

"Mother and Father panicked, of course, and wanted me married as soon as possible. So when Randolph presented himself, they were beside themselves with joy. Eminent family, very old, solid. He is older than me, which they thought would be good to keep me in tow." Julia's face became very grave then. "Which he certainly has done." She tried giving Henrietta a little smile. "But why talk of such things just now? This is supposed to be a happy luncheon filled with talk of silks and rosebuds and lovely wedding champagne."

But Henrietta was not to be put off so easily. "Did you love him?" she asked plainly.

Julia smiled tiredly. "I suppose I thought I did. He was very handsome. I thought his quiet demeanor was simply shyness, but it turns out it's not that at all. He's . . . let's just say he is quite strict. He has very old-fashioned ideas about correct behavior and decorum."

Henrietta nodded, trying to understand.

"I've been rather a disappointment to him, I'm sure, despite the fact that I'm a Howard."

"Is he . . . good to you?"

Julia paused as if trying to decide what to say. "He's been known to be rather rough," she said finally.

"He's not . . . not violent, is he?"

Julia did not respond but merely looked at Henrietta sadly.

"Oh, Julia!" Henrietta whispered, shocked. "Does your mother know?"

"If she does, she wouldn't care. I'm a woman now and married, rather well, I might add. If my husband chooses to beat me, well, I must deserve it, my dear. At least it's never in a place that shows," she said quietly, gesturing toward her face.

"Oh, Julia!" was all Henrietta could think to say. "How awful for you! I . . . I had no idea. You always seem so . . ."

"Happy?" Julia finished for her. "Yes, that's me. Happy-go-lucky Julia! Well, darling, sometimes things aren't always as they seem." It was a fact Henrietta knew all too well.

"But . . . but what about a divorce? Or a separation?"

"Impossible, darling," she said. "I must think of the boys. That's all that matters now."

Henrietta looked down at her plate, her mind reeling. "Does Clive know?" she asked tacitly.

"I think he suspects. He's always very short with Randolph—who feels the slight, by the way. Clive's asked me outright, but I've always lied, which you must do now, too," she said slowly, looking at her trustingly.

"But why? Surely he could help?" Henrietta asked, a nagging twinge reminding her that she and Clive had pledged only honesty from now on.

"How could Clive possibly help?" Julia asked despondently. "By giving Randolph a beating as he likes to do when he's playing police-man? Or killing him?"

"Surely he wouldn't kill him!" Henrietta scoffed.

"I'm not so sure," Julia said uncertainly. "I'm rather convinced Clive has it in him to kill a man. Surely it was part of his job as an inspector in the city—or at least in the war, anyway."

"Yes, but that's different," Henrietta argued, though she knew that Clive definitely had a violent streak. She had seen him throw Virgil up against a wall and thrash him, not to mention beating Neptune until his nose was broken. "Maybe he could perhaps . . . well . . . rough him up a bit . . ." Henrietta suggested tentatively.

"To what end? Randolph would turn around and take it out on me. Besides, that's not very civilized behavior, now, is it, for the lord of Highbury?"

"Well, it's not very civilized to beat your wife . . . or other things," she added, thinking of her mother's accusations about her father.

"No, don't fret, dearest. I've found ways to deal with him. It's not so bad as it used to be. Now, come. I insist we change the subject. This has been horribly irresponsible of me! Here you are, practically on the eve of your wedding, and I'm frightening you with my horrible tales of wedded bliss gone awry."

Henrietta barely managed a smile in response.

Julia reached out and gripped Henrietta's arm. "You've nothing to worry about with Clive," she said reassuringly.

"No, I wasn't thinking that . . . but I . . ." she broke off, fibbing a bit and not knowing what else to say.

"I've seen the way he looks at you; he's quite smitten. And Clive, at heart, anyway, is a very good man."

Henrietta couldn't help but smile. "Yes, he is, isn't he?" she murmured.

"He was always very gentle with Catherine; I'm sure of it."

This isn't the way Henrietta had expected the conversation to go, but now that the subject of Catherine had been broached, she couldn't help her curiosity. "What was she like? Catherine, I mean."

"Oh, Catherine was very shy. Pretty," she grinned mischievously at Henrietta, "but not as beautiful as you are."

Henrietta felt herself blush.

"She was a sweet person. I think she always had a particular attachment to Clive, ever since we were children, really. I don't think Clive ever thought of her in that way, but when he joined up, I think it was her older brother, Charles, that put it in Clive's ear. Clive had always looked up to him, and Charles must have known how his sister felt about Clive."

"Oh," was all Henrietta could think to say.

"I know Clive loved Catherine in a certain way, and I suppose he thought it was the honorable thing to do. Maybe he was just caught up like everyone else was at the time, marrying like crazy. As if that made sense. All it did was create a glut of war widows barely twenty-five years old."

A waiter appeared now with a fresh pot of tea, which Julia poured out as she continued. "They didn't have long before he shipped out. Catherine pined for him while he was gone; I remember her moping about the house all the time. She was so happy when she realized that she was pregnant. We all were, really. You should have seen Mother. But at the end, she wanted to go home to her parents to have the baby. We could understand that, that she wanted her mother." Henrietta shifted uncomfortably. "But something went wrong, and, well, you know the story. Neither of them made it. It was devastating. Mother wouldn't come out of her room for days. We tried writing to Clive; Father tried to wire his commanding officer, but there was a miscommunication. Clive himself had been wounded somewhere in France and was en route back to the States, so the letter missed him. Well, you know what happened after that, I suppose," she sighed.

Henrietta wasn't sure she really did, but she remained silent, trying to take it all in. It was so very sad that it was impossible to be jealous. "What about Charles?" she asked, thinking he might have been able to offer Clive some comfort upon his sad return.

"He was killed, too," Julia answered. "Too bad, actually, because I was terribly fond of him," she laughed. "So I ended up with Randolph, and Clive ended up running away to the city, poor thing." She looked up at Henrietta. "But here I am again! Telling tales of woe!" She took Henrietta's hand. "He adores you, you know. You're so wonderful, so good for him," she said seriously. "You're an answer to prayers, Henrietta. I'm so happy for him, and for you. We all are, really, even Mother, despite her snobbishness. Clive's her favorite, and though she goes on about Clive marrying well and carrying on the name and all that, she really just wants him to be happy. And you're the first person to light up his eyes in many long years. We've all noticed." She gave her hand a squeeze before releasing it again. "I know he'll make you happy, too."

Henrietta felt herself blushing again. "Thank you, Julia," she murmured. "I hope so."

Julia's comment about making Clive happy, however, as well as the honeymoon gift she had just been given, introduced another area of concern in her mind that had been nagging her for the last months. She had toyed all afternoon with the idea of asking Julia for her advice about the wedding night specifically; she so wanted to please Clive, but she wasn't sure how to go about it. And after hearing about Randolph's brutality, she decided that perhaps Julia was not the best person after all to ask for tender suggestions for the honeymoon bed.

Girls mostly learned about what to expect, Henrietta knew, from their mothers, but Henrietta had already heard her mother's version of marital unions and still felt sickened when she allowed herself to think of it for any length of time. Her father did not seem that type, but then again, she had been only thirteen when he died. Perhaps she hadn't realized what he was really like. And hadn't she herself witnessed several examples now of men she had thought harmless who had turned out to be brutal? Neptune and Jack being prime examples. But that was different, she argued with herself. She could never put her father in the same league as them. But had her father *really* forced himself upon her mother? Perhaps Ma's warped mind had simply imagined it. Or did she give in to "it" so rarely that it felt like being forced? And what about all of the ogling, grasping men Henrietta had met over the years as a 26 girl or during her stint as a taxi dancer and then an usherette? Yes, she had seen her fair share of "bad" men over the years.

A good person to ask for advice might have been Polly, her friend from the Promenade, but she was still in Missouri. Henrietta had invited her to the wedding, but Polly had declined, saying that her grandmother was in poor health and that she couldn't possibly leave her. She had sent some handkerchiefs, though, as a small wedding gift and hoped that she and the inspector would be happy after all. Polly, she remembered, had never really trusted Clive, but, then again, she had never gotten to know him.

Antonia, of course, had taken great care in instructing her on how to behave in society, but not necessarily on how to be a good *wife*, especially in that way, and Henrietta was loath to ask her. The unsaid subtext that seemed to permeate both of the horizontal worlds, rich and poor, that Henrietta balanced between was one of submission, at least according to both Ma and Julia, and even Mrs. Howard, to a certain extent. Likewise it permeated both of the vertical worlds of sin and grace, Henrietta had realized, though in perhaps not those exact words, remembering that submission had been the key not only to getting beyond the sordid green door at the Marlowe and the acts performed there, but to what the Church expected of women as well. Hadn't Father Michaels, albeit in a kind, patient way, instructed that Henrietta's role would be to *obey* Clive, while Clive's would be to cherish and protect her? But what did *cherish* mean, exactly? And protect her from what or from whom?

"Shall we go, then?" Julia asked, and Henrietta saw that her window of opportunity was over. "Mother will be expecting us back," Julia said crisply, "and besides, I'm sure you still have a lot to pack. It will seem strange without you at Highbury now." She stood up, a signal for the waiter to approach adroitly. "But not long now," she smiled, "and you'll be with us always."

Henrietta was indeed kept very busy for the rest of that day and the next, her last day at Highbury as a single woman. She would have liked to spend more of it with Clive, who spent most of his days, now that he had officially retired from the force, with his father at the firm or reviewing documents about the state of Highbury in the library. They were not granted any time alone, really, until the last evening when they were out on the terrace, Mr. and Mrs. Howard having retired even earlier than usual, suspecting probably that the two of them might have much to say to each other before they became man and wife in several days' time.

Clive handed her what had become their customary cognac. Henrietta dared then to bring up the subject of the cottage one last time, but Clive dismissed it once again as being unrealistic and impractical. Besides, he pointed out, didn't it hold unpleasant memories for her of being held captive by Jack Fletcher? Henrietta did her best to explain that somehow it did not, that the cottage had always been such a quaint, lovely place, so peaceful by the lake, and in her pre-wedding anxiety, she yearned for it all the more, despite any unfortunate events that had occurred there. And anyway, her capture by Jack was short-lived, an hour at most, nothing like what had gone on at the Marlowe.

"I hate thinking about what could have happened there," Clive said bitterly. "How you were almost . . ." He broke off here and looked out at the lake.

"But I wasn't," she said, putting her hand on his as it gripped the iron railing. "Let's forget it, Clive," she said, referring to the cottage. "It was just a silly idea. Honestly."

He turned to her now, his face still full of concern. "I'm sorry, darling. It's quite impossible, I'm afraid."

"Yes, I know," she said with a sad smile.

He tucked a stray lock of her hair behind her ear. "Are you ready?" he asked, gently changing the subject.

"To go home or for the wedding?"

Clive laughed. "Either, I suppose."

"I wish the wedding was tomorrow," she said, wrapping her arms around him now.

"Me, too. I want this to be over. I want you for my wife, for my own," he said, kissing the top of her head and breathing in her sweet smell. "I want you to belong to me and only me, and I, utterly, to you."

They spent the rest of the evening discussing the wedding and any small details that may have been forgotten, and parted, finally, for the last time, at the bottom of the stairs. The next time they would see each other would be at the altar at Sacred Heart, and the next time they said goodnight to each other it would be in the new master bedroom designed for them in the east wing. Clive took her hand and, turning it over, drew it up to his lips and kissed her palm, slowly and sweetly. Releasing it, he bent to kiss her lips, and Henrietta could feel his passion hovering just under the surface, but he kept it at bay as he wished her good night and let her go up the stairs, somewhat reluctantly, without giving in to it.

Chapter 4

Henrietta did not see Clive the next day, per their arrangement, as she groggily climbed into the back of the Daimler very early, Fritz arranging her cases for her in the trunk. She had slept rather badly, truth be told, tossing and turning all night and having several bad dreams in which she was in a big rambling maze of a house searching for Clive but never finding him. She tried to shake these thoughts as Fritz headed south back to the city, the landscape rushing by in a blur, and tried instead to concentrate on the many things that still had to be done at home in preparation—most of them, of course, made all the more difficult in that they involved Ma.

Since they had moved to Palmer Square and now owned a telephone, Henrietta had taken to calling them once each week on Sunday to check on them. At first they had all jumped when it rang, Mrs. Schmidt, the housekeeper, usually having to answer it for them, but they were gradually getting used to the sound of it, though no one ever rang them except Henrietta. Both Ma and Elsie seemed afraid of using it, and Jimmy and Donnie usually just giggled or repeatedly shouted, "Hello? Hello!" into it over and over. Henrietta exhaled deeply as Fritz pulled up outside the brownstone, knowing that she had her work cut out for her in these next few days.

—

As expected, none of them had as yet purchased any new clothes for the wedding, though Mr. Exley Sr. now provided them with a very generous monthly allowance. Elsie said she had tried to take them shopping, but no one would cooperate. Henrietta's first day back, then, was spent downtown with the kids finding suitable attire; the second day was devoted entirely to Ma, who, of course, initially balked at buying a new dress. Henrietta forced her, however, to go shopping with her, and, as arduous as it was, a little part of Henrietta enjoyed being back downtown, and she let herself, as they trudged from shop to shop, indulge in memories of her days as a curler girl at Marshall Field's.

It seemed odd, then, since she had been reminiscing so much about the past, when she was handed a telephone message by Mrs. Schmidt upon their return home to Palmer Square from the long shopping trip. She and Ma and Elsie had been sitting in the front parlor—exhausted—drinking coffee and observing all of the new purchases when Mrs. Schmidt had bustled in to give Henrietta the telephone message. Henrietta felt her heart leap, hoping that it might be from Clive, though he had told her before she left Highbury not to expect a call from him of a romantic nature, as he knew that the operators were forever listening in. Still, as she took the folded message from Mrs. Schmidt, she could not help feeling a moment of disappointment that it was indeed not from him, but she was equally surprised that it was from, of all people, her friend, Lucy.

Struggling to find someone to invite from her side during the grueling invitation sessions with Mrs. Howard, Henrietta had finally decided to invite Lucy and the gang from the Marlowe. She had debated their respectability, being usherettes as well as female homosexuals, but they were the closest thing she had at this point in her life to friends. And it had been them, really, that had saved her and Clive from Neptune. She at least owed them an invitation, she had eventually reasoned, which Clive had agreed with when she had asked him for his thoughts regarding the invitation list one night on the terrace. Yes, he rather liked Lucy, he had said casually as he smoked his pipe, and he, too, felt they owed her their gratitude in the form of an invitation.

Henrietta had kept up an intermittent correspondence with Lucy in which she had lately written to give her their new address—and telephone number!—in Palmer Square and at Highbury. Often Lucy had suggested that they meet up, but Henrietta was forever putting her off, saying she was much too busy and rarely in town. Indeed, Henrietta had half expected them to decline to come to the wedding at all, so she had therefore been delighted when she received the RSVPs announcing that Lucy, Gwen, and even Rose would attend.

The telephone message handed to her now from Mrs. Schmidt read to call Lucy at her earliest convenience, so after excusing herself from Ma and Elsie, Henrietta slipped into the hall where the large black telephone sat on a little table, neatly placed atop a crocheted doily and accompanied by a little pad of paper and a pencil to take messages that rarely came. Henrietta patiently waited for the operator to put the call through and felt herself smile when Lucy's excited voice answered. The two exchanged happy pleasantries, and Lucy went on to explain that she and the girls wanted to treat her before she "tied the knot," is how she put it, though there wasn't much time left now, and could she possibly come out with them tonight? It was the only night all three of them had off. They should have called her earlier, Lucy acknowledged, but Gwen had just at the last minute gotten out of her shift. What did she say? Lucy had asked, practically begging her to come.

Henrietta paused, not knowing what to say and trying to think quickly. She was touched that they wanted to see her, but she had so much to do! Really, it was unwise. And besides, Ma would certainly grumble, probably saying something like she had not been here two seconds before feeling the need to gallivant off again. However, being downtown these past two days had made her excited and antsy, unsettled despite her exhaustion. Maybe it would be good to spend one last night with them, she reasoned. And didn't she really owe it to them? she persuaded herself.

"Well . . ." Henrietta began.

"Please!" Lucy urged, before she could finish. "You should take a couple of hours off for yourself. It will be good for you! Besides, we'll make it worth your while . . ."

"All right, then," Henrietta acquiesced, laughing a little now that the decision had been made and hurriedly took down the details.

Ma had indeed grumbled, but Henrietta steeled herself to ignore her, though she did feel a little guilty when Elsie had wistfully said good-bye. She had thought about taking Elsie with her, but she wasn't sure that whatever Lucy and the gang had planned would be completely appropriate for Elsie's young eyes. She would try to make it up to her tomorrow, she promised herself.

Reluctantly she had arranged for Karl, the not-quite-elderly man servant employed by Mr. Exley to be both butler and chauffer for the Von Harmons, to drive her, having sworn to Clive that she would only take the Packard left for them by Mr. Exley and never a cab or—God forbid!—the motorbus. She knew he was still haunted by the fact that Neptune remained at large; she was, too, to be honest, but she tried not to let him see her fear anymore, knowing now how sensitive he was about protecting her. In fact, she was pretty sure he would disapprove of her going out at all tonight if he had known, but she felt certain she would be safe with old Karl. She felt guilty, though, because she knew she was taking him from his cup of cocoa and *The Shadow*, his favorite radio program. Still, there was nothing for it; she had already promised the girls.

As requested, Karl drove her to The Green Mill on Broadway, where the girls had suggested they meet. As they neared, he told Henrietta not to hurry, that he had his paper and his thermos, as well as the almanac, and that she should enjoy herself. Henrietta was touched by his generosity, not really knowing him all that well, though she thought he seemed fond of her. He had told her on the drive over that he had known her mother in her younger days, having once worked in the big Exley mansion as a boot boy back when they still had such things. Henrietta listened politely, but she found it almost impossibly hard to concentrate on Karl's ramblings just at the moment.

When they finally pulled up to the curb, Henrietta looked out at the bright lights of the Green Mill's sign and was surprised at how excited she felt. Karl shuffled around the front of the car to her side and opened the Packard's door for her. She took a deep breath as she slipped out, giving Karl a faint wave of farewell, and proceeded to enter the club. Carefully she made her way in, peering through the thick fog of cigarette smoke to see if she could see the girls. Almost immediately she spotted the beautiful Lucy at a table in the back, right near the stage. The girls saw her then, too, and waved excitedly to her to join them. Henrietta wedged her way through the crowd, delighted to see the old gang—it had been so long! As she approached, they all exclaimed over her, saying hello and commenting on how much older and certainly stylish she looked.

"Look at you, Gumdrop!" Lucy said after she embraced her, "all grown up!"

Henrietta smiled at being called by her old nickname as she squeezed in next to them. She looked out excitedly at the throng of couples on the dance floor; the band was playing "Blue Skies."

"You all look wonderful, too!" Henrietta shouted above the music.

"I'll get you a drink," Rose offered. "Your usual?" she said, and Henrietta nodded.

"So you've landed on your feet after all, kid," Gwen said, smiling at her. "Lucy told us you're to be lady of the manor up north or something like that. Who would have thought the old inspector was loaded? Well, good for you, sweets."

"You'll have to tell us all about it!" Lucy said eagerly.

"Wait for me, though," Rose said, coming up now with a glass of beer for Henrietta. Henrietta smiled again; she couldn't remember the last time she had had beer.

"Oh, why don't you tell me about all of you!" Henrietta exclaimed.

"I'm sure it's much more interesting, anyway. Tell me about the Melody Mill!"

The girls spent the evening exchanging news, in between Rose getting up and down to dance at times whenever a suitable man presented himself. Henrietta was asked several times herself, but each time she declined, thinking of Clive and relishing the warmth of knowing that there was someone waiting for her at home, guiltily realizing that the "home" that came to mind was indeed Highbury, not the old apartment and certainly not Palmer Square. Neither Lucy nor Gwen were asked to dance, however, which seemed odd considering how attractive at least Lucy was, but then Henrietta noticed that they both wore gold bands where a wedding ring would normally be. Henrietta had left her own large emerald-and-diamond engagement ring in her room in Palmer Square, though normally she was never without it, much to Mrs. Howard's annoyance, who preferred that it be kept in the vault. No one in the family had ever had the audacity to wear it on a regular basis, Antonia had intimated to Clive, as it smacked of ill-breeding. Henrietta, for her part, thought this line of reasoning ridiculous when Clive had laughingly repeated the conversation to her in private. "What good is a ring kept in a drawer?" she had insisted, thinking of poor Helen's sad story and her lost ring. And anyway, she wanted the world to know of her love for Clive, and wearing it, she had to admit, made her feel more confident, her token of authenticity, as it were, into this strange, foreign world in which she was choosing now to dwell. Clive had smiled at all of this and, against his mother's private protests to him, had allowed Henrietta to permanently wear it. She had had the wisdom, however, to leave it behind on such a night as tonight.

Henrietta pointed to Lucy's ring when Rose was off dancing. "Still a couple, then?" she asked with a smile.

"We wear these to stop men from approaching," Gwen said, holding up her hand briefly. "Doesn't stop all of them, though, the swine," she said, taking a swig from the glass of gin she held, reminding

Henrietta, again, of the Marlowe. "But, yes, we are still a couple," she said, giving Lucy a rare, amorous glance.

"What about Rose?" Henrietta asked. "Why is she dancing with men? Just for fun?"

"She's decided to go back the other way, she says," Lucy explained. "Gwen thinks it's a stage, but it might be real. Who knows? Sometimes girls just like to experiment. Or she might just want kids, so she'll put up with having to have a husband."

Henrietta peered across the dance floor to where she saw Rose being held tightly by a young man as they danced to "A Fine Romance" and tried to guess Rose's true sexual orientation, which was obviously impossible to do just by looking.

"Speaking of," Lucy said mysteriously, "we got you a little gift." Lucy reached into a bag on the floor beside her and handed Henrietta a box that looked curiously like the box Julia had given her not but a few days before. Henrietta hoped it did not contain something too outrageous.

"Thanks, girls!" she managed to say. "You didn't have to get me a gift!"

Rose came to the table now, flushed. "Hey! You said you'd wait for me!" she said, picking up her drink as she sat down quickly with a thud.

"Well, you're here now," Gwen said to her absently. "Go on, then, open it!" she said, giving Henrietta a nudge.

Henrietta slowly opened the box and pulled out a white, almost see-through silk negligee followed by a matching black one. Beside her, the girls giggled. Henrietta held them up and forced herself to smile, though the sight of such articles caused her stomach to clench up in fear from the memories it unexpectedly dredged up about the night she had been forced to wear such a thing and tied to a bed by Neptune. She hadn't realized that there was so much fear still in her, and she struggled to breathe normally.

"Thanks, girls," she found herself saying. "They're . . . they're lovely! You shouldn't have spent all your money!"

"Well, we had to give the inspector a bit of thrill, even though you'll be more than enough for the likes of him, I should imagine," Gwen joked. "We got both black *and* white depending on whether you're feeling naughty or nice!" she grinned.

"Yes, we couldn't have you go to your wedding night unprepared," Lucy agreed. "I'm sure all the swells you're living with now wouldn't think to get you something like this, so we had to come to your rescue, just like the old days, right, Gumdrop?"

Henrietta couldn't help but smile, despite her discomfort at seeing the negligees. She had missed the girls' company more than she realized.

"You sure you want to marry this guy?" Gwen asked, then, more seriously. "It's not too late, you know."

"He does seem a bit old," Rose put in. "I'm sure you could do better, Henrietta. I couldn't believe it, actually, when Lucy told us you were engaged to him."

"Yeah, but his money makes up for it," Gwen added, giving Henrietta a little wink before she could offer any protest. "For that much money, I could put up with some groping at night."

"You'd still have some man telling you what to do, though," Lucy said.

"Yeah, and instead you have Gwen to tell you what to do!" Rose laughed, causing Lucy to give her a playful shove.

"On that note, I think I'll powder my nose," Gwen said with a smile, as she slid out of the booth. Within minutes, the lovely Rose was asked to dance again, leaving Henrietta and Lucy momentarily alone. Henrietta looked out at the dance floor, trying to control her swirling thoughts. It was Lucy that broke her reverie, laying her hand on Henrietta's arm.

"You're afraid, aren't you?" she asked, serious now.

Henrietta momentarily considered bluffing but abandoned this idea just as quickly. She was too tired to keep up the facade, and if she was honest, she didn't really want to. She nodded. "Maybe a little."

"Hey, kid, don't worry. It's not that bad."

"How would you know?" Henrietta laughed despite her unease.

"You think I haven't been with a man before?" Lucy asked, incredulous.

Henrietta shrugged. "Well, if you have, you obviously didn't like it."

Lucy laughed. "It was passable," she said, giving her a wink.

Henrietta tried to conjure up a smile.

Lucy leaned closer. "Listen, sweets. You love the inspector, right? And he loves you; anyone can see that by the way he looks at you. He's kissed you, right?"

Henrietta blushed and nodded.

"And you liked it, right?"

Henrietta nodded again, this time not being able to contain a small smile.

"Okay then, you just keep going."

Henrietta thought back to the night in Clive's apartment where she had been ready to give herself to him, how he had lifted the folds of her dress and lightly caressed her breasts before he had stopped himself. She had been on fire, then, wanting him to keep touching her, to continue his soft kisses. Of course Clive will be gentle! she reasoned again. She couldn't speak for her father or Randolph or perhaps the man Lucy had been with, but surely she knew Clive, didn't she?

"Just try to relax," Lucy went on. "Follow his lead. You might just enjoy it," she smiled. "It's not shameful," she added, more seriously. "To enjoy it, that is."

"How do I . . ." Henrietta paused, trying to think of the right words. "How do I . . . well, please him?" Henrietta asked, her voice barely audible. She gave Lucy a sideways glance.

Lucy grinned. "He'll show you, I'm sure. And if he doesn't, ask him to—he'll love it." Henrietta considered this option; she hadn't thought of simply being honest with Clive. Asking him to guide her.

"If nothing else, try this," Lucy said and leaned closer to whisper something in her ear.

"Lucy!" Henrietta exclaimed, her face a brilliant shade of red by now.

The other girls came up, then, and the conversation thankfully turned in a different direction yet again, Henrietta laughing now and feeling oddly relieved to have finally confided in someone and to have had her fears heard and dispelled—at least for now.

When they finally parted it was past ten o'clock. The girls escorted Henrietta out and embraced her. They were going on to the Aragon and begged Henrietta to come with them, but she declined, knowing Elsie would be up waiting and feeling sorry for Karl as well. Besides, she was not now accustomed to staying out as late as she had used to and was, in truth, very tired.

They said goodbye, then, Lucy giving her hand a final squeeze as she embarrassingly climbed into the Packard that Karl had brought around, the girls whistling at the luxury of it.

"Good luck," Lucy whispered. "You'll be fine."

"Thanks, Luce," she whispered back.

"See you in a few days when you'll be Mrs. Howard!"

The girls waved as the car pulled away, and Henrietta settled back against the seat, her box of new negligees sliding across the shiny black seat as Karl made an uncharacteristically sharp turn onto Clark.

"Have a good night, Miss?" Karl asked drowsily.

"Yes, I did, Karl. Thanks," Henrietta replied with a smile, thinking how strange it was that the future mistress of Highbury received her first real, and only, actually, wedding-night advice from a lesbian cocktail waitress, formerly employed as an usherette at a burlesque theater.

Chapter 5

The big day finally arrived—October 19, 1935—Henrietta's wedding day.

The house in Palmer Square was all aflutter as Henrietta helped everyone into their wedding clothes. She had finally forced Ma to choose something at Field's, which had turned out to be a two-piece black skirt and jacket with a respectable hat. Henrietta had quite liked another in a shade of deep rose, but Ma had insisted on the black, saying it would be more suitable, seeing as she was presenting herself back into society now as a widow. Henrietta couldn't help but wonder if there was a deeper, more overt reason for choosing black, but she let it go, happy that Ma had at least agreed to buy something new, apparently choosing to finally relinquish—if only to herself— her pride, knowing as she must that Oldrich Exley had paid for it.

Mrs. Andrews, Mrs. Howard's own personal maid, had been dispatched very early this morning to Palmer Square to help the female Von Harmons to do their hair, as she really was a very talented hairdresser, and Henrietta had likewise come to trust her. Henrietta and Elsie were upstairs with her now as each in turn had their hair brushed and twisted up and set with pins of pearl. Henrietta had dubiously offered Ma Mrs. Andrews's services as well, sure that she would refuse them, and was therefore surprised when Ma begrudgingly accepted. She grumbled afterward, of course, that it wasn't what she had wanted, but had surprisingly left her newly coiffed hair just as Mrs. Andrews had styled it.

Ma had then made her way to the nursery to ask Nanny Kuntz if the children were ready. Mrs. Kuntz rather breathlessly replied that she had everything well in hand, thank you very much. In reality she had spent the morning puffing after Doris, Donny, and Jimmy in her effort to make them presentable, but their excitement was running high, and she was having a hard go of it. Ma, standing in the doorway, had quickly inspected the three of them and admonished them to settle down, for heaven's sake.

Apparently feeling, then, that she had fulfilled her maternal duty for the immediate moment, she turned on her heel, without a word of thanks to the poor nanny, and went back downstairs and wandered into the parlor to fretfully wait, phrases and bits of laughter from Henrietta or Elsie floating down the stairs to her as she sat, then paced, around the room.

Martha tried to drink some of the coffee that Odelia, the maid, had brought in earlier along with a plate of fresh buns from the kitchen, but it left only a bitter taste in her mouth, causing her to suspect that Odelia had burnt it yet again. How could you burn coffee? Martha had fumed many times. What was the use of having servants if they didn't know how to do anything? In her day, someone would have been sacked for something much less than that by her father.

Her father. She hated the fact that he had returned to her life now. She had tried so hard to put that life behind her, but he had found her out in her shame and humiliation, as she perhaps always knew he someday would. A small part of her had wanted to go to him and embrace him that day when he appeared in the apartment to meet them all, but her stubborn pride had held her back. She had refused to let him see her capitulate at that moment or—heaven help her—cry.

She looked forlornly around the tastefully appointed room in which she now stood. She hadn't wanted any of this, but what did it really matter? she sighed. One cage was the same as any other. She had lost control of her life long ago, and she was becoming too tired to keep fighting.

She heard Henrietta laugh again. How could she be this relaxed? She had to admit that Henrietta had adjusted to the life she herself had run from with seemingly perfect ease. From the sound of it—through Henrietta's own anecdotes about Highbury and all that went on there—she had no problems interacting with servants, dressing in beautiful gowns, and tending to a full social calendar, all the things that had always filled Martha with dread. Henrietta was already practically living at Highbury, and if she was bothered by Antonia Howard or any of the Exleys, for that matter, she never showed it. In private, Martha marveled at her daughter, as if she belonged to someone else. But it had ever felt that way. She had always seemed more Les's child than her own. Les would have been proud of Henrietta, especially today. He would idiotically have said something about Henrietta taking a step toward restoring the Von Harmons to greatness. But hadn't *he* done that by marrying an Exley? she countered with herself bitterly. No, he had never seemed to count that as worth much of anything. But neither did she, she reminded herself.

Martha forced him from her mind. There was no place for him here today, nor had there ever really been a place for him in her heart, excepting, of course, at the very beginning. After almost six years since his death she still hated him for what he had done to her, taking the coward's way out and leaving her here with the eight children she had never really wanted in the first place. But she supposed she had been learning to hate him by degrees over their whole married life.

He had promised her so many things that had never—she realized almost immediately after their hasty marriage—even had a chance to come true. So many times she had pondered how she had ended up the way she had and inevitably always traced it back to that fateful day in the butlers' pantry, reliving it in her mind over and over again.

She had been quite old, nearly twenty-five, but horribly sheltered by her parents, Oldrich and Charity Exley. Les had already made his morning delivery that day but had come back later in the afternoon to find his cap, he had said with a sly grin, that he could swear he had left behind. Cook was in her room having her nap, and there had been no one else around. Martha, who was given to haunting the kitchens and who never got enough of the butcher boy's smiles, had eagerly let him in the back door to look for the missing cap. She had followed him to the pantry, where he was sure he had dropped it, he said, though Martha didn't remember him being anywhere near the butler's pantry that morning. When they arrived back in the tiny, ancient room, he had lost no time in putting his arms around her thick waist and kissing her. She had never been so shocked in her life, but found, to her shame, that she quite liked his attentions. He had continued his kisses until she was breathing rapidly, and then he had pulled her down beside him (on the floor!) without a moment's interruption in his efforts. Why had she let him? He had seemed gentle at first, even laughing a bit, but then he grew increasingly passionate. Martha grew worried that someone might come in at any moment, but she found it difficult to stop, in truth, she being so starved for affection, for love, and he being so determined to have his way. She panicked, however, when she realized that he had reached below her petticoat now, and she felt his hardness against her leg. She had no idea what was involved in sexual relations, but she was sure this was not what should be happening. Panic overwhelmed her.

"No! Leslie! We musn't!" she said, struggling under the weight of him.

"Come on, Martha!" he panted. "I'm going to burst here! You can't just stop a man now!"

"No, Leslie, please!" she wriggled again, trying to get away.

But he didn't answer her except for the rough yank of her drawers and his hard painful thrusts, suddenly inside her now, which she felt sure by the force of them that they would split her in two. Desperate, she tried to scream, but he put his mouth on hers, covering it. He finished quickly, then, and rolled off of her as she remained frozen in fear and shock and pain.

"That wasn't so bad, now, was it?" he said, still panting.

Martha tried to speak but found she couldn't, and instead quickly wiped a tear that had rolled down her cheek.

"Hey," he said, looking over at her as if seeing her for the first time. "You're kind of pretty, you know that?" he said and gave her a quick kiss on the cheek.

He stood up then and held out his hand to her to help her up. After a few moments of staring at his hand, her mind a horrible swirl of confusion, she took it finally and allowed herself to be pulled, the first gesture in the long life of pulling that lay ahead of her. Ashamed, she turned away from him and adjusted her under things. She was pretty sure she was bleeding.

"Found it!" he grinned, pulling a brown, checked cap out of his back pocket. "Wonder how I didn't notice it before," he said with another sly grin. He put it on then with an exaggerated flourish, but in so doing, knocked over one of the tea cups lined up along the edge of the shelf. It shattered upon hitting the floor, but Martha barely noticed. She followed Leslie to the door as if in a trance. She wasn't sure what to think. Perhaps this is the way it was supposed to be. Les certainly didn't seem to think there was anything wrong. But could this really be the finale that happened in the romance novels she so adored when the hero and heroine disappeared behind a locked door after their blissful wedding? She had read of birds singing and glowing sunbeams and beating hearts, but this . . . this had been nothing of the sort, this had been painful and messy and bloody. Blood? How could that be?

Les paused at the door and kissed her quickly. "See you next week, kid," he had said, as if he had done nothing more than plop the weeks' worth of meat and sausages on the table, and sauntered out.

And then she had gotten pregnant and then she had run away. She hadn't really wanted to, exactly, but she felt she had no other choice. She had been ashamed—not only of being with child, but of being in some strange way in love with Les, despite what he had done, and she hadn't known which she hated herself more for.

Martha had tried to think of him sympathetically after he had died, tried to feel sorry, but she just couldn't. There was too much anger, too much hurt after his suicide. After all that she had given up, he had given up on her. Rarely did she allow herself moments of self-reflection, but when she did, like today, she suspected there was something terribly wrong with her. There must be. Why else would Les have killed himself? For one thing, she knew she should at least have deeper feelings regarding her children, and she secretly feared she was an unnatural mother. She loved them, yes, but she didn't seem to have the strength to worry much about them. Each day it was a struggle just to get out of bed. She hated to admit it, but moving into this fine house with servants, much as she had fought it, had allowed her more time than ever to sit and not have to do anything in particular. Her days of trying to force herself to do the little bits of washing and mending that trickled in were over now. There was someone to cook and clean now, someone to do her bidding, someone to care for the children. She supposed that Elsie and, to a certain degree, Henrietta, had already done that for her in the past, but now she didn't need to feel guilty. She wasn't sure what Elsie did all day now, Mr. Exley Sr. insisting that she quit her job at Dubala's, though she suspected she still did some work for the pining Mr. Dubala on the side. The boys were all at St. Sylvester's, and Mrs. Kuntz was of course in charge of Doris and Donny, taking them out most days or entertaining them in the nursery. How had they all managed before to live in the little apartment on Armitage with just its few tiny rooms?

And Martha knew she slept too much. She was allowed to sleep as long as she wanted now. She knew it was wrong, but she couldn't seem to make herself do anything. Nothing excited or motivated her, but she had been that way for so long, she didn't remember what it felt like to be otherwise. She knew she should have more patience now, now that they didn't have to scrimp and save, now that the twins didn't go hungry at night, now that they all seemed taken care of, but she found she was still just as short, just as cross with all of them. She knew she was being unreasonable at times, overly sensitive and constantly irritated, but she couldn't seem to help it. Elsie, she knew, took the brunt of her moods, quietly accepting her, which Henrietta rarely did, instead always wanting to challenge and criticize her, it seemed, always ready for a fight.

She and Henrietta had locked horns since Henrietta was a little girl, but after Les's suicide, she had had to rely on Henrietta almost entirely, and now it had come to this. This awful, horrible wedding that was sucking her back to a place she had run from—or had she been expelled? She dreaded going today, to have all the eyes upon her, watching her, saying that she deserved what she had got—but she knew she had no choice, and it threw her into a state of near panic.

She picked up the morning's newspaper sitting on the otherwise tidy side table and began fanning herself. She had broken out in a sweat again, her stomach clenched in terror at the thought of today's events. "Elsie!" she tried to call out loud enough for her to hear. "Elsie! Bring me those pills!" she called louder. She could always rely on Elsie, much more so than Henrietta. She had been having these attacks more and more, especially after the stress of moving, and Mrs. Schmidt had suggested calling one Dr. Lawson, who seemed to have a special knowledge for these types of "women's troubles." Dr. Lawson had been called in just last week and had given Martha something to take for her nerves. They seemed to help for a short time, but they wore off quickly.

Elsie appeared, then, pill bottle in hand, dressed in the light blue bridesmaid dress that Henrietta had chosen but which Elsie had insisted on altering herself. Despite her being stockier than Henrietta, painfully resembling herself, Martha thought she looked really quite beautiful. Why hadn't she thought of herself as beautiful when she had been Elsie's age? But she already knew the answer. It was her mother, Charity—a more ironic name for a woman there had never been—who had first taught her, perhaps unconsciously, to think so little of herself. The little time she had spent in her mother's presence had always been filled with corrections and disparaging comments. "Martha, sit up straight!" or "Martha, stop scowling: no man wants to wake up to a sour face!" or "Martha . . . girlish figure!" whenever she asked for seconds. Martha knew she was a mortifying disappointment to her mother—too big, too ugly, too clumsy, too shy, too introverted—but Charity's greatest sin, in Martha's eyes, was that she had let Martha know this, to feel it deeply, every day of her life.

Her mother had eventually despaired of her and had even sent her to a Swiss finishing school to improve upon her own obviously inadequate efforts, not to mention those of a long string of governesses, but it hadn't worked. Martha had hated it there and cried herself to sleep every night. But it had taught her one valuable lesson—that she could live without them.

"Ma, are you okay?" Elsie was asking now, handing her a glass of water and holding out a pill in the palm of her hand. Again Elsie worried about how she was going to carry this off. As Henrietta's maid of honor, she would of course spend the service on the altar with her and would have to sit next to Henrietta at the head table at the dinner. She would have to entrust Eddie with the pills. He could keep them in his suit pocket.

Selfishly she wanted to enjoy herself today and was torn between these base feelings and concern for poor Ma. She glanced at the clock on the mantel. The cars being sent from Highbury would be here soon to take them to the church, where she would help Henrietta to slip into her dress. It had been decided that it would be easier for Henrietta to dress in the bride's sanctuary in the back of Sacred Heart rather than so far away in Palmer Square, not having to be concerned, then, about dirtying it on the ride up to Winnetka. Elsie knew she couldn't rush Ma, and yet, they would have to hurry.

Stan was to meet her at the church and had agreed to ride up with the Hennesseys. She thrilled to think what his reaction might be to her beautiful new dress. She was looking forward to seeing him, as he had not been around as much lately. He had been predictably shocked when she had told him she was moving to Palmer Square, but not as happy as she had thought he would be.

"Gee whiz, Elsie, that's a bit far for a man to travel, especially to a neighborhood of swells. I'll have to dress up just to come see you!" he had complained.

"It's hardly far, Stanley. Just a few extra blocks, and, anyway, we've often gone walking together in Palmer Park," she had said encouragingly. "It's not just for swells. You know that."

"But now instead of us looking up at all the fancy houses, wondering what it would be like to live in one, now you actually do. Doesn't seem right somehow."

"Anyone would think, Stanley," she said in a chastising tone, "that you are begrudging me our good fortune."

"It's not that, Elsie, it's just that, well, I can't keep up with this! I can't give a girl this kind of life."

Elsie had laughed then. "Oh, Stanley! Of course I don't expect this! I just . . . I just want to be with someone I . . . care for very much," she had said with a hint of red on her cheeks.

Stan's feathers were not to be so easily soothed, however, and he was not as steady a fixture at their new abode as he had been at the shabby apartment on Armitage. Elsie felt his absence keenly, as did Ma, oddly, who had become rather fond of having Stanley about, especially with poor Eugene gone. When Elsie had finally worked up the courage to ask Stan about it, he had told her he had gotten a promotion from the warehouse onto the line at the electrics and was working extra shifts.

"A man's gotta do what a man's gotta do, Elsie," he had said with determined disgruntlement, and Elsie had smiled to herself at what was his obvious attempt to earn more money for what she believed would be their new life together, whenever that would be.

At least she *hoped* it would be their new life together, having convinced herself that Stanley was indeed over his silly crush on Henrietta. After all, Henrietta was marrying Clive Howard today! And if a doubt still occasionally nagged at the corner of Elsie's mind regarding Stan's first choice, she pushed it away as quickly as she could and would distract herself with something useful, such as embroidering for her hope chest. Henrietta had never put much stock in a hope chest, but Elsie clung to hers and was ever adding to it, perhaps feeling more in need of hope regarding marriage than Henrietta would ever be.

Over the years, Elsie had accordingly completed a whole table-cloth and napkins and was now steadily working on a "his and her" set of pillowcases, with a male and female robin on the edge of each, respectively, set among a perfect nest of twining flowers. Even Henrietta had complimented them when she had at last come home to prepare for the wedding, though Henrietta had teased her about who was to be the hopeful recipient of the hope chest and reminded her that a certain Lt. Harrison Barnes-Smith would be in attendance at the wedding and that his RSVP had not listed a companion.

Elsie had blushed to the roots of her hair at Henrietta's intimation. She should never have confided in Henrietta, and, yet, how could she not? She had no one else. She had told Henrietta that she had, as it happened, run into none other than Lt. Harrison Barnes-Smith in Palmer Park—of all places—several times now over the summer. Elsie had related how she had gotten into the habit of taking Donny and Doris there in the afternoons to give poor Mrs. Kuntz a rest, who, in Elsie's opinion, anyway, was perhaps a trifle too plump to be employed as a nanny, as the position required much running after children, or at least the Von Harmon children, at any rate. As a result, Doris and Donny had become quite fond of watching the bicyclists that frequented the park's perfectly oval track, and she herself had very little else to do anyway.

Elsie had been surprised, then, on one particular afternoon as she strolled among the cluster of shrub roses planted near the north end, when she chanced to see Lieutenant Barnes-Smith—at least she thought it was him—riding with one of the clubs just coming around the corner. Before she had a chance to think, she had waved to him, which she later decided was probably unladylike. At the sight of her waving, a look of puzzlement had crossed the lieutenant's face before he seemed to recall who she was. He had come over directly, then, his companions reluctantly dismounting to wait.

"Miss Von Harmon?" he asked as he approached. "I thought it was you! Do you remember me? I think we shared a dance or two at your sister's engagement party. Lt. Barnes-Smith, at your service," he said, bowing slightly in exaggerated politeness.

"Yes," Elsie had blushed. "Of course I remember you." She gazed at him now, and he seemed even more handsome than when she had met him at the party. He had thick black hair and dark brown eyes and a slight dimple in his chin. She knew she should say something more, but for the life of her she couldn't think what. Instead, she furtively looked over at Doris and Donny, who were climbing a fallen tree some distance away.

"Yours?" he said, eyeing Doris and Donny with a smile.

"Oh, no, they're my brother and sister . . . I . . . Oh! You were teasing, weren't you?" she said, blushing now when she saw the amusement in his eyes.

"I was, yes, but how cruel of me. Forgive me," he said, laughing a bit.

Elsie was silent for what seemed like ages and could not help but feel it was ungentlemanly of him to simply stare at her, leaving her awkwardly dangling for conversation. She might have made an allowance if she suspected he were shy, but he seemed quite the opposite—quite outgoing and, well . . . charming.

"Did you . . . did you enjoy the party?" she finally managed.

"Smashing, I'd say," he answered with a grin. "My uncle's always going on about what a capital fellow Clive is. So much so that I found myself getting a bit envious, actually."

"Yes, he . . . we're all quite fond of him." She looked up at the lieutenant now and wondered how anyone's eyes could be that mysterious. He reminded her of maybe an actor, like Douglas Fairbanks Jr., perhaps.

"And how about you? Did you enjoy yourself that night? I must say, I can't remember when I've danced so much . . . and with such a pretty partner."

"Oh, yes," Elsie said again, flustered, and then realized that she seemed to be agreeing that she was indeed a pretty partner. She felt herself dangerously beginning to perspire. In her panic, she glanced over at his fellow bicyclists, who were still apparently waiting for him. "Are . . . are you in a bicycle club?" she finally succeeding in asking.

He followed her gaze and laughed. "Yes," he said ruefully, "as a matter of fact I am. But don't mind them," he said, giving his companions a dismissive wave and watched as they remounted their bicycles and rode off, most with amused faces.

"Oh, don't stop on account of me!" Elsie said, worried that she had inconvenienced him.

"I'll catch up," he said easily. "Besides, I'd much rather talk with you."

At his words, Elsie felt a delight she knew she shouldn't and looked away. What should she say in response to that? "I . . . I almost didn't recognize you without your uniform," she finally managed.

He gave her a puzzled look and then laughed. "Oh, that!" he said, looking down at his argyle sweater vest and bicycle trousers, which, Elsie had noticed, fit him very trimly. "I'm stationed at Ft. Sheridan, but sometimes they give me leave on the weekends, so I come stay with my uncle."

"Oh, I see."

There was silence between them again, though he didn't seem the slightest bit unnerved by it as he continued to look at her.

"Is . . . is he . . . do you live nearby, then? I didn't realize."

"Not too far," he said noncommittally.

"We just moved here. Not long ago, actually. That's ours," she said, pointing to a narrow brownstone across the park on Palmer.

"The old Meyer place? Did you, now?" he asked thoughtfully. "I suppose that makes us practically neighbors. Perhaps I might call on you? Just to welcome you, that is," he suggested casually.

She didn't know what to say in response to this. She couldn't think!

"I could bring my uncle along, if it would be more seemly," he added in an amused tone.

"No, I . . . I'm just not used to . . . yes, of course you can call," she stumbled. "You don't have to bring your uncle. I mean . . . of course you can if you like!" She was growing unbearably warm again. "We'd be happy to meet some new people," she said, but then suddenly remembered Ma, and her heart sank. "Well, actually, my mother is . . . well, ill right now, so . . . perhaps some other time," she said, looking up at him eagerly.

"Of course," he said, laughing again. "I didn't mean this minute. But I'd very much like to in the future. I look forward to it immensely, Miss Von Harmon," he said, flashing such a charming smile at her that Elsie felt her stomach clench up. He was so dreadfully handsome that her breath caught in her throat. "You've quite made my day," he said, holding out his hand to her.

Not knowing exactly what she should do, Elsie awkwardly gave him her hand to shake, but he surprised her by putting it to his lips and kissing it. She blushed uncontrollably and looked away, unable to repress her large smile.

He released her hand, then, and remounted, riding back toward the path. "Goodbye, Miss Von Harmon!" he said, giving her a last glance before rounding the first corner. "It was an unexpected pleasure!" he called back and then disappeared altogether.

Much to Elsie's surprise, Henrietta had found the tale very amusing as she had related it to her over a late-night cup of cocoa when Henrietta had come in from her night out with her friends. Elsie had waited up for her as she had sometimes done back at the old apartment, usually whenever she had something on her mind. A cup of cocoa and a chat was a pleasure Elsie had not enjoyed in a very long time.

With a smile, Henrietta had asked if the lieutenant had ever really turned up at some point in the ensuing months.

"Well, no . . . not yet," Elsie had admitted. "I assumed he hadn't had any leave lately. Oh, Hen, do you think he was teasing?" she asked, the idea of it suddenly dawning on her. "I never thought of that! How silly of me. Of course he wouldn't really want to call on me . . . us."

"No, that's not what I meant at all, Els," Henrietta said gingerly. "It's just that, well, I'm not sure how trustworthy he really is. I was only teasing before when I said he was coming alone. I didn't mean that you should . . ."

"That I should what?" Elsie asked quickly, feeling an uncharacteristic irritation rising up within her.

Henrietta exhaled. "Listen, Elsie, it's just that Julia told me he's a bit of a 'ladies' man'—you know, a flirt."

"Why should that matter to me?" Elsie exclaimed. "He only said he was going to call—with his uncle, I might add—to welcome us. Nothing more!" This conversation was definitely not going as planned. Of course she wasn't *really* interested in Lieutenant Barnes-Smith!

"Look, Els," Henrietta said gently. "I'm sure you're right. No doubt he has the best of intentions, but just be careful."

Elsie gave her a muddled look. "What do you mean by that?"

Henrietta's brow furrowed momentarily before she seemed to force a smile. "Just that you wouldn't want Stan to get all upset, would you?" she said, giving her a little wink.

"No, I suppose not," Elsie said and could not help but let out a little laugh now as she imagined an annoyed Stanley. Thankfully, whatever small tension that had existed between the two sisters was broken then.

Of course Elsie didn't wish to intentionally make Stanley jealous, she had mused several times since that conversation with Henrietta, but, if she were honest, she could not help looking forward to seeing the lieutenant later today at the church in what she hoped would be his dress uniform, complete with charming smile. As she helped Ma on with her coat now, she remembered what a beautiful dancer the lieutenant had been at the party. Surely a dance or two today—if he even asked her, that is—wouldn't hurt, would it?

"Elsie, do you have my bag?" Henrietta called from the top of the stairs as she descended now, Mrs. Andrews following behind her, the small smile of pride on the older woman's face unmistakable. She had completed Henrietta's hair, sweeping it up elegantly and holding it in place with a net of tiny pearls in the back and three pins with large pearls at the ends toward the front. Mrs. Howard had hinted on more than one occasion over the summer that perhaps Henrietta should adopt a shorter style, as was all the rage right now, something perhaps like Loretta Young. But when Henrietta mentioned it to Clive, he had stopped short of forbidding her to cut her hair and had instead begged her to keep it long, and today, she had to admit, she was glad she had. Later, at the church, Mrs. Andrews would put her long lace veil in place for her. With Henrietta's permission, she had also applied the faintest of makeup to her eyes and lips as she sat before the mirror in her room, dressed simply in her old blue paisley dress so that she could unbutton and slip out of it easily in the bride's sanctuary at the church without disturbing her hair. She had gotten rid of all her old clothes except for this one dress, a reminder, she had told Elsie, of where she had come from, and she felt it particularly appropriate to wear today as she fully crossed from her old life to her new.

"Oh, Hen!" Elsie nearly gasped as Henrietta came down the stairs now. "You look beautiful!" she whispered, even as little tears formed at the corner of her eyes.

"Thanks, Elsie," Henrietta said, beaming and radiant, obviously pleased with Mrs. Andrews's work. "It's all down to Mrs. Andrews, of course," she said, looking back at the woman behind her.

"I'll say thank you, Miss, but the truth is that it's not hard to make you look beautiful," Mrs. Andrews said with a smile. "It was a pleasure. I'll just wait in the foyer," she said, giving Henrietta a last look of approval before she made her way out.

"She's right, you know," Elsie said. "And you don't even have your dress on yet! I can't wait to see you in it!"

Henrietta smiled. "Well, you look lovely, too, Elsie—a perfect bridesmaid!" she said genuinely as she observed Elsie in her floor-length gown of blue organdy with a gauzy sash that draped around her waist and trailed to the floor.

"Thanks, Henrietta," Elsie said with a happy smile as she smoothed her skirt down and adjusted her gloves. "I do feel rather elegant today!"

Henrietta finally dared to look over at Ma, who had remained curiously silent since Henrietta had come down. "You look nice, too, Ma," she said. "Your hat suits you."

Ma did look better in her new clothes and with her hair styled. She was not yet fifty years old, and yet she was gray and wizened. She looked twenty years older than she really was, perhaps because of the twisted look her face always held, as if she was constantly in pain or as if she had forgotten how to smile. She was looking at Henrietta now in an almost haunted way.

Henrietta was unsettled by the way Ma was staring at her as if she were a stranger. "Well, what do you think?" Henrietta finally asked awkwardly, gesturing at her hair and face. "It's just a little makeup, Ma. Mrs. Andrews insisted."

Ma sighed. "You look nice, Henrietta. Of course you do. I don't often say it, but you do."

"Thanks, Ma," Henrietta said quietly and hoped she wouldn't cry.

"You don't have to go through with this, though, you know," Ma said abruptly, instantly breaking whatever beginnings of harmony that might have been forming between them. "There's still time."

Henrietta felt an angry retort spring to mind, but she held it in, predicting she would need a lot of patience today, and she didn't want to start off cross. How could Ma, even now, not realize that she *loved* Clive? "Yes, Ma, I know, but I really do want to marry Clive."

"Well, suit yourself. I knew you'd be stubborn."

"Ma, I know marrying Clive will be . . . difficult in some ways, but isn't every marriage?" she said gingerly, not wanting an argument to erupt today of all days. She wanted the day to be perfect, and its perfection was already being challenged by, of course, Ma, the one person who should be her closest friend today, but who sadly was not.

"Well, I've already said all I'm going to say," Ma wheezed, hobbling over to the sofa and pretending to rummage through her handbag for some imaginary item.

"Ma," Elsie said, cautiously intervening, "surely today is not a day for Henrietta to have second thoughts. Today should be a happy day, shouldn't it?"

Ma looked like she was going to speak but stopped when Odelia suddenly burst into the room.

"Sorry to interrupt, Madam!" Odelia said breathlessly, "but the cars are here, and ain't they gorgeous!"

There was a general scuffle, then, as they all made ready to leave. Herbie, Eddie, and Jimmy clamored down the stairs, dressed smartly in navy wool suits, it being Jimmy's first time in long pants, and he was looking quite grown up. Doris and Donny had been put in matching navy blue velvet sailor outfits, Doris's, of course, being a dress, while Donny's consisted of short pants. It had been arranged that Henrietta, Ma, and Elsie would be driven by a chauffeur hired for the occasion in the Howards' Rolls Royce and that Eddie, Herb, and Jimmy would go in the Exleys' Packard with Karl at the helm. A third car had to be hired to carry Mrs. Andrews, Mrs. Kuntz, and Doris and Donnie, while Alcott and Antonia would be driven by Fritz in the Bentley. Finally, Clive and the major would arrive in Alcott's prize possession, the Isotta Fraschini Tipo.

Mr. Exley Sr. had tried again on several occasions to sway Henrietta in her decision to allow him to walk her down the aisle, but she had refused each time. She knew she was angering him, but it couldn't be helped. Instead, it had been decided that he would escort Ma to her seat. He had resignedly accepted this role, of course, but he did not seem to relish the prospect of finally walking down the aisle with his daughter twenty years too late. He would much rather have been escorting his stunning granddaughter who had snagged a Howard. Ma had also resentfully agreed to this arrangement, though she insisted that she sit with the children in her own pew behind Henrietta, separate from the Exleys.

Henrietta would have liked to instruct the chauffer to drive past their two old apartments, the company apartment they had lived in while her father had been an employee of Schwinn and the shabbier one on Armitage, but she was afraid there wasn't time, and, besides, she did not wish to expose her sentimentality to Ma, who would surely have made several derogatory comments, no doubt most of them aimed at her father, whom Henrietta was trying hard not to think about today. Instead she spent the drive north attempting to instruct and remind Ma and Elsie what their special roles were for the day—where they were to sit, when they were supposed to dance, what the photographer would want of them, where to stand, what to do . . . Elsie concentrated hard on her many instructions, but Ma merely looked out the window, seemingly ignoring Henrietta, all the while fitfully clutching and unclutching her handkerchief.

The drive to Winnetka seemed to go faster than it ever had before, and Henrietta soon found herself outside of Sacred Heart before she even had time to contemplate the momentous action she was about to take. The driver had delivered her to a back door, close to the rectory, so that she could slip out, being not yet fully arrayed in her gown, without being seen by any guests. The little assemblage had nothing to fret about, it turned out, however, as they were more than early enough to have arrived before anyone else.

Henrietta began to feel nervous now as they made their way into the bride's room. Edna was already there, having been entrusted with the dress as a result of being elevated to the position of personal lady's maid now to Henrietta. When Mrs. Howard had originally suggested Edna's advancement, Henrietta had intended to protest, saying that she did not want or need a personal maid, but had then realized it would be an easier life for Edna, not having to scrub floors and make beds anymore, so she had acquiesced. She still couldn't help feeling uncomfortable about the whole thing, however, and intended to use Edna's skills in a different way—make her her assistant, or secretary maybe—but that would have to wait.

Everything seemed to happen at once now. A chair was found in the corner for Ma, which she heavily sank down into, while Mrs. Andrews and Mrs. Kuntz took the children through to the church and helped them find their assigned pew. Meanwhile, Elsie, and then Julia, who had somehow appeared and been hastily and without incident introduced to Ma, helped Henrietta out of her old dress and carefully arrayed her in her wedding gown.

It was positively beautiful, a work of art. It had been ordered from Paris and had arrived just a few weeks ago. Mrs. Howard had been beside herself with worry that it wouldn't arrive on time and had actually purchased another dress from Flemings on Michigan Avenue as a backup. But the dress had arrived from Paris as scheduled, and besides needing a few alterations, which Mrs. Howard's seamstress had quickly seen to, it fit her perfectly. Elsie had not yet seen it, however, and she stood in awe of Henrietta as Edna continued to fasten the last of the buttons and Julia attempted to straighten the long train. Mrs. Andrews had reappeared as well and had delicately pinned the veil in place, stepping back now to assess that all was perfect.

"Oh, Hen!" Elsie said. "It's beautiful!"

It was a Chanel gown of long, close-fitting silk with an enormous train. It had been modeled, Antonia had told her during one of the fittings, on the dress Chanel had produced for Princess Dmitri of Russia, though this meant little to Henrietta. The dress had one hundred and twenty buttons running down the back and a rounded neck lined with a beaded roping that exposed just enough of Henrietta's neck to display a gorgeous diamond-and-pearl necklace that Mr. and Mrs. Howard had given her as a wedding gift.

"You do look beautiful," Julia said proudly. "Are you nervous?" she asked of Henrietta's reflection in the mirror as she stood beside her.

"Yes, I suppose I am," Henrietta said with a fleeting smile.

"Well, if it helps at all, so is the groom," Julia confided, turning to look at the real Henrietta, instead of her image in the mirror, and gave her hand a squeeze as she did so.

"Is he here already?" Henrietta asked.

"He is indeed, pacing at the front," Julia said, smiling. "He resembles a large schoolboy. I'll just pop out and check on him, shall I?" Not waiting for an answer, she disappeared.

The thought of Clive being in any way anxious was new to Henrietta. He was normally so confident, so strong, so sure of his actions. Only once, on that night on the terrace just after the Jack incident, had he come close to breaking down in front of her, revealing a deeper, more tender side, and she had loved him all the more for it.

Since she had returned to Palmer Square just this week, she had written to him daily, telling him of each day's events and always of her love for him, but she had not received any communication back. She had hoped for a note or a letter of some sort in return, but she had been disappointed and put it down to Clive's sometimes-aloof manner even still. She knew that a part of him, not just his shoulder, had been damaged in the war and that he could be quite old-fashioned at times, not liking to always show his emotions. He was indeed from a different generation, closer, actually, to her mother's age than hers, but she did not like to think about it, and, anyway, she didn't care. So he wasn't the romantic type, she had told herself; what did it matter? She didn't need romance necessarily. She only needed *him*, and today she would become his wife.

Henrietta smiled at the image of Clive being nervous, however. It somehow made her feel better that she was not alone in feeling jittery. She turned now to see her profile in the mirror. The dress really was stunning, she observed, and she was feeling an unusual wave of gratitude toward Mrs. Howard when oddly there was a little knock at the bride's door and none other than Mrs. Howard herself stepped through. Edna curtsied out of habit, though as a lady's maid she was not required to do so, but the anxiety of the day, not to mention her recent quick shift in duties as of late, had her confused. She quickly exited now, along with Mrs. Andrews, to whom Mrs. Howard gave a grateful pat on the arm as she passed. Elsie seemed to recognize her cue as well and gave Henrietta a reluctant smile before she excused herself to see if the florist had arrived yet with the bouquets.

Mrs. Howard somehow did not notice Ma, still sitting silent in the corner, dreadfully pale and perspiring, but saw only Henrietta and paused in admiration of her creation. She let out a small, satisfied sigh and walked swiftly to where Henrietta still stood before the mirror and kissed the air alongside both of her cheeks and took her hands in hers.

"My dear, you look absolutely gorgeous."

"Thank you, Antonia," Henrietta said, feeling awkward with Ma sitting so near. She was about to finally introduce the two of them, the two mothers in her life now, but Mrs. Howard rushed on before she had a chance.

"I just want you to know, my dear, that despite our initial differences, shall we say, I really am quite fond of you. You've made Clive happier than I've ever seen him, and I'm grateful. I've tried to warn both of you of the immense responsibility you're taking on, but I can see now that you will succeed brilliantly. I've come to almost see you as another daughter, and I hope you can rely on me, trust me, as you would a mother, especially since . . ."

Ma cleared her throat here, and Mrs. Howard, startled, peered into the shadows where Ma was heaving herself out of the rather deep-seated chair.

"I'm sorry," Mrs. Howard said stiffly, though her tone was anything but one of repentance. "I assumed we were alone. You should have made yourself known. Who is it?"

Ma snorted. "You don't need to concern yourself with me, Antonia Howard," Martha said, her voice slightly cracking. "I can see you two are managing quite well as it is."

"Ma!" Henrietta exclaimed, deeply embarrassed. "Let me

introduce you. Antonia, this is my mother, Martha Von Harmon. Ma . . . Mother . . . this is Antonia Howard."

The two women stared at each other, Mrs. Howard coolly assessing every small detail of Ma's attire and person, the quickness with which it was completed and the lack of accompanying facial response indicating that she was not impressed. She was the first to speak, however.

"Please call me Antonia," she said, smiling sweetly. "How very charmed I am to meet you . . . may I call you Martha?"

Ma did not answer.

"We were very sorry to hear that you've been so ill of late, but delighted that you are strong enough to attend today. You must be very proud of Henrietta."

Ma gave her a disparaging look. "I haven't been ill," she said, looking accusingly at Henrietta. "I just didn't want to come."

"Oh, Ma!" Henrietta said faintly.

Mrs. Howard looked Ma up and down yet again and managed another false smile. "Well, I misunderstood, then. Forgive me. I won't take up any more of your time. I'm sure you have much to say to each other. Henrietta," Mrs. Howard said, taking her hand again and squeezing it. "My very best wishes and my blessing," she said sincerely. "You look lovely; Clive's a very lucky man. I'll see you at *home*," she said, barely glancing at Ma as she said it, but the barb had hit. "Good day, Mrs. Von Harmon," she said, not looking at Ma, and then disappeared behind the thick red curtain that blocked them from view of the congregation.

"Why did you do that, Ma?" Henrietta hissed as soon as Antonia was out of earshot. "Can't you just get along? Isn't that what you always told me? All those years that I waitressed and got fired for slapping some cook trying to feel his way up my legs?"

"Always one for melodrama, aren't you?" Ma retorted. "Well, I'm glad your new mother is less of a disappointment."

"How can you say that to me?" Henrietta said, near tears now. "It hasn't been easy for me . . ."

Luckily, they were interrupted when both Edna and Elsie arrived back with all of the flowers, and Julia came in then, too.

"They're almost ready," Julia whispered, nodding her head toward the front of the church. The organist had started playing lightly in the background, and Henrietta felt her stomach clench. "Mr. Exley's in the back waiting for Mrs. Von Harmon," Julia said kindly, apparently not noticing the tension between the two of them.

"I'll go; I'm not really needed here, anyway," Ma said, the irritation in her voice unmistakable. For a moment she looked as though she was going to stumble, but Elsie caught her and helped her through the tiny door at the back which led into the narthex where the procession would begin, asking her if she was sure she would be okay, did she need water, anything?

"Ma!" Henrietta called after her, but Martha did not turn around. Only Elsie looked back at her, her face one of apologetic pity as she made her way out with Ma. Henrietta felt she might cry, her throat thick and aching with tears, but she steeled herself and tried desperately to push it down, turning to Julia instead.

If Julia thought the parting between mother and daughter odd, she didn't say so. Henrietta was too distraught to be embarrassed now and suddenly had a new surge of panic.

"Oh, no! What about Mr. Hennessey?" she cried. "Is he here?"

"Don't worry," Julia said soothingly. "He's in the Narthex, waiting patiently, though he does seem a bundle of nerves. He keeps loosening and retightening his tie, poor man. He appears positively unhinged. Whatever have you done to him, Henrietta?" she smiled reassuringly.

Henrietta responded with her own unexpected smile at the image of poor Mr. Hennessey fraught with anxiety, but she grew instantly sober again, almost frantic. "Oh, Julia! What am I going to do? This isn't what I thought my wedding day was going to be like!" she said on the verge of tears again. "Everyone seems cross, and I don't feel particularly happy, just horribly nervous. It's not anything like what I imagined it would be!"

Surprisingly, Julia laughed. "It will get better. Once you begin, there's no more thinking about it, just doing it. I was the same."

Henrietta reflected that of course one would feel distress to be marrying the likes of Randolph, but she didn't say so. She, on the other hand, was marrying the man she loved, so she shouldn't feel this anxious, should she?

An usher knocked on the door and poked in his head. "It's time," he said simply. "Are you ready?"

Henrietta nodded. "Just one moment," Julia said. Elsie came in, then, and handed Henrietta her long spray of roses and orchids just as she could hear the organ loudly begin Handel's "Air."

"She's fine. Don't fret about it," Elsie said soothingly, referring, of course, to Ma. "This is your big day. Be happy," she said, smiling at her. "Oh, Henrietta! I love you!" Elsie said, wiping tears from the corner of her eyes. "Good luck."

"I love you, too, Elsie," Henrietta responded, leaning forward and kissing her on the cheek, and she suddenly felt overwhelmingly sad at the prospect of leaving her forever.

"May I be so bold as to say I love you as well?" Julia said to Henrietta with a smile. "Would you mind another sister, Elsie?" she said as she held out her hands to both of them. Quickly the sisters reached for Julia's outstretched hands, forming a momentary triangle between them.

Elsie smiled shyly.

"Thank you, both. For everything," Henrietta said, squeezing their hands tightly.

Julia gave her a wink just as the usher reappeared, gesturing with more urgency this time.

As previously instructed, Julia walked out first to begin her long walk down the aisle of the packed church, Elsie following at a slightly faster pace, though she appeared to remember to slow down every few yards, concentrating on her steps.

Henrietta emerged into the Narthex, then, and saw Mr. Hennessey waiting, wringing his hands. A huge smile lit up his face when he saw her, arrayed as she was, her beauty absolute. As predicted, Henrietta detected two tears in the corners of his eyes. He held his arm out to her, "Ready, girl?"

At those simple words, Henrietta now felt in real danger of crying herself. "Oh, Mr. Hennessey. Thank you," she said hoarsely. "You've been so good to me."

"The pleasure has always been mine, girl. I knew you were something special, and now look at this. I'm so proud of you, as if you was my own daughter, and I mean it."

"I know you do," she said, kissing him on the cheek.

Edna had finished fluffing her train and appeared by her side now. "Ready?" she squeaked. Henrietta nodded and bent so that Edna could carefully pull the little front wisp of a veil over her face. The music changed then to Mendelssohn's "Wedding March," and Mr. Hennessey tightly gripped her hand, entwined through his arm. She turned her attention to the front of the church now and almost felt faint at the sight of the crowd. She peered toward the altar, but all she could make out was Randolph and Major Barnes-Smith. Somehow she forced her legs forward, though her heart was beating so hard that it was difficult to breathe.

And then she saw him.

The two couples of the wedding party had cleared now, and Clive, so dreadfully handsome in his black tails and white tie, slowly turned to look at her. The look of pure love on his face as he gazed at her melted her heart so completely she almost fainted, and she leaned, for just a moment, on Mr. Hennessey, who held her tight. As she drew closer, she could see that Clive's face was controlled, but she saw him swallow deeply and could tell by the way he clenched his right cheek that he was fighting his emotion. She smiled at him, then, her anxiety giving way to concern for him, and to her delight, he smiled back.

Clive looked at the vision floating toward him and felt as unnerved as he had before any battle, but in a strangely different way, of course.

Henrietta invoked such a fierce tenderness in him that it almost took his breath away. He was almost ashamed of how much he loved her. He never took his eyes from hers as she slowly walked up the aisle to him. Often when he had lain in the field hospital, listening to the shelling in the ever-encroaching front, he had drifted in and out of consciousness, and sometimes a vision had come to him, a vision of a woman that brought him warmth and peace, and he oddly felt that same way now as Henrietta walked toward him. He didn't care what anyone thought of him or his choice for one so young; he didn't see her that way. Yes, she was young, and beautiful as well, but he knew that that was not at the heart of his love for her, that there was infinitely more to it. As he stood waiting for her to come to him, he offered up a silent prayer to God that he would be the man she deserved and that God would not take her from him. Surely God would not be that cruel, to take his wife again, would He?

He had thought of Catherine this morning as he was dressing and hoped she understood. But of course she would; she had ever been that way. He had already had a wedding day all those years ago, so he had been thrown off by his disquietude today as he attempted to button his cufflinks on his own, fumbling them so badly that in the end he was obliged to seek the help of his father's valet. Unlike today's extravagant event, when he had stood at the altar with Catherine it had been in front of family only, and on that day his feelings, to be honest, had been mostly of duty, his new role in the war looming large, as opposed to the overwhelming feelings of love he felt now. Of course he had loved Catherine, but it had been almost a schoolboy's sort of love. What he felt now for Henrietta was infinitely different.

Often he had cursed himself, reliving in his mind the events of his first marriage and the war. If he hadn't married Catherine, he had reflected for what seemed a hundred times, she perhaps would be living now. Had his selfish sense of duty to Highbury and his country led to her death? It was too much to think about, and often he had chased away those nagging thoughts with a bottle of scotch. He prayed that God would forgive any sin of his against Catherine and that she, in heaven now, he felt sure, would forgive him, too.

And suddenly, Henrietta was here before him, and his heart was beating terribly in his chest. Mr. Hennessey, tears on his cheeks, lifted her veil for her and kissed her cheek, looking at her so lovingly, almost forlornly, that Clive knew Henrietta's stubborn insistence that he walk her down the aisle had been the right decision. Mr. Hennessey took her hand, then, and sturdily placed it in Clive's so that Clive could feel her trembling, making him want to tightly embrace her, but he manfully stood his ground.

"You take care of this girl, Clive Howard," Mr. Hennessey whispered to him fiercely. "She's come to be very precious to me."

Clive shook his hand and was about to answer but found to his dismay that he couldn't actually speak. He could only incline his head formally instead, but Mr. Hennessey seemed to understand, and, with one last look, took his place in the pew next to his wife, who was crying in earnest.

Fr. Michaels began the ceremony in prayer, during which Clive stood at perfect attention while Henrietta tightly gripped her bouquet, fearing that she might at any moment faint. Fr. Michaels had cautioned them both during one of their appointments with him to eat the morning of the big event, having seen his share of fainting brides, and even a couple of grooms, over the years, he had said, but she had not been able to get much down. As Fr. Michaels continued the Mass, reading the blessing in Latin from a big red book held by a small, wobbling altar boy, she tried desperately to hold on to his words, to formulate some meaning to them, but it was horribly nerve-racking knowing that the eyes of the whole congregation were on them, though they themselves couldn't see anyone besides Fr. Michaels, standing immediately in front of the two of them. She took a deep breath, trying to calm herself.

Just when she thought she could stand it no longer, Fr. Michaels mercifully came to the critical moment and was instructing them to turn and face each other and to join hands, Elsie stepping quickly forward to take her bouquet for her. Henrietta was able to focus, then, on Clive's solid face before her, his kind eyes seeming to hold her up and support her. He tenderly took her hand.

Fr. Michaels asked each of them if they entered into this union freely, to which they both, looking into each other's eyes, answered in the affirmative. Fr. Michaels then stated that since it was both their intention to enter into the holy sacrament of marriage, that they should state their vows now before God and the Church gathered together this day. He cleared his throat and asked Henrietta to speak first.

She took another deep breath and repeated, in a quiet, resolved voice, after him: "I, Henrietta Elizabeth Von Harmon, take you, Clive Alcott Linley Howard, to be my husband," (here her voice faltered a bit) "to have and to hold from this day forward, for better, for worse, for richer, for poorer, in sickness and in health, to love, cherish, and obey, until death do us part." She smiled at him, then, two small tears escaping as gently as her vows had.

Clive, his jaw clenching furiously, repeated likewise. "I, Clive Alcott Linley Howard, take you, Henrietta Elizabeth Von Harmon, to be my wife, to have and to hold from this day forward, for better, for worse, for richer, for poorer, in sickness and in health, to love and to cherish, until death do us part," he said in a clear, steady voice.

Major Barnes-Smith was asked to produce the rings, which Fr. Michaels blessed, and they were exchanged as well, each of them saying as they slipped the rings onto each other's fingers—Henrietta's still trembling dreadfully—"I give you this ring as a sign of my love and fidelity in the name of the Father, and of the Son, and of the Holy Ghost, Amen."

After more prayers and yet another blessing, Fr. Michaels pronounced them man and wife and told Clive that he may kiss his bride, which he did with surprising tenderness, as he looked at her with absolute love—as if no one else was present, as if no one else existed.

The Mass continued, then, again in Latin, Clive and Henrietta taking their place on the kneelers already set up for them in front of the altar. Henrietta floated through the prayers and rituals, unable to stop the beating of her heart, only occasionally glancing over at Clive—her husband!—who seemed, oddly, deep in prayer. When they did catch each other's eyes, however, they could not repress their happy excitement, their true joy. Henrietta, in her distracted happiness, managed to offer up at least one prayer of her own as well, that she would have the strength to be a better daughter, a better sister, and most especially, of course, the wife Clive deserved and prayed that she could make him happy in all things.

Before she knew it, the Mass was concluding, and Fr. Michaels told them to rise for the final blessing. He sprinkled them with holy water and then prayed over them with hands outstretched: "My dear friends, let us turn to the Lord and pray that He will bless with His grace this woman, Henrietta Elizabeth, now married in Christ to this man, Clive Alcott Linley, and that He will unite in love the couple He has joined in this holy bond. Father, keep them always true to your commandments. Keep them faithful in marriage and let them be living examples of Christian life. Give them the strength that comes from the gospel so that they may be witnesses of Christ to others. Bless them with children, and help them be good parents. May they live to see their children's children. And, after a happy old age, grant them fullness of life with the saints in the kingdom of heaven. We ask this through Christ our Lord. Amen."

He leaned forward then and shook each of their hands, whispering, "Congratulations!" to each of them, relieving the tension that they hadn't realized they were so dreadfully under. He motioned for them to turn to face the crowd for the first time, and he happily boomed out, "Ladies and gentleman, it is my very great pleasure to introduce to you for the first time, Mr. and Mrs. Clive Howard." A resounding applause erupted, and the recessional, Purcell's "Trumpet Tune and Bell Symphony," began its soaring notes as Elsie hurried forward to hand Henrietta her bouquet before her long walk back down the aisle, now as a married woman.

Lovingly Henrietta and Clive looked at each other before taking their first step, Henrietta's heart truly in danger of bursting with happiness. As they processed down the aisle, Henrietta could not retain her smiles, bestowed joyfully on the crowd as they passed by, and Clive's face exhibited a rare, broad smile as well, Henrietta now on his arm for good.

They had done it! For better or worse, for good times and for bad, they were married, and nothing could change that now.

Chapter 6

S tan stood anxiously at the Winnetka Yacht Club, gripping a glass of champagne and wishing it was something stronger, like whiskey, for example, but none seemed available just now. And, anyway, Elsie didn't approve of him drinking whiskey, though he had tried to point out to her that all the movie stars did it, like James Cagney in *The Public Enemy* or even William Powell in *The Thin Man*, both of which he had taken her to see, but she had remained unconvinced, saying that that wasn't real life.

But this wasn't real life either, was it? he thought, looking around disdainfully. He knew hardly anyone, of course. He had intended to stick next to the Hennesseys for the duration, seeing as Elise would probably be tied up with wedding duties, but they had disappeared somewhere. Photographs out by the lake, someone had said, though why the Hennesseys presence would be required for those, he didn't know. He thought he recognized the gaggle of young women over by the bar as being Henrietta's "friends" from the Marlowe, but he had no wish to converse with any of those girls of ill repute. Try as he might, however, he could not keep his eyes from wandering back toward them every so often. They were attractive; he would say that. And, of course, there was that pesky lieutenant sidling up to them now. Well, that was to be expected, he thought disgustedly, turning his back to them again and looking out at the lake itself, trying to shake the deep melancholy that threatened to overwhelm him.

Henrietta was married. He still couldn't believe it. His Henrietta! But she wasn't his and never had been, he mused bitterly and drained his champagne glass. Thankfully a waiter passed nearby, affording him the opportunity of wretchedly grabbing another glass with minimal exertion. It had all been in his head, hadn't it? Going all the way back to that day he had first seen her in the Dutch Girl costume on the motorbus, when he resolved that she would someday be his. So many times she had smiled at him, her sweet dimples turning his insides to mush; surely that meant something, he had told himself over and over. But no, he thought as he kicked the leg of a barstool now with his toe, it hadn't. Or maybe it had until the inspector had distracted her from him. That's all he had thought the inspector was at first, just a distraction, until he solved his stupid case, but before he knew it they were engaged! How could she? But then when he had seen the inspector's house—Highbury, he called it—at the engagement party, it had all made perfect sense.

He hadn't put Henrietta down as a gold digger, but he supposed she couldn't help it, poor kid. She'd been poor for so long, and the sacrifice she was willing to make for her family by marrying that old coot of an inspector almost overwhelmed him. He despaired for her! He supposed she could keep herself away from him during the day in that big of a house, but what about at night when she would have to . . . to give her body to him.

He shuddered, unable to think about it anymore without feeling nauseous. But the thing that confused him was how she didn't seem as repulsed by the inspector as he would have expected. Quite the opposite, actually. Whenever she was around Howard, Stan had observed (when he forced himself to really look at them), she seemed so maddeningly in love with him. How could that be? Surely it was an act? Well, he thought with a grin, she was a good actress, always had been. He sighed. There was nothing for it. He felt sorry for her in the end, but he just couldn't believe it, even now. He supposed he had been hoping that she would come to her senses perhaps at the last second, but she hadn't, and when she made her vow just an hour ago in the church, so prettily and so shyly, not being able to keep from smiling and crying all at the same time, it was as if he had been kicked in the stomach. He had had to grip the pew in front of him and was glad to be sitting next to the Hennesseys, who were blubbering quite loudly, conveniently masking his own gasp of sorrow as the sword entered his heart. And then, as she had walked down the aisle on the inspector's arm, he had thought that maybe she would catch his eye as she passed him by and that they would exchange a last look—acknowledging her sacrifice and perhaps regret—but she hadn't seemed to notice him at all in the crowd and indeed looked rather blissfully happy.

After that, he wasn't sure he would be able to endure the receiving line formed at the back of the church, but he willed himself to stand erect and take it like a man. Perspiring a bit, he looked ahead up the line and saw her, radiant, and the inspector, smug, of course, standing, shaking hands and embracing their guests, introductions proudly being made. As Stan slowly shuffled forward, he tried to think of something to say that wasn't reproachful or regretful, but he could think of nothing, so after dutifully shaking hands with Mr. and Mrs. Howard, who stood at the front of the line as the hosts of the day, he settled for "Congratulations, Howard," as he held out his hand, hoping upon hope that today of all days the inspector wouldn't call him Pipsqueak. He didn't think his pride could take it. Mercifully, however, Clive didn't.

"Thank you for coming, Stan. You've always been a good friend to us, especially to my wife, in our times of need, and your presence here today means a great deal to us."

He had said "wife" on purpose, hadn't he? Why did he have to say that? To rub it in? Why couldn't he have just said "Henrietta"?

"Oh, Stan!" Henrietta was saying to him then, knocking him out of the trance he seemed to be in. "I'm so happy to see you," she said, putting her arms around him, which immediately threw him into a panic. Awkwardly he put his arms around her, too, but was careful that his arms not linger on any part of her torso for even two seconds altogether. He hurriedly stepped back, nervously glancing at Clive, but the inspector was addressing the Hennesseys now, who were immediately behind him in the line.

"Say you're happy for me, Stan," Henrietta was saying to him.

"Course I'm happy for you," he said, forcing a smile. "Course I am. Why would you say that?" he said with more feeling than perhaps he should have.

"Well, thanks, Stan, for everything," she said, and before he could answer, her eyes darted to the next guest in line, which happened to be Mrs. Hennessey, and she exclaimed over *her* now, holding out her arms to her, inadvertently dismissing Stan, just as Elsie, next in the line near Mrs. Von Harmon (looking deathly pale, by the way), exclaimed, "Stanley!" and his attention had been reluctantly drawn to her.

Elsie. Yes, Elsie. He must think of her, and hadn't he, actually, a hundred, thousand times, convincing himself that she was by far the better of the two sisters? After all, who would want someone as wild as Henrietta when they could have the tried-and-true Elsie?

Actually, he thought, as he finished his second glass of champagne now, he was definitely better off without Henrietta. Good riddance! The inspector could have her, and, by God, he would have his hands full.

"If you'd care to take your seat now, sir," a waiter was saying, trying to usher the guests to their tables.

Stan fumbled in his pocket for his table card and found that he was at table thirty-three and began wandering around in search of it. He eventually found it near the back—of course—and further despaired when he saw who was already seated there. Those three girls from the Marlowe! Oh, God! he despaired. How could this day get any worse? Slowly he approached and purposefully took a chair opposite them; he had no desire to sit near them. Introductions were politely made, and though they didn't recognize him at first, one of them—Lucy, was it?—the blonde, after surreptitiously staring at him for the first ten minutes, finally identified him as the kid the inspector had locked in the squad car that night at the Marlowe, causing him to ask the waiter (who had just conveniently appeared with a fresh round of champagne intended for a toast for the wedding party's entrance) if there was any whiskey available, to which the waiter had rather rudely responded with, "That will come later, sir," further humiliating him. The Marlowe girls had the decency, however, to pretend they hadn't heard. Eventually another young couple took their places at the table as well as another single man. Where were the Hennesseys? Stan wondered, looking around rather desperately. Surely there was some mistake? He couldn't possibly be expected to sit here and make conversation with this lot. Casually he leaned over and saw that the card the couple had put down did indeed read "Table Thirty-Three" in elegant gold script. His eyes quickly perused the room until he finally spotted—to his utter disappointment—the Hennesseys, seated at a table very near the head table. Miserably he slumped in his seat, the slight obvious.

He made a pretense of studying one of the buttons on his suit coat until his attention was aroused, however, by some commotion at the doors. The orchestra struck up "Here Comes the Bride" as the conductor announced, "Ladies and gentleman, I give you Mr. and Mrs. Clive Howard!" Henrietta—in all of her glory—and Clive entered the hall now, both of them beaming, to loud clapping and even some cheers. To Stan, Henrietta looked so much like a heavenly creature, so much like an angel, that for one brief moment he thought he might die. He watched as the happy couple proceeded to the head table, Clive delicately assisting Henrietta to her chair, and desperately Stan wished that it was him who could bend close to her and whisper in her ear just as Clive was doing now.

The repeated clink of a silver spoon on a crystal goblet broke his reverie, and he looked to see Major Barnes-Smith standing next to the seated couple, grinning at them as though they were all in on some happy joke—which obviously Stan was not—before clinking the glass in his hand again.

A general hush came over the room now as the major cleared his throat and began. "Ladies and gentlemen. What a lovely day for a wedding," he said, smiling. "As many of you know, I had the very great pleasure of being Clive's commanding officer in the Second Calvary in the war. Today is not the day to recount battles and extreme courage under fire, however, but let me just say that a finer man has never served under me." Stan noticed that Clive looked down at the table now and that Henrietta's gloved hand had reached for his. "A more beautiful, lovely bride I could not have imagined for you, Clive," the major continued, "and a more fair, honorable man I have never known for you, my dear," he said to Henrietta. "I wish both of you every happiness, for you deserve it. I implore both of you to live the life you have been given, grasp it firmly, and embrace it for all the boys who are no longer here with us, for all the absent friends. We must do the living, all of us, for them—the eating, the drinking, the working, the dancing . . . the loving. Live for them . . . and be happy," he entreated, his voice growing more and more quiet. "And so," he boomed out toward the crowd now, as if suddenly remembering the purpose of his speech, "I give you, Clive and Henrietta Howard! May you have a long and happy life!" He raised his glass, and the crowd stood up and repeated, "To Clive and Henrietta!" and then drank down the contents as the couple leaned toward each other and kissed, the crowd lightly applauding them.

The dinner proceeded quickly, then, each course being brought out by what seemed an army of waiters. Stan ate his, of course, but he didn't much enjoy it. Too fancy and rich for his liking. Whoever heard of tiny pink bubbles that were surprisingly crunchy and salty on a layer of white stuff on a bit of toast? Then there was a clear soup with hardly anything in it, followed by what seemed like a bit of fish in a thick yellowish sauce with chewy bits in it. One of the Marlowe girls had exclaimed that it was a lobster hollandaise sauce, whatever that was, but it hadn't impressed *him*. Next came a laughable little ball of ice that Stan was able to eat in one bite, surprisingly tasting of lemon and vodka. He shook his head at the coldness of it and looked across at one of the Marlowe girls. Rose, he thought she said her name was. The single guy—Al, he thought his name was—was paying her particularly close attention. Stan had not really been listening during the introductions and explanations of how everyone at the table exactly knew Clive or Henrietta, but he thought this Al had said he was some distant friend of Clive's. That would make sense, Stan thought, rolling his eyes, as he seemed particularly lecherous. Well, it was none of his business! The beef that came next was barely cooked! (Henrietta had clearly been ripped off at this place.) And the tiny potatoes it came with weren't even mashed. Stan was about to attempt to mash them himself with his fork, but he noticed just in time that everyone else seemed to be simply eating them as is. Even the vegetables seemed undercooked, not mushy the way his mother always prepared them, which was what he preferred. All in all, it was a disappointment, but most wedding dinners were, weren't they? He himself was partial to the spread the ladies of the Altar and Rosary Society put on at St. Sylvester's, but that was just him. His mother always said that ham sandwiches or fried chicken were enough for a wedding, as most people, due to the large amounts of alcohol consumed, wouldn't remember much about it in the morning anyway. No use wasting good money on a wedding dinner, she always said, and Stan was inclined to agree. Not that Henrietta and Clive hadn't spent a lot for this rubbish, given that it was in a yacht club and all, but it hadn't been worth it. Again, his mother was right.

A chocolaty pudding was next, which he heard one of the girls call *mousse*, but he was nearly full now.

"Oh, they're cutting the cake!" exclaimed one of the girls, and Stan's gaze was drawn to the corner near the head table, where Henrietta and Clive were feeding each other bits of cake (disgusting!) and laughing while a photographer snapped pictures. Slices of cake were quickly delivered to the tables not long after, but Stan had found he was no longer hungry. Still, wouldn't it be a sort of sin not to eat Henrietta's wedding cake? he worried. Carefully he wrapped his piece in his handkerchief and slipped it into his pocket for later.

"Oh, goodness!" the girl he thought was called Rose exclaimed, her eyes on the dance floor now. The orchestra had been playing light dinner music, but now a woman in a beautifully flowing black evening gown had stepped in front of a big silver microphone and was smiling at the crowd. "That's Helen Forrest! They've got Helen Forrest to sing at their wedding!" Rose squealed. (Stan wondered who the heck Helen Forrest was and squinted blearily at the band, but nothing registered.) An excited buzz had erupted from the crowd now, and everyone at Table Thirty-Three arched their heads to get a better glimpse of the lovely Helen Forrest as the lights dimmed slightly and she began to sing "All the Things You Are," in a rich, velvety dulcet voice.

Clive walked manfully out onto the floor, holding Henrietta's hand, and when they reached the middle, he swept his other arm tightly around her waist and held her as they began to dance. Stan allowed himself, just once, to look at Henrietta's face, and he had to turn away when he saw the complete love there as she gazed up at Howard, tears on her cheeks. Damn it! he thought.

"Don't they make a beautiful couple?" the girls were swooning to each other. Stan took the opportunity to look more closely at them now that their attention was elsewhere. Lucy and the other girl next to her—what was it? Lynn? Gwen?—were wearing wedding rings, so where were their husbands? Probably at home having a good rest, thought Stan. Wise move. Only Rose did not wear a ring. He saw Al try to put his arm on her back as they watched the happy couple dance, but she shrugged him off. The crowd applauded now as the dance finished, and the conductor requested that the rest of the wedding party and parents take the floor and join the happy couple as "The Way You Look Tonight" began.

Stan watched as Elsie stood up to dance with the Major. No cause for concern, there, Stan assessed. After all, he was ancient and a bit of a cripple. Mr. and Mrs. Howard were dancing as well, as were Clive's sister and her husband, though they were a bit stiff on the floor. Stan allowed himself to glance once more at Henrietta and Clive, and this time was sickened, when he looked closer, to see that Clive seemed to be singing the words of the song to her! My God! That was a bit much! He looked away in search of Henrietta's mother. He caught a glimpse of her still seated at the head table. Mr. Exley Sr. was standing near her, gesturing toward the dance floor, but Mrs. Von Harmon was shaking her head. Stan watched uncomfortably as the older man finally went back to his seat, but many eyes from the surrounding tables, Stan saw, were watching, too.

Miraculously the song finally ended, and the conductor then invited everyone to please join the happy couple, the next song being Artie Shaw's "They Say." Henrietta positively laughed—laughed!—as Clive spun her around the floor. Stan tried not to watch them as he annoyingly heard the nearby Rose sing part of the lyrics . . .

They say I shouldn't dream of your face in the moon.
They say that all my dreams will be nightmares too soon.
Let them talk. Let them say what they want to
If it makes them feel happy that way
I know I'll always love you, no matter what they say.

The bride and groom had eyes for no one but each other, and Stan accordingly tried to force his eyes from them to search for Elsie instead. The major had retired back to the table with his stiff leg, his place on the dance floor being taken up by his nephew, the young lieutenant. Elsie's eyes, Stan noticed, held a pleasure he didn't appreciate. The young couple next to Stan had gotten up to dance, and Al had taken Rose off as well. The waiter had come back and announced that the bar was now open for after-dinner drinks of a wide variety should they wish to indulge.

"Is it free?" Stan asked, Lucy and Lynn . . . no, Gwen . . . suppressing a giggle at his question.

"It *is* complimentary, yes, sir," the waiter said with a curl of his lip and retreated in apparent disgust.

"I think you've offended him," Lucy said.

"Who cares?" Stan said roughly and stood up. "I'm getting a drink. Anyone want one?" he asked.

The girls shook their heads, dismissive of him now, and turned their attention back to the dance floor. Just as well, thought Stan. As he squeezed his way into a spot by the bar, he wished Eugene were here. Eugene could be a bit rough around the edges, but he wasn't a bad chap, not really. Stan actually found him a bit sad more often than not.

He tried to concentrate on his drink and, for lack of anything else to do, listen in on the conversations near him which concerned football, mostly, and some politics, his eyes wandering against his will every so often to the dance floor. Henrietta and Clive were no longer dancing, it seemed, but were mingling with their guests, never very far from each other, however. Elsie appeared to be dancing now with one of the Exley uncles. He turned back toward the bar and was just trying to decide about whether to order another drink or no when he felt a tap on his arm. Somewhat blearily, he turned and saw that girl, Rose (it was Rose, right?), standing beside him.

"It's Stanley, isn't it?" she asked quickly, to which Stan gave a brief nod.

"Yeah?"

"I know this is terribly forward, but could I ask you for a very big favor?" she said, looking behind her in a distraught sort of way.

"What is it?" he asked suspiciously.

"Would you dance with me? Just for a couple of songs?" she said, looking over her shoulder again, during which time Stan took the opportunity to quickly assess her. Not bad, he thought. Just his height, blond hair, green eyes, a bit on the thin side, but well endowed. She was dressed in a black-and-white striped dress with a black hat. Her scooped-neck collar was a bit too revealing, but she could pass for respectable, he decided. Still, he wasn't sure . . .

"Well, I don't know," he said, glancing at the dance floor. "I'm sort of with someone."

"You are?" she asked, confused, looking around to find his apparent date. "Well, it doesn't matter. It's just . . . just to get away from that Al that was at our table. He won't leave me alone, and I just thought that if he saw me dancing with someone else for a while . . ." she sniffed.

Was she about to cry? Stan wondered uncomfortably. He had no interest in dancing with anyone at the moment, especially one of those Marlowe girls, but his sense of chivalry was unfortunately piqued and was already beginning to work against him. He couldn't just leave this distressed girl to the lecherous overtures of some drunken buffoon, could he? What would his mother say? He looked around. "Well, maybe just a couple; I'm not very good, you know," he said hesitantly. He stiffly held out his arm to her, then, to begin the rescue.

"Oh, I don't mind," Rose said, taking it gladly. "I just need a warm body."

She seemed to brighten considerably as he led her away from the bar. He could have sworn he saw her wink at Lucy and Gwen as they passed by them, but he couldn't be sure.

Out on the dance floor, which seemed much smaller now that he was on it, he respectfully took Rose in his arms, keeping a fair distance between them as he began to concentrate on his steps. A waltz was playing now, and he wasn't the best at waltzes, though he thought the large amount of alcohol that he had consumed was definitely aiding in his technique, at least it seemed that way anyway. He looked up and saw Elsie swirling by with the lieutenant again. Damn it! He made it look so easy! Howard seemed to be a particularly skilled dancer as well, he fumed. Is that what the army taught its officers these days, how to dance well and impress young ladies? Shouldn't their focus have been on killing Krauts? Shouldn't . . .

"So, who are you here with?" Rose was asking him, bringing him back to the here and now.

Stan looked at her, puzzled.

"You know . . . you said you were here with someone," she said again.

"Oh," he said, shaking his head. "I'm . . . I'm here with Elsie, the maid of honor, but she's been a bit busy, as you see."

"Oh, her?" Rose asked, nodding her head to where Elsie was dancing now, the lieutenant's head bent toward hers, smiling and listening to what she was saying.

"Yes, her," he said firmly, looking beyond her to the large windows. The sun was beginning to set now.

"Well, I have to thank you for helping me," Rose said, more sweetly now. "You're a real gentleman; I can see that."

Stan bristled with pride despite himself.

"You live in the city, don't you?" she asked. "What part?"

"Logan Square. You?"

"Wicker Park, on Damen?"

"Oh! Nearby, then," he said, smiling for what reason he knew not. "I'm at the electrics on Western."

"No!" she exclaimed. "So's my brother! Do you know him? Billy Whitman?"

Stan had never heard of him, but that didn't mean anything. The electrics employed hundreds of men on different shifts. "I might have heard the name," he fibbed. "I'll look out for him."

"Oh," she said, as if considering something. "Well, you . . . you might not mention that we danced," she said, smiling up at him apprehensively. "He wouldn't understand."

Hmmm, Stan surmised, protective brother—must be a good family despite the Marlowe connection. After all, Henrietta had gotten mixed up there as well, and it hadn't really been her fault. It had been Clive's, actually, but he didn't want to go over all that again. Maybe something similar had happened with Rose. Personally, he wouldn't put it past Clive . . . Rose's eyes were very bright; he couldn't help notice. Very pale, pretty skin with just a smattering of freckles. She was an interesting combination of homespun and provocation. She reminded him of someone . . .

"You don't still work at the Marlowe, do you?" Stan asked with narrowed eyes.

"No, I just did that for a little while for the money," she explained hastily. "But it wasn't a nice place," she said, looking away. "I work at the Melody Mill now . . . just as a waitress."

That's better, thought Stan. Least she came to her senses. He felt her hand slip a bit lower on his back now. It was a seemingly innocent movement of her hand, no matching look registering in her face—in fact she was looking at another couple—but he felt an odd jolt of electricity run through him just the same. He found himself staring at her lips and was awash with panic, then, suddenly aware that he should not be feeling the way he currently was. It must be the alcohol, he thought desperately. He increased the space between them and looked around for Elsie. He could not initially see her, but instead surprisingly saw that Henrietta was actually quite close by, dancing with her new brother-in-law. Randolph was his name, wasn't it? He was about to look away when he saw that Henrietta's face looked upset and quite distressed, actually, so he looked closer. Randolph was holding her, he saw now, quite close and quite tightly, whispering something to her. Her face looked flushed and angry now, and he could see that she was trying to pull away. Stan was just about to intervene, to make a show of congratulating her or cutting in if he had to—poor Rose would just have to understand—but before he could make a move, the inspector had cut in, glowering at Randolph as he did so. Henrietta seemed relieved, relaxing into Clive's arms and whispering to him, after which Clive glided them to the other side of the floor. For the first time, Stan was glad that Clive had been there, that he was up to the job of protecting his Henrietta, and he felt a strange release then, a crack finally occurring in the burden he had been carrying around for so long, and the whisper of relief it brought made him feel strangely light and almost giddy. For the first time he was beginning to feel happy that she was happy, and it felt blessedly good.

"Everything all right?" Rose was asking him now.

"Yes, I just . . . I thought that guy was bothering the bride." (Why hadn't he said "Henrietta"?) "Probably just drunk."

"People usually drink too much at weddings, don't they?" she said, her eyes twinkling.

Why were her eyes so sparkly? "Would you . . . would you like to get a drink?" he asked, nodding back toward the bar. Why had he said that? How stupid! "I mean . . ."

"Hey, bub! Give a guy a chance, will you?" said a voice behind him as a finger tapped him, harder than need be, on the shoulder. Stan turned to see Al, standing behind him with a somewhat leering grin.

"Well, actually, I was just getting the lady a drink," Stan said stiffly, straightening up.

"Good! You go on and get her a drink, and I'll keep her company," he said, trying to step between them now.

"Hey!" said Stan.

"Oh, all right, Al, just one dance," Rose said, looking at Stan forlornly with a small shrug.

"I'll wait right here for you," he said, crossing his arms and standing on the edge of the dance floor. "Then we'll go get the drink together."

Al quickly whirled Rose out of sight, and as Stan craned to keep his eyes on them, they rested instead on Elsie, standing by herself, also looking out at the crowd. Regrettably, she caught his eye and excitedly waved. He sighed, knowing what he should do. Reluctantly he left his vigil and went over to her. This might be his only chance to talk to her. He looked around for the lieutenant and saw that he was dancing with Henrietta now. Was everyone going to dance with Henrietta? he wondered.

Elsie held her hand out to him. "Stanley! I've been looking all over for you! I was getting worried!"

"Gee whiz, Els, I didn't want to get in the way. Besides, the sarge seems to be keeping you company well enough," he said in a more aggrieved voice than he really meant.

"Stanley!" Elsie smiled. "He's just filling in for his uncle. The major finds it hard to dance with his leg, poor man. The *lieutenant*," she corrected, "is obliging me."

"Obliging? Is that what they call it?" he said sorely.

"Don't you want to dance?" she asked shyly, obviously trying to change the subject.

The thought hadn't occurred to Stan. "Yes, I suppose so," he said, looking around for Rose and Al as he led Elsie to the dance floor. "I didn't realize we could, though this one's almost over."

Stan waited to catch the rhythm and then carefully guided Elsie as they began dancing. They were silent for the first few moments, Stan trying to concentrate.

"I saw you dancing," Elsie finally said quietly. "She's very pretty."

"Yes, she is . . . I mean . . . I was just doing her a favor . . . it wasn't really like a real dance . . . she's . . . it's just that . . . she's trying to get away from that guy . . ." He saw Rose now and inclined his head toward her and Al. "See?" he explained to Elsie, "That guy's a bit of an ass." He continued to watch them.

"Well, that's nice of you," Elsie said and then remained silent, waiting for him to turn his attention back to her.

Finally Stan seemed to realize that no one had spoken for a few moments and that Elsie was patiently looking at him. He returned her gaze now and asked, "How's . . . how's it going? All this?"

"Oh, you mean the wedding?" Elsie said, perking up now. "Isn't it beautiful, Stanley?" she gushed suddenly, as if she had been just waiting for him to ask about it. "I've never seen Henrietta happier in all my life! Clive has been so sweet to her today! You can't imagine! Every whim of hers he's fulfilled. Even getting Helen Forrest to sing! Can you believe it? That was *his* doing! Can you imagine anything more romantic? Even Mrs. Howard didn't know about it, apparently. I heard her tell one of the Exleys that it was pretentious in the extreme, is how she put it. She pulled Clive aside and told him that several of the older guests were complaining that the music was too modern, but Clive just laughed. I actually heard him laugh! But he must have had a word with the orchestra because they started playing more waltzes, then. Still, Henrietta was thrilled. She's cried at least half a dozen times today, I'm sure! She seems so very happy. Ma seems to be relaxing a little bit, too. She finally found some older women to talk to that she hasn't seen for years. She's hiding out with them at a table in the back somewhere. Clive asked her to dance, but she had the rudeness to say no! Can you imagine? The shame of it, Stanley!"

But Stan was only half listening to Elsie as he watched Rose and Al leave the floor now. Where was he taking her? he wondered. "I don't know, Els! He's just trying to show off, I reckon."

"Who?"

"The inspector, of course, hiring a big-time singer. It's a bit much, if you ask me," he said, moving them to the right a bit to try to see Rose and Al.

"You don't have a romantic bone in your body, Stanley Dubowski!" Elsie said mournfully, though her tone suggested that she hoped she was wrong.

Just then, however, Stan finally spotted Rose and Al. Al had her by the hand and was now corralling her into a darkened corner near the main doors. He was obviously drunk. On instinct, Stan twirled Elsie, lurching to the side quickly to get a better view.

"Ow! Stanley! I . . ." Elsie stopped dancing now and gripped his hand through her glove. "I think I've hurt my ankle. You turned so suddenly . . ."

"Gee, Elsie, I'm sorry!" he said genuinely, but still taking a quick glance at the corner. Could no one else see a woman in distress? he thought, panicking. "Are you all right?" he said to Elsie, helping her off the dance floor now. "I . . . I think that Al guy is attacking that Rose woman . . . I just saw . . ."

"Might I be of service?" came a drawling voice from behind them. "I have some experience with injuries, you know."

It was the lieutenant, of course, Stan realized, turning to look at him now, and he did not like the way Elsie's face lit up at the sight of him. Elsie hobbled to a chair and sat down, the lieutenant going down on one knee in front of her.

"May I?" he asked her, as if Stan wasn't there.

"If . . . if you wish," Elsie said, and, even in the darkened room, Stan could see her blushing.

"Hey, bub! What's the big idea?" Stan said, his hands on his hips. The lieutenant gave him an exasperated look. "There is no big idea, my man. Just that I've had some training as a medic, if you must know."

"You've never seen any action!" Stan said, hotly.

"Neither have you, I presume," the lieutenant said coolly.

"Stanley! He's just trying to help," Elsie put in obligingly. "He's sort of like a doctor . . ."

As if he didn't know what a medic was! And why did she have to say it so dreamily? He rolled his eyes. Maybe it wouldn't hurt for the lieutenant to check her out, though, while he went to investigate . . .

"All right, fine . . . I'll be right back!" he said, dashing off now toward the front doors, hoping he wasn't too late. He could still hear Elsie calling "Stanley!" from behind him as he made his way through the crowd.

When he finally got to the corner, breathing a bit more heavily than he would have liked, Rose and Al were nowhere to be seen. Where could they have gone? he wondered anxiously, spinning around and searching the room. He took a few steps toward the bar, but he didn't see them there, either. He wouldn't have taken her outside, would he have? he worried. He went to the nearest window and looked out but could see nothing in the quickly descending darkness. He hurried back to the doors and burst through them, crossing the lobby in a rush, where the coat-check girls lolled, smoking. He went through the main doors to the outside now where he could instantly hear the lap of the waves from the lake.

"Rose?" he called, not seeing her in the immediate vicinity. "Rose?" he called again, walking toward the side of the building.

He heard a shuffle and then a startled, "Stanley?"

He came upon them, then. Al had her against the wall, though her arms, which she quickly dropped now, had been oddly entwined around him as if not in the least bit of distress. They had apparently been kissing, from what Stan could tell. Rose looked quite disheveled, and she instantly slipped out from under Al's arms, who let them drop sluggishly as he stepped back. Casually, as if nothing had happened, he pulled out a cigarette from the box in his jacket pocket.

"That was a long time getting a drink, Mack," he said, putting one to his lips and lighting it.

"Are you all right, Rose?" Stan asked, ignoring Al and taking a step closer to her.

"Yes, I'm okay," she said hurriedly. "Let's go inside, shall we?" she said, taking his arm.

"That it, then?" Al asked her, likewise ignoring Stan and taking a deep drag.

"Of course that's it!" Rose said angrily.

"Seemed pretty eager just a few minutes ago. Before this dope showed up," he said, flicking his ash at Stan.

"How dare you!" Rose said. "Don't listen to him, Stanley!"

Surprisingly, Al laughed. "Better watch this one, pal. She's pretty foxy. She knows what she's doin' all right. Might just find yourself trapped. I reckon she's that type."

"Hey! You don't talk to a lady that way!" Stan said, incensed now but trying to reign in the anger that had been brewing all day.

Al held up his hands in a show of innocence. "Sure she's a lady?" he said with a little laugh.

Something in Stan just cracked then, and before he knew it he drew his arm back and punched Al right in the nose. It felt surprisingly good, though it hurt his hand horribly.

"Hey!" Al yelled, momentarily stunned by what had just happened as he held his nose and stared incredulously at Stan. A look of fury crossed his face, then, and he lunged at Stan, shoving him backward so hard that he nearly fell. Rose let out a little scream. Quickly Stan got his footing and rushed toward him again, raising his fist to smack him when two doormen from the yacht club seemed to appear out of nowhere and pulled them apart.

"No fighting!" one of them said, pinning Stan by the arms.

"Yeah, okay, sorry," Stan said thickly. "Sorry." He glanced over at Al, who was glowering at him. The doorman let go of him with a shove. Stan collected himself, smoothing his hair back with the palms of his hands and breathing deeply while Al slunk off farther into the parking lot, dodging the parked cars.

Reactively, Stan quickly felt his pocket for Henrietta's cake, which was of course smashed now into a gooey mess, and he let out an anguished groan. He would never eat it now; it was ruined! With a deep breath, he stood up straight and raggedly held out his arm to Rose, as there was nothing else he could do now. Hesitantly she took it, and together they walked unsteadily toward the doors.

"Oh, no you don't, buster. You're not going back in there."

"But I have to! My date's the maid of honor!"

"Sorry, pal."

"Please, mister," Rose implored. "I'll keep an eye on him; I promise! Please? I'll get him some coffee. He'll behave now."

The doorman seemed to hesitate. "All right," he said reluctantly. "But one sign of trouble, and I call the cops. Groom's orders."

"Yes, sir," Rose said as they passed through the doors. "Thank you."

Rose dutifully led Stan to the shadows by the bar. "Are you hurt?" she asked. "I'm so sorry you got mixed up in that."

"Ah, it was nothing," Stan said sheepishly, though his heart was pounding at the near miss of almost getting thrown out! He would have died from the shame of it! Getting thrown out of Henrietta's wedding for fighting? He would never forgive himself.

"I think I need a drink," he said heavily.

"I told the doorman I'd get you coffee . . ."

"He won't know."

Rose hesitated. "Oh, all right. But stay here!" she implored as she left him slumped against the wall. He took the opportunity to look over the crowd again. Elsie was nowhere in sight now. The lieutenant must have spirited her away somewhere. He could not see Henrietta, or Clive, for that matter, anywhere at all.

Rose came up and handed him a drink. He was delighted that it was a scotch and even more surprised that she held one, too. They clinked their glasses together in a silent cheers.

"Listen," she asked. "I have a favor to ask . . ."

"Yeah?" he said, looking past her, still trying to locate Henrietta.

"I think my friends have left," she said worriedly. "Do you think you might give me a lift home? I just thought, since we live so close to each other . . ." her voice dropped off.

There was a commotion in the crowd now as people began clapping. Stan craned his neck to see. It was Henrietta and Clive. They had emerged from the back of the hall, dressed in normal clothes now, except that Henrietta carried a small bouquet, a replica of her bouquet from earlier in the day. They paused somewhere in the middle of the dance floor, which had hurriedly cleared for them to pass. Several women gathered around, and Henrietta laughingly tossed them the bouquet. Secretly he was glad that Elsie was not among them to catch it. The couple continued on then, Stan suddenly realizing with dread that this was it, they were leaving! That's why they had changed, stupid! he chastised himself. They were off to begin their honeymoon! Stan's heart was beating hard in his chest as he realized he had not had a chance to really talk to Henrietta, to dance with her one last time. He had meant to, but he just hadn't gotten around to it. And now his chance was over! They were passing so close to him now, so near the doors and their new life. She didn't see him, of course, and he wanted to call out to her, to say goodbye, but he didn't. Mortified, he felt hot tears in his eyes, which he furiously blinked away before anyone saw. What was it that Elsie had said to him? That he didn't have a romantic bone in his body? Well, for once in his life, he thought despairingly, he wished to God that he didn't.

Chapter 7

The gravel crunched faintly as the Isotta pulled up in front of Highbury. Clive had insisted on driving the short distance from the yacht club himself rather than involve Fritz. Henrietta was secretly glad. It was her first time alone with her *husband*—her heart fluttered in excited pleasure at being able to call him that—and she was eager to recount all the details of the day with him, alone. As they drove back on the almost empty streets, both of them concluded that the day had gone so very fast, as had the drive now to Highbury. They seemed to have barely scratched the surface of discussing all that had happened at the reception when they had already arrived back at the estate! Except for the servants, they were alone. By arrangement, Clive and Henrietta had left the reception early, as tradition held, while Mr. and Mrs. Howard would remain until the last of the guests departed. It was only eight o'clock in the evening, but the reception wouldn't end until ten. Still, it felt later than it was.

As Clive came around to open the car door for her, Henrietta suddenly fell silent, her excited chatter during the drive home fading away now as the massive Highbury loomed in front of them. She suddenly became very nervous, knowing what was expected next. She glanced up at the east wing and saw that it was dark, which somehow

made it seem all the more cold and foreboding. Clive gave her his
hand to help her out of the car, saying, "Why, hello, Mrs. Howard,
how very nice to see you!"

She laughed despite her nerves. It felt strange to be called that!
She didn't think she would ever get used to it. He wrapped her arm
through his, then, and said in a cheerful voice, "Let's not go in just
yet. Do you mind, darling? Let's walk by the lake. I would see my wife
in the moonlight."

"Yes, my lord!" she said, responding in kind, glad for an excuse not
to proceed to the wedding chamber just yet.

No staff were on the grounds, thankfully, at this time of night as
Clive led his new bride down to the lake. She was relieved at this
suggestion and wondered if he was delaying going into the house
on purpose to calm her. If so, she was very grateful. Despite the chill
in the air now, a walk was just what she needed after the noise and
chaos of the reception. The lake, by contrast, was blissfully quiet and
still except for the sound of the rhythmic lap of the waves. Clive carefully led her past the boathouse out onto the dock, where they stood
looking out at the bright reflection of the moon on the water and
held hands. Henrietta took a deep breath. She could not believe she
was married! That she belonged to this man, now, and he to her. That
all of this would someday be theirs.

"Happy, darling?" he asked gently.

"More than I ever thought possible, Clive," she whispered, looking
at him now.

"I love you," he said, squeezing her hand and kissing her softly,
"with all my heart." He gazed into her eyes, and she thought he was
going to kiss her again, but instead he said rather abruptly, "Come!
I've got a surprise!"

"A surprise! You've already surprised me with Helen Forrest!
What is it?" she asked, as she allowed herself to be led back to firmer
ground. "Oh, Clive, I didn't get you anything!"

Clive laughed. "I have all I'll ever want, darling, now that I have
you," he said as he led her up the path.

"Where are we going? Are we taking the long way back to the stables?" she asked, wondering if he had bought her a car, though she really couldn't drive that well. He had tried to show her a few times, but she had yet to really get the hang of it.

"You'll see."

Together they climbed the path up the slight hill that ran past the boathouse until they reached the ridge, and Helen's old cottage came into view. To Henrietta's surprise, a light was burning inside and smoke was coming from the chimney.

"Oh, no, Clive!" Henrietta whispered anxiously. "There's someone in there! Did one of the servants move in?" she said, gripping his arm as they walked toward it, a niggling feeling of unease overcoming her. She felt possessive of the cottage now, though she wasn't sure why, and it bothered her that someone occupied it, which was completely irrational, she knew.

"Yes, as a matter of fact, someone does occupy it," Clive said with a smile as they came upon it now and he pushed open the door with not a little effort. "That would be us!" he said, gesturing wide with his free arm, Henrietta still having hold of the other one.

"Oh, Clive!" Henrietta said as she gingerly stepped inside. She had never seen it so warm and inviting. Soft kerosene lamps and candles glowed everywhere and a roaring fire crackled in the fireplace, which was surrounded by cozy well-worn furniture procured from somewhere—a sofa and two small armchairs and an old Victrola as well. The whole place had been cleaned and patched and repaired to perfection. Henrietta's eyes traveled to the kitchen table, where a large bucket of ice housed a bottle of champagne and nearby stood a bouquet of wildflowers.

"Did you do all this?" she asked, incredulous.

"Well, I arranged it. Mother wasn't happy, as you might imagine. I picked the flowers myself, though, this morning."

She took a few steps more. "Are we to spend the night here?" she asked tentatively, her eyes darting to the bedroom beyond and then to him.

"If you wish it," Clive said delicately. "I will be guided by you, my love."

Suddenly it was all too much. "Oh, Clive!" she said, holding out her hand for him to take, tears coming to her eyes. "You've gone through so much trouble to please me this day. How can I ever repay you? I don't deserve someone so good!"

Clive laughed. "Nonsense!" He looked down at her now, more seriously, as he pulled her to him and held his arms loosely about her. "If you must know, you've already repaid me, darling, a hundred thousand times over, earlier today when you became my wife. You've given me a second chance at love. I want to do it right this time. I mean to make you happy, each and every day, and to keep you safe, always."

It was difficult to see him now for the tears in her eyes, and he appeared blurry in front of her.

"It's not permanent, you know," he added in a lighter tone, "before you get too excited and take to wearing gingham dresses and kerchiefs. But until we leave anyway, it is ours, and when we come back, well, it can be our special place. How about that?"

"Oh, Clive," she said, looking at him seriously. "Thank you. I love you so very much."

"Come on," he said with a smile, leading the way to the small kitchen area. "Let's get settled in our little abode! I'll pour us some champagne," he said, rustling the bottle from its firm nest of ice. "Why don't you put on some music?"

Henrietta, still stunned, walked to the Victrola and began to peruse the stack of records there. They were all her favorites. "How did you know?" she asked, gesturing toward the records. Clive laughed as he walked in then and handed her a crystal glass of champagne. "Well, I *am* a detective, or was," he grinned. "I happen to notice small details." He sat down on the sofa while she put on Benny Goodman's "And the Angels Sing" and joined him.

"That's one thing we haven't talked much about," she said seriously. "You leaving the force. You've had to feel it very much, and you haven't said a word about it, dearest."

A faint wave of something—regret, maybe?—passed across Clive's face then, but he quickly brushed it away. "Let's not talk of that tonight. No serious subjects! We'll speak about it later, perhaps on the ship as we idle our days away. Tonight is only for happy things."

Henrietta nodded and tried to smile. She was overwhelmed by Clive's attempts to please her (he was a romantic, after all!), to show her how very much he cared for her, and she struggled to mediate her mounting feelings of disproportion. She had gotten him nothing and brought so little to the table (she knew she wasn't supposed to think these thoughts anymore and fingered the gold band that now sat between her heart and her engagement ring), though she knew what she was supposed to give in return. And she *wanted* to give herself to him, but she was afraid. Afraid that it might be painful after all and more so, to be honest, that she wouldn't know what to do. Over the summer when she had found herself unwittingly alone at times with Clive—out on the terrace, upstairs in the darkened hallways, or even strolling through the rose garden—she had allowed him to kiss her and let his hands briefly roam. It had been exciting and dangerous, and she had thrilled to his touch. She had wanted to be intimate so many times, but now, now that it was expected, it seemed so contractual, so forced. It wasn't spontaneous! And as lovely as all of this was, she thought, as she looked around the cottage again and contemplated how much effort had been put forth, it only served to increase her sense of discomfiture, as if it were the build-up to the final act in a production for which she had somehow forgotten her lines. She looked over at Clive now, who was looking back at her. Carefully he took her champagne glass from her and set it down. He stood up then and held his hand out to her. "Come," he said, "let's do what we do best. Let's dance."

At his suggestion, Henrietta audibly breathed a sigh of relief and smiled. Clive put on "The Way You Look Tonight" and held her in his arms. She began to relax when she felt his strong arms around her. Thoughts of her father made their way into her mind suddenly, but she forced them out just as quickly. In the past, memories of him had always been a source of comfort for her, but now, after her mother's horrible insinuations about a darker side of him, thoughts of him left her feeling squeamish, if Ma's tales could even be believed. She didn't want to think about that now, though, and, annoyed, pushed those thoughts away. Instead, she closed her eyes and deeply breathed in Clive's scent. He usually smelled of crisp linen and cologne, but there was always a deeper, earthier, manly smell to him too that mingled with it and made her insides clench.

He was softly singing the words now to her . . .

Yes, you're lovely, with your smile so warm,
And your cheeks so soft,
There is nothing for me but to love you,
And the way you look tonight . . .

She looked up into his eyes and could not help a little laugh, or perhaps it was a little gasp, from slipping out, so very overwrought was she. He stopped dancing then and looked down into her eyes, the love in them palpable. Tenderly he brushed her cheek with the back of his hand. Her heart began to beat fast in her chest.

"You're still frightened, aren't you," he said gently.

The fact that he knew, that he understood her so well, made fresh tears come to her eyes as she nodded.

"Oh, my love," he said, "the last thing I would have is to force you to my bed. I promised you that we would go slow. We don't have to do anything tonight if you do not wish it."

Quickly she searched his eyes to ascertain his sincerity. "Honestly?"

"Honestly," he said with a small smile.

"But . . . but what about a child?" she asked, unable to push Ma's—and Helen's, actually—prediction from her mind.

"A child?" he asked, taken aback, and Henrietta almost thought he might be angry. "Who filled you're mind with that notion?"

"Well, Helen," she said, gesturing around the cottage. "And my mother, and Grandfather, and, well, Julia, in a way. No one else has

said it exactly, but I feel it. That I have to produce . . . Don't you . . .
don't you want a child, for Highbury and all of that?" she murmured.
He closed his eyes and sighed and then took her face in his
hands. "You absurd girl. Of course I don't care about any of that.
Put that worry from your mind. I only want to love you, to please
you. And if a child never comes, then so be it. I'm happier right
now, this minute, than I could ever be again. You have fulfilled
me . . . completed me . . . and I need not one thing more." He kissed
her forehead and then took up her hand and kissed it. "This life
we've entered into is about you," he said, kissing her hand again,
"and me," kissing her other. "Let's just be happy in our love; many
people never get even this chance."

He kissed the palm of her hand, then, and Henrietta felt her knees
weakening.

"As far as loving you, taking you to my bed, I will wait for you,
Henrietta," he said, his voice catching a bit. "I will wait for you to be
ready. I've waited years for my heart to come to life once more, and I
can surely wait just a little longer still."

Henrietta felt herself wanting to embrace him, to give herself to
this good man in front of her, to love him, but she wasn't sure how
to begin.

"Clive, I . . . I want to . . . to please you, but I . . . I want you to show
me. Show me what to do, help me," she whispered, blushing.

He studied her for a moment and then lifted her chin with his
finger. "Are you sure?"

"Yes, very," she said, smiling up at him, trusting him completely
despite the fear that still hovered near.

"Very well," he said quietly. He took her hand then and led her
to the bedroom. Helen's bed had been removed and a cherry four-
poster bed stood along the opposite wall in an attempt to differenti-
ate it from what it had been and to dispel any lingering memories of
Jack or that horrible night.

"What if . . . what if someone comes?" she said, looking back
toward the door.

"No one will come. I've given explicit instructions. No parents, no servants—especially the meddling Billings."

Henrietta smiled hesitantly, and Clive kissed her softly.

"I . . . I didn't bring any of my things . . ." Henrietta said, pulling back and thinking about the negligees she was supposed to wear. She still felt nervous and distracted.

"I had Edna bring some of your things over," he said, nodding toward an armoire in the corner.

"You did?" she asked and released herself from him to step over to it. Hesitantly she pulled the small brass knob of the armoire door. Neatly hanging inside was the feathery gown and robe from Julia, the negligees from Lucy and the girls, as well as her long cotton white nightgown hanging on a peg on its own, which Edna must have included for later, for when it was all over . . . She was embarrassed that Edna had had to handle such things and that she knew—that everyone knew—what she would be engaging in tonight. Still, the sight of her long cotton nightgown made her want to cry.

"What . . . what would you like me to come to you in?" she asked him now, trying to keep her voice steady.

She watched as he came closer and his eyes darted over the various articles. "I quite like this," he said finally, briefly touching her old cotton nightgown.

For a moment she thought he was teasing her, but she saw by his face that he was very serious and her heart melted once again. "Oh, Clive," she said, her voice wavering. "Are you sure?"

He smiled. "I have a weakness for old-fashioned things, being old, you see." His eyes twinkled.

She laughed despite herself. "You're not old!"

"I'm glad you think so," he said, laughing himself and catching her about the waist, kissing her. It was obviously intended to be a quick kiss, but it turned into a deeper one, Henrietta suddenly feeling a jolt of electricity run through her. He continued kissing her until she relaxed and began kissing him back. Timidly she pressed her hands to his back, lowering them a bit as she pressed her body closer to his, and she felt a shudder rip through him. This was normally about the time they would force themselves to break apart, and out of habit, Henrietta stood back. They gazed at each other, not knowing what to do next. Finally she leaned forward and kissed him again as her fingers fumbled to loosen his tie, as she had done so many times over the summer. She felt his hands graze her breasts then, but he stood back, breathing heavily now, with his head turned as if fighting himself. "I told you I would go slow, and I meant it."

"I . . . I want you to. I want you to show me what to do," she whispered. "Help me to know how to please you . . ."

He looked back at her now as if deciding something and then slowly took her face in his hands again and kissed her forehead, her cheeks, and then her lips, almost groaning as he did so. He reached for her buttons and began to undo them, gazing into her eyes all the while. She swallowed hard as the dress fell about her shoulders and hung about her waist. Timidly, she undid her brassiere as he watched and unbelted her dress so that it fell to the ground. Standing before him now in only her panties and silk stockings, she saw the male desire in his eyes and knew that he was pleased with what he saw, and a part of her was pleased, too. How many times had she seen raw desire in men's eyes, and now, only now, did she allow herself to answer it. She pulled the pins out of her hair, and her golden-auburn locks fell about her shoulders.

"My God, Henrietta, you're so beautiful," he said hoarsely, as he stepped forward to rescue her from her awkwardness, kissing her passionately as he pulled her to him. She could feel his hardness against her panties, and a strange pleasure shot through her as he fondled her naked breasts with his hands. She reached for his buttons as well, remembering Lucy's words to follow his lead, and he pulled back to help her, finally shrugging out of his shirt. Even in the darkened room lit only by candlelight, she could see the severe scarring on his shoulder, and her heart went out to him.

"Oh, Clive," she said, reaching out to touch it lightly, "you poor thing." She had not thought it would be so bad! He seemed to be studying her face for her reaction to his mangled shoulder, but if he was expecting shock or disgust, he found none. She ran her fingers through his hair and cupped his cheek. Instinctively, she knew now what to do and ran her fingers faintly down his back and over the scars of his shoulder. "I want to take care of you," she whispered, and his response was to grab her almost roughly and kiss her fiercely.

"Oh, Henrietta. I need you so much," he said thickly. "You've no idea how much."

She led him to the bed, then, and as she sat to undo the stays of her stockings, slowly peeling them off, he shed himself of his trousers and the rest of his clothes and stood before her, naked now except for his gold wedding band. Henrietta found herself wanting to look at him, at all of him, but she shyly turned her head away, reminding her of her days at the dressing room parties at the Marlowe where she had surreptitiously watched lovers in the darkened corners. She could feel her heart pounding in her chest now as she reached out her hand to him as she lay back on the bed. Calmly he took it and lay down beside her.

Softly she kissed his scarred shoulder, feeling him tremble, and any feelings of fear or doubt on her part were dispelled as she saw how much this man—her husband—wanted, no, *needed*, her. He drew her mouth to his now, kissing her tenderly, deeply, until she began to respond, her heart racing and a warmth spreading through her. She arched her body toward him as he pulled away from her lips and began traveling downward, kissing her neck and then her chest until he reached her breasts, cupping them with his strong hands and kissing them before coming back up to her waiting lips. Tentatively she put her hands on his hard chest, not knowing what else to do, and he took one of them and moved it lower, causing him to groan with pleasure as she felt her way. His hand had moved between her legs now, and he caressed her steadily, matching his movements with soft kisses, eliciting an ever-growing passion in her until she felt on fire, a pulse welling up inside her that amazed her in its intensity and the speed with which it overcame her. She was panting now, whimpering, "Clive, please . . . Clive . . ."

He moved on top of her, then, and his weight felt strangely comforting. She felt him gently ease himself inside of her now, breathing hard, and she knew he was trying to control himself. She gasped for a moment at a small pain as he pushed deeper, but she was engulfed then in an intense pleasure, his hand still caressing her as he began to thrust. She felt an almost blinding light, an explosion of passion as her body quivered uncontrollably. The ripples of passion continued in waves over her, as Clive, thrusting harder now, fully exploded inside of her, shuddering almost violently.

It was over, but he continued kissing her passionately, covering her face and neck, until he finally pulled away and lay beside her, taking her hand in his. Her heart was still racing as she lay thinking that this had been nothing like what Ma had described, nor Julia or Lucy, either, whose description at best had been to call it "passable." This was something so beautiful, so trusting . . . a breaking down of everything between them and the opening of a tiny window into each other's souls. She had never felt closer to any human being in her life.

Two tears rolled down her cheeks as she stared at the ceiling, and Clive, noticing, raised himself up on his elbow in alarm.

"Oh, my darling, did I hurt you? I tried to be so careful," he asked, dismayed.

"You didn't hurt me, dearest," she said, turning her head toward him with a smile. She ran her fingers through his hair now. "It was lovely. I'm so very happy, Clive. You've made me so happy."

The newlyweds spent that night, and still another, miraculously undisturbed, left to discover each other more and learning to be man and wife. Mary had stocked a small icebox with a feast that could have lasted a week, allowing them to stay cocooned in the cottage indefinitely. They only ventured out twice, once for a walk in the woods and once for a jaunt in the rowboat tied up by the boathouse, though they didn't get very far before they laughingly turned back to their hovel, more wet than dry from splashing each other with the oars. When they reluctantly emerged two days later, having to finish packing for their long journey, Mr. and Mrs. Howard were waiting for them in the morning room, busying themselves with reading the paper, as if to perhaps seem ignorant of the two days of carnal knowledge that was obviously occurring on the other side of their property.

Henrietta, for her part, felt a glorious freedom and met their eyes with not one ounce of shame. She was a real woman now, understanding all of the subtleties that went with it and instinctively, if not consciously, knowing in her sexuality the power she had over this man at her side whom she was, in turn, eager to love, obey, and cherish in all things. Yes, she had made love to this man, and she wasn't ashamed! It gave her great pleasure, great satisfaction to know how very much they pleased each other, fulfilled each other in a way no other person ever had or could. She knew that now and was confident, assured. Almost gaily she discussed the wedding over tea with the Howards, greeting them like old friends. Excitedly she finished packing, with Edna's help, of course, and let little bits of information drop about how the wedding night had gone, as Edna, very nearly engaged to Virgil now, was solicitous for advice just as she had been not so very long ago. Henrietta was glad to discreetly impart what she had learned, causing Edna to blush profusely, though she was ever so grateful for the information, carefully pondering it as she hung up Henrietta's discarded clothes.

As she and Clive locked up the cottage, which would stand empty again for who knew how long, Henrietta sighed deeply and left it with much regret. It had been a refuge of sorts for her when she had first come to Highbury, and any feelings of fear or sadness that haunted it because of Jack had been completely exorcised for her by her weekend of love and intimacy with Clive, endearing it all the more to her.

She had never felt safer or happier than she did now, leaving for their honeymoon on the arm of her new husband, waving goodbye to the Howards and the whole staff, as Fritz drove them to the train station. But Clive, proudly taking on the role of husband and protector of his precious, young wife with the almost intense dedication of a sacred trust, was for his part taking no chances in his new duty and had made sure, among other things, to pack his revolver.

Chapter 8

Elsie sat with her leg propped up on a little stool, her ankle carefully bandaged.

Her injury at the wedding had turned out to be a rather nasty sprain, causing Lieutenant Barnes-Smith to remain attentive to her for the rest of the evening, getting her a soda water from the bar ("Nothing stronger?" he had implored her. "For the pain? No?") and marveling at her brave countenance. Eventually he was asked to help her to the car, during which he insisted that she lean heavily on him until she was safely deposited in the Packard with Karl at the helm. Ma, more than happy to have an excuse to leave, joined her. Doris, Donny, Jimmy, and Mrs. Kuntz were rounded up and squeezed in as well, and the lieutenant was discharged with the duty of making sure Eddie and Herbert, both of whom veritably begged to be allowed to stay to the bitter end, made it home with Fritz—or, perhaps, Elsie suggested helpfully despite her pain, he might ask the Hennesseys to take them and spare the Howards their car and driver. She could not believe that Stanley was nowhere to be found! It was so unlike him to not be there by her side to be of help. He was so eager any other time. Perhaps he had gone to the aid of that poor woman he had been so concerned about? Rose was her name, wasn't it? She hoped he was okay, as the lieutenant helped her into the car now, his hand lingering for just a moment on hers.

"You'll look for him, won't you, Lieutenant?" Elsie asked, drawing her hand back, her face flushed, undoubtedly from the excitement of the night and not, of course, because the lieutenant was leaning so very close to her through the open window.

"Indeed I will, Miss Von Harmon," he said, as if taking orders. "It will be my special mission. Leave it to me; I'll see your brothers get home safely."

"Are you going to kiss her?" Donny asked shyly from where he sat near Elsie, a naughty smile on his face.

"Donny!" Elsie exclaimed.

"Would that I might, young man," the lieutenant muttered, giving him a wink and then looking over at Elsie. "Good night, Miss Von Harmon," he said more formally. "Might I call on you? To check your progress, that is?" he asked hopefully.

"Well, I'm not sure," Elsie murmured, flustered by his comment about kissing her. Surely he was teasing? And why did he talk that way? So formal and polite? It didn't seem to fit him at all, and yet she thought she liked it.

"Please. It would upset me greatly to not know how you're getting along with your injury," he urged.

"Oh. Well, it's hardly an injury," Elsie blushed, embarrassed by her clumsiness in the first place. "I'm sure it's fine."

"Please," he said so earnestly that she wavered.

"Well, I suppose so," she said hesitantly.

"Elsie!" Ma said from where she was slumped in the corner of the back seat. "Quit your talking. I want to get home!"

"Yes! You're right, Mrs. Von Harmon," the lieutenant said quickly. "My apologies. I shouldn't keep you. Ready," he said, standing up straight and nodding to Karl. "I'll call on you, then," he said loudly over the noise of Karl putting the car into gear and pulling away to begin the long drive home.

Elsie tried not to, but she couldn't resist looking back out of the tiny rearview window, just once, at the lieutenant as he stood waving goodbye. Another blush crept up her face as she turned back to face

Ma, glad of the cover of darkness. But it didn't matter anyway, as Ma already had her eyes closed, and Mrs. Kuntz was in the front next to Karl with Doris on her lap. Elsie held Donnie's hand, then, and looked out the window, trying to wonder all the way home what on earth had become of Stan and hoping that nothing terrible had happened.

It had been three days since the wedding now and still she had had no word from Stan. She would never dream of telephoning him, and though she had several times considered writing to him, she had abandoned the idea as many times again, seeing as he lived just a few streets over and it seemed silly somehow. If she were able to walk better, she might venture over to see him, but as it was, she was stuck here. She set aside her copy of *Sense and Sensibility* and shifted her weight in the overstuffed armchair in the front parlor, gazing out the window and hoping that Henrietta and Clive had made it safely on the train to the *Queen Mary*. She couldn't imagine travelling somewhere so far as Europe, and she admired Henrietta, not for the first time by a long stretch, for her bravery and her confidence. It was drizzling outside now, autumn having finally arrived in earnest, as if the warm air and the sun had been holding on until they saw Henrietta happily married and on her way. The sun, it seemed, was allowed to drop its heavy burden now and retreat, allowing the clouds to move in and take over. Indeed, it had stormed last night, and the wind had sent most of the remaining leaves on the trees surrounding Palmer Square to their soggy graves in the street below.

Elsie was debating whether or not she wanted to put forth the effort to hobble to the kitchen for some cocoa when she was surprised to hear a knock at the front door. She heard one of the servants—it sounded like Karl's shuffle—move to answer it, and, sure enough, she could hear Karl's voice as he opened the door, apparently in the role of butler for the moment. Though she strained to hear, she couldn't quite make out who the visitor was, but she hoped upon hope that it was finally Stan. Excitedly she smoothed her skirt and reminded herself that she meant to give him a good scolding!

She was rather shocked, then, when she looked up, just as Karl shuffled into the room, unceremoniously announcing, "A Lieutenant Barnes-Smith to see you, Miss," and found that very same person following at a modest distance.

"Oh, Lieutenant!" Elsie said, flustered, sitting up a bit. "I . . . I wasn't expecting you."

"Forgive my intrusion, Miss Von Harmon, but I came to see how you were doing," he said, gesturing toward her elevated leg. "You said I might," he suggested uncomfortably. "Do you not remember?"

Elsie just stared at him.

"But perhaps you were not quite yourself . . ."

"Oh, yes," she blushed, feeling embarrassed all over again regarding her injury. She was so clumsy! "I mean . . . yes, I remember, but . . . my . . . my mother is resting just now," she apologized, trying to imitate what Mrs. Hutchings would say and feeling sure that that venerable woman would not approve of the situation that was currently unfolding in the Palmer Square front parlor.

Mrs. Hutchings was the lady's companion that Mr. Exley Sr. had employed to educate his granddaughter in the finer points of society, mostly for the purpose of securing a respectable husband. Mrs. Hutchings had taken up residence with the Von Harmons in late September, during which time she had tried her best to instruct her charge, who had proven to be a most dedicated pupil, but the arrangement had, alas, been short-lived, lasting no more than two weeks, if truth be told. Mrs. Hutchings, as she later reported to her employer, Mr. Exley Sr., had never shied away from her duty in her life, but there was a first time for everything, she had said in a clipped tone, and had declared that she could no longer remain under the roof of Mrs. Von Harmon, finding that lady much more in need of instruction in the ways of polite society than her daughter ever was. Mrs. Hutchings found the arrangement unsuitable, nay intolerable, to her finer feelings and had accordingly put in her notice, saying that Mrs. Von Harmon's quips and quibbles and general refutation of all that she said was vexing in the extreme and completely counterproductive to the education of said Miss Von Harmon, whom, she added, she would personally be sad to be parted from as she found her company exceedingly pleasant and her nature a quite docile one. Mr. Exley fumed to have been thwarted yet again by the willful Martha, but, having been counseled by Gerard, agreed to let it pass until after Henrietta's wedding when the topic could be addressed with more circumspection.

"Well, I promise to be on my very best behavior," the lieutenant was saying as he smiled at her charmingly, and Elsie felt her initial reservations at being alone with him melt away. "May I sit down?" he asked, pointing to the chair opposite.

"Oh, yes! I'm sorry! Yes, please do sit down," she blushed. "Would you . . . would you like some tea?" she thought to ask. "I could ring for some," she said dubiously, having never actually done so since she had come to live in this splendid house, not wanting to bother the servants, though Mrs. Hutchings had been forever urging her to do so, instructing her to embrace her proper place in society's hierarchy.

"None for me, thank you. But don't let me stop you," he added.

Why did everything he said sound so . . . well, so romantic and debonair? He definitely had a charming flavor of John Willoughby to him, she surmised, her mind going back to the novel wedged by her side, pushed deep into the cushions when she had nervously shifted her weight upon the lieutenant's entering the room.

"No, I . . . I'm fine." She tried to smile.

"Are you?" he asked, concerned. "I see you've had the doctor 'round," he said, pointing to the bandage tightly wrapped around her ankle. "Is there anything you need? Any little service I might perform for you?"

Why was he so dreadfully handsome? With his dark hair and mysterious brown eyes, he completely paralyzed her, unnerved her with his beauty. She tried repeatedly to look away, and yet she could not stop herself, like a fragile moth drawn to the only source of light, no matter, in reality, how dull or inconsistent. "No, it's nothing, really," she stammered, embarrassed by his attention to her clumsiness. "I'll be up in a few days."

"It warms my heart to hear it, Miss Von Harmon. Perhaps when you are well, we might take a stroll in the park, if you're feeling up to it," he suggested, smiling, gesturing absently toward the window.

Elsie's mind raced at the suggestion, which she felt sure was inappropriate. What would Stanley think? Or Mrs. Hutchings? Or Ma, for that matter?

Not waiting for her to finish, he went on. "But I can see that I've distressed you. Forgive me," he seemed to say with real remorse. "It's just that," he glanced toward the window as if in despair, "I'm rather lonely sometimes and I do so enjoy your company." He looked back at her now with such woeful eyes that Elsie was positively distressed. "Forgive me for thinking that you may have felt the same." He managed to look hurt here.

"Oh, Lieutenant!" Elsie said earnestly. "Oh, you musn't think that! I mean . . . I do . . . *of course* I enjoy your company, it's just that . . ." How could she explain about Stanley? Was it possible that this young officer could really be in earnest? Surely that was impossible. A girl like her? He could have any woman, that was obvious, so why would he single her out? He couldn't really be lonely, could he? Surely he had a multitude of friends back at the barracks, and yet his eyes did look so sorrowful . . .

"You have another, is that it?" he said, not waiting for her to finish. "This Dubowski fellow?"

"Well, actually . . ."

"I understand," he said with a sigh. "It was foolish to think you were free." Another despairing glance out the window. "Mighten we still be friends, though, Miss Von Harmon?" he said, looking hopefully back at her after sufficient pause.

"Oh, I should very much like that, Lieutenant!" Elsie said, relieved now.

"Would it . . . would it be impertinent to ask you to call me Harrison?" he asked softly, as he gazed at her, turning her insides to jelly. "Seeing as we understand each other so well. . . now that we're to be just friends?"

"I . . . I suppose so . . ." she said, feeling wretched all over again. "I mean, no, I suppose it would be all right . . ."

"And, then, might I call you Elsie?" he asked, leaning forward slightly in a way that felt oddly intimate.

Elsie blushed. "Yes, I suppose that would be okay," she said awkwardly, knowing full well that Mrs. Hutchings would have been outraged.

"Splendid! Well, I can see you are fatigued, so I will not tire you further with having to converse with the likes of me," he said, rising now so that he stood over her.

"Oh, no, I . . . I enjoyed it," she said eagerly.

"I merely wanted to see how you were getting along. But I can see you're well looked after," he said, allowing his eyes to travel and linger the length of her body. "No doubt Mr. Dubowski's been very attentive."

Elsie did not say anything in response to this, as there was nothing she could say. Stanley had not yet appeared at all.

The lieutenant held out his hand to her, and when she put hers in his, he leaned toward her and brought her hand up to his lips. "I know I would be," he said smoothly.

Elsie felt her stomach flip and hoped he could not hear her swallow loudly.

"Goodbye, Elsie," he said wistfully. "I'll come again, if I may, in a few days to check on you."

Elsie blushed yet again and was afraid she might not be able to speak. "Goodbye, Lieuten—I mean, Harrison," she managed finally, and she could not keep from smiling long after he had descended the front steps into the rain.

Five and a half miles away, Stan could not hear the pelting rain as he stood on the line at the Sulzer Electrics Company soldering radios. In some ways it was easier than his job had been in the warehouse, which actually required physical stamina with all of the lifting and loading, but this required concentration. Well, it had at first, anyway.

Now it had become routine, and he felt he could actually do this in his sleep. There were no windows in the factory, but he could tell from the rumbling of his stomach that it was almost quitting time. He looked at his wristwatch, a gift from his mother on his last birthday, and saw that he was correct.

When the whistle blew ten minutes later, he gratefully made his way to his locker and gathered up his large lunch box and thermos as well as his coat before joining the crowd, hurrying now to get out. It wasn't until he stepped outside the main doors that he realized it was raining and put up the umbrella his mother always made sure he left the house with. For once he was glad he had brought it. He made his way past the big gray fence and the large wrought iron gate amidst his fellow workers, who normally joked and shouted to each other as they passed through the gates, but who today were silent, bent over against the lashing rain as they hurriedly made their way home. If it weren't for a car honking its horn at one of the more lightly clad employees who had dashed into the street without looking, Stan probably wouldn't have bothered to look up at all. As it was, however, he did look up to see where the noise was coming from, and, as he did so, was quite shocked to see what looked very much like Rose Whitman coming toward him. She didn't seem to notice him, however, but instead was determinedly walking toward the factory, swimming upstream against the current of men pouring out.

What was she doing here? Stan wondered, and, peering closer, saw that she was very wet as she made her way, shielding herself against the rain with her arm. Where was her umbrella? She would catch her death!

"Rose!" he called out, trying to move across the steady stream of men to catch her attention. "Rose!" he shouted again.

She heard her name called and looked around distractedly before finally catching his eye. "Stan!" she said, a hesitant smile breaking out on her face.

"What are you doing here?" he asked now that he was upon her, the crowd moving around them as he held his umbrella gallantly over her.

"I . . ." Rose began, her eyes nervously darting around before looking back at Stan. "I'm bringing my brother's lunch, or should I say, dinner, to him," she said, holding up a black rectangular lunch box. "He keeps forgetting."

"That's nice of you, seeing how it's raining and all," Stan said. "Didn't you bring an umbrella?" he asked, disapprovingly.

"I was in such a hurry, I guess I forgot," she said, smiling up at him, which caused a stray image of Elsie to pop into his mind somehow.

"Well, here," he said after a longish pause, during which he remembered—it being Tuesday—that it was his mother's chicken-pot-pie night, and the thought of potentially missing it caused him not a little anguish. He struggled to master these more base desires, however, and succeeded in finally offering, "Let me go with you," calculating that if he hurried, he might still make it home in time.

"Oh, no!" Rose said quickly. "That's okay. You go on home. I've gotten wet before, believe me, and I survived," she said, smiling, two small dimples appearing. For a second, Stan's heart constricted; in that moment he could have sworn it was Henrietta, but the vision evaporated as he shook his head.

"No, I insist," he said weakly.

"You're a real gentleman, you know that?" she said with a grin and put her arm through his in such an easy way that it surprised him.

"Your brother's in repairs, right?" Stan asked, bent on his mission now, peering through the rain as they walked. Since the wedding, he had looked up this Billy Whitman—just out of curiosity, mind—and had discovered that he was a decent-enough chap working on the repair crew, night shift, though some said he was touched.

"Yes!" she said, obviously impressed. "How did you know?"

"I know just about everyone here; I make it my business to know, you see."

"Yes, I'm sure you do," she said, giving him a coy smile.

They walked along in silence then until they reached the

maintenance shed, which was really more of a long, low building in the back of the factory yard. Ironically, it was surrounded by broken bits of machinery amidst the tall grass, peppered with stray bits of litter, stacks of old tires, and rusting barrels. On the threshold, Stan's insides quivered a bit as he recalled that it was an uncannily similar maintenance shed where Henrietta's father had hung himself all those years ago. He had studiously avoided the Schwinn factory ever since then and had avoided this place as well. Who knew what horrors had been committed here? He hesitated now, just inside the door, but Rose had already moved past him and was making a beeline toward the back of the building, where she said her brother's bench was. Stan had no choice but to force down his sense of the macabre and said a silent prayer against ghosts as he hurried to catch up with her.

The building was oddly abandoned except for Billy, whom they found standing over a workbench, upon which was what looked to be a large gearbox of sorts, partially disassembled, if Stan judged it rightly. Billy was a large man with broad shoulders and big hands, which made the image of him holding the tiny screwdriver in his left hand seem incongruous. His one-piece gray uniform seemed too tight and looked dirty already from grease and oil, or perhaps it had started the night out that way. From a distance he seemed a man to be reckoned with, but as they drew closer and Stan observed his close-cropped brown hair and the light brown eyes which held a slightly vacant look, he thought he looked more like an overgrown schoolboy. A red birthmark sprawled across his right cheek, making it look as though he was permanently slapped.

Billy looked up as they approached and gave a big grin. "Rosie!" he said happily with a dull, thickly idiotic voice. "What you doing here? Come to see me? Come to see me?"

Rose held up the lunch box. "You forgot this again, Billy," she said reproachfully.

"Ah, gee, Rosie. Sorry. Sorry. I forgot again."

"It's okay, Billy," she said, relaxing her frown. "Working hard, I see," she said, observing the guts of the gearbox splayed out in front of them. "Billy's a whiz with machines, aren't you, Bill?" Rose said encouragingly. "He can fix anything; can't you?"

Billy nodded dumbly in response and carefully placed his lunch on the back bench, adjusting it until it was perfectly aligned with the edge of the bench, tapping it slightly to perfect its position. Stan took the opportunity to survey Billy's work area and approved of its tidiness and organization.

"Uh, huh," Billy said slowly, scratching his head and turning back toward them, slack-jawed. "Most things." He looked at Stan now as if seeing him for the first time. "Who's he?" he asked thickly.

"This is my friend, Stan," Rose said, chancing a glance at Stan as if silently asking him if it was okay to call him a friend.

Stan gave an almost eager nod.

"He works here, too," she added.

"Doin' what?"

"I'm on the line," Stan answered with a slightly puffed-out chest. "Soldering mostly."

Billy ignored his answer, Stan's lofty new credentials seemingly lost on him. "You followin' her?" he asked.

"Following?"

"Billy!" Rose said.

"You followin' her?" he asked again.

The straightforwardness of the question confused Stan. It didn't seem to be threatening, and yet he couldn't think how else to interpret it.

"Lots a fellas follow Rosie," Billy said, his face scrunched up in distress now. "You should see. Don't like 'em much, I don't. Not nice to her sometimes. I can see out my window."

"Billy! We have to go now," Rose said hurriedly, putting her hand on Stan's shoulder.

"Once there was even a lady, but she only came once. That was a long time ago."

Rose's face had gone white now.

"Billy!" she said again. "You'd better get to work now before your boss sees you. Remember? And Stan and I have to go before we get locked in here for the night!"

Billy's face took on a look of concentration then as he focused his eyes again on the pieces in front of him. "Okay, Rosie. Bye," he said dully, seemingly dismissing them already.

"Bye, Billy. See you at home," Rose said awkwardly and turned now to go.

"Nice meeting you, Bill," Stan likewise added, but Billy did not respond. Stan hesitated for a moment as if he were going to say something more, but in the end he decided to simply follow Rose back to the front of the building. Her pace was surprisingly fast, and he hurried to catch up with her, which didn't afford him much time to make sense of the strange encounter with her brother.

"You musn't mind Billy," Rose said finally, as if she suspected his thoughts. They stepped out of the shed now, the sky nearly black with the fading light and the heavy clouds, the rain continuing its deluge. Stan again covered them with his trusty umbrella as they huddled closely under it. "He's a bit backward," she said, clearly embarrassed. "He doesn't mean anything. Don't listen to what he says. He gets in trouble a lot because he gets distracted easily, but when he's focused on his task, he can do wonders with machinery, actually. That's why it's good that he works alone . . . usually, anyway."

They had passed through the factory gate and stood on Western Avenue now, cars hurrying past and splashing water from the puddles that were collecting by the crumbling curbs.

"Here, let me walk you home," Stan offered. "Which way?"

"Oh, no! I'll be all right."

"In this rain? Without an umbrella?" Stan asked incredulously. "Not a chance! And, anyway, what's this about these guys following you?"

"Oh, don't listen to Billy. He . . . he gets confused . . ."

"But who are they? Are they dangerous?"

"Just stragglers from the Marlowe or the Melody Mill. You know how it is . . ." her voice trailed off.

Stan did very well know! It was just like Henrietta all over again.

"Listen, I'm walking you home, and that's final!" Stan mustered.

"Please, Stan. Not tonight. It's just my dad at home, and he's been drinking. You know how it is, right?" she asked again, attempting what Stan swore was a suggestive sort of smile. Or was she just trying to be brave? Stan couldn't tell exactly. The more he studied her, the more she just looked like a frightened young girl to him. "Well . . ."

"It's just a few blocks," she said, pulling back from under the umbrella.

Stan followed her, still trying to hover the umbrella over her.

"Please, Stan," she begged.

"Well . . . if you're sure. Here—" he thrust the umbrella into her gloveless hand. "You take this." When she tried to hesitate, he said more forcefully, "I insist!" And as if to prove his sincerity, he backed out from under its flimsy protection and stuffed his hands in his coat pocket, allowing himself to be fully pelted by the rain.

Rose stepped toward him now so that they were both covered again. She was standing so close to him that he could smell her perfume, made all the stronger by the humidity in the air. Oddly, it was rose-tinged, just like her name. She further shocked him, then, by reaching out her free hand and placing it on his cheek. "Thank you, Stan. It's too bad you have someone else," she said wistfully. Before he could say anything, she had turned and was already crossing the street. "I'll make sure you get this back!" she shouted, looking at him one last time before hurrying down the block.

Stan stood watching her for a few moments, horrified by the excitement her simple touch had elicited in him, and forced himself to think of Elsie instead. Slowly he turned toward home, knowing his mother would fret that he did not have his umbrella, especially as he was quickly becoming drenched. He should probably make his way to Palmer Square to call on Elsie, he thought, as he awkwardly struggled to pull up the thin collar of his coat, as if it would be the slightest help against the downpour. He hadn't seen her since the wedding, but it was already getting late, and he risked arriving home to a cold chicken pie if he delayed any longer.

Each morning he told himself that he would stop by to see Elsie after work, but each day as he was leaving the electrics, he found some reason not to. Like now. But he couldn't just turn up looking like a drowned dog, could he? A part of him knew he was just making excuses, but, gee whiz, nothing was the same now that they had moved, not like the old days when they had all been crowded in together in the little apartment. For one thing, when he did call, no one was ever around except Elsie herself. Eugene, of course, was gone, and the boys were always off somewhere in some other part of the house supposedly studying, but knowing Eddie and Herbert as he did, Stan wasn't buying it. And the little ones, to whom he had previously delighted in bringing sweets, were always shut up in the nursery now with the nanny or the maid, or whatever she was called. Even Mrs. Von Harmon wasn't around much, spending most of her time, Elsie said, in her room. Elsie seemed to think it was because Ma wasn't used to all that space, that she seemed more comfortable living the way she had always done, in just a couple of rooms. Indeed, Elsie had told him on one of his early visits, just after they had moved, that Mrs. Von Harmon seemed reluctant to occupy any of the other rooms unless someone else was there with her. And then there were the servants to deal with now, most of whom always made Stan feel somehow not himself. Karl seemed all right, but he had a pretty good idea that the housekeeper, Mrs. Schmidt, did not approve of the likes of him. He could tell by the way she asked if she could take his hat and coat, as if it were an odious chore, and when he did hand them to her, he could swear her face held a look of disgust as she gingerly hung his belongings in the hall. The only one who was always about was Elsie. She seemed to be always there, eager and available, with nothing else to do but wait for him to turn up, it seemed. But wasn't that a good thing? he asked himself as he crossed California. Of course it was a good thing, he argued, but he couldn't shake the feeling of being suffocated when he went to visit, as if there wasn't enough air in the new place, which didn't make any sense at all, considering how much bigger it was than the apartment.

Resolutely, he turned down Mozart toward his family's modest bungalow instead of north toward Palmer Square, deftly avoiding a rather large puddle as he did so. He promised himself that he would definitely go tomorrow. He tightened his coat around him, satisfied with his decision, and hurried now to get home. The problem, the way he saw it, was that the Von Harmons didn't seem to need him much anymore, and whether Stan realized it or not, he needed to be needed.

Chapter 9

Clive took a deep puff of his pipe as he watched the English countryside rolling by. Henrietta was asleep, leaning against his chest, and his arm was wrapped protectively around her. It was beginning to go numb, but he wouldn't for all the world disturb her. She had been bright and eager earlier this morning when they had docked at Liverpool, delighting in seeing a new country, and they had had just enough time to take tea at the Adelphi before catching the train to Derbyshire. After a couple of hours, the initial excitement had worn off, however, and the rocking of the train had momentarily lulled her to sleep.

Clive bent toward her now and breathed in her sweet smell, distributing a quick kiss. He could not remember being this happy in his whole life, but with that glorious feeling came the fear that it would be just as quickly taken away. Henrietta had confessed to him on the ship that she felt the same way, and they had both taken comfort, then, in their shared trepidation, as if because they both feared to lose each other, it would somehow prevent it from happening.

Henrietta continued to delight him, to swell his heart to the point he thought it might burst. He knew the danger of letting his emotions run this free, of allowing himself to feel this deeply, but he was past the point of return now and there was nothing for it but to go forward, to allow himself to be enmeshed in his joy and simply hope for the best and to try not to think about what might happen, what could happen, all the ways she could be taken from him and how he could prevent it. This tangled line of thinking, with its myriad of variables, often led to a very dark place, so he tried not to let his mind go there and instead concentrated on Henrietta herself, on pleasing and spoiling her.

He delighted in showing her, on the journey over, things she had never seen or heard of before, like shuffleboard or baked Alaska or sighting whales off the starboard bow. She was amazed at how huge the ship was—a floating town, she called it—marveling at the tennis courts, hair salons, lecture halls, ballrooms, dining rooms, and swimming pools, and she was forever getting lost or turned around. In her rapturous enthusiasms she was almost like a child, and he laughed along with her as if he were a schoolboy again. But at night in their first-class honeymoon suite, she was anything but a child; she was a woman in every sense of the word. She seemed to delight in exploring his body as much as he did hers, and their nights were spent in lovely passion such as he had never felt before. There was a true emptying of himself when he was with her. Somehow in her arms he felt more the child than her, the injured boy needing to be healed, needing to be filled, and she seemed always to know now how to do that for him, how to answer the sorrow and the angst that was never very far from the surface. Sometimes she still cried after it was over, from happiness she said, and though it distressed him immensely to see her tears, they seared her to him in a way he couldn't explain. With each day that passed, he felt love's tendrils reach out and further encircle his heart, and rather than fight this encroachment now, he willingly gave in to it, knowing he would be held captive by it for the rest of his days and not caring. Indeed, he desired to be held here forever.

And, if he was honest, there was an additional pleasure in being in society with her, showing her off as his wife, and he took pride in the fact that she seemed to stun so many. He was very much aware, as they sat each night at the captain's table or as they made their way to the dance floor, of how many men gazed at her, hoping to catch even a few utterances fall from her pretty lips or perhaps even just a lingering glance. But his heart positively ached when he correspondingly observed how utterly unaware, or uncaring, at any rate, Henrietta seemed of the attention of these other men and how her eyes never strayed from his.

There was only a small blip on their happy abandonment, however, which occurred on their very last night at sea. Clive, appreciating that this was their last night of truly being alone, knowing that the weeks ahead would be full of family obligations once they arrived at Castle Linley, ordered the ship's oldest bottle of champagne to be delivered to their stateroom. Later, as they drank it in bed, they reminisced—again—about their wedding day, turning it over and over to make sure they had found every jewel to hold on to. Despite the romantic nature of their discussion, however, a dark thought suddenly crept into Clive's mind—a memory from that day he somehow hadn't remembered until now. He uneasily recalled that he had seen Randolph, Julia's husband, dance with Henrietta and that she had seemed so distressed by him that Clive had felt obliged to step in. It was all coming back to him now. After he had rescued her, as it were, she had declined to say what it was about, saying that it was nothing, that she didn't want to spoil the day by discussing disagreeable things. In the day's euphoria, he had obeyed her wish, wanting on their wedding day to do anything for her, fulfill even the slightest request of hers.

But now, as they lay in each other's arms, he was bothered by the image of Randolph bent close to her and Henrietta pulling away, looking pale. Clive asked her, his fingers entwined with hers, if she might tell him now what had transpired between them. Clive unmistakably felt Henrietta's body tense, but she didn't move away.

"It was nothing, darling," she tried to say absently.

"I'd very much like to know," he said, running his finger along her shoulder.

"Just the usual leering, that sort of thing."

"Nothing else?" he asked after a pause.

Henrietta remained silent for a few more minutes, during which Clive patiently waited. Finally she spoke. "I'm sure he didn't mean it . . ."

"What was it?" he asked quietly.

"If you must know . . ." she began hesitantly. "He said that now that I'm in the family, I'm fair game and to watch myself," she finished, exhaling a deep breath and looking up into his face now.

"Did he?" Clive answered, his voice governed, trying to control the fury beneath. "And what did you say?"

"Just that he was a wretch and that I could take care of myself. Of course he just laughed and said he very much doubted it."

"And?"

"Oh, Clive. Let's just forget about it. I'm not worried in the slightest."

"Tell me," he said more sternly than he meant to.

Henrietta gave him a look of surprise and went on. "He just said that he's used to taking what he wants and that . . . that you're away a lot . . . that Julia is a frigid bitch"—she added, almost in a whisper—"and that it isn't really his fault if he occasionally needs some amusement." Henrietta looked at Clive apprehensively now.

"Bastard!" Clive said, bringing his fist down onto the mattress. He hated Randolph. He always had. He had never understood why his beautiful sister would have agreed to marry him. He knew his parents had pressured her, but still, he had thought she would have had more fortitude than to give in to them so easily. He had spoken to her before the wedding, pleading with her, but she hadn't wanted to hear it. "Poor Clive," she had said, touching his face briefly, which had utterly confused him. Wasn't she the victim here, not him?

He had been proven right, though, Randolph showing himself to be every bit the cad Clive had predicted him to be. As the years had passed, he was pretty sure that Randolph was violent with Julia, but he couldn't prove it. He had confronted her about it one Christmas Eve when he had had too much to drink, but she had denied it, of course. Even if he could prove it, he had realized morosely, what would he do?

He thought back now with fresh fury to the night before the wedding when he had gone to the major's home, whom he knew had felt obliged to give him a bit of a do as the best man. Little did the major know that having spent years now in what he felt was eternal bachelorhood, Clive had no desire to hang on to it, no desire to savor and prolong the prison it had become. Rather than glorious freedom, bachelorhood represented an aching loneliness that had seemed to stretch out forever. By contrast, a life with Henrietta, even bound by the societal confines of marriage, seemed a blissfully freeing and heavenly prospect. How appropriate, then, he had mused as he dressed for the major's soiree that evening, that he should spend the last night of his awful bachelorhood with the likes of Randolph. He had hated having to ask him to be a groomsman, but etiquette suggested it, considering Julia was to be a bridesmaid. He had so few friends left, most of them having died in the war, and when he had come back, he hadn't bothered making any new ones. Asking anyone on the force was out of the question, accordingly to Mother, anyway, so he had turned to his former CO, whom he looked up to almost as a second father, and which had left Randolph as the next obvious choice for a groomsman.

They had been playing billiards, Randolph already having drunk quite a lot, as he leaned against one of the bookcases and coolly looked on while Clive banked a shot. Randolph took the opportunity of congratulating Clive, not only for bagging the ball, but for bagging Henrietta as well, he had said crudely.

"She's rather fetching, Clive," he slurred suggestively. "But I suppose you know that already," he said, swaying slightly. "You'll have to be careful there," he grinned. "That things don't go astray, I mean. You'll have to keep a tight hold, that's my advice to you. There will be a lot of foxes around that chicken, let me tell you," he laughed, looking over at the major for encouragement, but whose face was instead quite dark. "Let's hope you've still got enough to, well, keep her rooted, one might say."

Clive was tempted to thrash him right there, but it would be unseemly, not only because he was a guest in the major's house, but because Randolph was his brother-in-law, as well as his groomsman, with the wedding being the very next day. Instead, Clive, his cue stick in hand, calmly walked toward Randolph and stood briefly in front of him, holding the stick dangerously close to his throat.

"Don't ever let me hear you speak of her again in that manner or tone, Cunningham. She is to be my *wife*, and I will not have her disparaged in any way. I've been waiting years to have a real reason to thrash you, so please give me one, and so help me God you won't thank me for it."

"Steady on!" Randolph tried to laugh as he leaned back from the cue stick with an exaggerated motion. "I didn't mean anything!"

The major coughed in the background. "Here now, let's have none of that. I think we all need a drink," he said, moving toward the decanter.

Randolph had laughed in earnest now, further infuriating Clive.

"Yes, Clive, just teasing, you know," Randolph said lightly, though he swallowed hard. "Don't be so sensitive. You're behaving like a nervous woman! Isn't that right, Major? We'll put it down to wedding jitters and leave it at that."

As Clive watched Randolph saunter over to where the major stood, he felt the hatred rise up in his throat, but he forced himself to let it go. This was definitely not how he had wanted to spend the night before his wedding, but he had no choice but to play the part of the gentleman and get on with it.

He looked down at Henrietta now, who had nestled back into the crook of his good shoulder, and he swore yet again to protect her, especially from men like Randolph.

"I think he beats her," Henrietta said quietly, her fingers entwining themselves in his chest hair. "I'm not supposed to tell you," she said guiltily, looking up into his eyes.

Clive felt his stomach clench. So it was true after all. "How do you know?" he asked, trying to keep his voice controlled.

"She told me. It was the day we had lunch together before I went back to the city. I had planned on asking her for advice about the wedding night," she smiled at him, "even though the groom was her brother, but she ended up telling me all of that instead."

"Fucking bastard," Clive said loudly. "I knew it! I'm going to kill him."

"Shh!" she said, putting a finger to his lips. "That's why she doesn't want you to know. She doesn't want you to do something foolish."

"Why doesn't she leave him, then?" he said angrily.

"And go where? Do what?" she asked. "What about the boys?"

Clive thought about this and let out a deep breath.

"Some men are just cruel, I suppose, Clive. I don't understand why, but you of all people will have seen that. In the force. And in the war."

"Yes, but this is my sister!" he said despairingly.

"We'll think of something, dearest," she said, running her fingers through his hair now, which soothed him immensely. "We'll find a way to help her, but killing him isn't it."

He felt angry and deflated at hearing this about Julia and Randolph, but it wasn't really a surprise—he had always suspected it, and yet he felt uncontrollably sad. So many good men died alongside him, and yet vile creatures like Randolph Cunningham had lived. It was difficult at times to fight down the feelings of gross injustice that sometimes welled up and threatened to choke him. For years after the war, the injustice of the world had filled him with something close to rage, but now it felt more like simple sadness, bordering at times on despair. He turned on his side toward Henrietta, who was looking at him, concerned, as she brushed his stubbly cheek with her hand.

"I love you, Inspector," she whispered.

He secretly loved it when she called him that. He gazed at her—his Henrietta, his love, his own *wife*, and felt a surge of love for her, a burning need for her. He desperately wanted to make love to her, yearned to, in fact, but he paused, wanting to make sure he correctly read a matching desire in her eyes. He would never force himself on her. As if she read his mind, she ran a hand lightly down his chest and lower still, and at her touch, a moan from deep within escaped him. He pressed his lips to hers and began to kiss her—fiercely, passionately—as if to quell whatever ghosts still haunted him, running his hands along her body and swiftly moving on top of her.

He made love to her quickly, almost wildly, his own pain and his despair hovering near, and she rose in kind to meet him, opening herself to him completely. When he finally collapsed on top of her, he was surprised that he was shaking. "Oh, God, Henrietta, did I hurt you?" he asked, still panting.

Her response was to gently kiss his mangled shoulder. "Of course you didn't hurt me," she answered, her voice still thick with passion.

Clive lay back on the bed, breathing heavily, and stared at the ceiling, deep in thought. Finally he spoke. "You're not afraid of me, are you, Henrietta?" he asked, looking over at her now.

"Of course I'm not. What a silly question," she said lightly.

Clive sighed and looked back at the ceiling.

"I can't imagine what that might feel like, though," she murmured. "To always live in fear of the person you're supposed to love."

Clive did not say anything, but he embraced her then, drawing her near him, and they drifted off to sleep.

Henrietta woke now, sitting up and stretching, smiling ruefully as she did so. "Sorry. Are we almost there?" she asked, moving stiffly to the seat across from him and peering out the window of their first-class carriage on the train.

"Nearly," he said, puffing on his pipe again. They were rounding through Derbyshire, headed toward the little village of Cromford, where hopefully Bradwell, Lord Linley's chauffeur, would be waiting with a motor to drive them to Castle Linley. The hills were more rolling here, and endless sheep dotted the green spaces, which were compartmentalized into neat little squares and bordered by what looked to Henrietta like ancient fences of stones piled up on top of each other. Henrietta wondered how they didn't fall over. She looked across at Clive, who, his arm free now, had picked up a newspaper and was beginning to peruse it.

"We should be there in less than an hour, I should think," he said, not looking up. Henrietta thought he looked every bit the English gentleman in his tweed suit and waistcoat and derby hat. She had been careful as well in her toilette this morning, donning the dove gray pinstripe traveling suit by Piguet with a fur stole and thin gray hat pulled down over one eye that Antonia had instructed her to wear upon meeting the Howards for the first time. To this ensemble, Clive had added a small white rose picked up at a florist in Lime Street this morning as they had hurried by.

"Clive!" she said, pretending to be annoyed. "Aren't you ever going to tell me about the Lord and Lady Linley? Or what the house is like?"

Clive peered across the top of his paper.

"You keep putting me off, telling me that you'll tell me when we get closer, but I think we've reached the limit now, don't you think?" she pleaded. "I must know something of the place before we arrive!"

"Quite right, darling," he said in a passable English accent. He could adopt one prettily easily, having spent many childhood summers here. "But there's not much to tell, really."

"You always say that, and then there is."

"All right, then," he said, folding the paper haphazardly. "What do you wish to know?"

"Is it grander than Highbury? I'm assuming it is, since it's a castle and home to a Lord and Lady."

"In a way," he said, considering the question. "Mind you, I haven't been there since the war. It's not really a castle, though; it's just called that. God only knows why. No doubt some ancient baron trying to set himself apart. Some chum of William the Conqueror, I think it was, that managed to live through the conquest."

"Does your family really go that far back?" Henrietta asked, intrigued.

"I believe so. Lord Linley would be the person to ask. Or Father, of course. The house has burnt down a few times, I believe, so it's possible it really could have been some sort of crude castle once upon a time. Now, it's really just a big estate house, Georgian, certainly bigger than Highbury, but not a castle by any stretch. The name's just stuck." He set the paper back down beside him and reached into his pocket for his tobacco. "I haven't been there in years, but from what I understand from Father, it's not well maintained. It was conscripted by the army during the war and turned into an officer's hospital. I always thought it a strange twist of fate that I did not convalesce there," he said, tapping his pipe against the window. "Since then, I believe, it's never really regained its footing. Father reckons it should be sold, but Uncle Montague won't hear of it. Keeps hanging on, hoping Wallace will marry well, I suppose." He stopped there as if that were the natural end to the story.

"Go on!" Henrietta urged.

Clive gave her a sly smile. "What else is there to tell? It's the same with all of these old houses and titled families across the country. They can't sustain themselves on the rents of the tenants, and no one's really recovered from the war. It's the same as at home, really. The war did something to all of us, and no one seems to know their way back to that old life," he said sadly.

"And the oldest son died, right?" Henrietta asked. "Your cousin?"

"Yes, Linley," Clive said grimly. "Died on the Somme. Wallace went to the front, too—the younger son—but he made it through, though just. Took a rather nasty bullet in the leg." He looked across at Henrietta and smiled weakly. "We all used to play together when Julia and I were sent over every August."

"Did you like Linley?" she asked in her soft way.

"He was by far my favorite," he said, pausing to light his pipe now. "He was everyone's favorite, I think. So honest and open, always had a laugh up his sleeve. In that way he was very similar to Julia. I used to envy him, really."

"You?"

He smiled sheepishly. "I know. But I think everyone did,

somehow. He was just that type. Everyone loved him, and everyone was unbelievably devastated when he died. He would have done Castle Linley well."

"And Wallace?"

"Ah, poor Wallace. He never could quite measure up to Linley, and, worse yet, he knows it, or at least once knew it. I'm not sure what his mental state is these days; I haven't seen him for a very long time. I'm sure he feels guilty that Linley bought it in the war and he somehow squeaked through. Everyone who made it out feels that way at bit," he said tacitly, looking out the window and then back at her eventually. "Yes, Wallace made it out but with a bum leg," he went on, "but from what I understand, his nerves are a bit shredded as well."

"And he never married?"

"Ah. Well, that's the conundrum, isn't it?" Clive said, taking a puff of his pipe. "He's never really settled. Aunt Margaret's been throwing women at him for years to no avail. I suspect the reception they're holding for us will serve as yet another opportunity for them to invite eligible women. Wait and see," he said, giving her a little wink.

"Oh, how exciting. I love matchmaking!"

"Well, don't get your hopes up too much; Wallace, it seems, is not the type that wants to be caught." Clive looked back at his paper. "He should go for an heiress, but they're damn difficult to find these days," he said, looking up at her with a grin.

"Clive!"

"I'm merely repeating bits of Aunt Margaret's letters to Mother," he said, affecting innocence. "Meanwhile, Castle Linley crumbles around them."

"You make it sound very bleak."

"Well, you wanted to know. Perhaps we'll be surprised. As I've said, I haven't seen it since the war. I fear, however, that you may be in for a disappointment."

Clive looked out the window now at the fields rushing by and was suddenly reminded of being on a very similar train, shipped from the field hospital bound for London. He had been barely conscious . . .

And then Henrietta, in that way she had for sensing what he was feeling, moved beside him once more and took his hand, and he was grateful that upon his return, she was at his side.

Chapter 10

Castle Linley was a monstrously large Georgian house that was starkly beautiful in an austere sort of way. The sheer size of it overwhelmed Henrietta as they came upon it, and she laughed to herself when she compared it in her mind to Highbury. This was easily three times the size of the house in Winnetka, but it lacked the charm that Highbury now possessed for her. It struck her as odd that Highbury, with its turrets and chimneys and gabled roofs and gardens surrounding it, looked more like an actual castle than this, the Howards' ancestral home.

Castle Linley, in contrast, was an immense tawny-gray rectangle of local stone with no shrubbery to keep it company except a long, pristine lawn that ran before it, interrupted only by a reflecting pool with tall, trimmed shrubs planted periodically beside it in neat rows, as if they were soldiers standing at attention. The long drive, stretching endlessly up to the house (at least a mile, Henrietta guessed) was tree-lined, but no trees stood near the house, as if they would have detracted from its straight lines and thereby somehow thwarted its air of formality.

Lord and Lady Linley were on hand to greet them, actually condescending to step out of the house and onto the pea-graveled drive as the car pulled up. Henrietta was nervous, but she felt a new confidence at being introduced as Clive's wife, Mrs. Howard, and held her head up as Clive presented her. Henrietta knew that Lord Linley was of course Alcott's older brother, but she had not been prepared for how much older he looked. While Alcott and Antonia seemed still in their prime, Lord and Lady Linley seemed by comparison to be almost elderly.

"Let me get a look at you, my dear," said Lady Linley in a high-pitched, quivering voice, almost like a fairy, as she peered at her, holding a pair of eyeglasses attached to a small rod close to her eyes. She was a slight woman with very white skin, which hung loosely on her, and gray hair that she had piled up on her head in the style of a bygone era. Her dress, too, was very old-fashioned, almost ethereal, like something from the Edwardian days just before the war. Her eyes, Henrietta noticed, were a watery blue, but they still held a spark of something that Henrietta would have called mischievous had Lady Linley not been so old.

"Yes, Antonia was right. You *are* quite lovely. Ah, yes, and very young, as Antonia wrote. But then again, Clive's always been one for the ladies, haven't you, Clive? We never got to meet—what was her name, Montague? Catherine, that's it!" she said before Lord Linley could offer an answer. "But Catherine, as I understand it, was quite pretty, too. Then there was Alice when you were no more than a boy here. Do you remember her? The Duke of Marlborough's daughter? Montague said at the time that it was no more than a schoolboy's lark, and he was right, of course. Still, it would have been a frightfully advantageous match, but, no, it was not to be. I'm never listened to. And wasn't there some society woman, your mother said?" She paused for a breath of air and took the opportunity to look Henrietta over once again. "No doubt you saw this one's hips, though, Clive. Ever practical, weren't you, my dear boy? Good for birthing. Yes, I see that . . ."

Henrietta gave Clive a bewildered look, which Clive responded to by merely opening his eyes wide as he tried not to smile.

"Margaret!" barked the estimable Lord Linley, finally. "Don't scare the girl! They've just arrived. They're in no fit state to listen to such prattle. Her hips are none of our affair, surely." He turned to Henrietta now and brought her hand to his lips. "Welcome to Linley, my dear. You're very welcome. Indeed."

Henrietta noticed that his own eyes lingered on her hips perhaps a little longer than they should have, but she was used to that. She turned to look at Clive and was pretty sure he had observed his uncle's wandering eyes as well.

Lord Linley had a broad chest, despite his age, though his hair was white, and he still sported thick white sideburns that ran all the way down his chin to connect with a busy white beard in a Victorian sort of style. One hand clutched a riding stick, though he was not otherwise dressed for riding, and one eye sported a gold-rimmed monocle. He was gruff and burly, as if he would be more at home on the battlefield than seated in the halls of parliament. In point of fact, he had been a decorated officer in the Boer War.

"Where's Wallace, Uncle? Surely he's about somewhere?" Clive asked, looking around.

"Having a bit of a lie down," Lady Linley answered for him. "He hasn't been well, poor thing. He'll be down shortly, no doubt. But come in, my dears, come in. Stevens will bring us a lovely cup of tea, and you can tell us all about your journey," she said as she gestured them toward the house, where the senior household staff stood lined up to greet the guests. Henrietta was a little embarrassed that all of the servants had just undoubtedly heard the whole exchange regarding Clive's past loves and her birthing hips, but she tried to shake it off, knowing that the listening ears of servants was to be her life now, whether here or at Highbury, and thought of Antonia for inspiration, which she also found odd in and of itself.

"Oh! I nearly forgot," Lady Linley said, turning back toward them now. "Will you be wanting separate rooms?"

Despite her newfound confidence, Henrietta did not know what to say and felt herself blush as Clive answered from behind her, "One will be sufficient, thank you, Aunt Margaret."

"Just as I suspected," she quipped. "One room, Stevens," she said to the plump butler standing by.

"Very good, my lady," he answered, bowing, as if she had been merely directing him to lay an extra place for dinner.

Later in said bedroom, Henrietta dressed for dinner with the aid of one of the upstairs maids—Phoebe, her name was—assigned to her while they were at Linley. Antonia had urged Clive to take a valet and Henrietta to take Edna as her lady's maid, but they had both refused, wanting to be as free of servants as they could be on their honeymoon. Henrietta had tentatively suggested that perhaps lady's maids were becoming a thing of the past, but Antonia would not hear of it. She insisted on sticking to tradition and warned them that leaving their servants behind would not be looked upon favorably in England nor the continent beyond and that it would be received as most unseemly, but neither of them had cared. And as if to prove them right, Lord and Lady Linley seemed not to give a second thought to the fact that they had to supply their guests with personal servants from their own staff, but Stevens was of the opinion that it showed just how low the Howard line had sunk since its transplantation on American soil—but that was to be expected, and he had, with a sigh, assigned the two prodigals a valet and a lady's maid for the duration.

Phoebe had just left, feeling confident that her mistress looked quite perfect, herself thrilled to be speaking to an American and longing to ask her about the films she saw on her Tuesday afternoons off in the village, but she didn't dare. "She's lovely," Phoebe reported to the rest of the staff below stairs, "not a bit high and mighty," and they had all marveled.

Henrietta was just pulling on her gloves, surveying in the mirror the deep green Schiaparelli gown that tightly hugged her figure as Clive stepped in from his adjoining dressing room.

"You look stunning, Mrs. Howard," he said, coming over to her and kissing her on the cheek.

"Would you like to tell me about Alice?" Henrietta asked coyly. "I believe I've already been introduced to "the society woman" Lady Linley was kind enough to mention, which of course must be your *friend*, Sophia." Her eyes sparkled as she looked up at him. "But Alice is new to me. Was she terribly young and pretty?"

"Minx!" he said, grabbing her about the waist. "There's nothing to tell. Only Aunt Margaret's ravings. She's quite dotty, if you haven't noticed."

"I'll be the judge of that," she said authoritatively, "when you tell me later in bed." Her eyes held a suggestive glow. "It seems you've been rather a naughty boy, and you'll have to confess."

"If I must," he said, his mouth twitching as he kissed her. Timidly, she touched her tongue to his as his lips met hers, causing him to stiffen and clutch her tighter. "I might have to take you now," he said, breathing deeply and pushing her against the waist-high mattress of the bed. It was a mammoth four-poster bed, complete with old-fashioned curtains that went all the way around it and a little stool to assist in climbing up.

"Clive! You'll crush my dress!" she said, pushing him away.

Clive obediently stood up, then, with a grin. "Lucky for you we're expected downstairs any minute," he said, his eyebrow arched as he straightened his ruffled tie. "*And* that this is some sort of princess-and-the-pea bed requiring a certain amount of wherewithal to get into it," he said, studying it. "No throwing the damsel on the bed in a hurried state and having my wicked way. This requires some skill," he said, looking it over thoughtfully.

Henrietta merely laughed and took his hand, and he led her down to join the rest of the family.

Dinner passed uneventfully enough, though it was on this occasion that Henrietta was finally introduced to the mysterious Wallace. He cut a strange picture, hobbling in with a walking stick, but was dressed elegantly in his white tie and tails. She was surprised that he looked nothing like Clive, with his thinning blond hair and dark brown eyes, which were red about the rims. He had a high forehead and almost gaunt cheeks, looking almost sickly compared to Clive's robust form. For the most part, Wallace was adequately polite but quiet, spending most of the dinner merely picking at his food. It seemed to Henrietta that his mind was perhaps elsewhere, as if he were just putting in his time here until he was free to resume his own entertainment, whatever that might be. She likewise thought she detected a peevishness to him that she couldn't quite explain.

It was rather an amusing dinner, all in all, the eccentric Lord and Lady Linley asking her the most ridiculous of questions. It was all Henrietta could do to not break into laughter, for example, when Lady Linley asked her how many Indians she had in her acquaintance.

"Mother! It's 1935, for God's sake," Wallace said, exasperated, before Henrietta had a chance to answer. "There aren't any more Indians!"

"Aren't there?" Lady Linley asked, quite mystified. "I'm sure I read that there were, Wallace, dear. Somewhere on the American frontier or other."

"Well, Chicago is hardly the frontier, Mother."

"Isn't it?"

"Of course not! It's a thriving metropolis. It's certainly bigger than Manchester, at any rate."

"That can't be! Surely not! Tell him, Montague."

"Actually, Aunt Margaret, Chicago is a rather large city," Clive put in. "There's over three million people, I believe," he said, taking a drink of his wine.

"Well, I never! Imagine that, Montague!"

Ignoring her, Lord Linley took his own direction in the unfolding dialogue, or, rather, interview. "I say, tell us about your work with the American police, Clive. Damned interesting, that," he said, signaling the footman for more wine.

"As a matter of fact, I've recently resigned, sir," Clive answered, only Henrietta catching the slight note of regret in his voice.

She had indeed brought up the topic on more than one occasion on their afternoon strolls on deck of the *Queen Mary*, getting him to finally admit how very hard it had been for him to leave the force. The chief, he had said, had even come to his office for a private word before he had left and had asked him to reconsider, that he would see about a promotion if he would agree to stay, possibly cut down the number of cases he was assigned to. It had been almost impossible to turn him down, Clive had told her, but he had no choice but to tell the chief that he had family obligations to attend to and that it couldn't be helped.

"Was he angry?" Henrietta had asked.

"Not angry, just disappointed, I suppose," Clive answered. "I had a final drink with him before I left from his private stash in his desk drawer. Told me he'd keep the door open," Clive said, looking out at the ocean and the rolling waves.

"Maybe it's not too late then?" Henrietta implored. "To change your mind, I mean?"

"Don't tempt me!" he said sternly. The force with which he said it took her off guard. "I'm sorry," he said then, attempting a smile. "That came out wrong." He sighed and went on to explain, again, that he had given his word to the board of Linley Standard and, more importantly, to his father. That his greater duty was to Highbury and to her. He needed to provide a life for her, a safer one than what the city might offer. His real fear, he had admitted with a forced laugh, was that he wouldn't be any good at running the firm, that he wasn't suited to it.

"Nonsense!" Henrietta had interjected. "Of course you'll be wonderful!" she had said encouragingly, but the conversation had been revealing and made her all the more resolved to help him in any way she could.

"I say, did you really?" Lord Linley said, surprised. "Whatever for?"

"Clive's taken a position on the board of Linley Standard," Henrietta said encouragingly.

"Yes," Clive said, shooting Henrietta a grateful glance. "Thought I'd better learn what I'm about before Father retires," he said stiffly.

"But Alcott's years from retiring, surely?" Lord Linley argued.

"Perhaps," Clive answered. "But it's high time I looked to my responsibilities, wouldn't you say?" he asked, as he took a drink of his wine.

"Well said, my boy, I'll give you that," Lord Linley harrumphed, flashing a severe look at Wallace.

Ignoring it, Wallace spoke to Clive. "So you're giving up being a police captain to be a captain of industry," he drawled condescendingly. "Is that it?"

"Something like that, yes," Clive said shortly.

"How very clever you are, Clive. We should all take a lesson from your book," Wallace said, an insincere smile creeping up his face.

"And how about you, Wallace? What have you been up to these days?" Clive asked, a bristle in his voice now.

"Oh, you know, a little of this and a little of that," he said, leaning back in his chair. Henrietta thought he was putting on a good show of disinterested nonchalance, but she thought his eyes looked sad, or perhaps worried.

"Would that it was more," Lord Linley harrumphed again. "Perhaps you should drive over to the Burrows with Clive tomorrow. Get his opinion on the matter. I daresay a fresh set of eyes might help."

Wallace shot Clive a glance to gauge his interest.

"I'd be happy to," Clive said, setting his napkin on the table, the servants clearing the dessert dishes now. "It's been a while since I've been down to the lower estates, but it would make a nice change. I didn't realize you could still drive, Wallace," Clive said directly.

"Oh, I manage most things," Wallace said bitterly. "You'd be surprised."

"Really! Must we talk of the estate's affairs!" bemoaned Lady Linley suddenly from the other end of the table. "Surely business can wait until after the reception and all of the guests have gone!" she implored. "They'll soon be descending upon us. No one is staying longer than a week, however, except of course the Earl and Countess of Ashforth. They always stay on and on; it's a terrible bore, really, but what's to be done? It wouldn't be so bad, but with the east wing closed off now, and most of the west, it makes it a bit of a squeeze, doesn't it, Montague? Then with all the extra servants running around . . ."

"Margaret!" Lord Linley interrupted.

Wallace chuckled. "Really, mother. Clive, here, will be thinking you're referring to him."

"Don't be absurd! Of course, I don't mean *them*. Clive's my nephew, and Henrietta's a lovely thing, aren't you, dear? Oh!" she said, suddenly despairing. "You have no idea what the house used to be!" Lady Linley sighed, looking at Henrietta, who decided to nod sympathetically. "We had such lovely parties! The prince himself once stayed with us. It's been so very long since we've had a party, a proper party, that is, and I'm quite looking forward to it!"

"I'm sure it will be lovely," Henrietta said appropriately, though she was a bit unsettled at the prospect of having to meet several more members of the aristocracy.

"It's the war's fault," Lady Linley said sadly, "that we've been reduced to this."

"No, it's not, Mother," Wallace put in, moving his crystal wine glass in slow circles on the thick white tablecloth so that the last of his wine swirled lazily. "It was changing before that. There's no place in the world anymore for monstrosities such as this. The old order has cracked apart, and well it should. It isn't right for certain families to have everything while the common man labors in vain until he falls into his grave, utterly spent and broken. And for what? So that we can throw ever more elaborate parties?"

Henrietta looked at him in surprise, as it was the most he had said all evening.

"Wallace!" Lord Linley boomed. "We have a duty!"

"A duty?" Wallace scoffed. "To what? To whom?"

"You must forgive my son's socialist tendencies," Lord Linley said to Clive.

"And what if I am a socialist, Father?" Wallace said wearily. "We have to be realistic. We can't keep clinging to the old ways no matter how much we might want to." Suddenly he let out a little laugh. "We have only to look to our dear king for an example of walking away from his duty. I rest my case there. Surely you can't expect more of me than the king himself?" he said with a sly grin.

"Wallace! For shame!" Lady Linley twittered. "How dare you speak of the king in that manner!"

Wallace remained unruffled by this scolding and finished off his wine.

"I must admit, Wallace, I have to agree with you on a number of scores," Clive said, looking at him with what seemed to be a new appreciation.

"You Americans have the advantage," Wallace said, addressing him alone now. "You're not entrenched in this bloody feudal hierarchy; you're able to start afresh. At least the common man has a chance to better himself there."

"On the surface, yes," Clive agreed. "But there *is* a hierarchy that exists, a rather brutal one, I might add. It's not as steeped in history, but it's every bit as unforgiving, maybe even more so because of its self-conscious youth. It yearns for the prestige of its parent," he said, inclining his head, "and so it follows the example laid out very carefully."

"But surely those days are numbered, Clive; you've said so yourself."

"Perhaps," Clive said thoughtfully. "In time, it may look differently; I'll grant you that. But meanwhile," he said, looking around the room appreciatively, "beautiful old estates such as this still exist, and something must be done."

"By Jove, yes!" interrupted Lord Linley. "Just what I've been saying to Wallace. Something must be done . . ."

"Yes, something must be done with this old hulk, Father, but restoring it to its former glory is not it. It should be made into something useful!"

"But it was a hospital during the war! Ghastly, that was, my dear," Lady Linley said to Henrietta. "Isn't that good enough?" she asked Wallace now. "Castle Linley did its duty."

"No, Mother," he sighed, "it is most assuredly not 'good enough.'"

"Well!" Lady Linley sniffed. "This is quite enough of political talk. It's become really rather tedious!" she said abruptly.

"Forgive us," Lord Linley said gruffly, though Wallace remained noticeably silent.

Lady Linley ignored the apology but for a slight inclination of her head. "Come, my dear," she said to Henrietta. "It seems we're quite in the way, so we'll leave the men to their port now, shall we?" She stood up, and the men attentively stood as well, including Wallace, who hobbled up rather nimbly on his crippled leg.

"We will withdraw," Lady Linley continued saying to Henrietta, "and you can entertain me with all of the wedding details! And don't leave a single thing out!"

Henrietta obediently followed Lady Linley, though she very much would rather have listened to the men's conversation than recount what all of the ladies at the wedding had worn and who had come with whom. As she passed Clive, however, he surprised her by defying not only English propriety but his own usual reticence at displaying his emotion publically and caught her hand, giving it a quick kiss before he released it, and her, to be swallowed up by Lady Linley.

Chapter 11

Elsie sat anxiously in the Chippendale armchair across from Aunt Agatha, trying to sit properly but not quite sure what to do with her legs. She tried sitting perfectly straight with her knees pressed tightly together, but it was a difficult position to maintain. She could feel perspiration gathering under her arms, not only from her strained effort but also because they sat very near the fire, Aunt Agatha apparently subject to frequent chills.

As that venerable lady now poured out the tea, Elsie stole a few glances at her and could not help but think how much Aunt Agatha reminded her of a large chipmunk, or maybe a rabbit, with her round, fleshy cheeks and her two front teeth that had an unfortunate tendency to jut out just a little too much despite what was an obvious effort on Agatha's part to hide them by smiling as little as possible. Elsie watched her carefully, trying to observe and take note for future reference, but she felt sure she would never remember all of these little rules and niceties. She wasn't as clever as Henrietta in this department, whom she still marveled at in her ability to adapt and change. How she had the courage to someday take on the running of Highbury was nothing short of amazing to Elsie, as well as terribly frightening. As Elsie took the teacup and saucer offered to her now, she tried to calm herself by contemplating that Aunt Agatha seemed by far the nicer of her two new aunts, Aunt Dorothy barely condescending to speak to her, but even so, Elsie couldn't help but feel that she had been asked here for a more specific reason than a friendly chat.

Ma had been invited as well, but, of course, she had declined. Elsie wasn't sure which was preferable, sitting here alone to face whatever Aunt Agatha meant to say to her or having to fret over whatever disparaging comments Ma would surely make if she were present. After careful consideration, Elsie thought she preferred to be here alone and had tried all the way up to Kenilworth to guess what the topic might be about.

They had begun with the usual exchange of pleasantries regarding the weather, the drive up, the wedding, and Ma's health before they had rather quickly come to the end of them. Looking solicitously at the tea service, Aunt Agatha now offered Elsie a scone, which Elsie politely declined, which apparently left Agatha no choice but to finally broach the subject she had been instructed to initiate.

"I must say, my dear," Aunt Agatha began, uneasily. "Father Exley," she said, making her grandfather sound, to Elsie's ears, anyway, jarringly like a priest, "was rather disappointed when Mrs. Hutchings left her position."

Elsie shifted uncomfortably. So that was it. It was to be about the companion. "Yes, I'm sorry about that," Elsie said apologetically.

"Well, that leaves us in a rather precarious state, does it not?" Agatha said, taking a sip of her tea. "I mean, what are we to do with you?"

"Must you do anything with me, Aunt Agatha?" Elsie asked tentatively, following her aunt's lead by also taking a sip of her tea.

"Of course we must do something, my girl! You must make a good match; Father Exley is rather set upon it. As I understand it," Aunt Agatha went on, "he plans to put a very large dowry upon you." Aunt Agatha drew herself up here and gave her a look that seemed intended to impart how impressed she was of said proposed arrangement. "Therefore you must somehow be brought out into society.

You're too old to be sent away to school or to come under the instruction of a governess," she said briskly. "A lady's companion such as Mrs. Hutchings seemed to be the perfect solution, but we see now that having an additional person in the house while your mother is . . . not herself, was also ill-conceived," she said with a small cough.

For a moment, Elsie allowed herself to think with amusement of the scene in *Pride and Prejudice* where Lady Catherine De Bourgh questions Elizabeth Bennet about the wisdom of all of her sisters being out in society at one time. If only that were simply her problem! Elsie thought forlornly. The concept of "making a match" terrified her, and she tried to think of a way to introduce Stanley into the conversation. She was pretty sure the Exleys would not approve of him, but she knew she would have to speak up sooner or later.

"But I'm not in need of coming out, Aunt Agatha . . . to find a husband, that is," she began hesitantly. "As it happens, I'm . . . I'm nearly engaged already. So, you see, there's really no need for all this fuss." Timorously she looked up into Aunt Agatha's wrinkled face, and, despite the startled expression she was met with, she felt a certain sense of relief and accomplishment at finally having revealed her secret.

"Engaged!" Aunt Agatha sputtered. "To whom, my dear? Surely not to Barnes-Smith?"

"Lieutenant Barnes-Smith?" Elsie asked, confused. "No . . . I . . . his name is Stanley Dubowski," she stammered, quite taken aback by the mention of . . . Harrison.

"Who?" Aunt Agatha seemed genuinely perplexed.

Elsie was surprised that her deep feelings of love—and her beloved, for that matter—were not more obvious to the greater world. "I . . . the man that I came to the engagement party with," she offered. "And my date at the wedding . . . though I didn't see much of him . . ." Elsie trailed off, hoping this would be enough to jog a memory.

By the pinched expression on Aunt Agatha's face, Elsie knew she was trying hard to place him, making Elsie feel all the worse that Stanley had obviously made so little an impression.

"Him?" Aunt Agatha asked eventually, seeming to finally put a face to the name. "I thought he was the Hennessey's son. He's your . . . your intended?" Agatha asked, looking mystified.

"Well, yes . . ."

"What does he do?" she said, peering down at her sternly, her buck teeth only partially showing.

"He . . . he works at Sulzer's Electrics. On the line," she added quietly.

"No, no, no, my dear!" Agatha clucked. "You can't really be serious! Father Exley would never approve—much less Gerard, I daresay." She shivered.

"But, Aunt Agatha . . . I . . . I love Stanley," Elsie said, blushing. "I always have! He'd be crushed if I throw him over. First Henrietta did, and I couldn't go and do that to him as well. I don't *want* to do that to him, as a matter of fact! He'd never survive it, and I'm afraid I wouldn't either."

"Nonsense! Has he declared himself?"

"Not exactly," Elsie said, her mind drifting against her will to his long absences, the current one since the wedding still stretching on and on.

"Just as I thought. He's no doubt seen the disparity in your positions. It is a schoolboy's fickleness, nothing else!"

Elsie looked sadly down into her teacup. "But he's not a schoolboy," she muttered.

"And what of the Lieutenant?" Aunt Agatha continued, ignoring her.

Elsie's head rose slowly. "What do you mean, what of him?" She began to feel apprehensive again. Did she somehow know he had come on several occasions now to visit her?

"He was rather attentive throughout the wedding," Aunt Agatha sniffed. "Several people, myself included, noticed—and commented. You must be careful there, my dear."

"What do you mean? I . . . he's nothing to me! Just a . . . just a friend."

"Well, I'm very gratified to hear it," Aunt Agatha sighed.

Her curiosity piqued now, however, Elsie dared to continue. "But he . . . he seems very much a gentleman. Very proper." It was all she could think to say as she accidentally put one too many cubes of sugar in her tea.

"Oh, I daresay he presents himself as proper," Aunt Agatha said stiffly. "But he's thoroughly unsuitable just the same," she continued sternly, "should the question ever happen to arise in your mind."

Elsie was beginning to feel slightly offended now. Was she to be warned off *every* man who took the slightest interest in her, as if she had no ability to discern for herself? "I . . ."

"He's a terrible flirt, you know. He's been engaged several times already," Aunt Agatha said now, discreetly wiping a bit of jam from the corner of her mouth with her thick linen napkin.

"He has?" Elsie asked incredulously and felt slightly sick, though she knew not why. What did it matter to her?

"Oh, yes, indeed!" Aunt Agatha added with a bit too much enthusiasm, suggesting to Elsie that in her weaker moments, Aunt Agatha might be one who was frequently tempted by and perhaps more than occasionally gave in to the sin of gossiping. Her austere, proper exterior relaxed for just a moment. "He's a scoundrel through and through!" she hissed conspiratorially as she leaned forward slightly to impart this particular bit of news. "I was surprised, actually, that Clive Howard enlisted the major to be his best man, but I suppose the uncle should not be tarred by the same brush as the nephew!" Aunt Agatha conceded reluctantly and reached for a strawberry. "Why the major had to drag him along at all, however, I'll never understand! Antonia swears she didn't invite him, but that the major brought him as his guest. Thoroughly unsuitable. The major ought to know better after the Alice Stewart scandal, but one can never account for certain others' actions, can one?"

Elsie desperately wanted to ask what the Alice Stewart scandal was all about, but she refrained. She couldn't help thinking about how Henrietta had told her that the lieutenant was a "ladies' man," and how Elsie had misunderstood her meaning entirely. But that was typical, wasn't it? she thought disparagingly of herself. She was always getting these types of things wrong. She looked up at Aunt Agatha now, fearful that her sharp chipmunk eyes might be able to see through her, that she would somehow know that in fact the Lieutenant had called on her several times already since the wedding and had even on the last visit induced her to walk out with him in the park. But he hadn't seemed a scoundrel at all; rather, he was very charming and funny. So different from Stanley's serious intensity. It had been a welcome break in the loneliness she had begun to feel more and more. She missed Henrietta more than she could say. While it was true that Henrietta had not been at home very often these last months, anyway, just knowing that she could quickly write or even ring Henrietta in Winnetka if she really needed her had made all the difference.

"Tut, tut!" Aunt Agatha was saying now. "Never mind, my dear! No need to be downtrodden! You will meet many eligible men. Which is the whole reason for this little conversation, actually. Since a companion cannot come to you, you must come to us, that is, your Uncle John and I," she added. "We will see that you meet the proper people," she condescended, surveying the tea tray now for any other bits she might nibble on.

Elsie felt a sense of panic welling up in her. "Oh, no, Aunt Agatha!" she blurted out. "I . . . I mean, thank you for the offer, but I really couldn't leave Ma . . . Mother . . ." (She had endlessly been instructed to refer to her as such now, but she kept forgetting.)

". . . and the kids."

"Oh, it wouldn't be permanent. Maybe for a few weeks at a time, perhaps; you'll still see them often enough, I daresay."

"Oh, please, Aunt Agatha. I can't come! Eddie's having a bit of a hard time, lately, and he . . . he likes telling me things in the evening, and Herbie, too. I . . . please! I'm not like Henrietta . . . I wish I could be, but I'm not!" she said in a panicked voice and was surprised that two hot tears had appeared in the corners of her eyes. Though her concern for Ma and her brothers and Doris was very real, a different fear was overwhelming her. She worried that if she went away, how on earth would Stanley ever call upon her then? She had a hard enough time inducing him to come to Palmer Square! If she went and stayed with the Exleys, that would be the end of his visits entirely, she was sure of it.

"Now, now!" Aunt Agatha said, disturbed. "No need for tears!" She shifted in her chair as she tried to come up with a solution. "What about weekends?" she finally asked. "You could stay with us for part of the week and then go back . . ." she said, bargaining.

"But that's when I see them the most!" Elsie said, despairingly.

"I'm sure we can come to some sort of arrangement," Aunt Agatha said uneasily. "Perhaps Wednesday to Saturday afternoon, then?"

When Elsie didn't immediately respond, Aunt Agatha saw her chance and continued delicately. "Wouldn't it be nice to get out from time to time?" she said encouragingly. "We'd take you to the theater and the ballet, lovely parties. A young girl like you should not be alone so very much."

Elsie was wavering. She would dearly love to see the theater, but how could she do that to Stanley? And, anyway, she wasn't sure she was brave enough to stay with them. After all, she barely knew them! And what would Ma say? There would be no end to her ranting.

"And John and I need some entertainment as well," Aunt Agatha continued smoothly, sensing victory. "What with Ernest and John Jr. gone and married now, you'd be doing us quite a favor. I always wanted a girl to go about with me and keep me company! Might you indulge us? And it would please Father Exley immensely, I must say," she said, her voice trailing off now.

Elsie was so confused. She wasn't sure what she should do. In her heart, she wanted to stay at home, but she didn't know how to say no. Aunt Agatha was being so kind, and she didn't wish to disappoint her. But wasn't that better than disappointing Ma and Stanley? Oh, why did she always find herself in these types of situations? Her only desire in life was to make everyone around her happy, to not create

waves or draw attention to herself. Why couldn't they have just carried on as they were? Yes, it was nice to have enough to eat and fine
things, but sometimes she missed Mr. Dubala's dusty old shop where
nothing ever changed and her Sunday afternoon walks with Stanley
in Humboldt Park. As she faintly set down her cup on the table, it
came to her as well that though Aunt Agatha was *asking* her to come
and stay, she probably didn't really have much of a choice if it was
her grandfather's idea. It was becoming clear to Elsie that he generally got what he wanted, thinking about how they had been forced to
move and how he had sent poor Eugene away. What was she to do?

"Well, might I know your thoughts, my dear?" Aunt Agatha asked,
somewhat eagerly, now. "Have I managed to persuade you?"

"Well, I . . . perhaps it wouldn't hurt to come and stay—sometimes,"
Elsie said tentatively. She didn't see any way out of this. She would
just have to tell Ma that grandfather had insisted, and, surely, given
the past, Ma would understand that, wouldn't she?

"Oh, I *am* glad, my dear!" Aunt Agatha said, noiselessly clapping
her hands together. "You've no idea how pleased Father Exley will
be. And don't fret! You'll have a lovely time, I'm sure." And as if she
could sense her anxiety regarding Stanley or even the lieutenant,
she went on. "You'll have so many suitors, you won't know whom to
choose!" Elsie rather doubted this, as men usually never gave her a
second look. Which is why Stanley's attentions (at one point in time,
at least) and those of the lieutenant's, if she were honest, were so very
welcome.

"In the meantime, my dear, you must give up this notion of
Stanley . . . Dubowski, was it?" she asked distastefully. "Put him
aside. Kindly!" she added when she saw the look of alarm on Elsie's
face. "No need for bad manners, but the sooner the better. I'm sure
you'll see the sense of this," she added in her previously authoritative
tone. "And now it's getting late, my dear. Perhaps you'd better go. We
wouldn't want your mother to worry, now, would we?"

As Elsie awkwardly rose to leave, then, Mrs. Exley having rung for
the chauffer, she had the distressful feeling of having been manipulated

and began to doubt her decision almost immediately, wondering if she was making a terrible mistake. Had she really thrown over Stanley and the lieutenant (not that Harrison was hers to throw over, she scolded herself) as well as Ma and the kids for fear of what grandfather would say? Or was it because she didn't want to hurt Aunt Agatha's feelings, or, worse yet, for the promise of the theater and the ballet? Whatever was the motivation, she was now quite disappointed in herself as she sullenly pinned on her hat and perfunctorily kissed Aunt Agatha on the cheek. She hated that she was so weak.

All the way home, these thoughts kept swirling around in her mind, and she again found herself desperately wishing she could talk to Henrietta. She had tried valiantly to fill Henrietta's shoes ever since she had left them all, which was really all the way back when she had started working at the Marlowe. That's when it had all started, when Henrietta had got involved with Clive in that mystery case. Then she had moved to Highbury, and now she was married and hopelessly gone on her honeymoon. Henrietta had given her the address of Clive's aunt and uncle in England; perhaps she should write to her. She was trying hard to be what Henrietta had always been to them—a second mother— but it was obvious she was failing miserably. Look at them! All split up now. But that hadn't really been her fault. And now she was supposed to give up Stanley as well. She couldn't really do that! she thought as she wiped a fresh tear now. And yet . . . a nagging doubt kept coming back to the forefront of her mind. Perhaps Stanley had already given *her* up. Why else would he stay away? she thought miserably.

She would simply have to seek him out, Elsie determined, as she blew her nose into her handkerchief, however uncomfortable it might be. She must somehow find a way to explain what was happening and impart to him how tenuous was the rope upon which they now balanced. She sighed as she leaned her head on the window of the car and wished with all her heart that Henrietta were here and hoped, for her sake, that she was enjoying herself.

Chapter 12

A s predicted, guests began to arrive at Castle Linley as the week progressed, Clive surreptitiously explaining who they were to Henrietta each morning in their bedchamber before the two of them emerged to attend the day's events and to be formally introduced. It was mostly to be a family party, an opportunity for the English relatives to meet Henrietta and to congratulate the new couple, but like Castle Linley itself, the family had been crumbling away for generations now and only a handful of stray cousins were left.

Indeed, Lady Linley had been quite at her wit's end as to whom to invite and had finally settled upon what she considered an acceptable assemblage. The Earl and Countess of Ashforth and their daughter, Lady Winifred, who was quite, by the way, past the optimum marriageable age, had come down from Durham, the countess being a cousin of some sort to Lord Linley as well as to the Prince of Wales himself, making them the highest-ranking pair there. Then of course Lord and Lady Fairfax had also been invited, who were not really relatives exactly, but who were still in possession of two passable daughters, which, Clive wickedly suggested, was perhaps the real reason for their presence at what was supposed to be merely a family affair, Lady Linley no doubt hoping that one of them might *become* family. There was also the Honorable St. John Sedgewick and his wife,

Elizabeth, who had made their way up from Bath, Elizabeth being an aunt to Alcott and Montague.

The rest of the party on the night of the reception would be made up mostly of some of the landed local families that the Howards would be expected to invite, most of them, coincidentally, with daughters. To make up the numbers, then, Lady Linley had been obliged in the end to ask some of Wallace's set, mostly former army officers, who could be counted on to behave correctly and to converse with the young ladies or make up hands at cards if required.

One of said officers, a Captain Bertram Foley, Clive seemed to happily recognize from the war when they had been stationed in France together.

"Hardly what Mother had in mind, I'm sure," Clive said, adjusting his tie once more in Henrietta's mirror, as he stood behind her. "Not quite the splash I think she was envisioning for us. I'll have to exaggerate in my letters," he smiled ruefully.

The last of the guests were arriving today, the morning of the reception, which, Henrietta thankfully discovered, was really just a big dinner party. No flaunted introductions or orchestras, just a rather formal dinner followed by a gathering of sorts in what the Howards called the reception room.

"She forgets sometimes, I think, that the English do it differently," Clive went on.

"I prefer it this way, don't you?" Henrietta responded, as she finished the last of the tea Phoebe had brought up to her. Henrietta had observed that everything in England had an air of tradition and heavy formality to it, a quiet muteness that pervaded all, like a painting so old that some of the color had leached out or faded. Not that it wasn't beautiful, she admitted. The country around was quite pastoral, and the house held a certain grandeur, perhaps majesty, even though, as Lady Linley had commented, a part of it was closed down. Highbury, by comparison, was much more . . . what would be the word? Henrietta ruminated. Ostentatious? No, that wasn't really fair to Highbury. It was more . . . dazzling. Brighter somehow.

As if it were meant to impress. That was it, Henrietta realized. With Highbury and the other North Shore mansions she had so far been brought to, Clive's parents and their circle at home seemed to try harder to impress, while Castle Linley, despite its crumbling mortar in places and the broken gate near the conservatory, commanded respect and awe without seeming to try at all.

Even the servants here were different, Henrietta had noted. At home, the servants really were more *staff* than servants, people who came and went, were fired or hired as need be. Here, they seemed to truly embody the word *servant*, as if they were born into it and had no other purpose in life. Though Henrietta had endured countless lectures from Antonia about fraternizing with the servants, she had not been able to help befriending some of them at Highbury, thinking fondly of at least Edna and Mary. Try as she might here, however, she could barely get one of them to even look her in the eyes, much less talk with her. The gulf between them was very wide and apparently unbreachable. For one thing, they had a distinct knack, more so than the servants at home, for remaining out of sight.

And then there were the guests themselves, who, like Castle Linley, also commanded a respect without seeming to put forth any effort. Henrietta was perceptive enough to notice that she and Clive seemed a sort of novelty to the other guests because they were American, not because they held some exalted position as they did at home. In fact, if Henrietta judged correctly, the other guests seemed almost to look down on them because they were Americans, as if they weren't quite the thing, Clive's having toiled in a common profession such as the police lowering them further still, all of which Henrietta found ridiculously funny considering they were probably wealthier than at least three quarters of the people in the house. Pedigree, she saw, was everything to them, though to boast of it was equally distasteful, and if Lord and Lady Linley were not his aunt and uncle, Henrietta guessed they would probably not be welcome at a country weekend soiree such as this. Henrietta was used to being regarded as the bottom of the barrel, however, and didn't mind in the slightest.

Antonia, she was beginning to meanwhile realize, knew what she was about, and Henrietta resolved to pay closer attention to her edifications. For the time being, however, it was wonderful to be out of the spotlight. Lady Linley had bigger things to worry about than the entertainment of her American nephew and his wife.

"I have to say that I do, darling," Clive agreed now. "It's one of the reasons I so enjoyed living in the city. I got to be just an ordinary person buying sausages from a wagon and drinking beer," he said, reminding her of the evening they had spent at Polly's apartment while she had sewed her costume for the Marlowe.

He held out his hand to her now. "Shall we attempt a real ride today?" Henrietta had of course never been on a horse before, so, earlier in the week, Clive and the stable groom had given her several lessons, cautiously leading her around the stable yard so that she could get the feel of it.

"Do you think I'm ready?" Henrietta asked tentatively.

"We won't go far, and we'll go slow. But we can get away from here and be alone," he said suggestively.

"We're alone now!" Henrietta laughed, giving her hair one last pat. "Oh, all right," she acquiesced. "It's better than having to listen to the countess drone on about Winifred's comings and goings, which I assume I'm meant to be impressed by. Or to have to listen to Lady Fairfax elaborate one more time about the many suitors who've made a claim for one of her daughters. It's frightfully dull, you know," Henrietta sighed as she put down her hairbrush.

"Ah, my poor darling," Clive said, his mouth twitching as he kissed her forehead. "I'll spirit you away from this life of drudgery."

Henrietta pinched him, but he merely grinned.

"Immediately after breakfast, then. Let's get away early before anyone offers to join us."

Thankfully, not many of the other guests were awake when they descended to the main floor, most of them having their breakfast in their rooms, so Henrietta and Clive were able to make their escape after informing Stevens of their desire to ride, allowing time for him to tell the grooms to ready two horses. After making pleasant conversation with Mrs. Sedgewick, the only other guest at breakfast, Henrietta dutifully went upstairs to change into riding breeches and a jacket.

"You're rather fetching, my dear," Clive said a half an hour later as he helped her up onto Daisy, the mildest of the horses. The air was crisp despite the unusual appearance of the sun, suggesting that it might be the last nice day before the weather turned.

With a nod to the stable boy still holding Henrietta's horse, Clive led them off across the vast acreage toward the village beyond, and Henrietta, though still unsteady with the huge bulk of the horse underneath her, felt a thrill just the same. It was wonderful to be out in the open air with her love, her new husband. She still delighted to call him that as she gazed at him, riding slightly ahead of her.

They rode for about a mile until they could just see the village down below them in the valley, Clive trying to explain the territory and showing her all of the places he and Julia spent exploring with Linley and Wallace when they were children. When they reached a little grove beside the worn track leading into the village, they dismounted and led the horses through the trees to a little brook that eventually ran down to meet the river alongside the village.

"This was one of our favorite places," Clive said as he walked closer to the brook, surveying it. "Julia used to say that it was a fairy bower," Clive laughed.

Henrietta smiled and looked around. A few fall anemones could still be seen arching toward any stray rays of sun that made it through the thick tree branches, almost bare now, their brown leaves lying all around them. Henrietta breathed in the heady scent of the decaying leaves mingled with the fresh scent of the brook and was almost overcome by a warmth of feeling, a connection to something eternal that welled up in her. As if he felt it, too, Clive took her hand. He looked over at her now and she at him, both of them searching each other's eyes. Finally Clive leaned close to her and softly kissed her lips. "I love you so very much, Henrietta."

"I love you, too, Inspector," she whispered.

He drew her to him, then, and rested his forehead against hers. "Sometimes I'm afraid of how much I love you," he whispered back, his voice slightly catching. Henrietta tenderly put her hand to his cheek and met his lips again with her own. He returned her kiss, slowly increasing his pressure, his hands going around her now and pulling her closer to him until he could feel her breasts against his chest. They continued this way until Clive's breath began to come faster, his arousal rising, and Henrietta could feel his excitement. They had already made love this morning, and the night before; indeed there hadn't been a night since the wedding that they hadn't come together, Clive proving a most patient and excellent teacher. He was always gentle with her and loving, and she felt no shame with him, no embarrassment at what he did to her, what he asked her to do. His attraction and passion for her never seemed to wane, nor hers for him, so much so that she secretly wondered at times if she were an unnatural woman. No other woman she knew of admitted to having pleasure in sexual intercourse, except of course the lesbian lovers she had witnessed in the dark corners of the Marlowe. They alone had shown pleasure, such that Henrietta's own desire at the time had been piqued.

Henrietta had never felt this happy, this alive, this confident in her fulfillment as a woman and now a wife, but she was beginning to realize, sadly, that hers must be a rare relationship, and felt a new sadness for her mother and Julia and the myriads of other women she knew who did not enjoy the attentions of their husbands but merely gritted their teeth and endured it. Her mother's words floated back to her: *Spread your legs and be quiet; don't struggle*, and *All men are the same—they only want you on your back. Either getting a baby put in or pushing one out.*

She had been lucky, she knew, and she would try to educate Elsie as best she could when her time came, to give her the advice that she herself had so longed for. And, yet, she couldn't imagine Elsie in the throes of passion, especially in the hands of Stanley

Dubowski. The thought of it made her shudder or laugh, depending on her mood. Her best advice would be what Lucy's had been to her, to just relax, to not think of it as shameful. Somehow, though, she didn't see either of them relaxing, imagining Stan, for his part, reading instructions from some sort of manual on the subject with the same seriousness he would attach to reading about how to defuse a bomb.

Those thoughts were far from her mind now, though, as she felt Clive fumbling to undo the belt of her trousers. Surely he didn't mean to make love out here in the open air just a few miles from the house? The thought of it excited her, however, but she felt nervous as he released her from the belt and undid her trousers, tugging them down around her thighs, when they both froze at the sound of something, or someone, crashing through the underbrush very nearby. Clive's hand went for the inside pocket of his jacket, and Henrietta realized that he was carrying his revolver.

"Shh," he whispered as he pulled her down beside him. They continued to stare in the direction of the noise until they finally saw a figure in the distance making his way through the woods. They peered closer. It was Wallace, limping along as fast as his crippled leg would allow him.

"Where's he going?" Henrietta whispered.

"It would appear he's headed toward the village," Clive whispered back. "But the bigger question would be why would he not take the road, or better yet, drive? He seems in too much of a hurry for a casual walk . . ."

"That *is* a bit odd . . ." Henrietta agreed, considering his poor leg.

"I've been trying to get him to take me down to the Burrows, but I can never seem to find him. And yet here he is," Clive muttered.

Together they watched him hurry by, and when they felt confident that he was safely out of hearing, they cautiously stood up, Henrietta's trousers ridiculously undone, and Clive's shirt pulled out.

"We look a mess!" Henrietta laughed.

"Foiled!" Clive added, the mood obviously shattered now. "So much for my plan to seduce you in the fairy bower. Be warned, though, fair maiden, I mean to have you here, so be on your guard."

"Oh, I shall, sir knight," Henrietta said, doing up her breeches. "Until then, I shall bestow upon you a favor of my regard."

"A token?" Clive asked, intrigued as he tucked in his shirt.

"Only this," she said, coming closer to him and planting a kiss on his cheek.

"I'll take it," he said, lovingly now, and took her hand as he went to gather the horses, happily nibbling the grass, long now after a summer of growth, by the brook.

Chapter 13

When they returned to the house, they were quickly absorbed into the fold of guests, their time alone for the day clearly over. Henrietta was approached by Sara Fairfax, the younger of the two Fairfax girls, as she and Clive made their way into the main hall, informing her that they were attempting one last game of croquet, probably for the year, "seeing as it is so lovely out today," on the south lawn if she wished to join, while Stevens informed Clive that his lordship would have a word in his study when it was quite convenient.

Clive decided to oblige his uncle first thing, before the shoot that was scheduled for later in the day. Henrietta made her way upstairs on her own, then, to change, removing her riding hat as she mounted the stairs, shaking out her long auburn hair, Clive wistfully watching her go as he made his way to the study.

Once in their room, Henrietta tossed her hat onto the bed and walked across to the window where she could see the croquet lawn below being readied by the servants. A small white canopy had been erected at one end of the court, where she could see Lady Linley seated near the countess. Stevens was walking toward them with what looked like a large tray of tea service, the under butler and a footman struggling behind, each carrying large trays of accoutrements as well.

Henrietta sighed. She had no real desire to play croquet or to face all of these aristocratic women on her own, in all honesty, but she knew she couldn't get out of it. She would have much preferred to stay indoors and write a long-overdue letter to Elsie and Ma, knowing that they would most probably be worried at not having heard from her in so long. She had sent a brief postcard from New York, and one from Liverpool, but that was all. She could potentially beg off from the day's events with a headache, but she didn't want to be perceived as the disagreeable American, nor did she want to begin down Ma's road of feeble excuses.

There was a knock at the door, then, and her maid, Phoebe, poked her head in and curtsied. "Excuse me, madam." (It felt strange to be called "madam" and not "miss.") "Would you like me to help you dress?"

"Yes, Phoebe, come in," Henrietta murmured and reluctantly pulled off her gloves. Any letter home would have to wait until later. Perhaps she would find time in the afternoon.

As it turned out, however, Henrietta had had little free time at all that day and had not returned to her room until it was time to dress for cocktails in the drawing room before going in to dinner.

Clive had come in late from the shoot, and Roberts, his acting valet, had run a bath for him. Henrietta had already finished her toilette, with Phoebe's help, of course, and was rather pleased with the effect. She sat waiting for him now in their bedroom rather than descend to the drawing room without him. When Clive finally emerged from his dressing room in his white tie and tails, she felt a surge of love all over again. His hair was combed back now in a rather elegant style, though she could see his few silver hairs just above his ears. It didn't bother her in the slightest, however. Indeed, she felt it gave him an air of refinement and added to his attractiveness. His warm hazel eyes caught hers, and she felt herself melt just as she had that first night at the Promenade. This was the longest they had spent apart since their wedding day, and she felt excited to see him, as if they had been apart for weeks. She went to him, and he put his arms around her.

"You look beautiful, darling," he said as he observed her dress. During the extensive packing sessions for the trip, Antonia had helped her to choose it specifically for tonight's reception. It was a Jeanne Lanvin creation of black velveteen with a scooped-out back and bare shoulders, the dress held in place only by thin straps of velvet. "Are you really my wife, or just some fantasy of my damaged mind?"

"I'm really your wife," she smiled up at him.

He gave her a quick kiss, careful not to disrupt her ensemble, and then took her hand. "Had a nice day?" he asked.

"For the most part. The girls were very eager to teach me croquet, though I'm certain that the countess put it down as a mark against me that I didn't already know how. Lady Fairfax, it turns out, is quite good at it and won. We moved on to bridge after luncheon, then, and I'm pretty sure they were rather shocked when Lady Winifred and I managed to win, which I, of course, have your mother to thank for."

"Well, well, you'll have to tell her. She'll be ever so pleased to hear it, coming from you," he said with an arched eyebrow. "Do I hear a hint of gratefulness from the neophyte?"

"Really, Inspector, that's hardly fair!" she said, narrowing her eyes at him.

"I have to tease you sometimes," he laughed, "as I so rarely get the chance; you are so perfect otherwise, you see."

"Flatterer! Still, I will forgive you," she said majestically. "Just this once." She smiled at him. "Now, you tell me about your day. How was the shoot?"

His face grew more serious and he reactively reached into his pocket for his pipe. "Bearable," he grimaced. "Just." He had located the pipe now, but he merely stared at it before absently returning it to its place in his jacket.

"What is it, Clive?" Henrietta asked softly, reading the shift in his demeanor.

"It's nothing. Just that the guns . . . the rapid fire . . . it unsettles me sometimes," he confessed.

"Yes, of course," she said sympathetically, resting a hand on his arm. "So many bad memories."

"Sometimes," he said, giving her a grateful smile and patting her hand.

"Shall we go down?" she tried to say cheerfully, hoping to change the mood.

Clive glanced at the little clock on the mantel. "I suppose we should," he said with a sigh. "Ready?"

Holding his arm out to her now, he led her out and down the grand staircase. And though she was the one to be anxious with the gala event upon them, it was Clive's hand that slightly shook as he grasped hers in his own.

"Here they are!" boomed Lord Linley from where he appeared in the doorway. "Stevens is about to ring the gong and you haven't even had a drink yet! Don't dawdle out here in the hallway!"

Clive gave her hand a squeeze then as they joined the others in the drawing room."Let them be," Mrs. Sedgewick was saying. "You know how newlyweds are!"

"I can assure you, madam, that Roger and I were never like that!" the countess said snidely. "We never forgot our duty, wedding trip or no."

Clive looked at Henrietta and gave her almost an imperceptible wink before they let go of each other to take the drinks offered them.

Dinner progressed as expected. It was a very lavish spread, which Henrietta thought odd, especially as the Howards, according to Clive, anyway, were so cash poor. She had hoped to be seated near some of the local families, thinking it might be easier to converse with them, but instead Henrietta found herself seated near Miss Jane Fairfax, who had been absent from the croquet match, but whom, it turned out, thankfully, was not in the least threatening and was, indeed, rather amusing, marveling as she did that she and Clive had

had Helen Forrest sing at their wedding. She then proceeded to ask numerous questions about jazz in general, as if Henrietta were the expert on the subject. Henrietta tried to answer as best she could, though she could see that Lady Fairfax did not approve of this particular line of conversation.

To her right sat the countess, who meanwhile seemed intent on asking her about the Von Harmon connection, claiming that Louisa Von Harmon was a distant cousin of hers whom she had met at court, as Louisa was a lady in waiting to Queen Mary and that she had likewise been a particular friend of Victoria Eugenie of Battenberg, who was Queen Victoria's granddaughter, of course, and who later became the Queen of Spain. After further, careful questioning of Henrietta and dissection of her limited answers, the countess abruptly determined that this same cousin, Louisa Von Harmon, that is, must have indeed been a cousin of sorts to Henrietta's father as well.

Henrietta rather quickly perceived that the countess's conclusion regarding the Von Harmon connection caused her to immediately rise in the estimation of all in the vicinity, and she smiled sadly to herself thinking that her father would have been so proud. She forced this from her mind, however, and instinctively looked down the table at Clive. He seemed engrossed in a discussion with Lord Linley and the Honorable St. John Sedgewick about hunting, and she wished she could join that conversation instead.

Anything would be preferable to having to listen to the countess, whose attention had shifted now, in her rather shameful attempts to thrust poor Lady Winifred at Wallace, who was deflecting her efforts with only passable grace.

"I say, Wallace, dear," the countess was saying, "Winifred does so enjoy a game of croquet, don't you, Winifred? Such a youthful game, I've always felt, wouldn't you say, Wallace? Yet suitable for any physical condition."

Henrietta winced at her patent reference to his injured leg.

"Yes, I daresay it is," Wallace put in tactfully with what seemed a false smile, though Henrietta thought she saw his jaw clench.

"Perhaps you might get up a game tomorrow, Wallace? Winifred, I'm afraid, missed today's match as she was suffering from one of her headaches again. She's quite delicate, are you not, Winifred?"

Lady Winifred did not respond but looked morosely into her wine. Henrietta felt sorry for her and tried to assess whether the poor woman resented being addressed as a child despite the fact that she was well over thirty, but it was difficult to tell. It was obvious that the countess still felt it the height of fashion for well-bred young ladies to be fragile and rather pale. Henrietta was of the opinion, however, that a stalwart war veteran such as Wallace would need someone with a bit more wherewithal to her, both mentally and physically, to attract his notice.

"If you wish it, Countess, then of course," Wallace said begrudgingly after a scorching look from Lady Linley, who had an amazing ability, despite the slightly dotty persona she often chose to present, to be part of several conversations at once. "Though it may be too chilly. One never knows what the weather will be. It's so very fickle these days," he said smoothly.

"Splendid," the countess said serenely, ignoring his insinuations, if they were indeed insinuations, confident for the moment in what she saw as her victory. Lady Winifred remained silent.

Lady Fairfax was not to be undone, however, and asked Wallace if he had enjoyed London and recounted with excellent detail how he had been so very kind to escort her Jane to the latest exhibition at the Tate when they had both been in town.

"Jane had a delightful time, did you not, Jane?"

"Oh, yes, M'ma!" Jane said enthusiastically.

Henrietta caught Lady Fairfax's look of triumph toward the countess. It was becoming apparent to Henrietta that Wallace Howard, future Lord Linley of Castle Linley, was considered quite the catch, though besides the title, Henrietta could not understand why. He was not exactly what one would call handsome, with his angular face and sunken brown eyes that seemed to hold a permanent sadness, a pain almost. He could be polite if need be, but he was distant and aloof, seemingly interested in nothing or no one around him. He would make a most disagreeable sort of companion, Henrietta mused. He was listless most of the time, unless, Henrietta had noticed, the discourse turned political, as it did now at Lord Linley's end of the table.

"Did I hear you say you plan to continue on to the continent, Clive?" Captain Russell, one of Wallace's friends, was asking.

"Yes, in a few weeks," Clive answered. "We're going to stay for a short time in London, and then on to Paris and eventually Venice," he said, looking down the table at Henrietta and catching her eye with a smile.

"You might think twice about that, old boy," Lord Fairfax put in. "What with Mussolini invading Ethiopia. Seems a bit of a mess just now."

"Yes, it's all the talk in chambers these days," the earl added solemnly. "There's a rumor that Mussolini plans to align with Hitler."

"Preposterous!" blustered Lord Linley. "Hitler's an inconsequential upstart."

"I wouldn't overlook him, Lord Linley," Captain Russell said carefully. "He's gaining more and more power. The Nuremberg laws are a perfect example."

"Agreed," the earl said, tossing his napkin onto the table now.

"Surely that has no bearing in Paris, however," Clive said quietly as he tightly gripped the stem of his wine glass between his thumb and forefinger.

"We'd be foolish not to think so," Sedgewick put in. "If we're not careful, there'll be another war. Just look at Spain. Even now French volunteers are swarming over to back the Republicans."

"And why shouldn't they?" Wallace said loudly, drawing the men's eyes to him. "They *should* be backing them! We should, too. Every one of us should be fighting against Franco and the Nationalists. I would if it wasn't for this bloody bum leg!" he said, giving his leg a look of disgust.

"And be aligned with the Soviets? Don't be ridiculous!" Lord Linley said.

"Better them and the working man than the Nazis and the Fascists!" Wallace argued.

"I do fear that what we're seeing in Spain and Italy is a microcosm of what might spread across all of Europe before too long," the earl broke in. "The writing is clear."

"Exactly my point," Wallace said bitterly.

"Surely not after all we've suffered in the Great War," a Mr. Cooper ventured to add quietly, not having spoken yet at all this evening besides the usual pleasantries. He was the owner of the local Masson Mill and had lost two sons in the war.

"Of course it's not over!" Wallace said hotly. "Hitler has taken up where the Kaiser's left off, and there's no one to stop him!"

"Wallace!" Lord Linley said with quiet fierceness.

"Gentlemen! Gentlemen! That is quite enough!" Lady Linley said querulously from the other end of the table. "You can continue this over your port. But don't keep us waiting, mind you!" she demanded, as she stood up now, a footman hurrying to hold her chair. "We've arranged for a quartet to entertain us," she added to the murmured delight of Sarah and Jane Fairfax.

"Oooh, might we dance, Lady Linley?" Jane asked hopefully.

"Jane!" Lady Fairfax barked. "Don't be impertinent!"

"I'm sorry," Jane said, somewhat remorsefully. "I didn't mean anything by it."

"Not at all, my dear," put in Lady Linley. "Of course the young people might want to dance. I'll see that Stevens has one of the carpets rolled back for anyone that wants to indulge," she said, her eyes resting on Wallace for a second, but his face did not reciprocate any enthusiasm as she swept out of the room, the ladies dutifully following her.

The reception room located in the front of the house was smaller than a ballroom but bigger than the drawing room and was aglow with soft lights as the ladies entered. The quartet had set up at one end of the hall near the grand piano, where straight-backed chairs with gilding and thick, light blue upholstery had been placed. There were also more comfortable armchairs in groupings around the room, including in front of the massive fireplace. On one side of the room, the servants had already removed one of the carpets. The older women took up residency by the fire, keen on listening to the quartet, Lady Linley bemoaning the fact that young ladies no longer stood up and sang to accompaniment for the evening's entertainment, a sentiment the assembled matrons were quick to agree and sympathize with.

The men, surprisingly, followed them to the drawing room rather quickly, which on the surface seemed to indicate an eagerness to enjoy the ladies' company and the music, but which was really, truth be told, the result of only having been allowed to indulge in one quick glass of port by Lord Linley, who fully understood the nature of his current duty, having been instructed in it earlier by none other than Lady Linley herself. Gruffly, then, he led the men into the reception room as he would have led them into battle, with a promise of cigars and a more explicit discussion regarding the evolving situation in Europe later, when the evening's entertainment had been endured for a sufficient amount of time, muttering as he went, something about losing the battle but winning the war.

The young ladies, however, were all but unaware of this apparent sacrifice as the men came marching in and were happy to leave behind their own idle chitchat in favor of a dance or two, their faces lighting up considerably now.

Clive and Henrietta felt obliged to stand up to several of the serene, elegant waltzes that proceeded, Henrietta whispering to Clive that they were sure to not hear any jazz or big band here in these ancient halls, to which Clive had quickly smiled his agreement. Henrietta noticed that Lady Linley looked on with approval as Wallace methodically spoke to each single woman in the room, his leg preventing him from dancing, though he did make one exception and singled out Lady Winifred to stand up to a waltz with him, her shyness and his bad leg making the endeavor painfully awkward to watch.

Henrietta was of course asked to dance by several of the other gentlemen, whom she felt she couldn't refuse, including Lord Linley, whose fingers she maddeningly felt a bit too low on her back and whose other hand grasped hers with more pressure than was necessary. Henrietta merely smiled graciously and was very glad when Captain Foley, Clive's friend from the war, interrupted.

Captain Foley was a handsome man with dark brown, almost black, hair and a set jaw. And though in tails just now rather than a uniform, he seemed every bit the dashing officer. He sported a rather stylish mustache and still kept himself trim. The way he looked at her now with a certain glimmer in his gray-green eyes led Henrietta to guess that he was perhaps the philandering type.

"Might I offer you my congratulations, Mrs. Howard," he said with a suggestive sort of smile, confirming Henrietta's assessment. "Clive's a very lucky man."

"Thank you, Captain," Henrietta answered smoothly. "I believe you knew each other in the war, isn't that right?"

"We did indeed," Captain Foley said seriously, any hint of flirtation quickly evaporating. "Never fought in the same trench, of course, but in the same battle."

"I should have liked to have known him then," Henrietta added. "What was he like? I can only imagine."

"Very serious in his duty."

"I'm not surprised," Henrietta said with a sad smile.

"No," Captain Foley went on. "Never shirked from his duty, did Clive. He was confoundedly brave; his men loved him."

"Yes, I'm sure they did."

"He risked his life for them many times, and they would have followed him to hell and back," Captain Foley continued grimly. He paused to twirl her. "But I'm sure he's told you all the old stories," he tried to say in a lighter tone once she was facing him again.

"No, not really," Henrietta admitted, suddenly feeling disappointed. "He . . . he doesn't like to speak about it."

"Understandable. Not many of us do. Too ghastly, really." He paused for several moments then before continuing. "And definitely not suitable for dancing conversation," he said, flashing her a rather charming smile again. "Especially with such a beautiful woman," he added, his previously flirtatious manner returning.

"Have you never thought to marry, Captain?" Henrietta parried.

Captain Foley surprised her with a brief chuckle and then leaned toward her. "I'll let you in on a little secret," he whispered to her, "but don't tell Lady Linley, or I fear I wouldn't have been asked down for the weekend."

Henrietta looked at him warily.

"I've very recently engaged myself to be married," he said waggishly.

"Captain Foley! How wonderful!" Henrietta whispered back. "Who's the lucky woman?"

"A Miss Rosalyn Edwards."

"I'm afraid I don't know her."

"No, you wouldn't, of course," he said, still smiling. "She's from Devonshire. Lord Huntington's fourth daughter. My father is his cousin, so not exactly arranged, but certainly encouraged and condoned. As it happens, Rosalyn and I find we are quite suitable for each other, as it turns out."

"But are you in love, Captain?" Henrietta asked before she could catch herself.

Captain Foley laughed again. "I can see you are a romantic, Mrs. Howard. But then," he said, observing her, "you would be."

"I'm terribly sorry, Captain!" Henrietta blushed. "I don't know what possessed me to ask such a thing."

"Not at all. I don't mind answering. At least you're honest," he said, smiling down at her. "No, not in love, certainly," he went on. "But we are fond of each other, and that's quite enough."

The dance ended, then, and Captain Foley bowed before releasing her. "I fear I've monopolized you quite enough at present, Mrs. Howard. I must away now and dance with all of these other lovely ladies, as I'm sure that was what I was asked here for. I trust you'll keep my secret?" he whispered with a knowing look.

"Of course," she smiled back at him and gave his hand a little squeeze. "Good luck."

He deposited her near Mrs. Cooper, the mill owner's wife, and then politely begged the honor of standing up with one of Mrs. Cooper's daughters who was hovering near. In response, the girl curtsied excitedly and quickly took his hand. Henrietta meanwhile took a glass of offered champagne from one of the footmen passing by, feeling relieved to finally have a moment's rest, when she was surprised by Mrs. Cooper, who apparently felt the need to prove her sagacity to the new Mrs. Howard and therefore began a rather awkward tête-à-tête about the latest fashions. Henrietta listened kindly and did her best to keep up, not being at all knowledgeable, actually, about the big Parisian houses now being elaborated upon by the plump Mrs. Cooper, but she couldn't help but wonder what the woman would have thought if she knew she was addressing a girl who had once scrubbed tavern floors and danced with men for money.

Fortunately, she was rescued before long by the Honorable Mr. Sedgewick, and though she spoke cordially with him as they danced, Henrietta could not keep her eyes from wandering to Captain Foley every now and again, wondering what it would be like to enter into a marriage with only "fondness."

As the night wore on, the music livened up as much as possible given the setting—the quartet playing an occasional jig now. Clive observed Henrietta being instructed in how to dance to such a tune by none other than Lord Linley himself and decided that this might be the perfect moment in which to step out and get some air and possibly a smoke of his pipe in peace. Accordingly, he took a large cognac and made his way to a set of French doors running along an outside wall toward the back of the room, hidden partially behind thick velvet curtains, one of which was tied back with a golden tassel. The doors opened easily enough to his touch and led into a vaulted Victorian conservatory. Tropical plants still resided within, basking in the warm air, though to Clive's eye, even in the darkened interior, there did not seem to be quite as many as there had been when he was a boy, but very probably he was remembering it wrong. He had surely forgotten about the heat of the conservatory, and having wanted to escape the heat of the reception room in the first place, moved toward the back, where he thought he remembered there to be a little door that led to the outside.

As he navigated the brick pathway that wound through the overhanging plants, he could see that the staff had been neglecting this room as well. Indeed since he had been here he could not help notice how badly Castle Linley was in need of repair. Crumbling walls, parts of the gardens overgrown, the stables not quite as clean and maintained as they should be. He tried in his mind to allow concessions for the fact that it had been requisitioned by the army during the war and not quite restored to its former glory when they no longer had need of it and had finally withdrawn, leaving the Howards to put it all back together, but he still found it hard to understand. It created a nagging guilt, however, that Highbury was in need of its share of repairs as well, thinking about the abominable servants' quarters over the stables that he and Henrietta had witnessed when confronting the suspicious Virgil earlier in the summer. If nothing else, this trip was spurring in him a desire to throw himself into Highbury upon their return, to take an interest where it should have been all along.

Indeed, it was about just such matters that Lord Linley had called him into the study this morning to discuss after he had returned from his ride with Henrietta. Though it was only ten in the morning, Lord Linley had offered him a cigar and a drink, both of which Clive had respectfully declined, discreetly consulting his pocket watch as he did so. Clive took a seat opposite him, curious as to the nature of this impromptu meeting, as it were, while Lord Linley took his time in pouring himself a drink, seeming reluctant now to broach the topic that was so obviously on his mind. Finally, after fiddling with several items on his desk and letting out a deep sigh, Lord

Linley proceeded to intimate that the estate's finances were woefully in arrears. He then asked, gingerly, how Highbury had fared through the war and the Depression. Alcott never wrote of any problems, Lord Linley confided, so he assumed all was well, was it not? Clive noted the eagerness in his uncle's voice and felt suddenly sorry for him, despite the unpleasantness of the current conversation. He had certainly aged since Clive last saw him; he seemed broken and sad, muddled at times and clinging to the past, whereas he had once been very astute and sharp. In looks, he resembled his own father very much, though his father had always been the smaller—and the more obliging—of the two.

"We were affected by the crash, it's true," Clive answered slowly. "But we've recovered well. We were lucky that Father invested so well."

"I see, I see. Very good, indeed," Lord Linley said, taking a drink of his brandy. Clive began to suspect that this exchange was going to uncomfortably veer into a request for funds from across the ocean, which Clive with almost certainty already knew would be a dead end. Montague Howard, against his own father's wishes, had married Margaret Beaufort, who, though an earl's daughter, had come to the marriage with not the excessive dowry that the estate so badly needed. It had fallen to Alcott, then, to marry well to attempt to shore up Linley, so he had dutifully married a very wealthy American, Antonia Hewitt. The contract that had been drawn up had accordingly allowed for a third of her fortune to be deposited in Castle Linley's coffers, but somehow even that vast amount had not been enough. As per arrangement, Alcott had gone to live in America with his new bride, and Montague had had to try to restore Linley with what he had, Antonia's father having made it quite clear that that would be the end of any further funds. Clive knew that even if his father could be persuaded to offer more pecuniary aid, his mother would not hear of it.

Thankfully for Clive, Lord Linley did not go down that path, however, but instead abruptly changed the subject while he puffed at his cigar. "Did I ever tell you, Clive, my boy, about my engagement in the

Boer War?" Not waiting for an answer, he went on. "Ah, we gave the Zulus hell, we did, Clive. That's when a man was a man, I tell you!" he harrumphed.

Clive wasn't sure what to say next, so he merely answered, "Indeed, sir." He had, in fact, heard these stories many a time during his summers at Linley.

Lord Linley sat determinedly puffing his cigar as his gaze travelled to his many trophy heads displayed and mounted around the room, several of them African in nature. A smile crept across his face, then, as if he were perhaps recalling happier days on safari, when one clearly understood who was the hunter and who the prey. But these memories seemed short-lived, however, and his face crumpled again almost instantly.

"Clive, what am I to do with Wallace?" he asked hopelessly, looking back at him now.

Of all things, Clive had not expected their exchange to turn in this direction and feared what was coming next.

"It should have been Linley, you know," the old man said angrily, his words already a bit slurred. "Linley would have been the man to . . ." He took a large drink and then mumbled, "Bloody war!"—an expletive Clive thought odd since he had just moments before been espousing the glory of the Boer War. "Wallace could bloody well care less," Lord Linley went on. "Doctors say to give him time, that he's experienced a great shock, but, look at you! Now, you know what you're about. You've taken up your responsibility like a man, taken a lovely girl. I've been to Highbury, you know, back in '92. Beautiful place Alcott has, I'll give him that. Small recompense, I suppose, for having to leave Blighty. Still, maybe it wasn't such a bad sentence. Look around you, Clive, it's all the same, all the old estates," Lord Linley said defeatedly. "Alcott was ever more judicious with you and Julia, I saw that early on," he mumbled, shifting gears again. "I thought him a fool, but perhaps he had the right of it. I was too hard on Linley and too soft on Wallace."

Clive again felt sorry for the old man slumped before him behind his mahogany desk; he had ever been fond of his uncle. He could understand the disappointment Lord Linley was feeling and felt a fresh wave of guilt at being awarded his uncle's praises when he himself had been the cause of his own parents' anguish, having very nearly walked away from Highbury as well. And yet he could sympathize with Wallace and his apathy, recognizing all too well the dark places in which Wallace's mind was probably sometimes dwelling and knowing firsthand the resultant despondency that often came without warning. Accordingly, he felt a kinship with Wallace, at least on that score.

"I don't know what he gets up to all day," Lord Linley was saying. "Bloody waste of time. Why won't he settle down and get married? Lord knows there's plenty of girls for the taking after the decimation we've just been through. Take Ashforth's girl, for example. A bit past the bloom of youth, perhaps, but plenty of money. Is it too much to ask? Picking a girl and bedding her? It can't be for lack of trying on Lady Linley's and my part. Do you know how many bloody weekends such as this we've had to endure? Always the same. Is it too much to ask for him to take up his responsibilities? If something isn't done soon, I will be forced to sell the estate," he said with a heavy sigh.

"Is it as bad as all that, sir?"

"Yes, I'm afraid it is, Clive, my boy, and yet Wallace feels no sense of urgency, no sense of despair or gloom over the matter."

Clive cleared his throat. "Would you like me to speak to him?"

"If you'd like, dear boy," Lord Linley said forlornly. "See what he gets up to, though I'm not sure how far you'll get. You've heard him. Pertains to be a socialist."

"Well, I wouldn't go that far."

"You don't know him like I do," Lord Linley put in. "The war's addled his brains."

Clive was about to argue this, but it occurred to him, then, before he did so, how he had seen Wallace slinking through the woods just this morning and reflected that perhaps he did not know his cousin as well as he once had.

—

Once Lord Linley had finally dismissed him, having come to no real conclusions about anything in particular, Clive began looking for a chance to get Wallace alone, but Wallace was strangely absent from the shoot. And now at the reception, Wallace seemed preoccupied by what surely were Lady Linley's instructions for the evening to converse with all of the young ladies present and make charming small talk, though Clive wasn't at all sure how charming Wallace could actually be these days. Maybe once, but now?

It was quite singular, then, as he tried to open the little glass door at the back of the conservatory, to see none other than Wallace himself again slinking off as fast as his crippled leg would allow him across the back garden.

Furiously, Clive tried to open the door, but it was either stuck or locked, and he cursed to himself. Why was everything here so confining, so locked and broken? he fumed. Clive tightly grasped the handle one more time and tried lifting it a bit as he put pressure on it and this time managed to get it open. As he burst forth, the pea gravel crunching underfoot as his feet sank into it, he could just make out the figure of Wallace disappearing into the formal maze of shrubbery beyond the fountain. Clive considered calling out to him, but even before he had a chance, he heard a voice behind him.

"Clive, old boy, there you are!"

Startled, Clive turned and peered back at the figure coming toward him through the conservatory and recognized it as Captain Foley.

"Bertram . . ." he said hesitantly.

Quickly Clive looked once more back across the garden, but Wallace was already gone. It would be no use going after him now, Clive sighed. He knew he could probably catch up with him, considering Wallace's bad leg, but the moment of surprise had passed, and he would have to make up some explanation to Bertram as to why he suddenly had to dash off. There would be another time, he knew, to catch Wallace. Maybe tomorrow.

208   Michelle Cox

"What the devil are you doing out here?" Foley asked now, his hand held out to him.

Despite his momentary distraction, Clive shook the proffered hand warmly. He had been pleasantly surprised when Foley had turned up as a guest for the weekend. Someone else who had lived.

"Just felt in need of some air," Clive said, stepping farther outside now into the chilly night.

"Yes, I bloody well know what you mean," Foley said, following him out. "Smoke?" Foley asked, holding out a cigarette case.

Clive held up his pipe.

"Ah," Foley said and took one out for himself. "I forgot you preferred a pipe," he said as he struck a match and lit a cigarette. He quickly inhaled and then removed it, considering it, as he gathered some stray tobacco bits from his mouth with his thumb and forefinger. "Congratulations are in order, of course," he smiled at Clive. "She's lovely."

"Thank you, Foley," Clive said graciously. "I can't believe it sometimes, you know."

"Doubtless, old boy. But you give us all hope."

There was a moment of silence before Clive spoke again. "What have you gotten yourself up to, then, since the war, that is? You're looking well. Stayed in the ranks, I see."

"Well," Captain Foley said, taking a drag of his cigarette. "Seemed the thing to do. Didn't know what else to put my hand to. Not a bad life, really, now that there aren't any Krauts firing at us, though who knows for how long." He gave Clive a strained sideways look as he deeply inhaled, his eyes squinting slightly, and then looked absently out into the dark grounds.

"Never thought to settle down yourself?" Clive asked pleasantly.

"Well, that's just it, old boy," he said, looking over at him again. "I just shared my secret with your wife."

"Oh?"

"As a matter of fact, I *am* to be married, very shortly, as it turns out."

"You don't say!" Clive said, his pipe clenched in his teeth as he reached out with both hands to shake Foley's. "Congratulations, old dog."

"It hasn't been announced yet, so, you know, keep it under wraps."

"Who's the lucky woman?"

"Rosalyn Edwards. She's a younger daughter of the Earl of Huntington."

Clive raised his eyebrows.

"Not a lot of money, of course, which I'm sure is why they're allowing her to marry a mere officer in his majesty's. Still, not a bad match."

"Well done, Bertram," Clive said. "Let's have a drink to celebrate." Clive made a move to open the conservatory door, but Captain Foley put his arm out to stop him.

"In a moment," he said hurriedly and then smiled crookedly in what seemed to be an attempt to counter his sudden movement. "I was hoping for a word, actually."

"About?" Clive asked as he stepped back, puzzled.

"It's damned, awkward, old boy, but I find I'm a bit short these days, and I, well, I was hoping you might lend a hand, as it were." Foley had the decency to look Clive in the eye as he asked, but Clive could read the anxiety there.

Rationally, Clive recoiled from the suggestion, knowing it would be a bad idea. As a rule, he loathed lending money, but, Foley, after all, had been a fellow brother in arms, and he felt conflicted.

"How much?" Clive asked stiffly.

Captain Foley held his gaze for a few moments before answering, as if trying to predict Clive's answer or to perhaps work up his courage. "A thousand pounds?"

"A thousand pounds!" Clive exclaimed. "Good God, man. What do you need it for? Surely your tailor's bill is not that high."

"No, no!" Foley said hurriedly. "Nothing like that."

"What is it for, then?"

Foley looked away.

"Gambling?" Clive asked, remembering that Bertram had stayed to play cards below last night after he and Henrietta had retired to their room.

Foley looked back at him with something like relief crossing his face. "Yes, something like that, I'm ashamed to say."

"Who fleeced you?"

"I'd rather not say, old boy. You understand, don't you? Not quite the thing to kiss and tell."

"Quite," Clive said, rubbing his hand through his hair.

"Listen, if you haven't got it, I'll find it somewhere. I would just like to . . . to go into this marriage with clean hands, if you know what I mean. Free and clear and all that."

Clive sighed. "Let me see what I can do," he said, draining his cognac now.

"Thanks, old man," Foley said, holding out his hand. Clive reluctantly shook it. "I'll pay you back—on the queen's life," he said, a bit too cheerfully for Clive's liking. And yet, what did he expect? Groveling humility?

"Can we have that drink now?" Clive said wearily.

"You go in," Foley suggested. "I'm feeling a bit closed in. Need a bit of air, stretch my legs," he said restively.

Clive merely inclined his head. "All right, then,"

"And, Clive," he said, calling after him. "Thank you."

Clive spent the rest of the evening on edge, stewing over Foley's request and wondering where Wallace had gotten himself off to. Clive hated to give Foley the money, but how could he not? For one thing, he would have to wire the States for it, which would be time-consuming and would cause all kinds of questions, especially from his mother. He would have to ask his father to keep it to himself if possible until he could get home and explain.

And as for Wallace, he did not return, at least to the reception room, so when Clive and Henrietta finally made their way upstairs after the last of the guests had gone, he stopped Stevens and asked if Wallace had somehow returned unnoticed and retired early to his bed. Stevens dutifully reported that indeed Mr. Wallace had not yet returned and would Mr. Howard like to be woken when he did return, though, Stevens took the liberty of adding, it might be quite late.

"He's done this before, has he, Stevens?" Clive asked.

"Many times, sir. Almost every other day would be a safe assumption," Stevens said emotionlessly.

"Where on earth does he go?"

"I really couldn't say, sir. Perhaps you should inquire of Mr. Wallace personally, sir."

"What about his valet?"

"Compton? I wouldn't know, sir. Shall I ring for him?" Stevens asked.

"No, not at the moment," Clive mused.

"Might I bring you anything else, sir?" Stevens asked when it became apparent that Clive had finished his questions.

"No, thank you, Stevens," Clive said dismissively.

Stevens bowed and left, and Henrietta and Clive resumed their way up the stairs.

"What was that all about?" Henrietta asked, trying to stifle an unladylike yawn.

"I'll explain upstairs," Clive answered wearily.

An hour later, when they were both finally in bed, Henrietta lying with her head on his chest, Clive related, at Henrietta's prompting, his sighting of Wallace again hurrying off somewhere and the exchange he had with Lord Linley earlier that morning in the study.

"Sounds remarkably like someone I once knew," Henrietta said playfully in reference to Wallace's apparent disinterest in the estate.

Clive kissed her shoulder. "He's gone now, that fellow."

"I see," Henrietta said. "Well, I have a secret to share. But I'm not supposed to tell."

"Perhaps you shouldn't, then," Clive said quietly. His interest was immediately piqued, however, and he raced through the evening's events in his mind. He remembered then what Foley had said to him out on the terrace: *I just shared my secret with your wife.* That must be it, he thought with a sigh of relief, but he remained silent, wondering what she would do. He knew it was wrong to test her, especially regarding something so trivial, but he couldn't help it.

Henrietta raised herself up on her elbow and searched his eyes. She knows, he thought, and felt a surge of love for her. She was really quite good at detecting small nuances. Surprising him further, she gave his chin a quick kiss. "Husbands don't count, of course," she said, giving him a little wink.

A deep breath escaped Clive as he pulled her to him. "Let me guess," he said ruefully. "Captain Foley's engaged to be married?"

"Clive! You brute! You've ruined my surprise," she said, giving him a little pinch.

"Ow!" he said in mock pain, rubbing his arm. He wrapped his arms around her, then, and kissed her deeply, happy that there were no secrets between them, though it did not even occur to him to tell her about Foley's request for money, as, after all, that was a business affair, and a sordid one at that.

Chapter 14

When Clive and Henrietta appeared in the dining room the next morning a bit later than usual, they found Lord Linley already seated and reading the morning paper. Lord Fairfax was also present with his two daughters, as well as Lady Winifred and Lady Linley.

Henrietta helped herself to tea and toast, not feeling quite up to anything heavier. She had drank a bit more champagne than usual last night, and she and Clive had stayed up shamefully late. The last of the guests did not leave until two, and Clive had kept her awake for at least another hour after that. Indeed, the birds were just starting to chirp, though it was still dark, as they finally fell asleep. Clive suggested having breakfast brought up to them as he lay next to her, running his fingers languidly through her hair, but Henrietta thought it horribly indulgent and did not want the servants to be scandalized.

Clive had laughed out loud and said she had better get used to it.

Dutifully, however, he dressed, and they went down.

Henrietta had just been seated when Sara Fairfax leaned across the table and said in an excited, low voice, "Have you heard the news?" Without waiting for an answer she went on. "A man's been murdered in the village last night!"

"Murdered?" Henrietta asked, looking over at Clive, who had taken a chair next to her, the strict seating arrangement for dinner thankfully not applying to the breakfast table. His face remained unmoved.

"It appears so," Lord Linley said, lowering his newspaper. "Just up your street, eh, Clive? What luck that we have an inspector with the American police staying with us, wouldn't you say, Margaret?"

"Former," Clive reminded him as he reached for his teacup.

"Were you really a detective?" asked Sara, almost worshipfully. Henrietta suppressed a smile.

"Yes, I was," Clive answered courteously.

"How dreadfully exciting! Don't you think, Father?"

"Nonsense!" put in Lord Fairfax. "There's nothing exciting about solving beastly crimes, you daft girl. I suggest you change the subject to something more appropriate for young ladies and allow Mr. Howard to breakfast in peace."

"Do they know who the victim is?" Clive asked Lord Linley, ignoring Lord Fairfax's injunction.

"Haven't heard, old boy. Nothing about it in the paper, of course. Rotters," he said, giving the paper a shake. "Stevens apparently got the news from the milkman when he delivered this morning."

"Doubtless the constabulary has it well in hand," Lady Linley put in in a querulous voice. "No need to disturb young Clive on his honeymoon."

"No one's suggesting that he be disturbed, my dear," Lord Linley said irritably. "He asked a question, and I answered it."

"Come, let us change the subject!" Lady Linley said cheerfully. "Did you sleep well, Henrietta?" she asked, turning to her.

"I did, yes, Lady Linley, thank you," Henrietta answered with a polite smile.

Stevens entered the room, then, and approached Lord Linley. "I'm very sorry to disturb you, my lord, but there is a Detective Chief Inspector Hartle at the door. He wishes a private word. Shall I say that you're at home?"

Lord Linley sighed and tossed his napkin onto the table. "You'd better had, Stevens. I'm finished, anyway, and I daresay this chap might know something of the murder, wouldn't you say, Clive?"

"Very probable," Clive answered calmly, though Henrietta could tell that he was keenly interested. She was beginning to know him in a way only time and intimacy could instruct.

"Show him into the study, Stevens."

"Very good, my lord," Stevens responded as he bowed before exiting.

"I say, Clive, you might just look in with me, what do you say? After all, this is your field, eh?"

"If you wish it, Uncle, I'd be happy to assist," Clive answered.

"Montague! Don't involve the boy! He's got a young wife to tend to!" Lady Linley decried.

"Asking him to speak to a police detective with me is hardly involving him, Margaret! And I daresay, Henrietta is quite capable of amusing herself for all of ten minutes, am I not right, my dear?" he said, looking at her now.

"Of course, Lord Linley," Henrietta responded respectfully.

"Oh, well, as you wish, of course," Lady Linley said in an injured tone and with a dismissive wave of her hand. "Clearly whatever I say has no consequence, whatsoever."

"I don't mind at all, Aunt Margaret," Clive said, addressing Lady Linley. "I'm happy to accompany Uncle Montague, though I doubt very much I'll be able to add anything of real substance." He stood up slowly and inclined his head in deference to the ladies present. "Excuse me," he said to them formally, but before he could move away from the table, Henrietta ventured to say, "Unless you'd like me to go with you, Clive?"

Clive looked down at her and shook his head slightly, his brow furrowed. "I think not, darling," he said, clearing his throat. "I think Uncle Montague and I can manage."

"Good heavens, no!" Lady Linley agreed. "Why ever would you want to hear all of the beastly details, my dear? No, indeed. Leave it to the men."

Clive gave Henrietta a last, hurried look, accompanied by a forced smile, before he strode quickly across the room, Lord Linley already having a head start. If he had meant it to be reassuring, however, it failed miserably. Henrietta slumped back into her chair and tried to keep from looking hurt. She took a sip of her tea and ventured a glance around the table, but no one seemed to have noticed what to her had been Clive's very obviously slight.

"Do you think he's come about the murder?" Sara asked her sister.

"Of course he has, you twit! Why else would he be here?" Jane responded.

"But what have we to do with it?" Sara continued.

"Perhaps the murderer is still lurking around, and the inspector's come to warn us!" Jane suggested, causing Sara to squeal with excitement and a simultaneous loud clatter to be heard at the other end of the table. All eyes turned in that direction, where an embarrassed Lady Winifred, beet red, was attempting to recover her spilled teacup.

"I'm very sorry!" she mumbled as Stevens stepped forward to assist her, having just reentered the room at this particular juncture, this time with a salver of mail to be distributed.

"Girls!" Lord Fairfax said, addressing his daughters as he looked up from his paper, exasperated. "Be silent! You're upsetting everyone with your absurd theories. I'm sure the police have it quite in hand!"

Stevens took this as his cue to continue his deliveries and, as it happened, placed a letter next to Henrietta's plate. Still stinging from Clive's apparent dismissal of her and glad to have somewhere to fix her eyes, Henrietta eagerly glanced at it and saw that it was from Elsie.

"Well, we can hardly help speculating!" Jane muttered in her own defense, and, perhaps sensing another impending rebuke from her father, she stood up. "Very well. Come along, Sara. I have something very particular I wish to say to you. But perhaps we might have a game of badminton after breakfast if the rain holds off. What do you say, Sara?"

"Yes, all right," Sara begrudgingly agreed.

"Lady Winifred?" she said, looking over at her. "Badminton?"

"No, thank you," the poor woman said, still not recovered from her faux pas. "I think I'll just lie down for a bit."

Henrietta thought she heard Jane sigh. "Mrs. Howard? Surely you'll play, won't you?"

Henrietta wanted nothing more but to escape to her room to nurse her bruised feelings and to devour Elsie's letter, but she knew she shouldn't be selfish, even if Clive chose to be. "Yes, perhaps later," she compromised with a small smile. "I have some correspondence to attend to first, if you'll excuse me," she said, glancing toward Lady Linley, who acknowledged her desire to retreat from the room with a preoccupied sort of nod, having already begun to read her own letters that Stevens had just laid beside her teacup.

Henrietta clasped Elsie's letter, then, and made her way across the room and slipped out. She paused at the foot of the staircase and shot a quick, longing glance down the hall to the study, where she knew Clive was even now discussing the case with Lord Linley and the police. Reluctantly, she turned and hurried up the stairs to her room, trying to console herself with the fact that she would finally be hearing some news of home, as it had almost been a month now since the wedding.

This did little to reassure her, however, as she entered her room and plopped in a rather unladylike way into the chair by the window, though the sky was very gray and did not afford much in the way of illumination. Henrietta had given Elsie the address of Castle Linley before she had left, but she wasn't sure Elsie would write or that a letter would actually find her here. The last two letters she had received from Elsie while she had been staying at Highbury had contained very bad news, and she desperately hoped that this one would not follow the pattern.

She perused the plain white envelope addressed to Mrs. Clive Howard and thought how strange that looked in print. Quickly she tore it open, then, and began to read:

Dearest Henrietta,
I hope this letter finds you well and happy and that you are
enjoying your time with your new husband. (How funny that
is to write!) We didn't have much time to talk either at the
wedding or after, but I want you to know how very tremendous

I thought it was. You were so very beautiful—as usual!—and Clive was very handsome, too. You made a lovely couple, like something out of a fairy tale. I was watching him while you danced, and it seemed to me that he is very much in love with you, and, oh, Henrietta, how wonderful for you. I pray Clive is as attentive to you as he has always seemed in the past and that your wedding night was not too distressful, or should I say surprising? Likewise, I hope the ship was not too arduous; I would have been terribly afraid, but, then, I am not as adventurous as you.

I believe everyone at the wedding enjoyed themselves, even Ma to the extent that she enjoys anything these days, having been reunited, it seems, with a couple of old friends. The food, of course, was so delicious! I've never tasted anything quite so lovely, though, as you know, I usually just like plain food. The best part, I must say, was the music. I still cannot believe that Clive hired Helen Forrest to sing! I've never heard of something more romantic, even in all the novels I've read. I had hoped that I might have more dances with Stanley, but it turns out I spent more time with Lieutenant Barnes-Smith, or Harrison, as he has asked me to call him. Indeed, I believe Stanley got into a bit of a scuffle in the parking lot over some friend of yours named Rose, whom, he told me, was in trouble.

At this point in the letter, Henrietta rubbed her eyes wearily before continuing.

I had not seen Stanley these many long weeks since the wedding until just yesterday, but I will get to that in a minute—as it is my main purpose in writing to you. Harrison, on the other hand, has been to see me a number of times to inquire after the state of my ankle, which I inadvertently twisted (did you know?) at the end of the reception. Luckily,

Harrison was nearby at the time to come to my aid and to help me and Ma get into one of the cars. Harrison has been quite a chum, really, coming to see me and making me laugh. I know what you're thinking, Henrietta, that I should not have received him without a chaperone, but Ma was upstairs and there are always servants hovering around, so I didn't think it would be so terribly improper, though I know Mrs. Hutchings would have said so. I have gone walking in the park with him on a number of occasions now, and find I enjoy his company very much and feel he has been wronged in many ways. Aunt Agatha has warned me that he is quite bad news, but I don't find him so at all.

But I am getting ahead of myself. Let me start again. It all began when Aunt Agatha had me to tea shortly after the wedding. She suggested that I come and stay with them, for extended periods of time, to which I could not agree. (What would happen to Ma and the boys and, of course, Doris, if I did that?) She informed me in no uncertain terms that it was Grandfather Exley's express wish that I come out into society to make a good match and that I must stay with Uncle John and Aunt Agatha to that end, as Mrs. Hutchings didn't work out. Under immense pressure (you believe me, don't you, Hen?) I agreed to come for a part of each week rather than abandon Ma completely. I expected Ma to rant and rave when I finally got up the courage to tell her, but instead she just gave a little gesture like a shrug and went back to her magazine. To tell the truth, Hen, I am very worried about her. She spends almost all day in her room. The pills that Dr. Lawson gave us help her, but she is very lethargic all day, as if she doesn't care about anything anymore. Not that she ever did before, but at least she would argue now and again. For the life of me, I never thought I would list her indifference as a good thing. Now she does nothing and seems to have no opinion on anything. I confess I am at my wit's end and don't know what to do.

But again, I am digressing. As I was saying, I have gone to stay with Aunt Agatha and Uncle John just one time so far and found that it wasn't so bad as I expected. They took me to see Twelfth Night, which I dearly loved. They are quite kind, actually, and tell me that I am to have a coming-out ball in the spring and are most anxious to introduce me to various young men.

And this is the terrible flaw in this whole arrangement—I am to give up Stanley, whom they say is unsuitable! At first this caused me great distress, as you can well imagine, and I resolved to hold on to him despite all. The problem, however, was that I had not actually seen Stanley, as I mentioned, in these weeks since the wedding. I determined, then, after Aunt Agatha's injunction to me to give him up, to seek him out no matter how brazenly bold that might appear so that I could be reassured of our mutual understanding before walking into the fire for him, as it were. Accordingly, I went to the electrics just yesterday and tried to time it for his shift's end, so that I might catch him as he came out, not wanting to go to his house and have to face his mother. I suppose I could have used the telephone, but I just couldn't bring myself to do it. I waited, then, outside the gate, and—oh, Hen—I can hardly write this—I finally saw him. I started to wave, but then I saw none other than this Rose, whom I mentioned at the beginning of this letter, come up to him from another direction and take his arm. And then—then she gave him a kiss on the cheek as they walked down the street together! They did not necessarily seem all that romantic, but how can this be explained any other way? It brought tears to my eyes, and, I confess, it has done on many occasions since. Oh, Hen! What am I to do? Perhaps I should do what everyone wants me to do and give him up, but the thought of it makes my heart clench. Still, another part of me is terribly distressed—shall I even say, angry?—to have seen him as such! Perhaps he is not the man I thought he was . . .

Meanwhile, I seem to have the opposite problem with

Harrison. I only meant to be friendly with him, but he seems to grow more attached each day, much to my distress. He is gorgeously handsome, I'll admit, which makes me a bit uneasy, really, as I feel I am so far beneath his notice. Be honest, Hen! I can't imagine what he finds attractive about me, and Aunt Agatha says he is clearly after the Exley money and that he has engaged himself to several young ladies in the past in the hopes of securing an easy life, is how she described it. She would be beside herself if she knew I walk in the park with him sometimes, but when I confronted him (I did, Hen! Aren't you proud?) about these engagements, he says that those are ugly, unfounded rumors that he has ever been the subject of, though he knows not why. He had a very sad and lonely boyhood, Hen, and I feel quite sorry for him. He says that he is frequently misunderstood by people and that he is not the villain people imagine him to be. Oh, Hen, I quite agree with him. If only people got to know him, they would see what a nice, honorable gentleman he really is. He told me the whole sad story of himself and a Miss Stewart, of which much misunderstanding abounds. I will not go into all of that here, but suffice it to say he was quite innocent of any wrongdoing!

So you see, Hen, I am quite at a loss as to what to do next. I thought I loved Stanley, but now I am not so sure. If I am honest, I must concede that he loved you first, not me, and that I was a sort of consolation prize for him. It cuts me to the quick to write it, but I cannot see any other explanation. My mind unfortunately wonders if you had a hand in encouraging him in this, but I realize I am being unfair to you, that you would never have done such a thing.

Henrietta bit her lip.

Meanwhile, Harrison seems to find my company interesting, and I his, but I am not to see him, and I'm sure grandfather would never permit him to court me, should he even want to, which I realize is awfully presumptuous on my part to even suppose.

As for everything else, it is going as well as can be expected, I guess. We have still no letter from Eugene, though I have heard from Aunt Agatha, who has heard it from Grandfather, that he is progressing well and that his commanding officers think highly of him. Ma I have already reported on. Eddie and Herb continue at school, though Eddie has been getting into more and more fights, and Herb has been sick again. Jimmy asks about you daily. I saw Mr. and Mrs. Hennessey at Mass last week, and they always ask after you as well. They have had some happy news. Their daughter it seems is going to have a baby, though she lives quite far away, as I understand it. Still, they were very happy and went on and on about it, as you can imagine. They send their love.

I must close this letter now, as it is quite thick and will be expensive to post all the way to England, though I suppose that isn't a worry for us anymore, is it? Still, old habits are hard to break, though I guess they weren't for you. I try to be like you, Henrietta, but I find it hard. Perhaps Stanley is just a form of old habit himself, not the love I once thought? And how should I proceed with Harrison? I do not wish to end our friendship, though I feel this would be the most proper thing to do, but I am often lonely, despite my visits to Aunt Agatha, and he makes me laugh. I would welcome any advice you have to offer, that is if you have any time to spare among all of the lovely parties you are surely attending. What is the library like? I'm sure it is immense! I hope that Clive is proving to be a kind husband and that you are happy. Please give him my love.

Your loving sister,
Elsie

Henrietta folded the letter and looked out the window with a sigh. Steaks of sunshine were trying their best to break through the autumn gray. How had things progressed so quickly? she wondered. And what was she to do with this mess? What *could* she do? She wished she were not an ocean away; clearly Elsie needed help and advice, something she should have been giving her all along. She felt like such a thoughtless, inattentive sister, unaware as to what was happening in Elsie's life, and yet when she left, she had thought everything was fine between Elsie and Stan; indeed, she had been expecting an announcement from them, especially given what Elsie had told her in whispered exchanges from time to time.

How dare Stan! she fumed as she stood up and began to pace around her bedchamber now. What was he thinking? Didn't he know that Rose was a lesbian? And what was Rose playing at? Meeting him after work and kissing him on the cheek? Something wasn't right, she mused, as she stopped pacing and took hold of one of the bedposts. She remembered then what Lucy had told her about some women subduing their true feelings for the sake of getting a husband and family. Or that some women were just experimenting. But had she meant experimenting with women, or experimenting with men? And to what purpose? And could women—or men, for that matter, uncomfortably thinking of Eugene—really change their inclinations? Perhaps through medical treatment or even prayer? Or was it just a state of mind? Henrietta wasn't sure and resolved to ask Lucy the next time she saw her. But why Stan? Was he Rose's target for a husband and family? Didn't she know he was Elsie's? She didn't think Rose would knowingly betray her after all they had been through at the Marlowe. Perhaps Elsie misunderstood what she saw? But why *had* Stan stayed away so long? Was he jealous of Barnes-Smith? Henrietta could definitely see that, but still. His normal reaction would have been to confront the issue with his inflated ego, not slink away in surrender.

And that was another thing. What about the lieutenant? From Elsie's description, she seemed to unwittingly be his latest conquest if

Henrietta was reading correctly between the lines, which actually distressed her more than the debacle with Stan. Elsie's reputation could easily be ruined by him, she knew, or worse. Henrietta enjoyed Major Barnes-Smith's company and did not dissuade Clive from asking him to be his best man, but she did not particularly like his nephew. She had seen this type before, very charming on the surface but with faulty manners that were somehow greasy. The type that was always on the lookout for the next opportunity and, much as she didn't want to admit it, Aunt Agatha was probably right, he was probably after what he assumed would be a large Exley dowry. Regardless, he was obviously toying with Elsie's sweet nature and compassion.

And what of this arrangement Agatha and John were forcing upon poor Elsie? It was obvious to Henrietta that Mr. Exley Sr. meant to use Elsie to make a good match, as she herself had done by marrying into the Howards, a particularly sweet coup for Mr. Exley Sr., though he had obviously not had anything to do with bringing it about. Who knew what or who he had in mind for Elsie. How dare they demand Elsie to give up Stan! Henrietta had worked hard to bring them together; they were perfect for each other, that was obvious! And yet, they seemed to be coming apart now of their own accord . . . Oh, Stan! she fumed again. This was clearly his fault; how could he be so stupid to give up the one woman who truly loves him for a . . . a lesbian?

Slowly she roused herself from her disjointed thoughts. Again she wished she wasn't so far away. Clearly she would have to get a letter off as soon as possible. She considered ringing for Phoebe, but for what purpose she wasn't sure. She didn't need to change just yet if she were staying in her room to write. She supposed she just wanted someone to talk to, but Phoebe was not Edna, nor was she Elsie, for that matter. And the one she really desired to talk with, she realized with an irritated sniff as she sat at the little desk arranged neatly by the other window, was at the moment beyond her reach and apparently did not wish for her to join his conversation.

—

As Clive accompanied Lord Linley into the study, he tried to keep his mind clear. He missed detective work more than he had thought he would, and he could not help feeling more than just slightly interested in the case before them. He reminded himself, though, that it was not his case and that the local constabulary would most probably resent any help he might offer, anyway. Besides, he wasn't so sure how much help he would really be, having lost some of his confidence after the last two cases. But that was because they had also involved Henrietta, he countered with himself, and he had been biased in his assessment of the details and the level of the threat. Still, he could not help feeling unsure of his abilities as he walked into the study, but he was determined to hide his misgivings.

Inspector Hartle was standing in the middle of the room, hat in hand, swirling it lazily with his finger while he peered at some of the masterpieces on the wall. When he saw Lord Linley enter, he approached him with just the required amount of deference, but no more, and reached out his hand to shake that of his superior.

"Detective Chief Inspector John Hartle at your service, Lord Linley. I'm very sorry for the disturbance. I hope I didn't call you away from your breakfast."

"Not at all. Quite understandable, eh? Given the circumstances, that is." He turned to Clive and gestured toward him. "This is Mr. Clive Howard, my nephew. Lives in America, but we won't hold that against him, will we, Inspector? Heh, heh!"

John Hartle's upper lip curled up in a kind of polite attempt at a smile.

"As it happens, we're his first stop on his wedding trip," Lord Linley continued. "I asked him to step in, though, if you don't mind."

"That's all very well, my lord. But a solicitor won't be needed. We're just making the rounds, wondering if anyone has seen anything suspicious."

"Solicitor?" Lord Linley queried and then laughed. "No, by Jove! He's not a solicitor, he's a detective inspector of the Chicago police!"

"Former," Clive added quickly.

At this bit of information, Hartle examined Clive more closely, though he kept any emotion from his face.

Detective John Hartle was a short man with close-cropped, graying hair and a gray mustache. Half of him was illuminated by the sun, weak though it was coming in through the large east windows, which revealed at least one side of his face to be deeply pockmarked. The other half of him was in shadow. He looked to Clive to be about in his fifties, but there was an air of youthfulness to him. His gray-blue eyes were very astute and keen. He was obviously able to handle himself well with the aristocracy, but Clive sensed he did not suffer fools gladly.

"Well, we'll have to make sure we're on our toes, then," Hartle said slowly. "You'll find we do things a bit differently than in the States, I'm afraid, Mr. Howard."

"Murder is murder, though, is it not?" Clive responded with a slight incline of his head. He stuck out his hand then to shake. "Not to worry, though, Detective Chief Inspector," Clive said, making sure to use the man's full title. "I don't mean to interfere. But if you need any help, I'm yours for the asking."

"Thank you, Mr. Howard," the inspector said dismissively. "I'll let you know."

Lord Linley cleared his throat. "Shall we sit down?" he suggested, gesturing toward the leather chairs by the fire. "No need to stand up like cattle!"

Clive and the inspector dutifully moved toward the chairs.

"Scotch, Chief Inspector?"

"Not for me, Lord Linley," Hartle answered, barely able to conceal his glance at the walnut clock on the mantelpiece.

"Clive?"

"No, Uncle. I've not yet had breakfast, shamefully. We were up rather late last night, I'm afraid."

Lord Linley pulled the servants' bell. "Tea it is, then."

"Yes, let's start there, shall we?" Inspector Hartle said, taking a notebook from his pocket. "You were up late, you say?" he asked Clive.

"Yes, we were having a dinner party, bit of a celebration. Clive's just married, you see," Lord Linley answered for him.

"Hmmm." The inspector scribbled away.

Stevens knocked then and entered silently. "You rang, my lord?"

"Tea, Stevens,"

"Very good, my lord," he said adroitly and disappeared.

"Why don't you tell us what happened?" Clive asked.

Inspector Hartle looked at him curiously. "All in good time, Mr. Howard. As it is, *I'm* asking the questions."

"Yes, of course. I beg your pardon," Clive responded.

The inspector looked at him to assess whether he was being sarcastic, but, seemingly convinced for the moment that he was sincere, he continued. "House party?"

"Yes," Lord Linley answered.

"All the guest staying here? Not at the Inn?"

"Well, most of them," Lord Linley added and proceeded to relate the names of all of the guests staying at Castle Linley as well as the local families that had gone home in their motorcars.

"Notice anything unusual?"

"Not that I can say," Lord Linley said thoughtfully. "It would have been difficult to notice, what with the music and all."

"Notice anyone coming or going?" Inspector Hartle asked Lord Linley, causing Clive to suddenly remember then how Wallace had disappeared across the grounds in the night and likewise how Captain Foley had stayed outside for a rather long time before Clive had noticed him sneak back in and join the card table, much to Clive's particular annoyance, as Foley was clearly already in debt.

"Not that I know of . . ." Lord Linley answered absently.

"You?" he asked Clive.

"Not that I can recall," Clive lied easily before he had time to think. Why did he want to keep this information to himself? "There were a lot of people mingling about, Chief Inspector."

"What about the servants? Might I have a word with them later?

They might have noticed something you didn't in all of the *excitement* of the party." Clive heard the sarcasm in his voice. Hadn't he himself used it often enough in the inspector's position?

"I say, Inspector! It's going a bit too far now. Are we suspected of something? If you wish to involve the household, you'd better tell me now just what's going on!"

Hartle acquiesced. "All right, then, a man was murdered in the village last night."

"Yes, we know that bit!"

"Can you give us some of the details, Chief Inspector?" Clive asked calmly.

Inspector Hartle looked at Clive for a few moments as if deciding whether or not to share any information. He finally seemed to reach a decision and eased back into the chair, resting his hat on his knee.

"We don't know much, really," he exhaled deeply.

A footman entered then with a large tray holding the usual tea accoutrements as well as a plate of biscuits.

"Thank you, Fennington," Lord Linley said, as the servant set it down carefully on the low table between them. Fennington gave a brief bow and dutifully disappeared while Clive leaned forward to pour out the tea.

"Do you have a name?" Clive asked as he offered the inspector a cup, which Hartle declined with a wave of his hand.

"Not for me, thanks. We do. He was one Ernest Jacobs of London, apparently. Wallet was still on him, but no money. We are in the process of tracing the address in his wallet to see where it leads us."

"How did he die?"

"Blow to the head. Heavy object of some kind, like a branch or a club perhaps. Maybe a walking stick. He was seen at the Horse and Coach until about eleven, maybe eleven thirty. Stumbled outside and got about five hundred yards down the lane before he was set upon and killed."

"What's the innkeeper say?"

"Says he came in about six o'clock off the London train. London accent. Tongue got loose as the night wore on, drinking gin apparently, said he was up looking at some property for the estate agents he worked for."

"Why would they be interested in property in Matlock?"

The inspector inclined his head approvingly at Clive's line of questioning.

"Did he have a room?"

Another inclination of the inspector's head. "Not at the Horse and Coach. Said he was staying with a relative and wandered off."

"Any case or bag with him?"

"Innkeeper said he had a little carpet bag and a black attaché case with him."

"What time did he leave? Eleven, you said?"

"Thereabouts, the innkeeper says. Well and truly full of drink by then."

"Simple robbery?"

The inspector shrugged. "Seems that way. Hopefully the London address will tell us more. He had a wedding ring on, so maybe there's a wife somewhere."

"Do you have a list of names of who was in the pub?"

"Pretty much. Checking on that as we speak," Hartle said, fingering his hat. He looked steadily at Lord Linley with a piercing gaze before he continued. "I should tell you now, my lord," he paused again. "One of them was your son, Wallace Howard, and he was seen leaving just after eleven."

Lord Linley stared at him, incredulous for a moment before he exploded. "That's preposterous, Inspector! There must be some mistake! He was here the whole time! I saw him!"

"Be that as it may, your lordship, three people identified him. He must have left the party at some point."

"It doesn't make him the murderer, though, Chief Inspector," Clive said evenly.

"No, it doesn't, but why would the Honorable Wallace Howard be sneaking about the countryside and frequenting the village pub when there's a house party unfolding at Castle Linley, where I'm sure his presence is not only welcomed but required? After all, it was a party celebrating his cousin's wedding, didn't you say?" The inspector let his eyes rest on Clive, who, in turn, carefully kept his face and his own suspicions hidden.

"Is he here?" the inspector asked of Lord Lindley after a pause, though he kept his eyes on Clive.

"Of course he's here! What are you suggesting, man?" boomed Lord Linley.

"May I speak with him?" he asked, turning his gaze to the older man, now.

Lord Linley seemed on the verge of refusing Hartle when Clive interrupted.

"I think it would be best, Uncle Montague."

"Oh, very well, but this is a bloody waste of time. You are trespassing dreadfully on my patience, Inspector. I'll not have my son accused in my own home!"

"No one's accusing anyone, Lord Linley," the inspector said with an arched eyebrow. "He simply may be able to help us identify anyone suspicious or even give us some clues as to the dead man."

Clive knew a bluff when he saw one, but he said nothing while Lord Linley rang for Stevens.

"Yes, my lord?" Stevens said, stepping in with amazing speed as if he were, for example, listening close by.

"Would you be so kind as to ask Mr. Wallace to attend us?"

"I'm afraid that is impossible, my lord. His valet, Compton, informed me this morning that Mr. Wallace did not come to bed last night at all. Indeed, he's not anywhere to be found."

Chapter 15

S tan shifted uncomfortably in his chair at the Green Mill, where he sat very close to Rose, and gratefully reached out and took the glass of beer handed to him by Gwen. He and Rose had already danced to four songs now, and he needed a break. Dancing was not his forte, nor was it a particularly enjoyable diversion, and yet he had agreed to come along. As he looked out over the dance floor, he wasn't exactly sure how he had gotten himself into this position, not that it was bad, necessarily, he mused, as he glanced over at Rose, laughing now at something Lucy had just said to her.

He had never been inside the Green Mill before and was surprised at how dim it was and how it gave off an air of seediness that he couldn't quite explain. He had heard that Al Capone had frequented this place in the past, and he couldn't help looking over his shoulder every now and then, even though Capone and most of his gang had been locked away in Alcatraz for several years now. He couldn't quite put his finger on what made him so uneasy—maybe it was because the lights all gave off a red glow, or maybe it was the scantily clad waitresses, or perhaps it had something to do with the slow seductive jazz that the band seemed to prefer rather than the big band hits he was used to. More than likely, it was some combination of all three.

Rose had asked him to come along with them, and he couldn't understand why the girls would choose such an establishment in the first place. He wondered what Lucy and Gwen's husbands would think if they knew and decided that they must be awfully understanding, that or perhaps they didn't know. Stan had asked on more than one occasion why they never brought their husbands along on any of their nights out, and they had just giggled and said that their "fellas" were working. It was obvious to Stan that Lucy and Gwen were very good friends, having frequently caught them leaning very close to each other and whispering things in each other's ear. And once—just tonight, as a matter of fact—he could have sworn that he saw Lucy rub Gwen's arm, and—if he didn't know better—he would have said it seemed more like a caress than anything, but he was obviously mistaken there. It must be the dim light or the copious number of beers he had already consumed. He hadn't meant to drink this much, but Gwen was always handing him a fresh drink, which bothered him for more than one reason, actually. As a man, he shouldn't be accepting drinks paid for by a woman! And yet they kept appearing.

In an odd way, however, it was precisely because of Lucy and Gwen's close relationship that Stan had gotten involved, if one could call it that, with Rose in the first place. Not only did Lucy and Gwen have husbands, but they had each other as well. It hadn't taken Stan long to observe that Rose was the odd one out in this threesome. Ever since he had accompanied her to the maintenance shed to deliver her brother's lunch (no—actually, it went all the way back to Henrietta's wedding!), he had felt sorry for this poor girl, who apparently had no other friend in the world, well, except Lucy and Gwen, and, in Stan's opinion, anyway, they weren't very good friends, often leaving Rose to her own devices, sometimes only in the company of some other girl to find her own way home after an evening out. Stan couldn't bear the thought of her making her way home from the Melody Mill at night, fretting about her dimwitted brother and having to go home to her probably drunken father. It tore at his heart, it did, and he didn't know why. Surely there were plenty of girls out there that fit this same bill, and he obviously couldn't follow each one of them home every night, nor protect all of them. In fact, he could barely keep up with Rose.

He had somehow fallen into the habit of arriving at the Melody Mill on the nights she was working—or on as many as he could manage, anyway—so that he could walk her safely home. In the weeks that had followed since he met her, he had come to genuinely enjoy her company, so that what had initially started out as a benevolent duty on his part had now become something, he had to admit, that he looked forward to. Even at the wedding, Rose had reminded him of someone, and as the weeks progressed he realized, with not a little trace of shame, that she reminded him in some strange way of Henrietta. She looked different, of course, but she had that same vivaciousness, that same—gumption, would he call it?—for life. She had an independent streak, like Henrietta, but she seemed much more willing to rely on him, to need him, to expect him to help her, and, he had to confess, it was beginning to be very attractive to him. It was exciting to have this new friendship, as he liked to call it, and yet it made him feel wretched at the same time. He knew his feelings for Rose were crossing over into a more amorous state than mere friendship, and he was not a free man, was he? He knew his allegiance lay with Elsie, and yet he could see now, with utter regret, that he just didn't feel the same way about her.

He felt terrible about it, but it was true. Try as he might—at first to please Henrietta and then because he genuinely felt sorry for Elsie herself—he had tried to love Elsie. And he *did* love her, in a certain way, but not in *that* way. She was just too . . . what word would describe her best? Plain? Plain and needy, he supposed would be the best choice of words. Not needy in the way that Rose was needy. That was different somehow. Elsie felt more like a sister to him, if he was honest. And anyway, now that she was rich, apparently, and locked up in a fancy house on Palmer Square, she seemed all the more removed from him. Let's face it, he had told himself over and over as he stood on the line at the electrics, analyzing the situation exhaustively, Elsie was a sweet girl, but she never got his heart racing the way Henrietta had or, truth be told, the way Rose was beginning to.

He knew that he needed to have a serious talk with Elsie, but every time he worked up the required courage, usually with the help of a couple of swigs of whiskey (a beverage which, he noted happily, Rose did not seem to mind his drinking in the least), to call on her, she was out—either staying with her new aunt and uncle, Karl had told him when he sleepily opened the door to Stan, or supposedly walking in the park. The second time Karl had offered the walking-in-the-park excuse, Stan noted the nervous shifting of his eyes and, putting two and two together, was having none of it and demanded to know in whose company she walked.

"I don't think it's proper to say, sir," Karl had said hesitantly, obviously knowing full well what side his bread was buttered on as he backed himself up against the front door of the Palmer Square house in response to Stan's threatening steps toward him.

"I don't care what's proper, Karl; you're going to tell me," Stan said, pointing a finger at Karl's concave chest, wincing at the realization that in so doing he maddeningly reminded himself of none other than Inspector Howard. Promptly, he thrust his hands in his pockets.

"Oh, all right," Karl said wearily now that he was not being immediately threatened. "She's with the lieutenant." This revelation, plus the fact that said person was referred to so casually by the household staff, was alarming to Stan.

"Where'd they go?"

"I wouldn't know, sir. He said something about sailing, I think," Karl said with a small shrug.

Sailing! Stan thought, infuriated. How dare that rascal take her sailing! This seemed to go beyond a friendly walk in the park! Who did he think he was, obviously taking advantage of a girl like Elsie? And, come to think of it, why had Elsie agreed to go along? he wondered as he slowly turned to retreat down the stone front steps of the Palmer Square house. Obviously she must have felt trapped and obligated, and he became even more infuriated.

"Should I tell her you called?" Karl asked listlessly.

"Don't bother!" Stan said with a toss of his hand. "I'll come back."

Stan felt Rose's hand on his arm now, startling him from his thoughts. Lucy and Gwen had disappeared somewhere, and Rose, leaning toward him to be heard over the band, asked him if he would take her home now, that she was tired, she said, as she snuffed out her cigarette. Stan did not like the fact that Rose smoked. He thought it quite unladylike and had questioned her about it early on in their acquaintance. Rose had merely laughed at him and carried on just as she wished.

Stan, also eager to leave, stood up adroitly at her request and looked around, annoyed, for any sign of Gwen and Lucy but was unsuccessful, as usual. They were always doing this! Always disappearing somewhere. Rose had told him often enough not to let it bother him, but he could not help thinking that it was terribly inconsiderate and possibly dangerous. What if he weren't here, for instance? What would Rose do then, all on her own? Carefully, he wove through the crowd, trying not to knock anyone's drink or inadvertently bump into anyone—not particularly desiring a fight. Rose squeezed along behind him.

Once outside, the icy wind hit them head-on. It was welcome at first after the sultry heat inside the club, but as they began to walk, they quickly grew cold. Rose wrapped her scarf around her tighter. Stan could see that she was shivering and contemplated putting his arm around her to warm her further but then thought better of it. He didn't want her to get the wrong idea, after all.

When they finally arrived at her little brick bungalow, there was only one light on upstairs. Stan thought he saw someone looking out the window, but when he looked again, whoever it was was gone. He was pretty sure it had been Billy.

"Want to go in and make sure everything's all right?" Stan asked, referring, of course, to her father. A routine had already sprung up between them that consisted of Stan waiting outside on the sidewalk while Rose went in to make sure her father wasn't in a particularly violent mood. If he was, the two of them would simply continue walking around the block or would go and get a cup of coffee, now that the weather had turned colder, until Rose was sure that enough time had elapsed for her father to have passed out.

"Nah, it's okay. Billy's home tonight." Billy indeed served as a sort of protector of her, mindless though he was, never allowing their father to harm her in any way, she had said, well, physically at least. Mr. Whitman was a big man himself, but when intoxicated, he seemed to cower in front of Billy. His revenge, however, was to lash Billy with his tongue, calling him every form of known obscenity during these altercations. Billy never seemed to mind the violent barrage of words hurled at him, though, or, if he did, he didn't show it, but just made his slow way upstairs to his room, where he whittled small animals from scraps of wood he stole from the electrics.

"All right," Stan said somewhat wistfully. "Goodnight, then."

Normally at this point, Rose would disappear quickly into the house, but tonight she lingered in front of Stan as if waiting for something, though Stan couldn't imagine what it was. He always tried to avoid looking into her eyes, as if that were some sort of betrayal of Elsie in and of itself, but tonight she seemed to take him off his guard and he found himself staring at her big green eyes, mesmerized. He felt his heart speed up for some reason and, despite the cold, his hands felt warm and clammy. He was so desperately confused. He had an overwhelming desire to kiss her, *really* kiss her as he had seen in the movies, and the strain of resisting caused him to let out a deep breath and look away.

Rose reached out a hand then and turned his face back to her. Slowly she leaned forward and kissed him. Lightly at first and then harder. It was his very first kiss ever, and she tasted of something sweet, something delightfully fresh, like candy.

"Do you like it?" she whispered, her lips still dangerously near his, and she kissed him again, this time allowing the tip of her tongue to gently touch his.

Stan felt his whole body go rigid in reaction, and he awkwardly put his arms around her, wanting more of this delicious sensation. The passion that was coming alive in him, however, sent out warning bells, and he shortly pulled himself from her grasp, breathing heavily.

"I . . . I shouldn't be doing this, Rose," he said apologetically, almost frantically.

"Do you really have someone else?" Rose said, her eyes looking like big, sad pools of water. "Lucy says you do."

"Sort of, yes . . ."

She ran her hand down his back and he suddenly felt himself quiver. "Is it all that serious?" she asked.

His mind suddenly went blank as he felt her hands creep lower. They were on his lower back now. He tried to think. *Was* it serious?

"I mean . . . you never seem to spend any time with her . . ."

That was true, he was able to reason for a mere second or two, thinking again of Elsie's many absences when he called on her and, worse, her apparent sailing date with Barnes-Smith. What kind of a name was that, anyway?

But his thoughts were abruptly curtailed when he felt her hands ever so faintly come to rest on his buttocks, causing several things inside him to explode. Where was the demure Rose he had come to know? he wondered briefly, but right now he didn't care. He felt wildly attracted to her and enormously grateful that they weren't pressed tightly together so that she wouldn't observe his excited state. Oh, God, why couldn't he think? He looked at her again as if for direction, and when he saw her big green eyes again, he lost all control and grabbed her to him, kissing her fiercely, though it was a bit more awkward than he had hoped. Why did it look so glamorous in the movies? Sobering suddenly, he pulled himself away.

"No, Rose. I . . . I shouldn't be doing this. I . . . I'm supposed to be engaged soon."

"Engaged?" she said with what might have been pretend hurt. "It doesn't seem like it to me. Are you sure?" she asked seductively, running a finger along his clean-shaven cheek. (He always considered himself lucky that no ugly stubble ever appeared on his cheeks as each day wore on. Boys at school had always seemed so proud of their scratchy hairs, but not him. He preferred his smooth skin.) He felt his insides melt at her touch.

"Because I could have really cared for you, I think," she said as she kissed him softly on the lips again. Before he could say or do anything more, though, she turned and disappeared into the house, leaving him hot and fuming on the frozen, deserted sidewalk.

The very next morning, a Sunday, as it turned out, he was determined to have it out with Elsie. Obviously they could not go on this way. Well, *he* could not go on this way. He had hardly slept a wink last night. He simply could not get the memory of Rose's lips on his, of her hands on his . . . well, on his body . . . out of his head, re-envisioning the scene outside her house over and over. In the dark depths of the night as he lay staring at the ceiling of his bedroom, it had made perfect sense for him to split with Elsie. It seemed inevitable, really. He realized now how very much he liked Rose, with her pretty hair and long legs, so graceful in every way and usually so ladylike, last night being an exception. (But such a nice one!) She was kind at times and witty, he ticked off on his fingers, and she liked hearing about his work at the electrics and his model airplane collection. And look how patient she was with Billy. For all of his faults, Billy was an okay guy, Stan assessed. Better than Eugene, really. He had never actually met Rose's father, but he had heard him before, swearing inside the house as Stan waited on the sidewalk. That was a bit of an obstacle, Stan worried, but wouldn't it be so much better for Rose if he could get her out of that situation? He assumed her mother was dead, as Rose never spoke of her.

Speaking of mothers, Stan thought, as he rolled over on his side, what would his own mother say if he threw over Elsie for Rose? He and his parents had all discussed, many times—usually over his mother's pot roast or some other equally delicious dinner—his prospects with Elsie, and they had jointly decided that she would make a good addition to the Dubowski family. Even his mother had begun to like her despite the fact that she was a Von Harmon and obviously came from deficient stock, not liking to speak openly of what the whole neighborhood called the father's cowardly, sinful act. And now that Elsie was well-connected and living in Palmer Square, his mother had been all the more accepting of her and had irksomely begun to inquire every other day or so as to Elsie's well-being, charitably willing now to put the past, or Mr. Von Harmon's past, rather, behind them. In fact, Stan was pretty sure that his mother assumed he was out with Elsie most of the time when really he had become consumed of late with dogging Rose. His mother would grow to love Rose as well, though, he was convinced. How could she not? There was so much more of her to love, and he again recalled the incident on the sidewalk one more time in his feverish mind.

But how, he wondered nervously, as he determinedly marched down Dickens toward Palmer Square, cutting across Humboldt Boulevard to save time, would he break it to Elsie? How could he explain to the poor kid that he had fallen in love with someone else? As he walked, another unnerving realization made its way up to his conscious mind. He understood clearly now that if he gave up Elsie, he would no longer have any reason to be near Henrietta, that his connection to her would be well and truly severed. But wasn't that for the best? he thought as he angrily kicked a rather large stone out of his path.

Stan did not perhaps have the wherewithal to completely analyze his feelings, but he certainly was able to feel that something had died inside him the day of her wedding, the final nail being her and the inspector's kiss on the altar and the priest announcing them as Mr. and Mrs. Clive Howard and watching her beaming face as she had walked down the aisle on his arm. Before then he had enjoyed believing that Howard had somehow beguiled or deceived her, had somehow made her an offer she couldn't refuse and that she had somehow offered herself up as some sort of sacrificial lamb, but he knew, sadly, as he watched her face that day, that it was no sacrifice on her part, that she truly loved him. And after that, if he was honest, the luster of his feeling for Elsie, already a bit dim in comparison to what he felt for her dazzling sister, dimmed further, then, almost beyond recognition.

No, he thought resolutely now, it would be better for him to give up the Von Harmons entirely. Henrietta was gone and there was no changing that, and Elsie, he supposed, had never really had a claim on his heart. The thought of her devastation when he told her, however, nearly crippled him as he climbed the steps of the house now. How could he explain it to her? And what would Henrietta say when she found out? But what did he care? he told himself angrily. He paused before knocking, taking a deep breath, his courage nearly leaving him completely. He wasn't sure he could actually go through with this and found himself hoping that she might be out after all. But no, he said, gathering himself up straight and boldly taking the brass knocker in hand and forcing images of Rose to the forefront of his mind. It had to be done.

Chapter 16

Detective Chief Inspector Hartle had eventually departed from Castle Linley, but not before asking the rather distraught Lord Linley if he might further make use of his study to speak to Wallace's valet, Compton, and maybe one or two of the other servants or guests.

Lord Linley's temper had flared up, demanding that the police use their skills to find his missing son, not interview his household as to the murder of some unknown man in the village! Was their duty not to the living? he had challenged the inspector, not to the dead? The inspector, for his part, again rationally explained that the two might in the end be linked and that he felt relatively sure, given that it had come to light that this seemed to be a particular habit, albeit a mysterious one, of the Honorable Wallace Howard, he was therefore probably not in any great danger. Lord Linley had grumpily relented, then, and retired to his rooms, but not before instructing Stevens to assist the two gentlemen in his study by summoning Compton and any other personages they might request.

Once Lord Linley and Stevens had finally left, the inspector slowly paced the room, his hands behind his back, before sitting down at Lord Linley's desk as he waited for the valet to appear. Clive had remained as well, having not been specifically instructed to leave. He casually removed his pipe from his jacket pocket and lit it.

"Don't you have a sergeant, Chief Inspector?" he said through narrowed eyes as he puffed deeply to ignite the tobacco.

"I do. He's on an assignment just at the moment. Looking into the London connections of the dead man."

"I see."

The inspector eyed him. "But you'll do for today. If you've a mind to."

"I was under the impression that I already was."

Hartle's jaw shifted to the left. "But I'm doing the questioning," he said sternly.

There was a faint knock, then, at the door, and Stevens and a quivering Compton entered the room. The inspector asked him the routine questions, Clive listening closely, but little more was forthcoming than was already known—that Wallace had left the party at around ten o'clock, that, no, none of his things were missing, that, no, he did not know where he took himself off to, and that, yes, he often did this, Compton had reported, visibly trembling. Timorously, the servant suggested that he shouldn't think anything of it if he were the sirs in front of him now and that no harm had surely ever come from it before. The inspector had dismissed him eventually with a sigh, and Compton had hurriedly left.

As they waited for one of the gardeners to be brought in who claimed to have heard something in the night, the inspector eyed Clive once again. "And you say you didn't see anything?"

"I did see Wallace cross the grounds last night, yes, when I stepped out for a moment. About ten o'clock, just as Compton said. Didn't think anything of it, really. I'd seen him do it before."

"Were you ever planning on sharing that detail?" the inspector asked intently. "Are you working for me or against me, Mr. Howard? Something else you're not saying, perhaps?"

"I wasn't aware that I was working *for* anyone," Clive said evenly. He wanted to say more, but he held it in, not wanting to make an enemy of the inspector. "I had forgotten about it," he said, referring to the detail about Wallace. "I've only just remembered."

"That's handy," Hartle said, studying him closely for several moments. "Bit of a nutter, this Wallace?" he asked finally.

"No, I don't think so," Clive said thoughtfully, aware of what the inspector was doing—trying to momentarily distract him. "Maybe hiding something, but not a murderer," Clive suggested.

Hartle actually laughed. "They all say that; you of all people should know that by now."

Clive allowed only a small smile to escape. "I suppose you're right."

"See anything else while you were out there?" the inspector continued more seriously now, and Clive knew that he suspected that he was holding back. He hesitated about reporting Foley's short absence; after all, it was probably nothing. He had been gone for only about fifteen minutes, surely not enough time to get to the village pub, murder a man, and get back. There was something off there, however, but Clive was almost positive it was unrelated. Regardless, he didn't want to share it with the inspector just yet.

"Not that I can recall," Clive said nonchalantly, keeping the inspector's gaze.

A commotion could be heard outside the door now, the shrill voices of the Fairfax girls rising up.

"Me first, Sara! I want to be questioned first!"

"But I'm the oldest! Of course they'll want to speak to me first!"

Stevens knocked then and stepped in. "I beg your pardon, sirs, but two of the young ladies wish to be interviewed. They claim," he said with a disapproving sniff, "that they have something rather urgent to report."

"Show them in," the inspector sighed.

Miss Jane and Miss Sara Fairfax then rushed in, their faces both aglow—that is, until they saw the imposing figure of the inspector himself, which somehow caused them to slow their steps and become suddenly shy. After a few routine questions from Inspector Hartle, their flustered testimony was found to consist of reports of strange noises in the night, though the time said noises were heard varied widely with each retelling of the story, and never did the two ladies ever quite agree. Finally, the inspector thanked them for their help and himself walked them to the door, where he turned them over to an apologetic-looking Stevens. The inspector and Clive then saw the gardener, who had been patiently waiting in the hall all this time, as well as a few other servants, though nothing new came to light, most of their statements being of little interest and much the same.

The inspector eventually took his leave of Castle Linley with a decided air of reluctance, Clive suspecting that he was waiting around should Wallace suddenly reappear. But, he said, he could no longer afford to stay and had other leads to check up on. He had instructed Clive, as he carefully placed his hat back on his head, to inform Wallace, whenever he happened to turn up, that he should step down to the station in the village double quick to give his statement, or the inspector would be obliged to send his men round to fetch him.

Alone in the study now, Clive tried to collect his thoughts, wanting to lose no time in following up on his own suspicions. His first objective was to find Wallace, of course; his second was to find Foley and discover what he might know. It was past midday now—where the bloody hell could they have gone? Clive wondered. He hurried across the study, intent on beginning a real search, but as he passed through the heavy door leading out into the hall, he nearly tripped over Henrietta.

"Darling," he said, startled. "Whatever are you doing here?"

"I'm waiting for you, of course." She looked up at him now, and he could see she wanted to speak, but neither of them did. She bit her lip slightly, and he knew she was upset about something, but he hadn't the time just at present to fathom it out.

"I've had a letter from home," she said finally, breaking the stalemate.

Ah. That was it. "Oh?" he asked, trying to be interested, but he could feel his mind reverting back to the case. "Everything all right?"

"Well, not exactly . . ."

"Why am I not surprised?" he sighed. "Listen, darling, perhaps you might tell me about it later. I'm in a bit of a hurry just now."

"Oh. Yes, of course. How . . . how did it go? With the inspector, I mean?" she asked tentatively.

"Fine, I suppose. Seems a simple case of robbery to me. Still . . ." He broke off, a new thought occurring to him.

"Is it true that Wallace is missing?" Henrietta asked, breaking his concentration.

Clive looked at her keenly. "How did you know that?"

"Sara Fairfax."

Clive felt his initial alarm give way to mild aggravation. "I'm afraid he is, yes, but I really must speak with Captain Foley. Have you seen him, by chance?"

"I can't say that I have. I've been stuck up in our room writing letters all morning."

"Listen, darling," he went on hurriedly. "I know we were supposed to ride to the Heights this morning, but would you mind terribly if we did not? I really must get to the bottom of this."

"You can't keep from being the inspector, can you?" she smiled suggestively, reaching up to touch his cheek.

"A man's been murdered, Henrietta!" he said, pulling away. "And Wallace seems unfortunately to have been in the vicinity. It doesn't look good. Lord Linley's quite upset."

"Of course we don't have to go riding," she replied quietly as she lowered her hand.

Instantly he regretted being so forceful. He was just about to say so when she spoke again.

"Why don't I come with you?" she asked tentatively. "To look for Wallace or Captain Foley?"

"Darling," he said, trying to be patient as he took her hands. "I'd rather you didn't. It may not be safe. Why don't you stay here and join the ladies?"

She pulled her hands slowly from his, and he knew that he had truly upset her now.

"If that's what you wish," she said quietly.

"Henrietta, please . . . you've got to understand . . . I . . . I need to find Foley on a private matter."

"I see," she said and stood looking at him, her eyes boring into him. "Isn't it a bit soon to be having private matters?" she finally asked.

"What? No! My God, it's nothing like that. I . . . it's regarding a different matter. I'll explain later. I promise." As he searched her eyes now, he knew he was disappointing her, but it was for the best, for her own good. She would just have to understand.

"Very well," she said resolutely. "I'll walk into the village later and post my letters."

"Just give them to Stevens. There's no need to walk into town."

"I fancy a walk," she said coolly.

Now she was angry, he could see. How could she be so unreasonable? Didn't she see the bigger picture?

He exhaled deeply. "If you insist on walking, at least take someone with you. Perhaps Lady Winifred. Don't go alone."

She gave him a disparaging look. "Is that a command, Inspector?"

"Yes, it is," he tried to say gently. "Promise me, Henrietta. A man's been murdered, and I don't want you out on your own."

"Very well, Inspector Howard," she said coldly. "I won't."

She turned and left then, leaving him in turmoil. He was angry at what he perceived to be her willful misunderstanding of the situation, but he felt he had no choice. Well, he thought, as he turned in the other direction to find Foley, he would have to sort it out later.

Henrietta angrily pinned on her hat as she looked in the clouded mirror of the antique cherry vanity in their room, its thick legs carved with cherubs intertwined with leaves and small animals. The edges of the mirror were spotted with age, but Henrietta could still make out her image clearly enough. She stood up and placed her two letters, one to Elsie, of course, and one to Julia, in her handbag. She had written to Julia as the only person she could think of who might be able to guide Elsie while she was away and hopefully steer her clear of the lieutenant, if he was really as bad as Aunt Agatha had reported.

How dare Clive require her to stay behind! she thought as she turned sideways in the mirror to assess the tweed suit Phoebe had laid out for her. She had been willing to overlook this morning's slight at the breakfast table, but her inflammation flared up again now at this new sting. As if looking around the house and grounds for Captain Foley or Wallace was so very dangerous!

She was angry—but wretched, too. She had believed Clive when he told her that she was his equal, but it was clear, *again*, that she was not. He had done this before, hurt her, and then had promised that he wouldn't again. And yet here they were. She thought for sure he would have called her back to him when she walked away from him just now, but he had not. Her throat was still aching from holding in her tears as she had quickly climbed the stairs to seek solace in their room and to collect her things.

She picked up her gloves now, and, as she yanked them on, she angrily tried to force Clive and his insufferable behavior from her mind and to concentrate instead on Elsie and her sad woes. She had no idea how long it would take for her letter to reach her, but she hoped it would be in time for the advice she offered. Poor Elsie, she sighed, successfully forgetting her own troubles for the moment and resolving to take Elsie more in hand once she got home.

Henrietta made her way to the drawing room in search of a companion to walk into town with her, though she was tempted to go alone just to spite Clive. He was positively turning into an old woman! Jumping at every noise and worrying that someone might be after them, or at least her. It was becoming tiresome in the extreme.

She first asked Lady Winifred, but, after a questioning look to her mother, at which the countess gave an almost imperceptible shake of her head, Winifred politely declined, saying that she had the beginnings of another headache. Jane and Sara Fairfax, on the other hand, sitting nearby and having thus overheard her, excitedly volunteered to go.

"I thought you were going to play badminton," Henrietta pointed out.

"Well, we can't very well play with no partners. And it would be terribly dull with just the two of us," Jane said. "Besides, we've decided it's too damp for badminton."

"Yes, please, Mrs. Howard, let us go with you! I'm sure M'ma wouldn't mind," Sara implored.

"Oh, very well," Henrietta said, trying to force a smile. They weren't her ideal companions, nor would they have been Clive's choice of protectors, she knew, but that fact alone was enough to convince Henrietta. Besides, they were pleasant enough, and so Henrietta waited patiently in the foyer for them while they ran to get their hats.

The subsequent walk into Cromford on the path beside the main road was uneventful except for the delightful scenery they passed, though Henrietta found she could not enjoy it as much as she might, given the current state of her irritation. The Fairfax girls were light and bubbly as they walked, helping to distract her from obsessing on her two problems, which threatened to endlessly chase each other for dominance in her mind.

Henrietta shook herself and tried to concentrate on what the Fairfax girls were saying, marveling that they were actually older than her by a few years, as they seemed remarkably silly and immature. Most of their conversation consisted of discussing the eligible men at the reception last night, which accordingly produced a large amount of giggling between them. Sara, Henrietta soon gathered, had been quite smitten with the squire's son, a stalwart lad by the name of Albert Cooper, about whom Jane delighted in teasing her, adding with savored sternness that P'pa would never allow a marriage such as that, the Coopers being so much lower on the social scale.

"But he does have a lot of money!" Sara retorted, "Which might go far with P'pa."

"What a goose you're being, Sara," Jane said smugly. "He only danced with you; it's not as if he made a declaration!"

"Yes, but six times!" Sara managed.

"Only because there were so few gentlemen. Of course he was obliged to dance. He at least has fine manners, I'll give him that," said Jane begrudgingly.

"And what about Captain Russell, or even Captain Foley?" Sara added with a sly smile. "They both seemed quite attentive . . ."

"Don't be absurd, Sara! They're both too old for me. For the life of me, I'm not sure why Lady Linley asked them! I was hoping that Lord Devereaux would have been asked. He has three lovely *younger* sons."

"I suppose she didn't want any competition for Wallace."

"Oh, Wallace! She should give up on getting rid of him! He seems not the slightest bit interested in anyone she throws in front of him."

"If I didn't know you better, I'd think you sound bitter, Jane," Sara laughed.

"Don't be ridiculous! Who'd want Wallace Howard? He's an old curmudgeon!"

"Yes, but you'd get to be Lady Linley! All of this would be yours," Sara gestured widely.

"No, thank you!" Jane retorted. "Though M'ma would be terribly pleased, would she not?" she smirked. "I'm sure that's why we're here. But Lady Linley would stand a better chance marrying him to some rich Irish girl or possibly an American who doesn't know better! Oh! I do beg your pardon, Mrs. Howard."

Henrietta could not help but smile. She found their banter pleasantly amusing, made more so by the fact that they seemed not at all aware that the situation they were so easily deriding was very nearly hers.

"Say, Mrs. Howard, you don't have any rich friends back in America, do you? Or maybe a sister?"

Henrietta laughed. "You both seem decidedly keen to be rid of poor Wallace."

"Then we wouldn't have to come to Derbyshire so very often and be made to make pleasant conversation with him. It's dreadfully dull here. But M'ma and P'pa are quite in earnest, you know. Why won't he take up with Lady Winifred? She's more his age, anyway."

"Lady Winifred! You can't be serious, Jane. She's a dull dolt if I ever saw one!"

"But didn't you notice that she was the only one he danced with?"

"Only because he was obliged to, most probably."

"For shame, Sara! She's all right in herself when you get her away from her mother. Fancy having the Countess of Ashforth for your mother-in-law, though! No wonder Wallace runs the other way!" Jane laughed.

They had reached the village now, and Henrietta paused to take it all in. It was delightfully quaint, with white plaster buildings trimmed with dark, thick planks of wood. It was like something from a storybook, and Henrietta wished Elsie could be here to see it, too. It reminded her of the novels Elsie was always reading aloud to her, back when they lived on Armitage and shared a bed. Suddenly, Henrietta missed home very much. Somewhat wistfully, she looked over at the Fairfax girls but saw that their gaze had drifted to two men lounging outside what seemed to be a pub. "The Three Jugglers" was written on a thick wooden sign hanging from an ancient, weather-beaten pole.

"It's Captain Russell!" Sara whispered excitedly. "What's he doing here? I thought he had gone home this morning."

"Obviously he got diverted!" Jane said, giving the men, who were already making their way toward them, a little wave. "Or perhaps he has a secret!"

As the two men came up, they lifted their hats in deference. "Good afternoon, Mrs. Howard," Captain Russell said with a genuine smile. "What a pleasant surprise."

Captain Russell had asked her to dance several times last night, and Henrietta had been taken by his easy manners and charming repartee. His large dark eyes were his best feature, Henrietta had concluded, as he was not what one would call traditionally handsome. He had a large nose and a scar running down his cheek, and yet there was something about his manner that both charmed and soothed. She could quite easily understand why Jane Fairfax—despite her protestations to the contrary—might be attracted to him. The man standing next to him eyed the two girls shyly. He was very broad across the shoulders, with light brown hair and soft gray eyes, and he was dressed well, if not expensively. He had a pleasant, ruddy face to him.

The captain, perhaps observing her gaze, said quickly, "Where are my manners? May I present my cousin, Maxwell Fielding. This is Mrs. Howard, Miss Jane Fairfax, and Miss Fairfax," he said, nodding at each of them in turn.

"I'm delighted to make your acquaintance," Maxwell said. He spoke well, but his Derbyshire accent was thick, and Henrietta remembered that Captain Russell had said last night that he had family in this area. Obviously not wealthy or important enough to have been invited to Castle Linley, however, Henrietta noted.

"I thought you'd already left, Captain," she commented. Several of Wallace's friends had caught the early train back to London.

"You've quite found me out, I'm afraid, Mrs. Howard. I *did* leave Linley this morning, but I couldn't leave the area without stopping to see my aunt and uncle. They live in Matlock Bath. Country house parties are not really my game, present company excepted, of course," he said, looking at Jane briefly, which caused a blush to creep across the poor girl's face. "I only came as a favor to Wallace. That and to see Maxwell, of course, though I was delighted to find so pleasant a party assembled."

Henrietta smiled affably, and Sara stifled a giggle.

"I say, would you care to take tea with us?" he continued. "It seems a shame not to, given that fate seems to have thrown us together in this way, does it not?"

"Oh, no, Captain, we couldn't possibly impose on your time with your cousin. I'm sure it's very limited, indeed," Henrietta said, wanting to get to the post office and possibly some shops to buy some souvenirs for everyone back home. The last thing she wanted to do was to sit politely with Captain Russell and his cousin and make conversation.

"Not at all. I assure you, we would be improved by the company."

"Mrs. Simpson's down the street does a capital tea!" Maxwell suddenly put in eagerly.

"Max is just up from Oxford, revising," the captain explained. "So you must forgive his rather shameful use of the vernacular."

Henrietta smiled.

"He's the family scholar, you see," the captain went on, patting him jovially on the back. "Come now, what do you say? We'd be delighted if you'd join us."

"Oh, please, Mrs. Howard!" begged Sara.

"Yes, let's, Mrs. Howard!" said Jane. "We'll only be forced to play bridge if we return too early!"

The captain laughed. "A fate worse than death, poor girls."

Henrietta hesitated. It was obvious that the four of them wished to be together, though Henrietta couldn't think why, as the aging captain and his young cousin couldn't possibly be potential suitors, if Lord and Lady Fairfax had anything to do with it, which, of course, they did, but Henrietta didn't want to disappoint them all. She astutely realized that as the married woman in the group, although the youngest, she was required to be the chaperone. The girls were looking at her so pleadingly that she finally gave in.

"Thank you, Captain," she said, then, trying not to audibly sigh. "We'd of course be delighted to join you."

The little group accordingly walked to Mrs. Simpson's tea shop, where a cream tea was ordered and promptly delivered. The conversation unfortunately, thanks to the perhaps impropriety of the Fairfax girls, quickly turned to the story of the murdered man and the surrounding circumstances, such as they knew them to be, which were sketchy at best.

"It seems I missed all the excitement," Captain Russell said as he took a scone from the plate held out to him by Henrietta.

"Yes! A detective inspector came to the house and everything!" Sara exclaimed. "Asking all sorts of questions! They even interviewed Jane and me, didn't they, Jane?"

"Yes, they did. And he was ever so severe!"

"Was it Inspector Hartle?" Maxwell asked.

"Yes, I believe that was his name," Henrietta said, trying to remember.

"He *is* rather severe," Maxwell agreed. "He has a bit of a reputation around here. But then, again, I suppose all inspectors have to be a bit brutish. Goes with the territory, I'd say."

The captain cleared his throat. "Mrs. Howard's husband is a former police inspector. In America."

"You don't say!" Maxwell said with admiration. "I thought I detected an accent! I knew an American once—studied for a while at Kings. Jolly good laugh, he was. I do beg your pardon, Mrs. Howard."

Henrietta smiled. "No offense taken, Mr. Fielding," she said, though she did not appreciate being reminded of Clive just at the moment.

"And do you know what else?" Sara said, eager to bring the discussion back to the murder. "They think it might be Mr. Wallace!"

"Sara!" Jane exclaimed. "For shame! That's not true!"

"Why else would he be missing? And, anyway, Jane, it's no use taking the moral high ground; you were listening at the door, same as me!"

Jane blushed a very deep shade of red and took a sip from her tea.

"Wallace Howard?" Maxwell asked.

"Do you know him, Mr. Fielding?"

"Not well. He's a friend of my older brother's. You wouldn't think, I know, us being common sorts," he said with a sideways glance at Captain Russell. "My brother works at the Masson Mill. Don't know how he came to be friends with the likes of Wallace Howard, but Howard doesn't go in for all the ever-so's, prefers to socialize with the lads. Rory's always going on about how Wallace tries to get them to organize. But, God love 'em, that sorry lot just wants a pint at the end of each day and they're happy enough. Don't want anything more, though Howard's always trying to stir them up. Even brought in some foreign chaps one time to speak to them. He's missing, you say?" he asked thoughtfully as he took a drink of his tea. "For the money, I'd say he's at the Merry Bells," Maxwell said hopefully.

"The Merry Bells?" Henrietta asked.

"It's a pub in Matlock proper. Place where the mill workers go usually."

"For myself, I can't believe Wallace had anything to do with it," Captain Russell interrupted, clearly upset by the news. "He has strange ideas, but he's honorable to a fault. Robbing and killing a man goes against everything he purports to stand for."

In her mind, Henrietta had to agree with Captain Russell, even from the little she knew of Wallace, and yet why did he stay away? Perhaps he was in trouble, too? Or worse, what if he, too, was lying dead in some ditch?

The conversation drifted then to more pleasant topics before Henrietta decided they really must be getting back. The captain offered to drive them in his motor, causing the girls to look pleadingly at her yet again. She preferred to walk, but she was anxious to tell Clive about the Merry Bells in Matlock . . . perhaps they could make it there yet today if they hurried . . . so she accepted the captain's offer, stopping briefly at the post office to deposit her letters, before allowing herself to be helped up into the car.

Chapter 17

Clive felt certain Foley was holding something back as he stood across from him now in Lord Linley's billiard room, having finally cornered him here, but he of course couldn't prove it.

Foley, as it turned out, had remained quite elusive, causing Clive to embark on a bit of wild goose chase to find him. After searching fruitlessly throughout the house and grounds, he had finally gone below stairs to seek out Stevens, who had hurriedly got up from his chair by the servants' fire to attend him. Captain Foley, a flushed Stevens had reported, had breakfasted in his room and had then gone out riding. No, he had not left the estate, Stevens said, thinking carefully in response to Clive's question, as his things had not been packed, nor had he asked to be driven into town, where he would have had to go to presumably catch the train back to London. Clive had no choice, then, but to wait for Foley's return and had employed his time by instead seeking out Lord Fairfax and the honorable Mr. Sedgewick to ask them a certain few questions regarding the card game last night. He would also have liked to talk to Captain Russell, whom, he was informed, had also joined in the game, but he later learned that Captain Russell had taken his leave very early this morning.

Not having anything else to do, Clive occupied himself by searching the nearby woods for any clue of Wallace's possible whereabouts but found nothing besides a well-worn path through the tall grass. Clearly, Wallace made this trip often. Clive was pretty sure it led down to the village and was sorely tempted to follow it, but he was eager to catch Foley upon his return, so he forced himself to make his way back up to the house. Stevens was nowhere in sight, so he inquired of the footman who seemed to perpetually stand at attention near the front doors and was told that Mr. Wallace had not yet returned, nor had Mrs. Howard and her party. Clive felt agitated as he paced around the house, trying to avoid other guests, as he was in no mood for idle chitchat, and finally tried to settle in the library with a book. He was beginning to regret his decision to separate from Henrietta for the day, as it had so far come to nothing. He closed the book he held limply in his lap and took out his pipe instead.

It was midafternoon when Stevens discovered him in the library and informed him that Captain Foley could presently be found in the billiard room. Accordingly, Clive hurried through the house and, upon entering the heavy, masculine room, indeed found Foley alone, lazily shooting balls about the table.

He seemed pleasantly surprised to see Clive as he quietly entered the room.

"Ah, Howard. Just the man. Didn't expect to see you away from your lovely wife. Care for a game?" Captain Foley said, indicating with his cue stick toward the table.

"Not just now," Clive answered aloofly, trying to read Foley.

"Heard you got mixed up with the DCI," Foley said, bending down to take aim. "But then again, that's right up your alley, eh?" he said, taking the shot. "Ghastly business, this." He walked around the table for his next shot. "Don't know what Blighty's coming to; a man can't walk home from a pub without being murdered and robbed." When Clive didn't respond, he looked up at him questioningly. "Everything all right, old boy?"

"Where did you go last night after I went back in? I recall you stayed out for a bit of time." Clive said disinterestedly.

"Just around, you know," Foley said, puzzled by the question. "Felt like I needed some air; frightfully stuffy in there, wasn't it?"

"How did you know the man had been robbed?" Clive asked steadily.

Foley slowly stood up straight now. "Look here, old boy," he said, the realization of what Clive suspected seeming to dawn on him. "I rather think I don't appreciate your tone. Just what are you implying?"

"Just answer the question."

"You can't really think I had anything to do with this . . . this murder business!" he said, incredulously. "You're coming unhinged, man!"

Clive held his gaze. "You don't think it vaguely suspicious that the very night you ask to borrow money, a man turns up dead and robbed of a large amount of cash?"

"This really is the limit, Howard! Don't play chief inspector with me! All your bloody work with the American police must have addled your brains."

Foley tried to stare him down, but Clive did not flinch.

"Look, if you must know," Foley relinquished with an exasperated sigh, "I felt damned ashamed of having to ask you for the money. I took a walk down by the fountain to cool myself down, as it were. Tried to regain some dignity; I do have a shred of pride left, you know," he said with a grimace. "I couldn't have been gone more than fifteen minutes! I came back in, then, and joined the card game . . . in this very room, if you must know!" he said with an air of indignation, though Clive thought he caught a trace of anxiety. "Ask Lord Fairfax!"

"As a matter of fact, I have," Clive said evenly, watching Foley's face pale a bit. "Something about your story didn't ring true. I didn't recall you being a gambling man, and unless it's a habit you've picked up since the war, which seemed unlikely, I deduced that you must be lying to me. I would have wagered a large amount of money on it," Clive said wryly. "As it turns out, you haven't played a game all weekend. Merely watched. So now I'd like to know why you need a thousand pounds from me. I don't like being lied to."

Captain Foley let out a deep breath and rubbed his forehead with his hand. Balancing the cue stick in the crook of his arm, he pulled out his silver cigarette case from his front jacket pocket and extracted a cigarette. He lit it and inhaled deeply, blowing smoke out of his nostrils as he gazed remorsefully at Clive.

"Sorry, old boy. You're right. It's a not a gambling debt, though I never specifically came right out and said that, merely implied it. Still," he said, taking another deep drag, "I should have been more forthcoming, though the wretched situation I currently find myself in *was* a bit of a gamble on my part, you could say. Just turned out wrong."

"Blackmail?" Clive guessed.

The captain oddly laughed. "In a way, I suppose."

"Let's have it, then. The truth this time."

The captain walked to the rack hanging along the wall and carefully placed his cue stick in the empty spot, taking his time.

"It's a bit tricky, old man," he said, looking at the wall.

"Try me."

Captain Foley turned around slowly and gave a small shrug. "I did gamble. With our upstairs maid, as it is, and now she's pregnant. Just one of those things, you know. Damned pretty, but, well . . . It was amusing while it lasted, but then she went and got herself up the duff."

"And she wants a thousand pounds?" Clive asked incredulously. "To get rid of it?"

"No," he said regretfully. "If only it were that easy. She's a damned Catholic. Insists on having it," he said, rubbing his brow again.

"And she wants you to buy her silence?"

"Not in so many words. I can't have the upstairs maid walking around pregnant, though. Mother would guess it immediately. I've done this sort of thing before, you see, if you must know," he said and had the grace to actually look ashamed. "Father took care of it, but with the understanding that if I did it again, I'd be cut off and have to take the chips that fell." He took another drag of his cigarette and walked to the fireplace to knock his ash. "So I'm setting her up. A cottage near her village somewhere in Ireland. A thousand pounds should do it. I agreed to educate the brat when the time comes. Problem is, I don't have any ready cash at the moment, and now is not the time to ask Father or let it be known about that I need cash, not with my upcoming nuptials to the very refined Rosalyn Edwards."

"Jesus, Foley! You've done it this time," Clive said, leaning on the billiards table with his arms crossed.

"Quite."

"Did you not think to marry this girl?" Clive asked.

"Thoroughly unsuitable, old man," Foley almost laughed. "You should know that!" he said, peering at him through his exhaled smoke.

"Do I?" Clive asked reproachfully.

Foley seemed to recognize his faux pas, then, and fumbled to correct himself. "No offense given, I hope, Howard. Surely."

His response, however, told Clive all he needed to know. Clearly, it was common knowledge that Henrietta was not originally of the gilded set.

"It's 1935, Foley," he said, piqued. "It's not unheard of."

"Look, old boy, it's different in America," Foley almost whined. "An entirely different thing altogether. And anyway, you're well set. You can marry whom you wish. Beggars can't be choosers," he said bitterly. "It doesn't matter, anyway. I'm engaged to marry Rosalyn, and I have to go through with it. Even if I weren't, I wouldn't marry Ada. We're not suited. You're lucky, Howard. Some of us aren't."

"I'm not so sure it has anything to do with luck, Foley. Maybe you should stop sleeping with the servants. Seems it's proving an expensive hobby. Like gambling."

"I say, Howard, that's a bit . . ."

They were interrupted, then, by a faint knock at the door, and Henrietta poked her head in.

"There you are! I've been looking everywhere for you!" she said, stepping into the room now. "Oh, Captain Foley, forgive me. But I . . ."

"Henrietta! This really isn't a good time," Clive said, surprised and somewhat irritated, though the sight of her made him catch his breath. Briefly, he realized that he had missed her. He suppressed these feelings, however, as his current conversation with Foley obviously took precedence at the moment, though he could see, by the way she stood her ground in the doorway, that she did not recognize that, or, worse, if she did, she didn't care. He would have forgiven the interruption if it were an emergency, but judging by her unruffled manner it clearly was not. To his further surprise she did not withdraw immediately, but instead stood looking at him impatiently.

"As I was about to say," she had the audacity to say, "I'm sorry to interrupt, but I really have some urgent news." She flashed an expectant look at the captain, then, obviously waiting for him to excuse himself. Clive was stunned.

"But of course, Mrs. Howard," Captain Foley said, crushing the butt of his cigarette against the bricks of the fireplace. "Forgive me. I was just on my way out," he smiled cordially and arched his eyebrow at Clive.

"This isn't over, Bertram," Clive said to him as he walked toward the door.

"No, I expect it isn't," Foley said before giving a brief smile. "Mrs. Howard," he said, inclining his head to her, and he disappeared.

"Henrietta!" Clive said, turning to her as soon as Foley was out of the room. "That was important!" he said, chastising her. She looked at him intently, her blue eyes blinking. He could tell that she was angry, but so was he. How dare she interrupt his interrogation! His mother, he couldn't help noting, would never have interrupted his father closeted in his study with a business associate.

"So is what I have to say," she said, clearly peeved. "Unless you don't want to hear it!"

"Unless you are hurt," he said sternly, "which you obviously aren't, or someone has died, which they obviously haven't, I don't know what would warrant this. What is so damned important?"

—

Henrietta stared at him, trying to control her anger. She had been so excited all the way home, barely listening to the idle chatter between Mr. Fielding and the ladies as they jostled in the back of Captain Russell's motor, to inform Clive of Wallace's probable whereabouts, and this was her reception? How dare he take the high hand yet again! Why was he acting so strangely, so aloof? Everything had been so perfect between them until that inspector had turned up asking about the murder. She could see that it had propelled Clive back into his previous role, and she wasn't sure she liked it. It was showing her a side of him that she didn't particularly appreciate. It was definitely a position that did not include her, and she wondered what would have happened if they had chosen that life in Chicago instead of the life at Highbury. She searched his hazel eyes, normally so warm and soft, but they were at the moment very cold.

"Don't you dare swear at me!" she said angrily, her voice wavering a bit, despite her attempt to control it.

Clive closed his eyes and looked away. "Forgive me," he said, his voice softer now, though he was clearly still upset. He looked back at her, concern now in his eyes. "I'm sorry. That was uncalled for." He reached for her hand, but she moved it away.

"I only wanted to tell you that I think I may know where Wallace is," she said stiffly. She watched his face for his reaction, but instead of the delight she had expected to see, his brows furrowed.

"Wallace?" he asked abruptly. "Where is he?"

"There's a very good chance he's at a pub called the Merry Bells in Matlock."

"Matlock?"

"Apparently it's a working man's place. He drinks there quite frequently, it seems, trying to stir up trouble among the local workers."

"How do you know this?" Clive asked, his eyes narrowed. There was still no sign of the pleased, grateful husband.

"I heard it in Cromford. We ran into Captain Russell and his cousin, Maxwell Fielding. We had tea with them, and of course the conversation turned to the murder, and Mr. Fielding said that Wallace is a friend of his brother, a mill worker at the Masson Mill, I think he said, and that he—his brother, that is—can be found most days at the Merry Bells," she said in a rush. "He said he believes Wallace goes there quite frequently as well."

"So that's where he goes," Clive muttered as he leaned back against the billiard table, his arms crossed, deep in thought. He abruptly took out his pocket watch to check the time and then snapped it shut. "I must go," he said, his eyes meeting hers now.

"Is that all?" she finally asked, incredulous.

He looked at her quizzically. "What do you mean, 'is that all'?"

"I thought I might get at least a thank-you."

"Oh, yes, of course. Thank you, darling," he said, as if nothing had happened between them! "Well done." He gave her a quick smile. "You'd better tell Lady Linley that I won't be at dinner tonight. I'll be back later, hopefully with Wallace, if I have any luck."

"What do you mean?" she blustered. "I had thought we might go together." She stared at him, and the realization slowly hit her that he had no intention, again, of including her. Why had she expected anything different? she thought as she bit her lip.

"That isn't going to happen, though, is it?" she asked stiffly.

Clive did not respond, but the look he gave her, however, suggested anything but.

"I should have known," she said bitterly and walked slowly out of the room.

Chapter 18

By the time Clive reached the Merry Bells in Matlock, having had to ask Bradwell, the chauffer, for a car and directions, it was growing dark. Bradwell had been reluctant to advise him, wanting to drive him himself, but Clive was adamant that he go alone—the days of having to be driven around by a chauffeur hopefully well into the distant future, if he or fate or God had anything to do with it.

The pub, when he finally found it, was a very old one; by Clive's guess it must have been at least five hundred years old, and it reminded him of a place his father and Uncle Montague had some-times taken him and Linley and Wallace to at least once each summer. Clive wished he could remember the name of the pub they had fre-quented; he hadn't thought of it in years. It had had a cemetery next to it, and the three boys had often played hide-and-seek there while their fathers drank beneficently with the locals.

Clive made his way now through the smoky haze to the dark wooden slab of a bar and ordered a whiskey. When he asked for Wallace Howard, setting a five-pound note on the bar, the innkeeper's eye lazily surveyed him and then gave a slight nod toward the back. Clive responded with an accompanying nod of thanks as he picked up his whiskey and made his way through to one of the dingy little back rooms. Clive had half expected to find Wallace surrounded by a group of disgruntled workers as they debated their situations, but instead he found him strangely alone, sitting with his head in his hands at a little back table in the corner, a whiskey and a pint in front of him. Several other groups of people were peppered throughout the room, smoking and talking mildly, and nearby three men played darts so that a periodic thud could be heard every so often through the haze of smoke. It struck Clive as peculiar that Wallace was alone, as if he didn't fit in in either world.

Clive set his whiskey on the table and pulled out a battered stool. "Mind if I sit here?" he asked.

Without looking up, Wallace said, "So you've found me." He glanced up at Clive, then, with one eye squinted shut, though it was by no means bright in the pub. "See? I always knew you were a better detective than you let on."

Clive sat down.

"Let me guess—you've been sent to fetch me. I'm always being fetched," he said, slightly slurring his words.

"Something like that," Clive said, taking a sip of his whiskey and eyeing Wallace carefully. He hadn't shaved, and he looked haggard. "Been here all day?"

"Long enough," he said with a wry smile. "What do you want?"

"The police have been round to the house," Clive said carefully, and he thought he detected a slight wave of concern pass across Wallace's face, though it disappeared just as quickly.

"Some excitement for you, then. Just like home! Something to break up what I'm sure you've discovered is a terribly dull existence. What was it? Father finally broke? Did the bailiffs come to repossess the house?" He broke into a deep laugh.

"It was regarding the murder," Clive said, taking another sip of his whiskey.

"Oh, that. Shame. Poor sod," Wallace said, sobering a little and looking at the two drinks in front of him as if trying to decide which one to partake of. Finally he chose the whiskey and threw it back in one go.

"You were seen leaving that same pub just after the dead man did," Clive said evenly.

Wallace's brow furrowed. "So? I remember him. Chatty little fellow. Up from London, I think."

"The police would like to talk to you."

Wallace took a drink of his pint now. "Regarding?" Wallace asked, his eyes locking on Clive's, making Clive wonder if he was really as inebriated as he was acting.

"Damn it, man! This is serious. It doesn't look good. You leave the pub, then this chap goes out and ends up dead, and you don't return to the house for going on over twenty-four hours. Instead you're found hiding out in a pub in Matlock, drinking. What conclusion would *you* draw?"

"Not that one, old boy," he said with a flicker of anger in his eyes now.

"Well, I wouldn't put it past this chief inspector to find it suspicious. He wants you at the station to give a statement."

"Or to arrest me?"

"Don't be absurd. Just go in and tell them anything you know about the man. If you spoke to him at all, any clues you can give, if you saw anyone. Say you were distraught once you heard he'd been murdered and stayed away. He already knows that you disappear from time to time. So play on that."

"Disappear?"

"He questioned your man and some of the other servants, too. They told him you frequently disappear off the estate and stay out until the wee hours."

Wallace looked away, clearly disturbed. "Did Father hear them say that?"

Clive was taken off guard by the question. He tried to remember. "He may have. Why?"

Wallace didn't answer, and Clive sat in the silence, watching him. Finally, he spoke. "Where *do* you go, anyway?"

"Mind your own business," Wallace said angrily.

Clive calmly took a sip of his whiskey and leaned back. "I found your trails through the woods. Easy enough to figure out where they go."

"Sod off!"

Clive waited a few moments before continuing. "Look, if it's any consolation, I don't think you murdered this bloke. But you must see it doesn't look good. I'd like to help you, but it would be a hell of a lot easier to do if you leveled with me. God knows I don't want anything to happen to you. Then I'd be left with Linley, and I've quite enough to handle just at the moment."

Wallace unexpectedly let out a laugh.

"Come on, drink up," Clive urged, taking advantage of the break in tension, and stood up. "Let's get over to the station and get this over with so that we can go home."

Wallace obediently drained his glass and wobbly stood up. He looked around for his walking stick. "Bloody stick. Always losing it."

Clive waited for him to make his way out from behind the table without it, leaning heavily on its deeply scarred surface instead. "Be honest, Wallace," Clive asked, watching him. "Where *do* you disappear to?"

"Leave it, Clive," Wallace said steadily, despite what Clive was sure now was his genuine drunkenness. "It doesn't have anything to do with this business."

When they finally reached the station back in Cromford, Detective Chief Inspector Hartle was just coming down the front steps, presumably to go home. Clive parked in front and got out, walking up a few steps to meet him and leaning forward to quietly relate what had happened.

Wallace, who had fallen asleep on the drive over, slowly climbed out of the car. Hartle signaled to one of the constables standing by the front door, and he hurried down to help the crippled man. Wallace's brief nap did not seem to have helped his mood any, as he immediately lashed out to Inspector Hartle.

"What's this all about, anyway?" he said loudly. "I had nothing to do with this bloody murder! You're wasting your time, as usual," he said indignantly, pushing the constable aside and gripping the iron railing himself instead.

"Just routine, Mr. Howard," said the inspector from where he and Clive stood by the ancient front doors, studded with iron bolts. "Just a few questions."

When they got inside, the constable led them to a small, cramped cross-examining room, which, Clive noticed, seemed ancient compared to the one at his old station in Chicago. That had been nothing glamorous, of course, but this seemed positively medieval with its thick stone walls, resembling more a dungeon than a modern police unit. Wallace slumped in a chair next to him, and Hartle, with careful, exacting movements, took the seat across from them. He sat back and looked at Wallace, as if deciding his guilt then and there simply by his observations, letting the silence build. Finally he reached into his pocket and took out a package of cigarettes and, after methodically tapping the pack against his palm, pulled one out and slowly lit it with some matches that already lay on the table, still watching Wallace as he took a drag and exhaled.

"Well, let's get on with it, shall we?" Wallace asked impatiently. "I'd like to get home if you've nothing really to say."

Despite Wallace's angry demeanor, Clive could read his distress. Doubtless Hartle could, too.

"Why don't you tell me where you were last night?" the inspector said calmly, his eyes narrowing as he took another drag.

"You already know this! I was at the Horse and Coach. And, yes, I saw the dead man. I didn't say two words to him."

"What can you tell us about him?"

"Nothing!"

"Come, come, Mr. Howard, think. Several people saw you talking with him."

"Jesus! I don't know. Idle chitchat. He . . . he was up from London."

"What was he doing up here?"

"I don't bloody know!" He was silent then, thinking. "Said he was an estate agent," he finally added, blearily. "Up here to look at property, I think he said. Bit of a git, if you must know."

"Why's that?" Hartle asked, inhaling again.

"One of those types that are just asking for a good seeing to, I guess you'd say. Very superior. That type."

"What time did he leave?"

"I don't know!"

"Roughly?"

"I don't know . . . eleven? Eleven thirty?"

"And when did you leave?"

Wallace grimaced, trying to think. "A little after, I suppose."

"Did you see him outside?"

"No."

"Any idea where he was going?"

"No! Wait," he said, his brow furrowed with the effort of remembering. "Said he was going on to Matlock, I think."

"At that hour?"

Wallace shrugged.

"Did he have a car?"

"I don't bloody know!" Wallace shouted now.

Inspector Hartle gave a slight nod to the constable standing by the door, who promptly disappeared and came back in carrying a walking stick. He held it carefully at the bottom, his hand encased in a handkerchief, and carefully laid it on the table.

"Recognize that?" the inspector asked, snuffing his cigarette now.

"Yes, that's mine," Wallace said nervously.

"That was found about a few hundred feet from the body, thrown into the woods. One of my men found it this morning. Blood on the end," he said, pointing to the silver knob at the top. "Matches the head wound. We've sent samples to see if the blood is a match. We'd like your fingerprints, Mr. Howard."

Wallace was thrown into a panic now. "Well, obviously my fingerprints are on it! It's mine! But there's been some mistake!" he said hurriedly, looking at Clive now, who shifted in his chair as he examined the walking stick. "I didn't kill this chap! Look. I left, and I didn't see him. I . . . I do remember not being able to find my stick, but I'm always leaving it."

The inspector was unruffled and reached for another cigarette. "Where'd you go after you left the pub?" he said, lighting it. "The truth," he said, pointing at him, the cigarette held tight between his two forefingers.

Wallace's face blanched. "I . . . I can't say."

"Can't or won't?" he said, looking at him, and, to Clive's surprise, Wallace's face became stubbornly resolute. Clive thought Wallace would have crumbled by now.

"Wallace," Clive said, leaning toward him, knowing what Hartle would do next. "Best tell him. It could go very bad for you if you don't."

Wallace gave an almost imperceptible shake of his head, closing his eyes as he did so.

John Hartle blew out a deep sigh accompanied by a cloud of smoke and snuffed out his cigarette. "You leave me no choice," he said grimly, as he wearily stood up. "Wallace Howard, I'm arresting you on suspicion of murder. You do not have to say anything, but it may harm your defense if you do not mention when questioned something that you later rely on in court. Anything you do say may be given as evidence. Do you understand?" Not waiting for an answer, he gave a nod to the constable, who reached to stand him up, but Wallace swaggered unsteadily to his feet himself, almost overturning the chair from under him.

"You swine!" he shouted. "I didn't kill him! You bastard, Clive! You lied! This is your doing, isn't it?"

Two constables took hold of him, then, and secured him, pulling him back. Wallace struggled to get loose. "You said it was just questioning!" he shouted, looking wildly at Clive. "I'm Wallace Howard!" he said, turning his attention back to the inspector. "You can't do this! When my father hears of this, he won't take kindly to it!"

"Happy enough to claim your lineage now, aren't you?" the inspector said calmly, still seated. "Last chance," he said with a shrug.

"Sod off!"

Hartle gave another nod then, and the constables pulled him back toward the cells.

"I'll do what I can, Wallace," Clive offered loudly over the noise of the struggle, feeling Wallace's accusation and blame very deeply. But how could he have foreseen that this would happen? He hadn't known about the new evidence.

"Don't bother!" Wallace shouted from somewhere outside the room now.

Clive felt unreasonably irritated with Hartle, as if he had been tricked as well, but he knew he would have done the same in the inspector's place. "A word?" Clive asked him crisply.

Hartle inclined his head. "Come on," he said, and he led him down the hallway to what was presumably his private office.

It was a tiny, plain room with no ornaments of any sort. Just a desk littered with papers, a chair, and a telephone. Two rickety chairs sat opposite the desk. Hartle tossed his jacket onto one and pointed at the other one, indicating that Clive should sit. On a shelf behind his desk stood a bottle of whiskey and a few glasses, which the inspector took down now, pouring each of them a large glass full.

"You don't seriously suspect him, do you?" Clive asked as he took a large drink.

"I haven't ruled it out. It's the best lead I have at the moment," the inspector said, following suit with his drink.

"Can't you at least let me take him back home until the samples come back?" Clive asked, though he already knew the answer.

"The law's the law, Howard. You know that."

"You could argue it's circumstantial," Clive said, raising an eyebrow hopefully.

"Barely." The inspector lit another cigarette. "No alibi." He shrugged. "Listen, I'll do what I can. But I have people watching me, too, Howard. I have to at least make a show of it. Until I can dig up something more plausible, this will have to do for an explanation. I'm under scrutiny right now myself, and I can't afford to make mistakes." Clive exhaled thoughtfully. That was one part of his former occupation that he didn't miss—having to be under the scrutiny of various authorities and even political figures at any given time. And he knew what it was to have to follow commands, sometimes seemingly illogical ones, from his days in the war. He wondered how he would fare in the private sector, running Linley Standard, his father's company, being master of the ship, as it were. Wearily he rubbed his forehead. He knew he was not going to sway Hartle to release Wallace, but what was he to tell Lord and Lady Linley?

"Any idea who he's shielding?" Hartle asked, his eyes flicking to Clive.

"None."

"Well, I've been doing a little digging. Seems Wallace has made several trips abroad in the last couple of years. Once to Berlin and once to Leningrad and several to France. Odd, is it not?" The inspector stared at him. "Six months ago," he went on, "a fight broke out at the mill in Matlock. Six foreign nationalists were locked up. Wallace was reportedly on the scene." The inspector took another drag of his cigarette while he looked for Clive's reaction.

"So?" Clive said, wanting to shift his body but forcing it to remain frozen, not wanting to make any suggestive movements, something he himself was always watching for. "Doesn't mean he murdered this man, Jacobs. Surely you must have other leads, other people in the Horse and Coach that night."

The inspector scrutinized him carefully, one eye involuntarily twitching. "I really shouldn't be discussing the case with you," he said, taking a deep drag, during which Clive knew better than to say anything. "I'll make an exception with you, however," the inspector said, neatly blowing out smoke. "Though there's not much to relate."

Clive felt his body relax.

"It seems the victim was indeed a London man," Hartle began, as if Clive had always been his confident. "One Ernest Jacobs. Chelsea address. Wife says he was coming up to Matlock on business. Didn't say what. No enemies that she knows of. Solicitor confirms that a large amount of cash was drawn out, by Mr. Jacobs himself, from his account not three days ago."

"How much?"

"A little over five thousand pounds."

Clive whistled. "Where'd he get that kind of money?"

"Apparently it was the wife's. Got a little inheritance when her father died a while back."

Clive mused over this. "Occupation?"

"Estate agent."

"Spoken to the employer?"

"Not yet."

"Any idea who he was meeting?"

The inspector held out his hands emptily. "Not yet. No one's come forward, which throws a potentially shady light on the whole thing. If it really was a simple property sale, why wouldn't the other party have come forward by now?"

"Maybe they haven't heard yet."

"Unlikely in this part of the world."

"Any more information from the innkeeper besides his initial statement?"

Hartle nodded. "Says this Jacobs had a bit of a swagger to him. Itching to let it out that he was a big man up from London to make a deal. Couldn't hold his drink all that well. Said it was obvious that he was carrying something valuable in the case by the way he held on to it."

"This seems more and more like a simple case of robbery to me."

"More than likely."

"Then why hold Wallace? It could have been anyone in that pub."

"True, or anyone who happened upon him on the road. But we have the rather disagreeable problem of the walking stick."

"He could easily have left it and someone else picked it up."

"Then why not explain his whereabouts?" the inspector said with a shrug. "We're back at the beginning now," he said and poured them another round.

"Does the innkeeper recall any exchange between him and Wallace?" Clive asked.

The inspector sighed, his eye twitching again. "Nothing more than the usual. Said Wallace is pretty quiet if he does stop in from time to time, which isn't all that much, apparently."

Clive's attention was aroused. "That's odd," he said, absently taking a drink. "His valet says he goes down to the Horse and Coach quite often."

"Or he thinks he does. Sounds like he's actually frequenting the Merry Bells."

"Bit far to go, isn't it?" Clive suggested.

"Must be some sort of attraction in Matlock, I'd say. Why else would he go all that way?"

"Maybe he prefers the company?"

The inspector snorted. "Not really a gentleman's pub."

"Is there such a thing?" he asked dubiously.

"I suppose you're right there, Howard. But look, we know he's involved with these socialists . . ."

"Do we?" Clive asked evenly.

"We've at least one man says Wallace has held several meetings in which unionizing was one of the topics," Hartle countered heatedly.

"But not social unrest?"

"Isn't unionizing a form of social unrest?"

"I'd have thought you'd think differently, Inspector," Clive said coolly as he sipped his whiskey, having already guessed Hartle's common roots.

"What I think doesn't come into it," Hartle replied.

Clive set his whiskey down. "Okay, let's assume for a minute that Wallace is a socialist . . . stirring up trouble and the like, urging men to unionize—against his own father, I might add."

"Stranger things have happened," Hartle interrupted.

"Even so, what does that have to do with murdering Ernest Jacobs?"

"Opportunity?" the inspector offered up. "They need funds perhaps?"

"Wallace Howard?"

The inspector shrugged.

"I admit he's up to something secretive, perhaps something social-istic, but he wouldn't murder a man for money."

"Maybe he was desperate." The inspector seemed reluctant to let his theory go. "Maybe he's being blackmailed, needed some ready cash."

Suddenly an image of Foley came into Clive's mind. He shifted slightly despite trying to control his body movements. "Look, you must have some other leads, surely? Who else was in the pub that night?"

Hartle looked at him intensely before continuing. "As a matter of fact, there *were* two others in the pub that left around that same time. A bloke named Crawford, who left a little after Jacobs and Wallace did. Lives with his brother and sister-in-law, and they tell us he took off for York last night. Said he planned it a long time ago, they say, to visit relatives, and that he popped down to the Horse and Coach to have a farewell drink with the lads before he left. We're still looking for him in York."

"And the other?"

"The innkeeper says he remembers another man, by the name of O'Brien, works at the Cromford Mills, left about a half hour *before* Jacobs left."

"But it would have been hard to leave with Wallace's walking stick if Wallace was still sitting there."

"Exactly."

"He *could* have taken it, though," Clive mused.

"Maybe . . ." Hartle seemed doubtful.

"Did Jacobs speak to Crawford or O'Brien, do you know?"

The inspector smiled. "First-rate procedure, Howard. Yes, I asked the same. Not that the innkeeper can recall."

"Hmmm. Did you pick O'Brien up?"

"We did indeed. Says he left early and was home with his mother."

"Did she confirm the time?"

"Didn't get in to see her. Happened to be indisposed at the moment we turned up."

"Convenient."

"Quite."

"So not much to go on," Clive mused and sat silent for a few moments. "I still don't think it's Wallace," he said finally. "Something's not adding up."

Hartle snuffed his cigarette now and shifted in his chair. "I'll see if I can get him out on bail in the morning, but I can't promise."

Clive recognized his cue to leave and stood. "Thanks, Inspector. I'll do what I can on my end."

"I appreciate your help, quite honestly, what with my sergeant down in London. He should be back by tomorrow, though," he said, which Clive understood to be his dismissal from further duties. The inspector looked at him closely. "Why'd you give it up? If I may ask."

"I'm my father's only son, so I felt obliged to behave as such and take over the family business, as it were," Clive answered with a regretful smile.

"The local gold mine, eh?" he put in, reminding Clive again that they were from two different classes. He thought he detected a bit of resentment on John Hartle's part, which surprised him, as Clive wouldn't have thought it of him, and which Clive had not experienced with his own chief in Chicago.

"Something like that," Clive said quietly as he walked out of the room and down the now-darkened hallway. A sleepy constable sat at the front desk. The inspector walked across the tiny lobby behind Clive, who paused at the door and held out his hand to him.

"You should think about PI work, Howard. You'd be good at it," he said, grasping his outstretched hand.

"Discovering if Mrs. Jones's husband is cheating on her or finding the neighborhood vandal?" Clive laughed. "Not quite my cup of tea," he said ruefully, "but thanks just the same."

Clive hurried down the steps, then, easily dismissing the inspector's suggestion as he slid into the Bentley. He instead chose to turn over the facts regarding the murder as he navigated the curving narrow road back to Castle Linley, trying to decide just how to tell Lord and Lady Linley that Wallace had indeed been found but that he was now being held in the local gaol on suspicion of murder.

Chapter 19

By the time Clive made his way into the front hall of Castle Linley, he found he was exhausted from the long day's events and did not relish the task ahead. Stevens met him and informed him that he had missed dinner and that the family and most of the guests could presently be found in the drawing room. Should he like to join them, or would he prefer to have something brought up to his room, perhaps?

Clive was horribly in need of a bath and something to eat, but he was equally desirous of seeing Henrietta. His first duty, however, he knew, was to speak privately with Lord Linley. He sighed as he handed his hat and coat to Stevens and adjusted his tie, trying to think of how best to explain what had happened.

"I'll just step in for a moment, Stevens," he said to the immovable butler. "I'll have something to eat in my room later."

"Very good, sir," he said with a bow and disappeared.

Clive slipped noiselessly into the drawing room with its deep red walls, along which hung a patchwork of portraits and landscapes, half-hidden in shadow in the dim lighting. He quickly looked about the room in an effort to find Henrietta. She was sitting next to Lady Winifred on one of the plump, paisley-patterned divans, apparently in deep discussion. Clive had hoped to catch her eye, but she did not look up, even when Lord Linley called to him.

"Clive, my boy! There you are!" he said, walking over to him and clapping him on the back. "We'd quite given you up for the evening."

"Forgive me, Lord Linley. I was detained," he said formally. "My apologies," he muttered, noting, after another quick perusal of the room, that all were present, except, of course, Captain Russell, as well as the Honorable and Mrs. Sedgewick. In the corner at the baby grand piano sat Bertram Foley, smoothly playing show tunes while Jane and Sara Fairfax looked on. Foley did not pause in his playing but merely gave Clive a deferential nod of the head, a maddening smirk residing on his face. Damn the man! Shouldn't he show some sort of humility given the trouble he was in? Clive was in half a mind to refuse him the money merely for his impudence, but he knew he was being unreasonable.

"Any news on Wallace?" Lord Linley asked eagerly.

"Yes," Clive said, leaning toward him, his attention redirected. "It's rather delicate, though, I'm afraid. Perhaps we could speak somewhere?"

Lady Linley joined them now from her perch by the fireplace, where she had been in what had seemed a very rapt conversation with Lady Fairfax. "What is it, my dear?" she said, looking at Lord Linley's worried face. "Ah, Clive! You poor boy! Shall I ring for Stevens to run you a bath? Perhaps something to eat? You must be positively famished!"

"No, Lady Linley, thank you. Later perhaps," he said to her, though his eyes couldn't help but again stray to Henrietta. Shouldn't it be her by his side, inquiring after his well-being? he thought, his irritation flaring again.

"You'll excuse us, my dear," Lord Linley said in a low voice. "Clive has some news to relate to me in my study."

"Is it regarding Wallace?" she asked in an anxious voice.

"Shh!" Lord Linley hushed her and looked around to see who might have heard. The earl and Lord Fairfax were near enough to have heard, Clive observed, though they made a pretense of having not. Clive took the opportunity to again look at Henrietta. Lady

Fairfax, robbed of her companion by the fire, had moved now to stand behind Henrietta and Lady Winifred and was asking them to make up a hand of cards. Clive expected Henrietta to decline in favor of talking to him, so he was stunned when he heard her respond that she should very much like to.

"Be quiet, woman!" Lord Linley was hissing to Margaret. "I'll tell you later!" He looked at Clive and gestured with his hand that he should proceed him from the room. With one last look at Henrietta, Clive, seriously perturbed now, followed Lord Linley to his study to relate the news.

It was very late when Henrietta finally came into their bedroom.

Clive had bathed and eaten and had sat in his dressing gown in one of the chairs by the fire attempting to read the letters from home that Stevens had delivered to him, but he grew more and more incensed as each hour passed. He had hoped that the letters would appease his disquiet, but they had instead added to it.

The first one had been from his mother, the first part of which, predictably, was devoted to a recapitulation of the wedding, including a list of additional gifts that even now were still arriving and a clipping from the *Tribune*'s society pages, which had devoted a full half page to the write-up of the lavish Howard wedding and which Clive had tossed to the side, not even bothering to read it. She had then, also predictably, inquired about their crossing and whom had they been seated with at the captain's table. She of course asked after Montague's and Margaret's health, and dear Wallace's as well, of course, and asked how many functions they had so far attended in Derbyshire and whom they had seen. She knew, she had written, how very tiresome he probably found her questions, but she implored him to make an effort. (Yes, so she can tell everyone at the club, Clive thought to himself as he poured another cognac.) Antonia had then gone on to ask after Henrietta—how she was holding up, whether she found Castle Linley agreeable, how her health was? This last question, Clive realized grimly, was no doubt a not-so-subtle way of asking if she were perhaps yet with child. Only briefly did Antonia mention Alcott, saying that he had enjoyed himself immensely at the wedding, perhaps a little too much it seemed, because now he was frequently out of sorts and locked up in his study for hours at a time. "It's almost as if he's pining for you," Antonia wrote, "which is absurd, considering you were never much around anyway." This last remark regarding his father troubled Clive, and he thought about what it might mean as he absently put down his mother's letter, barely finishing reading her salutations and greetings to be passed on to various family members, most especially, of course, to Henrietta, their own daughter now, she had written.

Concerned, Clive picked up his father's letter and opened it eagerly, quickly skimming it for anything obviously foreboding, but found nothing, at first glance, anyway, too amiss. It mostly contained details about various transactions at Linley Standard and listed a few contacts he hoped Clive might call on when he was in London, saying that having a body and a firm handshake on behalf of the Howard name would go far to calm certain investors. He would have his right-hand man, Bennett, telegram Clive with the details should he indeed be able to arrange a meeting for him with some of his London associates. It would be seemly as well, he said, for Clive to introduce himself and to get to know the men he would spend the rest of his career negotiating with. His father then abruptly turned his attention to familial concerns, saying that Antonia was moping about of late, both the excitement of the wedding being over as well as Julia having to consequently retreat back to her own abode, having a decidedly negative effect on Antonia's mood. "She tries to disguise it, of course," Alcott wrote, "but she will be very glad to have you back." He then went on to ask about Castle Linley and Montague and hoped that Clive was enjoying the ancestral home, wishing he could have come along, though he knew it, of course, to be quite out of order. Still, he had written, it reminded him that he had been away too long, and it prompted him to contemplate a trip there perhaps next summer. Clive was to tell Montague as much. He longed to see the old place again, he had added with what seemed to Clive to be a deep melancholy, and that it had been too many years. The letter took yet another turn then. Alcott went on to say that he was immensely proud of Clive, that he had done well, that he knew the sacrifice he had made and that he felt it very deeply. He had much to discuss with him upon his return but that, he said, could wait. Almost as an afterthought he had then gone on to ask if Clive remembered the night in the study at Highbury when Clive had asked him if he were making a mistake with Henrietta. His answer then, he reminded him, and which he would now repeat, was a most emphatic no. She was perfect for Clive, Alcott wrote, perfect for Highbury, and he hoped they would find much happiness in each other just as he and his mother had had. He had closed the letter then with all the other usual valedictions, and asked Clive to pass along his love to his brother, Montague, and most especially to Henrietta.

Clive had absently set the letters on the side table and had sat looking at the fire as it crackled in front of him, so many thoughts going through his mind. His father's letter upset him, though he wasn't sure why. Perhaps it was the request to meet with his business associates that was wearing on him, the mixing of business with pleasure? But was that really too much to ask, considering he was here in Europe and especially in light of him joining the firm soon? He conceded that it was actually a rather wise move. And as far as mixing business and pleasure, wasn't their participation in the events at Castle Linley and beyond a form of business transaction for his mother? And what about his involvement in this murder case? Wasn't that a form of business for himself? Or was it pleasure?

He sighed, wondering how Henrietta fit into all of this. Why couldn't they just be alone? None of this tension would exist between them if they weren't perpetually caught up in something or someone else's troubles. But wasn't that the way of life? How could they possibly escape it? He thought he understood then, finally, why Henrietta had wanted to live in the cottage.

Or was there a different reason his father's letter had disturbed him? There was such a feeling of finality to it. Was it because Alcott acknowledged the fact that he knew that taking up the reins of Highbury was a *sacrifice* to Clive, not the vaulted *privilege* that he should be looking forward to? Or was it his reference to and approval of Henrietta? He had glanced at the clock again, angrily wondering where she was and debating whether or not to call a servant, when Henrietta herself finally appeared.

He studied her face as she entered now, and he could tell that she was surprised to find him still awake, but she ignored him. She went at once into her dressing room to change and seemed to take an extraordinarily long time to emerge. As she walked to the bed in her long white nightgown, brushing her long auburn hair as she went, Clive felt a jolt of excitement despite his anger. Finally she acknowledged his presence as he sat, still in the armchair by the fire, with a single sulky glance before she looked away again.

"Henrietta," he said sternly. "It's very late."

"So it is," she said without looking at him.

"What on earth has come over you? I thought you might have been a bit concerned that I was late getting back. That you would have wanted to at least find out what happened. Whether or not I found Wallace . . ." he said with a trace of bitterness.

She turned to him, then, from her perch on the side of the bed, her eyes flashing, though she kept her voice controlled. "I'm sure that's none of my business. It's a much too dangerous affair for me to even discuss!"

"Are you still upset about . . . about before?" he asked, incredulously, standing up now.

"Can it be that you would imagine me not to be? That makes it infinitely worse!" she said, her voice rising.

She was still very hurt that he thought so little of her, that he treated her almost like a child, not a wife, and certainly not like an equal friend. It was obvious that despite all of his flowery language, he really just wanted a submissive, dutiful wife, and she had fought back tears all evening at the realization of it. Her mother had been right. Clive did not command her in bed at night, but he certainly expected her to lie back as concerned their day-to-day life. He was staring at her, and she found it disconcerting. She knew he was angry, but so was she!

"You didn't really expect to go along with me to Matlock, did you? You yourself said that the Merry Bells was a rough place!" He ran his hand through his hair. "Information, I might add, that you found out while having tea with Captain Russell, a notorious flirt if I ever saw one, and some stranger who claims to be his cousin! I quite take exception to that, as a matter of fact!" His face was growing increasingly red.

"Are you accusing me of impropriety? How dare you, Clive!" she exclaimed, completely taken aback by the insult of it. "I was forced to act as chaperone, if you must know, which should have been an obvious deduction, especially for someone who claims to be a detective!"

The force of her comment stunned him, and he was surprised by the hurt he felt, that she had taken something she knew he felt was a weakness and turned it against him. At the same time, he was amazed at her ability to fight back.

"Not impropriety, necessarily, but perhaps ill judgment!"

"Ill judgment! What else was I to do in that situation?" she threw back. "Besides, it garnered valuable information, which you seemed barely thankful of!"

"Are you such a child that you need to be praised constantly, Henrietta? I find your behavior disconcertingly similar to your mother's, and it is not attractive," he said with a bitter relish.

Now it was her turn to be stunned by his hurtful blow. How could he dare to compare her to her mother! She fought back the tears that were forming in the corners of her eyes now. She refused to cry in front of him! But how could he be that insensitive?

"Well, I'm sorry you feel that way!" she shot back. "It's obvious that you've made a mistake. You don't want a partner, you want a . . . a pretty pet! In that case you should have stuck with Sophia; she would have made you a perfect wife!"

Clive took a step toward her. "Don't be ridiculous, Henrietta! You're overreacting! Is all of this really about me not taking you to Matlock? It's absurd! I cannot take you on police business merely because you want to go."

"But it wasn't police business! You went to look for your cousin! Surely I could have accompanied you on such a task," she retorted.

"You are willfully misunderstanding the situation, and you know it!" he shot back.

"You're going back on your word!"

"What word?" he asked, incredulously.

"That I am an equal . . . a . . . a partner!"

"That has nothing to do with this," he said dismissively.

"Of course it does!" she shouted. "It has everything to do with it!"

"We've been through all of this before, Henrietta," he said tiredly. "It wasn't safe tonight. I thought you understood. I can see now that I was wrong," he said disgustedly.

"Yes, you were! About a lot of things." She stared at him. "I'm not a china doll, Clive. I'm not so easily broken. Sooner or later, you're going to have to face your fears!"

"I did face my fears—for an eternity—at the front, looking at the face of hell day in and day out!" he shouted. "A man is changed after that. Irrevocably," he said bitterly and roughly took hold of her upper arms as he searched her eyes. Why did she have this damned power over him? And as proof of it, his desperate anger turned suddenly to desire as he gazed at her beautiful face. Something in him crumpled, and he contemplated kissing her. But before he could, he saw tears forming in her eyes, now, and, worse, an unmistakable trace of fear.

"Don't," she whispered.

Slowly he released her, then, stunned that she could fear him, and it cut him to the quick. In an instant he was ashamed of all that he had said to her, whether it was true or not.

"What did you think I was going to do?" he asked, his eyes anxiously searching hers.

"I'm tired, Clive." Her voice was trembling now. "I wish to go to bed," she said, taking a step back.

"Answer me!" he commanded.

"I don't know," she whispered.

They stared at each other for what seemed a long time, the moments ticking away, each one filled with pregnant hurt, before Clive turned and slowly walked out of the room. Never had he felt more like a failure than at this moment.

Chapter 20

Elsie could not help observe the irony of the situation. She had been pining for Stan to come and visit her these many weeks, but now that he was seated, nervously it seemed, in the front parlor across from her, she wished with all her heart that he wasn't. Had she known that it was him at the front door, she would have been tempted to have Karl say that she was out, but she hadn't known, and so, without warning, Karl had naturally shown Stan to the parlor and had dutifully, if a bit uneasily, went to fetch her from the back garden, where she herself had been listlessly wandering among the last of the flowers, long dead now from the first frost.

She wondered, as she offered Stan some tea, or maybe coffee?— both of which he declined—if this was to be the long-awaited proposal she had been expecting for months and which the two of them had all but outright discussed several times in the past. He seemed very fidgety as she glanced at him again, convincing her that this must be his intention. She longed to put him at his ease, but she couldn't speak first, of course. She would have to wait for him to initiate what was sure to be a painful conversation, and her stomach clenched as she sat wondering how she was going to break it to him that she could not marry him, that she had already, in truth, engaged herself to Lieutenant Harrison Barnes-Smith.

She hardly knew how it had happened, but it had, and for better or worse, she couldn't change it now. Not that she wanted to, of course, but it had all come about in a manner very unlike how she had always imagined it would, and, had she begun her study of Jane Austen with *Pride and Prejudice* instead of *Sense and Sensibility*, she might have been able to better predict the eventual outcome of the romantic dilemma she now found herself in.

She hardly knew how to explain her engagement to Harrison, even to herself. As of yet no one knew about it, and the "lovers" had promised to keep it that way. Their courtship had evolved quickly since Henrietta's wedding, with what had begun simply with Harrison calling in every other day or so to ascertain that her ankle was indeed mending. These little visits had then progressed to short walks in the park until he had begun calling in earnest every day. From there, he had persuaded her to begin going to see various attractions in the city, though the lieutenant's choices of destination had at times a slight flavor of perhaps not perfect respectability, places that perhaps Mrs. Hutchings might raise an eyebrow at, for example. Often they went to Riverview, the amusement park on Belmont, where Elsie had thrilled to ride the new wooden roller coaster and the Ferris wheel. Harrison had urged her into the fun house as well, which was dark and terrifying, causing her to frequently bump into him and embarrassingly cling to his arm. He had persuaded her, too, to see the freak show, which she felt afterward had been decidedly inappropriate, as one of the "exhibits" was a scantily clad woman with four arms, but she had to admit she had been curious. When it was over, however, she felt more than a tinge of guilt that she had looked, though she didn't know why. Wasn't that the point of a freak show? To look at the freaks? Still, she could not help feeling that it had somehow been wrong, and when Ma had asked her later that night where she had gotten herself to that afternoon, she had lied and said the library, making the whole thing infinitely worse.

And once Harrison had even hinted that perhaps they go see a burlesque show at the Gem, but when she blushed and exclaimed

"Oh, no, Harrison!" he had been quick to say that he was merely kidding and didn't she know a joke when she heard one?

It was a pleasant sort of relief, then, when, one afternoon, he suggested that they go sailing for the day, though Elsie hesitated at first, not only because she couldn't swim, but because it seemed too late in the year for such an adventure and, ultimately, because she questioned whether it was wise to spend the whole day alone on the lake with him without a chaperone. The fact that she would never have had pause for concern had Stanley proposed such a plan oddly did not occur to her at the time.

Apprehensively she voiced her hesitations to Harrison, blushing slightly as she did so, worried that he might take it the wrong way—he was so temperamental at times! She was delighted, then, when he was not only *not* annoyed, but when he had hurriedly assured her that his uncle would be coming as well, that he must have forgotten to mention it—that is, if she didn't mind. Relieved, Elsie replied that if this were the case, then, yes, she would be delighted to go. As it happened, she had enjoyed meeting the major at the engagement party and had appreciated his gallant attempts to dance with her at the wedding. Yes, she would look forward to the opportunity of getting to know him better. And surely with the major in attendance, even the austere Mrs. Hutchings would have had no cause for complaint, Elsie convinced herself, had that venerable woman still been in the Exley employ in the role of watching over her.

It was regrettable, therefore, to find when they reached the Marina where Harrison was borrowing a fellow officer's vessel, that the major had suddenly taken ill, Harrison explained, and would not be able to attend. The major had apparently just now sent a hurried message to the front desk of the adjoining yacht club with his deepest apologies, though Elsie did not get a chance to see the note or even a messenger departing.

Harrison appeared utterly cast down by the news, sulking that his plan had been thwarted. It was a blasted shame, he said, having gone through the trouble of securing the boat and buying provisions and all, and now they would surely be wasted. Yes, he said in response to Elsie's comment about his poor uncle, it was too bad for him as well, stuck in bed, but what a lovely day he had planned and wasn't it too bad that they couldn't perhaps go anyway?

Elsie hated seeing him so distressed, but what was she to do? What would Henrietta do? she tried to think, and she decided that Henrietta would attempt to be brave. Yes, Elsie could envision Henrietta gaily sailing around the world with Clive. Elsie steeled her resolve, then, and suggested, with still more than a little trepidation in her voice, however, that it would probably be just fine for the two of them to go alone . . . unless, of course, Elsie added quickly, he thought he should go and spend the day with his uncle instead. Brightening considerably, Harrison hastily assured her that the best thing for his uncle would most definitely be undisturbed rest.

The matter settled between them, Harrison lost no time in untying the boat and getting it ready to sail. Elsie, meanwhile, stepped gingerly down into it on her own, gripping the sides for support as she went and cautiously sitting on the weathered, slightly warped bench in the bow. After all, she asked herself as she watched the lieutenant scurry about, what could happen? Harrison was always the perfect gentleman, though she was in truth sometimes not at her perfect ease around him, as if she never quite knew what he was going to say or do next. He was at times sulky and quick to criticize her, but at other times he bestowed upon her such charming smiles and even occasionally a pinch on her cheek so that she easily forgot his temper and his slights. She thrilled for those times when he was benevolent—they more than made up for his periodic contrariness. He kept her guessing, and though it was at times unsettling, it filled her with a strange excitement such as she had never felt with anyone, even Stanley.

As it turned out, she had nothing to be concerned about, and they had a lovely day out together, Harrison enjoying showing off his boating skills and telling her, as the boat gently rocked, about his sad childhood—losing his mother at a young age, his estranged father, and having to make his own way in the world. Elsie listened, her tender heart nearly breaking for him as he related all his sad troubles, how his lack of progression in any set profession wasn't really his fault, that he had been handed a raw deal at every turn. Only his uncle, it seemed, had taken pity on him and had allowed him to live with him if he agreed to enlist in the army. So he had not had much of a choice, he said wistfully, as he looked out at the other boats in the distance. And even now, in the army, he was not progressing as fast as he thought he should. Everyone seemed always against him, he said, dipping his fingers in the water.

Elsie earnestly asked what he might have liked to do, had he not been forced into the army, that is, and he answered, tentatively—after first extracting a promise from her not to laugh—that he might have quite liked to be a poet or maybe even a sculptor. Elsie's heart quickened. A poet! Might he not share some of his work with her? she practically begged. She would dearly love to hear any that he might wish to share with her, she pressed, immediately mourning his talent, wasted now as a mere foot soldier.

Harrison sighed and said that of course he would be more than happy to share some of his work with her—if she was serious, that is. Elsie assured him that she was indeed quite serious, that she was a great reader, actually. Upon hearing that, however, Harrison abruptly changed the subject. Noticing a decided shift in his tone, Elsie put it down to a poet's natural sensitivity. No wonder he seemed overwrought and moody at times. So much made sense now.

By the time they eventually tied up back at the Marina, the day's light was fading quickly. Having secured the boat tightly, Harrison helped Elsie out, who was grateful to be no worse for wear besides having procured a slightly wet and now torn hem on her dress. Once they were both on the dock, Harrison turned to her awkwardly, as if he were perhaps embarrassed that he had possibly shared too much about his past and his woes. Elsie could read his discomfort and longed to dispel it, to thank him for, well, talking so much with her, but she couldn't think of any words. He seemed like he wanted to say something, but he didn't. Most probably he was worried about his uncle, she reasoned, which prompted her to suggest that she make her own way home so that he could get back to him faster. Harrison hurriedly exclaimed, then, that he was hoping—seeing as they lived so close to each other—that it would not be too much of an imposition for her to come back to his uncle's with him—if only for a few minutes—to accompany him in his duties as "nurse" so that he might not be alone in them. And his uncle, he went on quickly, would dearly appreciate a look-in from Miss Von Harmon. Elsie was touched in a way she couldn't explain and said that of course she would accompany him and sit with his uncle for a time.

Thus they made their way to the elevated train, Harrison apologizing that he did not have the money for a taxi and Elsie not daring to offer the fare herself from her grandfather's exorbitant allowance, a generous portion of which was tucked away even now in her handbag. Fortunately they did not have long to wait before a train screeched into position along the platform, where Elsie stood shivering. The warmth of the car as they stepped inside was a welcome relief after the day spent on the chilly lake and the ever-dropping temperature she had felt on the walk to the station. Seated now, Elsie felt an odd sort of contentment as they jostled along, Harrison sitting very close to her, his hand just grazing hers.

She was a bit startled, then, when with a fast, swift movement, he moved his hand on top of hers and lightly squeezed it. She tried hard not to gasp.

"Thank you for today, Elsie," he said in a throaty voice.

Her stomach clenched again at his words and the feel of his hand in hers, and she prayed that her own would not become clammy as a result. Where were her gloves? Shyly, she looked over at him, and he flashed her such a charming smile that she almost laughed out loud. He was so . . . what was the word? . . . so debonair! What could he possibly see in a girl like her? she thought for the hundredth time. She was nothing special; she knew that. Besides, she was not free, she reminded herself, as she delicately pulled her hand away now and looked out the window, trying to call up images of Stanley, but, try as she might, they wouldn't stay. It was true that she loved Stanley—in a certain way—but not, she had to admit, in the way Harrison made her feel. He made her feel extravagant and giddy, nervous and trembling. She knew that she was smiling too much in front of him and that her eyes were giving away her growing attraction (Henrietta was always warning her of this), but she couldn't help it. She liked him. Very much.

When they finally arrived at the major's home, Harrison let himself in with a key, sheepishly admitting that they only hired servants when they entertained, except for a cleaning woman that came in in the mornings. It was an old brownstone, not quite on the Square as he had at other times led her to believe, but rather several streets over, which unfortunately cast a mild flavor of shabbiness on it. It was big and drafty and not at all a home, Elsie observed sadly. Oddly, as she looked around, nowhere could she see any evidence of the major's hat or coat, or any of his belongings.

"But what do you do for a cook?" Elsie asked, concerned, as he took her own hat and coat, his apparent, noble sort of poverty endearing him all the more to her.

"Oh, we make do, Uncle and I," Harrison said with a shrug. "I try my best," he said with a smile.

Elsie felt her heart go out to the two of them and couldn't help but think of how dreadful it would be if her own brothers had no one to look after them. They would be just as lost, she knew.

Harrison clapped his hands together now and pointed to the front room. "Why don't I start a fire for us? It's damned cold in the evenings these days," he said, pushing past her. "Isn't it?" There was a change in him now which Elsie couldn't quite put words to. He seemed more relaxed in some way, more like a regular joe than the dashing, elegant lieutenant he normally presented, and Elsie, though she barely perceived the difference, wasn't sure which persona she preferred.

"That would be nice, thank you," Elsie said, not knowing what else to say. "But don't go through any trouble on my account. I don't want to intrude."

"Oh, you're not intruding, not by any stretch," Harrison said, smiling as he bent to light the kindling already laid. Elsie gingerly sat down on the long day bed that passed for a sofa as she watched him work, pleased to be able to observe him unawares. His dark hair was growing out and becoming almost unruly, more so than she would have thought the army would allow. Bent over the fireplace now, he seemed thinner and smaller than she had first envisioned him, though she knew him to be her own height or even a little taller. She thought him desperately handsome. Despite being in the army, he wasn't a bit practical, as Stanley always was. Harrison, by contrast, had an almost boyish whimsy to him that she found irresistible. He had a way of talking her into doing things that she almost always felt guilty for later, like jumping onto the back of the trolley without paying and jumping off again before the conductor could stop them. She had never done something so daring, but she didn't regret it in the slightest. It was just a way he had about him that kept her from saying no to him. And when she did try to stand up to him, he pouted and sulked until she gave in. It should have bothered her, she supposed, but instead it made her laugh, as though it were a little game they were playing— she the indulgent mother and he the naughty little boy.

As the fire finally caught now, sputtering and crackling to life, he stood to the side and held out his hands to it, warming them.

"Aren't you going to check on your uncle?" Elsie finally asked.

Harrison started. "My uncle? Oh, yes! Of course," he said, rubbing his hands together again. "I'll just pop up. Won't take a minute."

"Oh, don't rush! Sit with him. I'll be fine down here. Unless you think I should go up as well?" she said, beginning to stand up. "You said he might enjoy my company."

"No!" Harrison said, rather forcefully. "No," he said again, this time with a hasty smile. "He . . . he might be asleep. Let me just check. And, anyway, now that I think about it, he might not like you to see him when he's not feeling so well."

"Oh, but . . . yes . . . of course," she stammered, puzzled at how contradictory this was from what he had said at the Marina. "I . . . I was just . . . I just thought he might want to see me, you said . . . But that's all right. You'll . . . you'll give him my regards, though, won't you?" she faltered.

Without answering, the lieutenant hurried from the room, then, and up the stairs.

In his absence, Elsie sat back down again and took the opportunity to make a study of the room's décor. In this room, anyway, she thought she could see the major's influence. It was very different from anything she had seen before, and she thought how odd it was to be sitting in a man's front parlor other than Stanley's, though that was actually his mother's, and which, in contrast, had always exuded an air of modest proportions and decoration. Only a few cherished possessions, some of them incidentally won at the St. Sylvester bingo over the years, were allowed to be displayed in the Dubowski home, as well as a few books—the Bible, of course, being one of them.

Here, the atmosphere was very different, the major obviously having collected various exotic pieces from his many campaigns in foreign parts, and Elsie marveled at a particularly large display of what she assumed were some sort of African tribal masks. They filled her with a certain sense of fear or dread, and she crossed herself, hoping they weren't evil. She tried to avert her eyes to other parts of the room, which was sparsely furnished and seemed overall a bit forlorn. In the corner of the day bed, she spied a ratty, greasy quilt, hastily tossed aside, and she resisted the urge to fold it. She was glad, then, when Harrison suddenly reappeared back in the room.

"How is he?" Elsie said, twisting so that she could see him better.

"Sleeping. He seems to be a bit better," he said, not meeting her eye. "But I thought it best not to wake him."

Despite this favorable report, however, Harrison still seemed anxious, Elsie thought, observing him closely, as if he were disturbed about something. Perhaps she should go after all. She rose.

"I should be going then, Harrison. I'm sure you're very tired.

You've been such a peach to put up with me when I'm sure you've been eaten up with worry. I'll be going now."

"No, Elsie! Please," he said, stepping forward a bit. "Don't go just yet, will you? I . . . I have so few visitors. I . . . I'd be so glad of the company . . . of *your* company." He smiled at her. "The truth is that my uncle is always dashing off somewhere, so I'm often here on my own, and I'm not ashamed to say I'm sometimes, well . . . lonely."

Elsie drew in a breath as she listened to his plea, able to relate so very much to his declaration of loneliness, having felt it herself nearly every day, cut off as she was now from almost anyone except the servants. And even the servants were not very obliging toward her attempts to socialize with them. She had tried on more than one occasion to befriend Odelia, but Odelia, in actuality, was painfully dull and did not seem to appreciate conversation of any sort, especially with those she considered her betters. Indeed, Odelia had almost seemed to resent her efforts, despite Elsie's attempts to convince her that she was very much *not* her superior. Her timid suggestions had fallen on deaf ears, however. Mrs. Kuntz and Mrs. Schmidt were no better, even when she offered to help them with their tasks, which they did not seem to be grateful for, nor which they had ever taken her up on. She had lost Mr. Dubala and the stream of customers she had gotten to know over the years, not to mention, of course, Henrietta, Eugene (not that he had been a great companion), Ma, and now even Stanley. The truth was that she had begun a slow steady slide into despair herself, and it took her breath away that here was a person—an utterly handsome, charming person, no less—before her who found himself, at his own admittance, in exactly the same position as she. It was almost too much to contemplate!

"Of . . . of course I'll stay." Elsie's voice was tight. "If you wish it," she said with a shy smile.

"Please, sit down . . . I'll get us something to drink," he said happily now, his face lit up, like a little boy that had gotten his way.

A disturbing thought, however, regarding Harrison's sad situation suddenly occurred to Elsie as she looked over at him. "But aren't you usually at the barracks?" she asked, confused. "I would think you're never lonely there."

"Oh . . . I . . . yes, well, I'm on leave just at the moment," he said, not looking at her. "I'll be right back," he said as he dipped out of the room, leaving Elsie to ponder his answer.

"Don't go to any trouble . . . tea or coffee is fine."

He returned quickly with a bottle of whiskey and two glasses. "Is whiskey all right?" he asked apprehensively. "I'm afraid we're all out of coffee, and Uncle never drinks tea."

Elsie had never had whiskey, though Stanley was always trying to get her to taste it, but she didn't want to disappoint Harrison or to appear too high and mighty.

"Yes, I suppose that would be fine," she said, taking the empty, proffered glass and smiling hesitantly.

At her acceptance, Harrison quickly removed the bottle's cap and poured a large portion for her, though she tried to indicate with her free hand to only give her a little. He poured himself an equally large portion and, putting the bottle down, then, looked at her expectantly.

Elsie brought it to her nose to smell it, which didn't help the prospect of drinking it, as it smelled strong and slightly medicinal. Tentatively, she took a sip and grimaced as it burned its way down.

Harrison grinned and took a huge gulp of his as he sat down heavily beside her. "Thank you for coming, Elsie. It was a smashing day," he said, looking at her sideways.

"Yes, thank you, too," she said furtively and tried another sip. "Perhaps . . ." she stopped to cough slightly. "Perhaps you might read me some of your poems," she continued. "If you . . . if you want to, that is . . ."

"Poems?" he asked, a slightly puzzled look on his face. "Oh, yes! My poems! Well," he said, looking around, flustered. "I . . ."

"Only if you want to . . . I was being presumptuous, I know . . ."

Harrison stood up uneasily, then, and began to peruse the book-shelf until he found the book he was apparently looking for. To Elsie it seemed to be a part of a bigger set, but she couldn't read the title from where she sat. Was he published? she wondered excitedly. Or maybe he just kept his notes in the thick bound volumes for safekeeping?

Harrison flipped through the book as if looking for something, his eyes quickly darting over the pages and lingering on some entries longer than others, almost as if he were reading them for the first time. Finally, he seemed to find what he was looking for and cleared his throat. "Here's a rather good one, I think," he said and proceeded haltingly:

Wilt thou go with me, sweet maid,
Say, maiden, wilt thou go with me
Through the valley-depths of shade,
Of night and dark obscurity;
Where the path has lost its way,
Where the sun forgets the day,
Where there's nor life nor light to see,
Sweet maiden, wilt thou go with me!

Where stones will turn to flooding streams,
Where plains will rise like ocean waves,
Where life will fade like visioned dreams
And mountains darken into caves,
Say, maiden, wilt thou go with me
Through this sad non-identity,
Where parents live and are forgot,
And sisters live and know us not!

Say, maiden; wilt thou go with me
In this strange death of life to be,
To live in death and be the same,
Without this life or home or name,
At once to be and not to be—
That was and is not—yet to see

Things pass like shadows, and the sky
Above, below, around us lie?

Harrison looked up, then, with what could be described as a dis-traught sort of look, causing Elsie to wonder if he were trying to tell her something.

"Did you like it?" he asked, sitting next to her again, the book still in his hands.

"I . . . I did," she smiled. "But you didn't write that one, though, did you?" she asked hesitantly. "It sounds vaguely familiar. Maybe one of the Romantics? I confess I don't know much about them," she added shyly.

A flicker of indecision seemed to cross the lieutenant's face before he smiled and said "No! Of course not! Surely you recognize that one. It's . . ." he glanced at the book again quickly. "It's John Clare."

"Ah! That's it," Elsie said and cursed herself for spending so much time reading Victorian novels instead of stuff that obviously mattered, like poetry. She had read some, but not much. She would never have guessed that Harrison would have a predilection for the Romantics, though; he continued to surprise her at every turn.

She racked her brain for any scrap to come back to her, and, mirac-ulously a tidbit finally surfaced. "There is a comfort in the strength of love; 'twill make a thing endurable, which else would overset the brain, or break the heart," she offered and looked at him expectantly, allowing him a chance to guess. Seeing that his face was a blank, however, she added, "It's from Wordsworth's poem 'Michael.'" She took another bashful sip of whiskey. "We had to learn quite a lot of it at school. Mr. Keegan was very set on Wordsworth," she murmured.

Disappointingly, Harrison did not appear impressed with her knowledge, but merely sat staring at her. Without warning, he further surprised her by leaning forward suddenly and kissing her, a quick sort of kiss like the one he had given her once on the front step of the Palmer Square house but which he had never repeated since. This time, however, instead of instantly pulling away, he kissed her again, deeply this time, harder, and she felt herself weaken as a tremor ran through her. Slowly he pulled his lips from hers but remained close, and she was embarrassed that her breathing had sped up. She hoped he didn't hear her swallow hard.

Abruptly, however, he just as suddenly pulled away and turned from her. Hunched over now, he put a hand over his eyes. "I'm sorry, Elsie! I don't know what's come over me! I . . . I know I shouldn't take advantage, but you're so . . . so . . ."

"So?" Elsie encouraged.

"So *wonderful*," he said, looking at her in a way that disturbingly reminded her of a performer in a melodrama. Was he toying with her? "I've never met anyone like you," he went on with what seemed like real sincerity now. "I . . . I can't help thinking about you all the time!"

"You do?" Elsie asked, not being able to contain her elation. "I do, too! Think of *you*, that is."

"Oh, Elsie," he groaned loudly. "Can't I kiss you one more time?"

Elsie hesitated. She knew she shouldn't be doing this, but the bottle of wine they had shared on the boat and now the whiskey, plus the warmth of the fire before them, not to mention their foray, albeit brief, into poetry, was beginning to cloud her reason. In truth, she was feeling a bit inebriated. "I . . . I don't think . . ." she began timorously.

"Fine," Harrison said shortly, his brow furrowed now. "I knew it would be this way." A faint scowl appeared across his face. "I thought you liked me is all," he said, turning away from her.

Elsie was horrified that the mood had changed so quickly and was desperate to recreate it. "Oh, but Harrison, I do! I really do!" Elsie said eagerly, laying a hand on his arm and setting her whiskey glass down.

He looked over at her, his face one of hurt, and Elsie was entranced by his sad brown eyes.

"Just one more time, then," she said softly.

With a grin, he leaned toward her as if to kiss her, but then he stopped short, causing her, as she leaned forward in anticipation, her eyes closed, to awkwardly bump into him. He laughed at her as she pulled back, blushing deeply. She was about to apologize when he suddenly lunged forward, then, startling her as he kissed her now with real passion. This second kiss was so unexpected that she didn't have time to think but simply let her lips be engulfed by his. His manly smell was so close to her and his breath on her cheek was so hot that Elsie felt a shocking flood of passion. She couldn't explain why she was feeling so . . . what was the word? Fervent? His hands, which were beginning to roam now, excited her more than she thought possible. He continued kissing her lips, briefly grazing her neck and her cheek before returning to her eager, awkward lips. Elsie's heart was beating alarmingly fast, and her breath was coming so rapidly that she was forced to breathe loudly through her nose.

She knew she should stop him—she had said just one kiss—but it was so very difficult. He leaned into her so much so that she was forced to lie back, and as he kissed her neck again, she struggled not to let a moan escape from her lips. With one hand he began to caress her breasts, albeit through her cotton dress, and she felt a corresponding ache in her lower regions. It shook her, and she was about to protest, but he moved his hand away of his own accord before she could say anything. Feeling that the danger had passed, she relaxed then, only to have his hands wander to her breasts again, and this time she couldn't help moaning in earnest. Seemingly inspired by her response, he moved his hand lower, lifting her dress and brushing the inside of her leg. Elsie was in a state of desperate confusion. She knew she should stop him—any minute she would, she convinced herself—but she was starved for attention, for physical contact of any kind, even a hug from her mother. Months and months she had waited for Stanley to even kiss her cheek or take her hand, but he never did, and she didn't know how to encourage him. She had tried to suggest on the night they had rescued Henrietta from Jack that he might kiss her sometimes, but he had not gotten the hint. And now, here was this terribly handsome lieutenant, desiring her, kissing her, making her groan with pleasure. She knew that it was up to the woman to put a stop to a man's passions, but the shameful truth was that she didn't want to. She was tired of always being overlooked, sick to death of it actually, often lying in her lonely bed at night and aching, really aching, to be held by someone, anyone.

He lifted her skirt now and was frantically undoing his trousers with one hand as he kissed her. Panic in earnest set in then as he kissed her fiercely and moved on top of her. "Harrison, no!" she said, suddenly realizing that it had finally gone too far.

"Elsie, please!" he said, shifting to the side and kissing her on the lips and neck until he reached the lace collar of her dress. He fumbled to unbutton it, but after a few failed attempts, he tore it open instead, exposing the tops of her large, heaving breasts that she normally tried hard to disguise from the world. Elsie was simultaneously terrified by the violence of his actions but oddly aroused as well.

"Harrison, your uncle . . ." she panted, wondering how much damage he had done to her dress.

"He won't hear; he's asleep. Come on, Elsie, I'm going to fucking explode," he said, breathing heavily, his flowery language well and truly gone now in the heat of the moment.

"It isn't right, Harrison," she said, groaning, as he kissed her breasts and crudely grasped between her legs. She felt in extreme danger of exploding herself. She didn't know how much longer she could stand it.

"God damn it, Elsie! I love you. Does that make it better, huh?" he said almost angrily, his hot breath against her cheek again. Elsie's eyes fluttered open, and the tribal masks hanging on the wall came into her view, sending a shudder of fear through her, and she knew somehow in that moment that all was lost. She knew then that she did not have the power, the strength, to fight him off, nor did she really want to. And hadn't he just said that he loved her? She supposed she loved him, too, she thought, as he roughly kissed her again, his lips open and wet with passion. She knew what was going to happen next, and she set her mind to it, knowing that it had gone too far to stop now anyway, hadn't it? She knew she shouldn't give in to his passions, or, worse, to hers. Women, she knew, were to be the voice of sensibility and control . . . And yet, he said he loved her, and no one else ever had. She knew she was weak. If only she could be more like Henrietta, but she would never be as good as Henrietta; this she knew and had accepted long ago.

She relaxed her tight grip on his shirtsleeves.

"That's it, yes," he said huskily into her ear as she did so, and quickly he moved on top of her again. His sudden movement caused her to panic all over again, however, knowing somehow that it was going too fast.

"Harrison, wait . . ." she tried to protest, wanting him to slow down and to explain she knew not what, but he was far from listening. Crudely he pulled at her underthings and, without any further prelude, wolfishly thrust himself inside of her, coarse and fast. She felt an intense pain as she struggled to make sense of what was happening and was shockingly overcome when her body betrayed her by responding, almost against her will, to his actions. Harrison groaned deeply as he continued on top of her, thrusting faster and faster. "Marry me. Marry me, Elsie," he grunted as he neared his climax.

Elsie, carried away by her own conflicting emotions, could not believe what he was saying but said hoarsely, "Yes, Harrison. Yes."

And it was done.

In the short time it takes for the autumn sun to dip below the horizon or to pluck the last of the summer roses, for better or worse, Lieutenant Harrison Barnes-Smith had deflowered Elsie Von Harmon in his uncle's drawing room and had simultaneously extracted a promise from her to marry him, and nothing could change that now.

Elsie could think of nothing else for days afterward as she paced around the house, reenvisioning the fateful night over and over, sometimes mortified, sometimes distraught as to what it all really meant, sometimes, if she were honest, tingling at the memory of what his kisses had evoked in her, causing a thin film of perspiration to erupt under her arms and on her neck as she thought of it. Harrison's hook in her was complete, whether she wanted it to be or not. When he had escorted her home that night, a sleepy Karl letting them into the front hall before disappearing off to bed, Harrison, almost certainly drunk by now, had violently grabbed her to him in a farewell embrace, kissing her and whispering in her ear, "You're mine now, Elsie. Body and soul." And it had both excited her and filled her with an awful dread.

Harrison had subsequently appeared the very next day, having remarkably reverted back now to the role of polite, charming suitor, only once revealing what might be considered the more insidious side of his personality. It happened as they sat awkwardly in the front parlor on Palmer Square when Elsie asked him if he had really, you know, meant it about them getting married or was it perhaps something one usually said in the . . . in a moment such as the one that occurred between them?

Before Harrison could answer, however, Odelia entered the room, dutifully delivering a vase of water as requested. Elsie quickly stood up to take it, noticing as she did so that Odelia most definitely gave both of them a skeptical once-over with her eyes before she left the room, the nature of which Elsie rather thought bordered on insolence, or perhaps just plain rudeness, and she fretted that somehow she perhaps knew what had happened between her and Harrison.

Taking the vase with trembling fingers, Elsie set it on a small table and began to arrange the limp bouquet of white asters Harrison had nabbed from Palmer Square Park on the way over, saying as he handed them to her that wild flowers were so much preferable to hothouse flowers, didn't she think? Elsie merely hoped they really *had* been from the park, as they looked suspiciously like the ones growing in the front yard of her neighbors, who would most certainly not appreciate them being ripped from their prized garden.

"Of course I meant it!" Harrison said, a touch of annoyance in his voice. "You're not trying to back out of it, are you? I knew it was too good to be true!" he exclaimed, managing to insert a small whine.

Elsie quickly turned to him. "Oh, no, Harrison! I . . . I just wanted to be sure is all," she crookedly smiled, turning back to the flowers now. They were so limp she wasn't sure she could revive them. "It's just that it might be difficult with my grandfather, he . . . I think, that is, I think he had other plans for whom I should marry."

"No doubt someone better than me," he said bitingly from where he still sat on one of the armchairs.

Elsie fought down the memory of the conversation she had had with Aunt Agatha, in which she had specifically warned her away from the lieutenant. "Well . . . it's just that . . ."

"Because it's awfully hard to unload damaged goods," Harrison said quietly, the sullen woefulness in his voice having been replaced by a certain knowing edge. Elsie felt herself tense. She caressed the smooth silkiness of one of the petals, finding momentary comfort in it before she pulled it from its center as she turned to him. He was sitting, quite relaxed, his legs crossed casually and his head propped up by one of his fists, his arm balanced on the side of the armchair, as he gazed at her with a wickedly confident air about him.

"What do you mean by that?" Elsie asked delicately, not looking at him but bleakly guessing his meaning.

"Just that, you know, some might see you as damaged goods now, making you all the harder for old Exley to unload, is all."

His implication hit her full force, and she gasped. "Harrison! How could you say such a thing?" she whispered, turning to him now, shocked not only by the unkindness of his words but by the level of hurt she felt.

To her surprise, Harrison laughed. "It's all right with me, kid. I don't mind, but some of the upper crust, well, you know how they are. Or maybe you don't . . ."

Elsie could not believe his cruelty. "But how would anyone . . . or Grandfather even . . . how would he ever know?" she asked faintly.

"Oh, I don't know," Harrison drawled. "Exley's a shrewd man of business. I wouldn't put it past him to have one of the servants keeping an eye out for anything untoward," he said with exaggerated delicacy.

Elsie's mind raced back to last night. Only Karl had seen them come in. Surely sleepy old Karl was not a spy? But what did it matter, anyway, she thought defensively. Coming in late with the lieutenant didn't prove anything! And she had been careful to cover her torn dress. Karl wouldn't have been able to tell she had been . . . interfered with . . . would he? But why was Harrison acting this way? It was ungentlemanly, to say the very least, especially after . . . after what had happened between them. Tears suddenly filled her eyes and she quickly wiped them before they spilled down her cheeks.

"You're crying?" he said derisively. "I'm only kidding! Can't you take a joke?" he asked with real scorn on his face. "You take everything too seriously, Elsie. Come here!" he commanded her, holding out his hand from where he sat.

Reluctantly Elsie walked over and took his hand, tying to muster up a smile. "Come on, kid," he said, pulling her down to balance uncomfortably on his knee. "Don't worry about any of that. We're getting married, you and me. You're happy about it, right?" he said, putting a slightly bent finger under her chin and forcing her to look up at him. She quivered under the sharp stare of his brown eyes. "You're not going to throw me over now, are you?"

Try as she might, Elsie couldn't make herself speak. She could only manage a slight shake of her head.

"That's my girl," he beamed. "I knew I could count on you to be sensible," he said, rubbing his hand along the side of her face. She hated herself for feeling a quiver at his touch, but she made herself stand up.

Quickly he stood up, too.

"What's the matter, kid? Hey, Elsie!" he said, more seriously now, taking her hand. "I'm crazy about you. You know that, right?"

Elsie couldn't bring herself to say anything.

"Elsie, come on! I need you! It's not my fault I've had no one to teach me the right things. I guess things got a little out of hand last night, but . . . you know, I couldn't help it. I thought you liked it . . . you seemed eager enough," he added with a certain level of disdain in his voice.

Elsie blushed profusely and looked away. Was this how a gentleman—a lover?—behaved? Talking about it openly? But maybe she
was just being naive. An image of Jane Austin's poor Lydia Bennet
appeared before her, but she angrily thrust it away.

"I thought I could count on you," he said sulkily. "Come on! Don't
say you don't care."

With great effort, Elsie made herself look into his eyes, then, and
tried to decide if they held cruelty or something else altogether, like
perhaps fear. She couldn't help but be infuriatingly attracted to him,
even now. Despite everything he had just said, particularly that she
was now damaged goods, Elsie could not help but to ultimately feel
sorry for him. He had been through so much, after all. No wonder
he was a poet—he obviously struggled with so many emotions. He
didn't mean to be cruel, she reluctantly decided; perhaps he had just
lost his way a bit. After all, he had lost his mother at such a young
age. His behavior last night she had all but convinced herself was out
of character, possibly due to the alcohol, and he seemed genuinely
sorry for what he had said just now.

She looked at him closely. They could take care of each other, she
thought. Better than anyone else because they both understood loneliness. Yes, she could see herself as his wife, she told herself, pouring
her love out onto him. Perhaps that's all he needed to be a better man.
Perhaps this is what God intended for her. Maybe this is why she had
been alone for so long, so that He could lead her to Harrison, who
so obviously needed her. She felt a certain sort of fatalism, then, an
acceptance that this was to be her role in life. She would simply have
to overlook his rough edges until she could smooth them out.

She forced herself to smile at him.

"That's more like it," he said with a grin. "I hate long faces. You
aren't sore, are you?" he asked in such a way that Elsie felt he would
surely be provoked if she indeed answered in the affirmative.

"No! Of course I'm not . . . not sore," she finally stammered. And
though she knew he wasn't referring to her physical well-being, her
mind went to the blood she had found in her underthings. "But . . .

but it does concern me a bit, Harrison . . ." she tried to say delicately. "What are we . . . what are we going to do? How will we live?"

"I'll figure it out! Surely your grandfather will set us up . . ." he said with an eagerness that was painful to hear.

Elsie felt a stab of panic, not only regarding what her grandfather might say, but also at the thought that perhaps it really was true that Harrison was merely after the Exley money as Aunt Agatha had suggested. Hurriedly she pushed the thought from her mind. "I'm not so sure, Harrison . . . he's . . ."

"Just don't tell anyone for now," he interrupted her, not listening. "You haven't, have you?" he demanded.

"No! Of course not!"

"Not even your mother?" he asked, suspiciously.

"No," she answered with a sad shake of her head. "She hasn't been down yet." Indeed, Elsie had been waiting for her to come down, all the while trying to decide how much she should reveal to her, when Harrison himself had appeared, ironically rescuing her from that particular decision.

"Good. Good," he repeated, deep in thought.

"Have you . . . have you thought what you might say to Grandfather?" she asked hesitantly, not wanting to upset him again.

"No, not yet. But leave him to me. I'll think of something."

"It . . . it does seem a bit rushed, Harrison . . ." she ventured. At the sight of his irritated face, she quickly added, "not that it changes how we feel, of course, but perhaps we should wait awhile. After all, we . . . we really don't know each other all that well."

He gave her a wicked stare. "After last night? I think we know each other well enough," he said coolly.

Elsie looked down at the ground. He did have a point, but did he have to say it that way? "I'm sorry. You're right, of course."

"Nothing's going to keep you from me," Harrison said testily. "Not even you."

Elsie, not knowing what else to do, forced herself to look at him and couldn't look away again, even though she tried. She was mesmerized. Harrison took hold of her shoulders, then, and kissed her, roughly, his thick lips coarsely moving against hers as they had last night. Elsie was initially caught off guard, but then she shamefully felt herself responding. She had convinced herself in bed last night that what had happened between them was a one-time thing, that she could not let things get out of hand that way again until they were properly married. She knew she had been at fault, not stopping him, and had prayed the whole rosary for forgiveness.

But now here she was, again letting him kiss her and caress her beyond what she knew to be proper, even between an affianced couple. He pressed himself against her as he kissed her, forcing her against the wall, and she could feel his hardened excitement as he kissed her again and again, her face almost wet now. Elsie was not sure what would have happened next had Mrs. Schmidt, the house-keeper, not happened to pass through the hallway just outside the parlor, making an uncharacteristically loud noise as she did so, which caused the lovers to quickly separate.

"Let me see you tomorrow," Harrison said breathlessly, bracing his arms against the wall on either side of Elsie's face, momentarily trapping her. "God damn it, Elsie! I need you!"

"All right, Harrison," she said quietly. "Why don't I come and sit with you and your uncle and visit?" she suggested.

"Don't be stupid," he said. "He's not up to having visitors just yet, and, anyway, I want to be alone with you." He paused, thinking. "How about the pictures?" he asked, to which she nodded, ashamed that the prospect of sitting next to him in a darkened movie house excited her.

The lieutenant abruptly left, then, and Elsie watched him go from where she stood now by the window. She attempted to adjust her hair back into place as she watched him saunter off down the street. She studied him, trying to envision him as her husband leaving for work on any given day. He seemed very pleased with himself, she decided, as she watched him pause halfway down the street to pull out a cigarette. But as he bent to light it, she saw him turn his head, then, to watch two attractive women walk past him. It was a seemingly innocent gesture, but something about the grin now on his face and the way he carelessly flicked his ash as he went on his way cut her to the quick.

What have I done? Elsie suddenly thought, her arms forlornly dropping to her sides, a feeling of extreme panic threatening to overwhelm her. Had she really engaged herself to this man? she thought frantically, bringing one hand up to her mouth as if to hold back a scream and feeling herself break into a sweat. She saw a black hole open up in front of her, but before she became enveloped by it, she turned from the window, breathing hard and scolding herself for being ridiculous. She was being silly! She just needed some rest, she thought, as she climbed the stairs back to her room, and resolved to stop thinking about him. After all, what was done was done.

But as she lay on top of her bed, still fully clothed, she found she could not, after all, stop thinking about him, about what had happened. She had to admit she cared for Harrison very much, admired him, no, *loved* him—she was sure. He was the first man to show her any real attention, the attention that she so craved, and though her intellect might tell her one thing, she could not completely rein in her emotions. Unexpectedly and certainly unbidden, thoughts of Stanley then entered her mind, and, for the first time, she did not relish them. He must never find out what had happened between her and Harrison, she thought desperately, but, then again, what did it matter? She didn't belong to him anymore, she thought angrily, with tears sometimes coming to her eyes. Hadn't she often compared him to Harrison over the last couple of months, Stanley clearly coming up inferior to the lieutenant in so many ways? she tried to remind herself. And, more to the point, hadn't she come to the conclusion that he had given her up as well?

While it was true, she admitted, that one could say that Harrison had taken advantage of her in a certain way, he had said that he loved her and wanted to marry her, which is more than Stanley had ever done. Surely that should count for something, shouldn't it? she thought as she rolled onto her side. Absently she traced the raised rows of the chenille pattern on her bedspread with her finger. She was not, as she had so often feared, to be left to the side as the years inevitably slipped by. She desperately wanted a romance of her own, just as Henrietta had.

She curled her knees up into her chest now as she remembered how she had more than once in the past thought about what it might be like to enjoy the dashing lieutenant's kisses. Now that she had, however, it wasn't nearly as romantic as she had imagined it might be. But perhaps that was her fault, she reasoned. Perhaps it was her own ignorance in knowing what to do, her lack of experience, which had made it less than she had expected.

Only once did it occur to her how similar her situation may have been to Ma's, but she quickly dismissed it. For one thing, she told herself hastily, Harrison was an officer, not a butcher's boy, and, according to Ma, her father had forced her, almost raped her, which Harrison, she insisted to herself as she quickly wiped away a tear, had most certainly not done. She had *let* him, she told herself, though it shamed her to admit it. But Ma must never find out what she had done! She would treat her worse than she had treated poor Henrietta, always accusing her of low morals, when, in fact, as far as Elsie knew, anyway, Henrietta had always been beyond reproach, despite her seedy surroundings. But maybe she and Clive . . . No! Elsie insisted to herself. Henrietta would never have been as weak as she had been. Yes, Ma would hate her if she knew. Cast her out, perhaps. But what did it matter, if she was getting married soon anyway? That was another difference. Ma had gotten pregnant, which had forced her into marriage. Harrison, Elsie consoled herself, had asked her to marry him before he had . . . well, *while* they had coupled. Surely that made all the difference! Nonetheless she prayed she wasn't pregnant.

Ma was only part of her worries, however, her grandfather being a bigger one. She knew little of the Barnes-Smith family, but she felt relatively sure that they were not the wealthy, connected family her grandfather was scheming for, especially as Aunt Agatha had already warned her off from him. Again she felt a sense of panic and wondered if it might be best to decline Harrison's offer after all and pretend none of this had ever happened. But what about Harrison's rather dismaying insinuation about her being ruined now for any other marriage prospects her grandfather might have had in mind? But he would never know that, would he? Was sleepy old Karl indeed a spy? It seemed unlikely. But what if she *was* pregnant? Surely it would be better to cast her lot now with Harrison in case she was and before it became obvious?

Yes, she would cast her lot with Harrison, she resolved, telling herself, repeatedly, that she was lucky, actually, to be loved by such a man as Harrison. Her conscious mind did not let herself dwell on the achingly painful fact that he had taken something so very tender and intimate from her, only to then descry her as damaged and undesirable because of it, as if she had been solely at fault for its loss. Somewhere deep in her heart—a part she didn't dare listen to—she was vaguely aware that not only was he, in truth, Stanley's inferior, but he was hers as well, causing a part of her to hate not him, but herself, for accepting him as worthy of her love. But she fought furiously to keep these thoughts from bubbling to the surface. No! she almost said out loud. She had begun this course, and she was determined to stick to it. She only hoped that Harrison would prove true to his word and have a plan.

The immediate challenge, she contemplated uneasily, was to convince poor Stanley of her happiness as he sat across from her now in the parlor. She again offered him some tea.

"No, Els, I'm not . . . you've already asked me that. No, thank you," he said with exaggerated deliberation. "I . . . I just thought I should see you." He stood up and walked across the room to the window. He looked out, distracted for a moment by some activity outside before suddenly remembering the task at hand and forcing himself to turn back to her. "How's your ankle?" he asked, pointing to it.

"Fine. Thank you," she said, her brow furrowed in confusion.

"Look, Elsie, there's no use beating about the bush. I . . . I have to tell you something." He thrust his hands in his pockets and stared at the carpet as he continued. "I know in the past there was sort of an . . . understanding between us, let's say. But . . . I . . ." he glanced up at her nervously. "Gee, Els, you seem different somehow," he said, looking at her closely as if trying to determine what it was.

Elsie blushed and was mortified that he might be able to guess what had gone on between her and Harrison.

"Go on," she encouraged.

Stan shook his head. "Yeah, well, I was saying . . . I know there was a sort of understanding between us . . . about, you know . . . about getting engaged at some point . . ."

"Yes?" she said encouragingly, grateful that he had finally come to the climax of what he wanted to say; he looked so wretched, milling about with his thoughts.

"It's just that I . . . I'm not so sure we're really suited for each other . . ."

Elsie was about to agree with him, but he cut her off.

"Now! Before you say anything . . ." he said, holding up a hand. "I want you to know I'll always care for you . . . as a friend, that is!" he added hurriedly. "I'll care for all your family, really, and I'd still be glad to help any time, though I'm not sure how much help I'd really be," he said, wistfully looking around the well-furnished room before turning his eyes back to hers. "I'm awfully sorry, Elsie . . . I . . ."

"Perhaps it *is* for the best, Stan," she interrupted, which completely threw him off guard. He had come expecting tears and denials and perhaps some awkward begging on Elsie's part, but not a quick acquiescence! What was going on? Suddenly he smelled a rat . . .

"What do you mean?" he asked, his voice full of surprise and suspicion. He paused to think. "Hey! It's that lieutenant, isn't it?" he asked, the obvious suddenly dawning on him like a ton of bricks.

"He hopes to catch you, doesn't he? Or maybe he already has!" he exclaimed, eyeing her carefully. "What gives, Elsie?"

Elsie swallowed hard. "It's true, Stanley." She managed a weak smile and sat up straight. "As it happens, I am engaged to Lieutenant Barnes-Smith," she said quietly and made herself look at him, fearing the worst.

"Engaged!" he shouted. "You barely know him! Have you lost your mind?"

"No," she tried to reply firmly. "I have not lost my mind, and I know him quite well, actually. Well enough to marry him."

"Engaged?" he muttered, and he began to pace about the room, studying the carpet. "Engaged?" He stopped his pacing to stare at her. "Does Henrietta know?"

"Not yet. We . . . we haven't announced it yet, so . . . I'll write to her soon."

"Do you love him?" he asked incredulously, a tinge of hurt in his voice.

"That's none of your business now, Stanley," she answered and oddly felt like she might cry when she heard the hurt in his voice.

"I can't believe it!" he said, barely above a murmur, turning as he said it toward the window.

"Anyway," Elsie went on, speaking to his back. "I believe you have someone else as well. Isn't that so, Stanley?" she asked softly.

He turned back to her now, mystified. "How do you know that?" he asked, suddenly sounding fearful.

"I . . . I saw you. It's Rose, isn't it? Henrietta's friend?" she asked hesitantly.

Stan just stared at her.

"I saw you outside the electrics. She took your arm and . . . kissed you . . . I'd come to talk with you, but . . ."

Stan wiped his eyes. Whether there was a bit of sand in them or merely some unaccounted for liquid, no one was sure, but he wiped them just the same.

"Yes," he finally said. "I was with Rose. I . . . I like her. Very much."

Elsie cleared her throat. "Well, it's all worked out for the best, then, hasn't it?" She forced a smile. "Are you . . . are you engaged? To her, that is?"

Stan still looked at her as if in a daze. "Not yet . . . but I was considering it. I . . . I thought I should see you first."

"Well, thank you for that, Stanley. It's more consideration than I gave to you," she said sadly and stood up. "Perhaps it would be best if you went now," she made herself say, though she was crumbling inside, suddenly afraid she would never see him again.

He shook himself as if waking from a dream. "Yes, I suppose I should." He walked slowly to the door, Elsie following him.

"I guess this is goodbye, then," he said, putting his hat on now and giving the front foyer one last gaze.

"You can still stop by and say hello, you know," Elsie said encouragingly. "Ma . . . Mother . . . would like it."

"Yeah, maybe," he shrugged noncommittally. "Goodbye, Elsie," he said forlornly and held out his hand to her awkwardly.

"Goodbye, Stanley," she said, taking it, and she leaned forward to kiss him on the cheek as well. "I'll miss you."

He left then, without another word, and as he closed the door soundlessly behind him, Elsie could not help but begin to sob violently, and loudly at that, there being no one close by to hear her anyway.

Chapter 21

Clive softly knocked on the bedroom door the morning after his argument with Henrietta, having spent the night in the adjacent guest room. He had had time to think about what had been said between them and regretted very deeply his reference of Henrietta to her mother. He knew this was shockingly unfair. But he also knew that this was not the heart of the matter, that he was being unfair in a much deeper way. It was again his persistence in trying to protect her, to keep her safe. And yet, hadn't he been thwarted even when he tried to wall her up, as it were, at Highbury this past summer? She had been in danger anyway. It had found her despite his best efforts. His natural reaction, perhaps subconsciously, had been to try all the harder to ensconce her, but he realized now that this had backfired. He saw in front of him a life in which Henrietta would not be content to sit quietly at home, and wasn't that the very thing that had drawn him to her? Hadn't her enthusiasm and spark for life jumpstarted his own weary heart? Having found this wonderful elixir, however, his tendency was to hide and protect it, but he knew it was no use. Henrietta wanted to be at his side, and though it terrified him, it excited him as well. He should have taken her to Matlock with him as she had wished, but, then again, would Wallace have really talked if he had? And if he had sensed that Wallace would talk privately, what would he have done with Henrietta? Sit her on a stool in the pub to wait for him? Have her stroll up and down the streets? Damn it! Each option filled him with dread, but he knew he would just have to try harder to make her feel involved. He would pick and choose the opportunities, of course, but he knew he couldn't just leave her behind any longer. After all, he further considered, she had survived two attacks from Neptune and seemed remarkably unaffected, after the initial trauma, that is. She was stronger, he concluded, than he had originally thought, in more ways than one. He would have to let her come along, at least some of the times, anyway, and he would simply have to grin and bear it, at least, that is, until she had a child to care for.

She was still asleep when he poked his head round the door, and, closing it noiselessly behind him, he carefully lay down beside her and watched her sleep. She was so achingly beautiful, and his heart almost stopped as he observed how very young she looked as she slept. Finally he reached out and brushed back a lock of her hair that had fallen across her face, and she stirred. Upon seeing him, her first reaction was to smile, which warmed him through, but she quickly stiffened, then, obviously remembering their quarrel. She sat up and pulled the sheets around her as best she could, despite him partially lying on them, and scowled.

"Henrietta, I'm sorry," Clive said genuinely, looking up into her blue eyes. "I'm sorry about what I said. I didn't mean any of it. And when I took hold of you," he paused, "I didn't mean anything by that either. I merely meant to apologize, even at that moment."

She didn't say anything but continued to stare at him with a look of nettled hurt.

"Henrietta, you must believe me. Try to understand. It's difficult for me sometimes to remember that I have a partner now, a wife . . . a friend. Give me time," he said gently, "time to get used to sharing my life with you . . . *all* the parts of my life. I need you to help me, to be patient, to show me how to be a good husband." He reached for her hand and brought it to his lips and kissed it.

—

As he did so, Henrietta looked at him and, despite herself, felt her heart go out to him. A part of her was indeed hurt, but she, too, regretted last night and had reflected that she had again gotten caught up in playing the role of the impudent child, a role she seemed to have perfected since meeting Clive, she sighed. She *did* feel that he had been wrong to exclude her in the way that he had, but she should never have called into question his ability as a detective. She had been wrong there, and she knew it. Not only because it wasn't true but because she knew it was a low blow, a sensitive issue for him, and she had willingly used it against him, knowing it would sting. And here he was, asking her for her forgiveness when really it should be her asking for his.

"No, Clive, I'm the one who should be apologizing," she said, reaching out and running her fingers through his hair. "I said some awful things, and I'm sorry," she said genuinely. "I didn't mean to hurt you. I know I should be more . . . more . . ."

"Wifely?" he asked with a smile, and she couldn't help but laugh.

Clive's look of strain disappeared as he lay his head down on the pillows now, still looking at her. "I missed you last night," he said suggestively. "I didn't realize how much I've already grown used to having you close to me. Especially since I'm apparently in need of a . . . how did you put it last night? . . . *a pretty pet* . . ." With mock concern, he pretended to look for said pet on the huge bed. He looked back at her then and shrugged as if giving up the search and threw himself back on the pillows. "I suppose you'll have to do."

"Clive!" she exclaimed and found herself laughing again. It felt good to not be angry with him anymore. In truth, she had slept terribly. She gathered up a pillow and hit him on the head with it.

"Minx!" he said, shocked by the force of it, and he sat up on his elbow, where he was greeted by another whack of a pillow as she laughed. He grabbed her, holding her by the arms as he forced her down, her hair spread out wildly on the remaining pillows. He bent and kissed her and thrilled when she responded in kind, running her

tongue along his lips as she ran her hands down his naked back, his
robe having come undone.

"Do you mean to have your wicked way?" she asked him with a
mischievous grin that caused a certain euphoria to travel through
him, no sign of what he had perceived to be her fear of him last
night—if it *had* been fear. It was clear in this moment, anyway, that
she desired him, wanted him, and he knew then, as he began to make
love to her, that all was well.

Wallace was eventually released on bail later in the morning, Stevens
being discreetly sent by Lord Linley to collect him, as it simply
wouldn't do for a peer of the realm to be seen at the local gaol. Clive,
having spent the morning closeted with Henrietta, unfortunately did
not have the opportunity of seeing or speaking with him after his
arrival home, as Wallace, upon returning, had likewise locked himself in his rooms like a child, refusing to speak to anyone. Lady Linley
had been beside herself as to what they would tell their guests and
suggested that they say he had irresponsibly gone off to London to
visit—no, help!—a friend, but Lord Linley had insisted that the truth
be told, that Wallace had been held—wrongfully, to be sure—by the
local constabulary overnight. He was sure the tale would eventually make its way to the ears of their guests, anyway, and he did not
wish to appear as a liar. As it was, all of the guests, whether they had
guessed the truth or heard it from the servants, began to make their
excuses to depart earlier than scheduled in the wake of what was
obviously a family crisis.

Now devoid of extraneous persons, a pallor of sorts had come over
the house, as if it were shrouded by the murdered man himself and
his as-of-yet-unknown killer. Bereft of their guests, Lord and Lady
Linley spent most of their time in their private rooms, as did Wallace,
which left Clive and Henrietta quite alone to wander about at what
should have been their leisure, but which was fraught instead with
an unnamed unease.

Clive took the opportunity to relate to Henrietta all he knew about the murder case thus far as they took a turn in the garden. Henrietta, listening intently and secretly thrilled that he was sharing the case with her, agreed that there was not much to go on, and, like Clive, she felt sure that Wallace was not the murderer but that he was obviously hiding something. Clive believed, based on what Maxwell Fielding had told her over tea in the village with Captain Russell, that it must have something to do with organizing the workers in Matlock or possibly Derby, or that perhaps he was part of a bigger socialist movement abroad and was a local leader. Nothing criminal, necessarily, but not exactly above board, either.

Clive had telephoned Inspector Hartle since Wallace's release, asking if any new light had been shed on the other two suspects. The inspector had begrudgingly told him that they had found Crawford in York just that morning, staying with family, who all, by the way, vouched for his whereabouts the night of the murder. That just left O'Brien, who had an alibi, albeit a fishy one, and Wallace. The only other remote possibility, of course, was that it hadn't been someone in the pub at all. That Wallace had dropped his walking stick as he hurried along and some stranger had picked it up, attacked Jacobs as he walked along, hoping just to rob him but killing him in the process, perhaps by accident? But there were several flaws to this theory. First of all, it would be one thing for Wallace to forget his stick inside the pub, but it seemed a bit unlikely that he wouldn't notice he had dropped it as he walked along. Second, why would a stranger randomly attack Ernest Jacobs? How would he have known he had such a large amount of money on him? Had it just been a random robbery that had proved exceptionally fruitful for the thief? It all seemed too coincidental. For his part, Clive was betting on O'Brien.

Stopping under one of the trellises now where only a single white rose was still in bloom among the dying vines, Clive asked Henrietta if she thought it possible for them to speak once again to this Maxwell Fielding.

"I believe he's returned to Oxford, I think he said," Henrietta mused, having been deep in thought. "But his brother, Rory—I think that's his name—may be of more help anyway," she said hopefully, wanting desperately to contribute and prove her worth to Clive. "He's the one who's Wallace's supposed friend."

"He drinks at the Merry Bells, too, I imagine?"

"Yes, I believe so."

Clive examined his pocket watch. "The shift won't end for a few hours yet," he murmured almost to himself. "Plenty of time to check out these trails of Wallace's," he said, holding his arm out to Henrietta. "We should probably have done this before now. Shall we?"

Henrietta wrapped her arm through his and could not contain her smile as she leaned into him and they began to walk across the wet grounds. He was inviting her to accompany him, to help him, and she felt her heart thrill.

It took longer than they had expected to reach the paths beaten down through the woods, as they had been on horseback the first time they had come upon them. It had rained this morning, and the ground was very soggy and the air still damp and cold, so much so that they could see their breath, the moisture heavy in the air. The sky was a slate gray, and a wind had picked up. Henrietta wished as they tramped along that she had worn a warmer coat. Clive paused when they came upon the place she now recognized as the fairy bower, though it was nearly bare now of any vegetation, and the sound of the cold brook gurgling beside them, full after the rain, made her shiver further. Standing among the dead bracken, Clive wrapped his warm arms around her and kissed her on the forehead. "We've missed our chance, I'm afraid," he said wistfully.

She looked up at him and did not think she could love him more than she did right now. He seemed to sense it and kissed her tenderly on the lips. She rested her head against his chest, then, and breathed in his smell—a deep manly scent of tobacco and linen—still unmistakable even through the soft tweed he wore now. She relaxed against him as she took in the scene around them. Though the branches were stark above them, with a thick, sodden blanket of reds and golds underfoot, Henrietta doubted they would see anything half as beautiful on their upcoming trip to Europe.

"We'll just have to come back," she said into Clive's chest. "Promise me," she said as she looked up at him. "Promise me that we'll come back to this spot and that you'll make love to me right here in the open."

Clive looked at her with an arched eyebrow, his mouth twitching. "That's a promise easily given," he said, kissing her again softly. "But," he said, after holding her close for a few more moments, "we musn't tarry, my love. The game's afoot!" he said, stepping back and taking her hand, and she stifled a little laugh at his joke, forgetting for a moment that they were investigating a serious case and that a murderer was still at large.

Wallace's path through the woods led them through a meadow, which soaked their legs completely as they waded through the wet grass until the path finally opened up onto the road itself, which, Clive deduced, must be about halfway between Cromford and Matlock. Having come to what was apparently a dead end, they paused to rest while they contemplated what to do next. Henrietta sat on a rather large rock covered in moss by the side of the road, while Clive leaned against the stone fence running alongside it, methodically digging in his pocket for his pipe as he tried to think. This did indeed seem to be very much a blind alley. Why on earth would Wallace trudge all the way through the woods simply to reach the lane that he could quite easily access with one of the cars from the garage, and with a bum leg to boot? It didn't make sense and furthered the air of mystery surrounding Wallace's movements. What did he do once he reached the lane? Clive wondered as he puffed deeply, searching the vicinity with his eyes. If he wished to have some secret rendezvous in the village, this would not be the fastest way to it.

"Any ideas?" he called across to Henrietta, who seemed to be gazing vacantly at the sheep in the adjoining pasture. A few weak rays of sunshine had broken through the cloud cover and illuminated Henrietta as she sat, causing Clive's heart to positively ache for her.

Henrietta looked over at him and shook her head, her disappointment obvious. Her gaze went beyond him now, though, down the road a bit, and suddenly she sat up stiffly, focused on something that had caught her eye. So intently was she staring that Clive turned to look as well.

"What is it, darling?" he asked, unsettled, but not seeing anything out of the ordinary.

Henrietta stood up and marched down the road a bit to what looked like a scrub pine bush off to the side. Clive followed her, intrigued, and watched as she pulled at several of the pine branches to reveal an old motorbike, painted a dull gray, complete with sidecar, an obvious remnant of the war.

"I saw the sun flash off the chrome," Henrietta explained, "or I probably wouldn't have noticed."

"My God," said Clive. "Well done, Henrietta!" he said, looking at her appreciatively, to which she could not help but smile. "Obviously this must be why Wallace tramps down here. This must be his. But why not keep it in the garage up at the house? And where does he go with it?" he asked himself, looking up and down the road.

"My guess is Matlock," Henrietta suggested. "If he went regularly to Cromford in this thing, he'd be seen for sure. And he obviously wants secrecy, hence he hides this thing down here."

"Yes, I agree," Clive answered. "All the more reason to find this Rory Fielding, I think. Perhaps he can shed some light on Wallace's activities in Matlock." He looked down at his drenched, shivering wife. "Come, my dear, let's get out of this cold," he said, taking her small hand in his. He was surprised by how chilled it felt. "What? No gloves?" he asked as he raised their intertwined fingers to his lips to kiss them. "Whatever would Mother say?" he asked, a wry grin on his face.

"Cheeky," she answered, clearly suppressing a smile.

The village was not far at this point, and they soon came upon the Horse and Coach, sitting, as it did, on the lonely road just before it forked into the village proper. After hesitating a few minutes, they decided to go in rather than continue on to the village, where Clive had planned to telephone the house for a car to come fetch them. Henrietta had begged to stop here instead, however, wanting to see what a real English pub looked like so that she could tell Elsie. Clive complied, thinking that it might be nice to sit before the pub's fireplace and drink an ale with his lovely wife. It would also be a good chance to conduct his own little investigation with the innkeeper. He had resisted the temptation before now, not wanting to step on the inspector's toes, but as chance had put him here, he saw no harm in asking a few questions.

Henrietta sat waiting for him at a small table by the fire, looking around curiously and resisting the temptation to put her feet on the fender. The pub was dim and smoky, inhabited at the moment by what looked like local farmers, sitting in little groups talking quietly. Everything seemed muted here, and Henrietta could not help but compare it to the loud dance halls in Chicago or the noisy taverns. A quiet, cozy hush enveloped this place, and Henrietta held her hands up contentedly to the fire even as she heard the rain pelting the windows outside. But for her damp feet, she wished they could stay here all day.

Clive appeared, then, and handed her a small glass of lager, he called it, and sat down heavily across from her with his own large glass, though his looked much darker. "He isn't offering much more than we already know," he said in his own muted tone as he leaned toward her, referring of course to his conversation with the innkeeper. "Confirmed that Crawford and O'Brien left around the same time as the dead man. Says that Wallace did, too, though." Clive took a long pull of his beer. "Something's not right here. I can feel it."

The innkeeper approached them now, carrying two heaping

plates of steak-and-ale pie and chips, which he put down roughly in front of them. "There ya are," he said plainly. Henrietta felt her mouth water and the sight of the steaming meat pie in front of her. She hadn't realized how hungry she was.

"Hope you don't mind that I ordered for us," Clive said with a wry grin. "Thought we could use some food."

"That and you were hoping for him to give you more information, I presume," Henrietta said as she tasted a bite and nearly groaned with the pleasure of it. "But, yes, I'm famished."

"Darling, you surprise me at every turn," Clive said, taking a bite himself. "Very astute."

They were silent for a few minutes while they eagerly ate, Henrietta swearing she had never had something this delicious in her life, to which Clive responded that her high opinion was probably due to the fact that she was cold and wet.

"There's another odd thing," Clive said, pausing to eat a chip from the end of his fork. Henrietta thought it delightful to see him eating something so common. "The innkeeper confirms that Wallace rarely drinks here, which is not what our friend Compton says, as we've already been informed."

"Didn't he say anything else?" Henrietta asked, wiping her mouth carefully. It would never do to appear back at Castle Linley with gravy on her lips.

"Not really. He clammed up. When I tried to explain that I'm a guest of Lord Linley and that I'm trying to help the police in a round-about sort of way, he suggested I "find yerself a badge, then," Clive repeated irritably.

Henrietta could not help but let out a little laugh. "Serves you right, I suppose," she added, draining her beer. "Did you ever think that it could be a woman?" Henrietta asked, leaning back now. "Maybe that's what this is really all about."

Clive looked at her appreciatively. "It did cross my mind at one point, but it doesn't seem to fit. Why the secrecy and the elaborate ruse?"

"Perhaps she's unsuitable. Not worthy of being Lady Linley and all that. Stranger things have been known to happen," she said mischievously.

"According to Compton, though, this has been going on for a couple of years already. I would have thought he would have grown tired of such an amusement by now."

"Perhaps she's more than an amusement."

"If so, then why wouldn't he force the issue with Lord and Lady Linley? He seems willing to force any other issue."

"True," she admitted.

Clive stood up then and held his hand out to her. "Come, my dear, our carriage awaits," he said, inclining his head toward the window.

Henrietta took up her soaked coat, which had not had nearly enough time to dry out yet, and bent to look out the nearest window. She could see that Bradwell had pulled up with the Rolls. She looked at Clive questioningly.

"I took the liberty of calling the house from the bar when we first came in. Told Bradwell to give us an hour."

"How clever, darling," she said, slipping her arm through his and kissing the stubble on his cheek. "Your timing is impeccable."

They stayed at Castle Linley only long enough to change clothing. Henrietta longed for a warm bath, but she knew they hadn't time if they were to make it to Matlock as the men emerged from the Mill. This time she put on a thick tweed skirt and made sure to take her heavy overcoat.

On their way out, they encountered only Lady Linley, sitting in the darkened drawing room and illuminated only by the fire as she sat on the smaller of the two sofas, petting two small dogs on her lap. It struck Henrietta as they passed through that she looked rather lonely and forlorn. Lord Linley was nowhere to be seen. When Clive addressed his aunt, excusing them from dinner due to some urgent business in Matlock, she had seemed startled, as if deep in thought. Clearly the trouble with Wallace had upset her greatly.

When it became apparent to her what Clive was actually saying, his apologies regarding dinner finally sinking in, Lady Linley seemed to rouse herself, then, and exclaimed that surely he didn't mean to take Henrietta out on a night such as tonight in this very vexing rain? "She'll catch her death!" she fretted. Had everyone lost their sense?

Clive tried to explain that he very much needed Henrietta with him on a particular errand, but Lady Linley seemed only to be half listening now, as if she already sensed her defeat.

"Oh, well, off you go, then," she had said, waving her hand dismissively at them as she went back to watching the fire. "No one ever listens to me; why should you?"

"Are you sure, Clive?" Henrietta asked as they bounced along the road toward Matlock, Clive having once again secured the Bentley for their purposes. "You don't really need me. You're just being kind, and I love you for it, but perhaps I should stay behind with Lady Linley. It seems cruel to leave her there alone. She seemed so sad."

"Nonsense!" Clive answered. "Wallace is there if he'd stop acting like a scolded child and come out of his room to attend his mother. And as for you, I *do* need you, as it happens. I need you to help point out this Rory Fielding; hopefully there will be some sort of family resemblance, and you'll be able to recognize him."

Henrietta acknowledged this in her mind to be a bit of a flimsy excuse, but she smiled anyway.

As it turned out, they missed the men coming out of the mill and decided to drive on to the Merry Bells, hoping that Rory might already be there. Perhaps it would be better this way, anyway, Clive mused as he drove, less conspicuous, though he felt uneasy about bringing Henrietta to a working-man's pub. He tried hard, as they parked and got out of the car, to remember her words about not being a China doll.

As if she could sense his fear, she put a hand on his arm just before they went in. "Clive," she said softly. "I'll be okay. Remember who I am. I'm just a 26 girl and a taxi dancer. I've seen quite a few things."

"Of course, darling, I know," he said, giving her hand a quick squeeze, making a show of his confidence.

Henrietta had no trouble finding the man who looked like an older version of Maxwell, but Clive hesitated before approaching him. What was he to do with Henrietta? Put her in the corner with a drink and hope no one harassed her? No, he would keep her near. Besides, the pub was crowded, and there weren't many free seats. Accordingly, they both approached the man they assumed was Rory Fielding, Henrietta holding out her hand to him as she asked him if that was indeed his name before Clive even had a chance to say anything. The man looked at them appraisingly before nodding and asking, "What of it?"

Again before Clive could interject, Henrietta hurriedly explained that she had had the pleasure of meeting his younger brother several days ago in Cromford. Rory still seemed suspicious, but when Henrietta prettily asked if she might sit down, he absently waved his hand at the lone chair in front of him. Clive resorted to leaning against the thick, timbered pole that the table butted up to, his arms crossed in front of him in an attempt at casualness.

After Henrietta was seated and leaning toward Rory in what could very possibly be interpreted as a rather alluring, confiding posture, Rory's countenance changed to one of interest and then concern, though he tried to hide it, and he asked how she had come upon Max and was he in trouble? The man could not help looking at Henrietta, and Clive could see, much to his entertainment, that she was giving him her best smile, complete with dimples, and batting her eyes every now and then. The man appeared mesmerized, and it slowly dawned on Clive that having her along might be less a liability than he imagined. Indeed, having her along—in some cases, anyway—might decidedly be an advantage in getting certain suspects to talk. The strong-arm method worked most of the time, but the attention of a beautiful woman had its charms as well. He watched, amazed, as Henrietta stopped short of outright flirting with this man, assuring him that Maxwell was not in trouble at all, that he was a perfectly delightful boy—*Boy!*—Clive thought, knowing as he did that Henrietta was certainly not the Oxford man's elder, and yet she came off as convincingly older than she actually was, a ruse that he himself had fallen for, he remembered, as he absently rubbed his chin, still watching her.

No, she was saying, it was their very good friend, Wallace Howard, who might be the one in trouble.

"What you want with Wallace?" Rory asked, suspicious again, taking a deep drag of his cigarette as he looked Clive up and down through narrowed eyes. "You with the police?"

"Not at all!" Henrietta laughed pleasantly. "This is Clive Howard, Wallace's cousin. The police seem to think it was Wallace that night, and we're trying to find out otherwise."

"It weren't Wallace," Rory said, exhaling heavily.

"How do you know?" Clive couldn't help but put in.

"Cause I knows where 'e was," Rory said, turning his eyes back to Clive and letting them rest there.

"Did you see him?"

"No. But I knows all the same where 'e was."

"Can you tell us?" Henrietta asked, drawing his attention back to her. "It's very important! You must see that, don't you?"

"He may go to prison for a crime he didn't commit," Clive said. "Or worse, hang."

They could both see that Rory was hesitating, but he gave a slight shake of his head as he drew on his cigarette again.

"If Wallace ain't already said, it ain't my place ta say, either. 'e's no idjit. 'e has his reasons."

"Does it have something to do with the socialist party?" Clive asked. "Or even the communists?" He was quiet as he said it, but even so, Rory's eyes darted round the pub nervously.

He looked back at Clive, puzzled. "Who said anything about that?"

"No one in particular. Just heard that Wallace was involved."

"That's 'is own business, too, mate. It ain't a bloody crime who a man votes for. At least not yet."

"No, but murder is."

Rory actually sat back and grinned. "Yer tryin' ta connect the dots, ain't ya? But there aren't enough bloody dots. Wallace didn't murder that bloke."

"Do you know who did?"

"No, but I can guess."

Clive's hands felt sweaty at the prospect of a revelation. "Go on," he said steadily.

"Can't say for sure, like, but if I was a copper, I'd go sniff out a lad by the name of Terrance. Terrance O'Brien."

Clive felt the hair on the back of his neck rise a little, but he fought to remain calm. "They have. He says he was in all night with his mother."

Rory laughed wheezily. "'is mother's on death's door. She wouldn't be able ta say if Terry were alive or dead, much less whether 'e sat in with her that night."

"But if he really stole all this cash, wouldn't someone have noticed by now?" Clive asked.

"Yer right, there, mate. 'e's lying low, but 'is cousin, Joe, ain't. Strangely paid off a lot of gambling debts, did Joe. I know 'cause me sister's married ta the local bookie, man by the name of Briggs. They lives over Chesterfield way, same as Joe. Briggsy tells me Joe paid 'im for all 'is debts, then up and bought a new suit of clothes, and then, off 'e goes ta London. Now that's odd, ain't it?" he said, leaning over his beer and giving them a sideways glance. "People gets ta wonderin' how 'e came upon such good luck. Says 'e won it on a horse, but Briggsy knows the troof, 'e does."

"Why hasn't anyone told the police this?" Clive asked.

Rory shrugged. "Not their bleedin' business, is it? Jist like it ain't yers, I'd reckon." Rory's eyes flicked from Clive to Henrietta. "This yer da?" he asked, nodding at Clive.

Henrietta laughed. "Mr. Howard is my *husband*, Mr. Fielding, thank you for asking," she said with perfect politeness, as if he had just asked after her health. Clive sensed it was time to go, trying to ignore the fact that he had just been confused as being Henrietta's father. His thoughts anyway were racing with this new information, though he cautiously wondered at the same time why Rory was so eager to prove Wallace innocent. Maybe it was to throw them off the scent. After all, the information he had rendered was all speculative, nothing hard and fast. All the same, he was anxious to relay it to the inspector and quickly calculated in his mind whether Hartle might still be at the station. Perhaps if they hurried . . .

"Thanks, Mr. Fielding. You've been helpful," Clive managed.

"Don't kid yerself. I'm trying to help Wallace. We was mates in the war. Like brothers, we was," he said, which, Clive noted, was all the more reason for him to cover for Wallace.

"Thanks just the same," Clive said, tipping his hat, as Henrietta stood up, following his lead. "I'll give him your regards, shall I?"

"Suit yerself," Rory said, taking a drink.

Clive motioned to Henrietta to make her way toward the door, but before he followed her, he turned back to Rory.

"Just one more thing. Does Wallace drive an old Royal Enfield?" Clive watched Rory's face intently and thought for sure he saw a ripple of acknowledgement pass over it, but Rory merely shrugged. "Not that I've ever seen," he said noncommittally, but Clive was sure he was lying.

As luck would have it, the inspector was indeed still at the station, and when Clive and Henrietta were shown forthwith into his office, Clive almost smiled at the hasty way in which the inspector jumped to his feet at the sight of Henrietta. Clive watched as the inspector took all of her in and then gave Clive a puzzled look. Clive was not sure whether to be amused or irritated, but he was becoming used to men's reactions to Henrietta's beauty.

He cleared his throat. "Detective Chief Inspector Hartle, allow me to introduce my wife, Henrietta Howard. Henrietta, Chief Inspector Hartle."

The Inspector barely controlled the startled look in his eyes, taking the cigarette from the side of his mouth and inclining his head to her with deep respect. He held out his hand. "Mrs. Howard. Delighted," he said with a rare smile. "Please sit down. May I offer you some . . . tea?" he said, looking around worriedly, as if wondering where he would procure some tea if she did say yes to his offer.

"No, thank you, Inspector," Henrietta said, confidently taking the seat across the desk from him. "I don't believe we can stay very long, isn't that right, darling?" she said, looking at Clive, who returned her gaze with amusement. She was wonderful in public, growing into her role with amazing speed and ability. She had been somewhat shy on the cruise over, still adjusting to being *Mrs. Howard*, but now, sitting in this musty police station in the middle of England, she positively shone. The inspector, Clive noticed, was trying not to stare.

"No, indeed not," Clive answered her. He related, then, what he had heard from Rory about O'Brien's cousin. The inspector, lighting yet another cigarette, seemed delighted to have new information, though Clive warned that Rory had seemed overly eager to shield Wallace, perhaps innocently due to some wartime allegiance, but perhaps because they were connected to something bigger, he suggested.

The inspector nodded at this observation, pondering it.

It was obvious, Clive continued, that they still needed to discover Wallace's whereabouts that night, that or get a confession from O'Brien. Possibly he and his cousin, Joe, were in on it together, or perhaps Joe was merely sloppy in his handling of his cousin's new fortune. Clive then proposed that while the inspector and his men follow up with O'Brien, he might be allowed to put into motion a plan for catching Wallace in the act of whatever he was up to.

"I assume you have someone watching him," Clive stated matter-of-factly, and the inspector, taking a drag, gave the slightest nod of his head, as if Clive had scored a point. "I need you to call him off for a few days. I have an idea, but in order for it to work, Wallace has to believe he's completely alone."

"But what about you? You don't think having his cousin in the house who happens to be an American detective is going to deter him?"

"I'll arrange for us not to be there; don't concern yourself on that score."

Henrietta looked up at him questioningly, but she remained silent.

Hartle stood up and walked to the little window behind him, so foggy and dirty that the outside world was barely visible through it. "All right," he sighed. "I'll give you a few days."

"Thanks, Inspector," Clive said. "That's all I need."

Hartle turned back toward them and nodded. "It was a pleasure to make your acquaintance, Mrs. Howard," he said to Henrietta as she stood up now.

"Thank you, Inspector." She smiled as she shook his hand. "I'm sure we'll meet again." She turned and walked toward the door, and Clive could not help but notice Hartle staring at her legs as she did so.

Quickly Hartle moved from behind his desk to open his office door for Henrietta, and, as Clive passed through after her, Hartle leaned forward and whispered, "You're one lucky bastard," in Clive's ear.

"I know," Clive said with a smile, as he firmly placed his hat on his head, and followed Henrietta down the stone steps to the Bentley.

Two days later, Clive and Henrietta, as arranged ahead of time between them, made a large show of leaving on a sightseeing trip to Buxton.

Clive had cleverly announced at dinner the night before that he would like to show Henrietta a bit of the local environs before having to leave for London, that it would be a shame not to. Lady Linley had said that by all means they should see the countryside but could not help but comment that, really, it was very short notice and she would have to inform Stevens right away. She seemed to be of the opinion that it would somehow be a great inconvenience for the servants, though Henrietta rather thought they would be happy to have two less people in the house to look after, but she did not say as much. Lord Linley did not bother to comment at all, having grown very silent since Wallace's return. Lady Linley then added that she would indeed be sorry to see them go, that they were quite abandoned since all the guests had so quickly taken their leave after the disagreeableness that had occurred. Again, Henrietta observed this to be contradictory, thinking back to how put upon Lady Linley had originally seemed at the prospect of housing and entertaining the house full of guests. Wallace had not been at dinner, but Clive suspected some one among the servants would inform him of their impending departure.

"Do you think it will work?" Henrietta asked as they sped down the country road toward Buxton. Clive had related his mysterious plan to her on the drive home from the station the other night. He explained that they would announce their departure from Castle Linley, but instead of going on a sightseeing trip, they would actually lie in wait for Wallace to make a move and attempt to follow him to whatever mysterious rendezvous he got himself to.

Clive was not only eager to prove Wallace's innocence in the murder of Ernest Jacobs, but he also hoped to put a stop to any of Wallace's unfortunate associations, socialist or otherwise, before he did something truly foolish. Clive had chosen his words carefully as he asked Henrietta if she would join him on the case, despite his private feelings of foreboding. He had forced himself to ignore his better judgment and ask Henrietta to help him track Wallace. Whatever anxiety he had felt, it had been momentarily dispelled by her excited acceptance and the resultant joy he read on her face. He tried to remember that now as he shifted the car into a higher gear and looked over at her, smiling and radiant.

"I'm hoping so."

"Do you think he suspects?"

"Given how self-absorbed he is, I'd say no. I don't think he's thinking about us much at all."

"Hmmm. So where are we going to wait for him?"

"At the Coach and Horse, of course."

"But this isn't the way to the pub," she mused as she looked out the window.

"Darling, we can hardly sit outside, or inside, for that matter, the Horse and Coach all day. We must meander a bit until it's time."

"I see," she said, nodding. It was thrilling to be on a real case with him, even though it only involved his cousin's wanderings. Doubtless it would turn out to be nothing. Clive seemed determined to think Wallace was involved in something dark, but she did not have that feeling at all. She thought him too passionless to be a revolutionary. He could talk impressively when it came to politics, but she didn't think he was really a leader in that way, despite what Inspector Hartle had said about him trying to organize labor and bringing foreigners in to stir up trouble. Still, it was unsettling that he kept making trips abroad. Why? she thought as she watched the scenery whip by.

"I wish we were really going sightseeing," she said now to Clive. "It's exciting to be on the case, of course," she added. "But I wish we really were going to Buxton. As tourists, that is."

"Yes, I know what you mean."

"I'm rather looking forward to our trip once this whole Wallace business is resolved. I want to be alone with you . . . just you . . . traveling about, stopping at a café or a pub, just as we did the other day. Somewhere where we don't have to be the ever-so-proper Mr. and Mrs. Howard of Highbury or Lord Linley's nephew and his wife, but we can just be Clive and Henrietta, two unsuspecting tourists."

Clive laughed. "I'm not sure if I'll ever be unsuspecting."

"You're right," she smiled. "Okay then, just Clive and Henrietta."

They were silent then for a few moments before Clive spoke again, clearing his throat, having decided to proceed with a topic that had disturbingly been on his mind the last few days when he wasn't preoccupied with thinking about Wallace's case, which was naturally almost always. Still, there was this other matter . . .

"As a matter of fact," he began, "what you're saying reminds me of something Inspector Hartle said to me the other day."

"What was that?" she asked, trying to adjust her hat without the benefit of a mirror.

He paused for a moment before continuing. "He suggested I go into private investigations," he said carefully, letting it sit there. "What would you say to that?" he asked, glancing sideways at her now.

"Private investigations?" she said more to herself than him. "You mean back at home? But what about Linley Standard?"

"Yes, I've been thinking about that," Clive went on. "But Father is still going strong. If anything, seeing Uncle Montague these past few weeks has shown me just how much. And, as it currently stands, it's just a matter of me learning the business. So between sitting in on meetings with him and looking through the ledgers, I suspect I may have some extra time. Highbury, of course, needs some tending to as well, but . . . I just thought that maybe . . ." He looked at her again. "If you were to help me with the investigations, we might, well, we might make rather a good team."

Henrietta broke off her machinations with her hat to stare at him, disbelieving. "Oh, Clive! Do you really mean it?"

Clive broke into a grin, though he kept his eyes on the road.

"We'd be a team? Truly?"

Clive laughed. "Well, I wouldn't get that excited. I'm sure the cases will be painfully dull, a missing locket here, and break-in there. Still . . . it would be a way to . . . keep my hand in, as it were. And something for us outside of Highbury. You'd still be under my mother's tutelage in terms of our role there, however . . ."

"Oh, I know that," Henrietta said dismissively. "Oh, Clive! It's a wonderful idea! Superb!" she said, leaning over and giving him a kiss on the cheek. "I can't wait!" she exclaimed, the countryside whipping by. "It's the best news I've heard in a long, long time."

—

The rest of the trip was filled with their happy, excited talk about what the new business would be like and how they would handle it in light of their duties at Highbury. Both of them could not help laughing at how much Alcott and Antonia would positively hate the idea, which, Henrietta admitted shamefully to herself, was in and of itself a small, added attraction to the plan, at least for her, which made her feel quite wicked for all of several moments.

They were so absorbed in their conversation that Henrietta was actually startled when Clive pulled up in front of the Palace Hotel in Buxton. She looked around, perplexed, as a porter quickly opened the car door for her, gazing at the rolling landscape that unfolded in front of her. The hotel itself was rather majestic, looking out over the whole of Buxton and the vale beyond. It was beautiful, to be sure, but Henrietta could not help being confused as she walked with Clive up the front steps. "But I thought Buxton was just a ruse," she said, taking his arm.

"It *is* part of the ruse, darling. After all, we need somewhere to stay the night or maybe more, depending on how long it takes to catch Wallace in the act. Besides, it's only ten in the morning, and, according to Compton, Wallace doesn't usually venture out until closer to evening. So you see, you're partially getting your wish to be a tourist, if only for a few hours, anyway."

Henrietta smiled and waited patiently by the front desk while Clive signed the guest book as Mr. and Mrs. Clive Howard, and she allowed herself to be led to her first stay in a hotel, grateful that it was in the company of her husband and that her husband was Clive.

Chapter 22

I t was nearly dusk when Clive rolled the Bentley into the grassy side
lot that served as a car park of the Horse and Coach. As if by way of
keeping its name, the old pub still had a watering trough for horses,
a throwback to its days as an actual coaching inn, though a few farmers did still use the trough, clinging determinedly to the use of a
horse and cart in lieu of the new tractors popping up with increasing
frequency along the roadsides. The inn was conveniently situated
at the crossroads of the Hill Road that led into Cromford and the
Derby Road that led to Matlock Bath and Matlock proper beyond
that. Clive felt certain that from this vantage point they would spy
Wallace pass by on the motorbike, presumably en route to Matlock.
Henrietta sat beside him in the front seat, restive and excited and
not at all sleepy, she said, after their long afternoon in bed. She had
wanted to see the Roman Baths in Buxton, but Clive had persuaded
her to participate in a different activity altogether and promised her
that they would see the Baths before they left England.

She sat now, eagerly watching the road with him. At one point
she turned and proposed that they play a game of rummy while
they were waiting, and he had burst out laughing. Pretending to be
perturbed, she had asked him what he found so terribly funny, and
he related how very different a stakeout was with her rather than

Michelle Cox

the hundreds he had been on with the likes of Charlie or Kelly, for example. Henrietta smiled at this, but then asked how he instead proposed to spend the time. He brushed her hair back behind her ear and said that he could think of lots of things, but she pushed his hand away and said that this was a serious case.

Clive certainly did not need reminding of this and had prayed several times on the drive over that Wallace's rendezvous would prove to be something entirely innocent. He wondered if he was making a mistake not only in bringing Henrietta along tonight, but also in proposing that they set up a private investigation business. Was he merely trying to overcompensate for his own nagging, perhaps irrational, fears? Was he being guided too much by his heart and not his head? Joining up at barely eighteen and marrying Catherine were decisions made from stirred-up emotions of honor and duty, not of practical sense. And look where that had led him . . . death and more death. But then, again, it had eventually brought him to Henrietta, so perhaps it all made sense somehow—

"There he is, I think," Henrietta whispered excitedly, pointing to a man hunched over a dark gray motorbike heading along the Derby road, the loud sputtering of its exhaust dying away into the night as he passed.

"Yes, I think we've got him," Clive said with determined calm, putting the car into gear and pulling slowly toward the main road. He wanted to make sure he had plenty of distance between them.

"Clive, hurry!" Henrietta said nervously. "We'll lose him!"

"Patience, darling. There's nowhere for him to turn off just yet, and we don't want him to suspect he's being followed."

That being said, Clive did accelerate a bit and quickly regained sight of him in the distance. They followed him in anxious silence all the way through Matlock Bath and on to Matlock itself, at which point they were forced to follow closer, the trade-off being that there was now at least a few other motorcars about, which afforded them a bit of camouflage as Clive darted behind them every so often. They

followed Wallace's twists and turns through the town and were surprised when they found themselves not only passing the Merry Bells,
but continuing on the Derby road until they emerged on the other
side of town, heading north now.

"So it's not Matlock, after all. The mystery grows," Clive said,
intrigued. "Perhaps he really is headed for Derby." He dropped back
some now that they were back on an isolated country road, so much
so that they nearly missed him turning off down a lane that appeared
off to the left and which was almost hidden by overgrowth, though
the frosts had turned it brown and gold. It was Henrietta who spotted him. Clive hesitated to pull in right behind him in case he was
close, so he idled the car for a few minutes in the road before nosing
the car gently in. The lane ahead was unpaved and absent of Wallace.
He had disappeared.

"Damn it," Clive muttered, as he steered the car slowly down the
dark lane.

"Well, he must be somewhere up ahead," Henrietta suggested
encouragingly, "unless he drove the motorbike into the brush." She
peered out the window to check her theory, but the darkness was
complete now, and it was difficult to see whether any of the grass was
beaten down with tire tracks. Finally they spotted lights up ahead,
coming from what looked like a small cottage.

Clive eased the car down the lane a bit more until the cottage was clearly
in view and then killed the motor, allowing the car to eventually roll to
a stop. They could see the abandoned motorbike just outside the cottage
itself, which told Clive by the lack of any attempt to hide it that Wallace did
not suspect he had been followed. There were no other cars in sight, but
that didn't mean there weren't other conspirators inside the cottage. Clive
prayed they weren't dangerous or armed. They gingerly opened the car
doors and got out, Clive motioning to Henrietta not to slam hers shut.

Carefully, they crept closer to the cottage, Clive holding up a finger
to his lips to signal quiet. They were standing outside the door now,
Clive inclining his head to listen, but the oak of the tiny arched door
was too thick to hear anything beyond it. He pulled out his revolver,

then, and cocked it, indicating with a nod of his head that Henrietta should stand behind him, an instruction she quickly obeyed.

He took a deep breath. "Ready?" he whispered.

Henrietta nodded, and Clive knocked loudly.

There was no sound from within.

They stood there waiting in the cold dark, Henrietta shivering either from the damp night air or the excitement of it all, and it suddenly occurred to Clive that there could possibly be a back door which Wallace and his cohorts might even now be escaping out of. What should he do? He couldn't very well send Henrietta around the back to check, but he couldn't abandon her here, either. Damn it! He had to make a decision and quickly.

"Stay here," he whispered to her, and he dashed off to check the back of the cottage.

It was very overgrown with dying weeds and bramble, but it took only a few moments to ascertain that there was thankfully no back door. Hurriedly, he crept back to the front, where he saw Henrietta knocking again. What was she doing?

"Wallace?" she called out sweetly. "It's Henrietta! May I come in?"

"Henrietta!" Clive hissed. "What are you doing?"

He cursed to himself as he rushed back to her side, his revolver still ready, just as the door opened to reveal Wallace standing in the doorway, holding, of all things—a child!—who looked to be no more than a year or so old.

Wallace looked them over, a scowl on his face. "I suggest you put that thing away," he said, nodding at Clive's gun.

Looking first at the child and then at Wallace, Clive lowered the revolver as if in a trance and obediently put it back inside his jacket, utterly stunned at what they had discovered.

"Well, it seems I have been found out," Wallace said thinly. "I suspected you might figure it out eventually, but I had to at least try to keep up the pretense." He looked at the toddler he was holding and then back to Clive. "This is my son," he said with a touch of pride despite the situation. "Linley Wallace Gustave Howard."

Clive could only stare in disbelief. No one said anything for what seemed a long time.

It was Henrietta who broke the silence. "He's lovely," she said with a smile and reached out and rubbed the baby's chubby arm. "You look exactly like your Papa," she said, looking up at Wallace now. Wallace gave her a grateful look and the first real smile he had given her since her arrival in England.

"Come in," he said gruffly and stood aside. "You might as well."

Clive and Henrietta followed him inside, Henrietta giving Clive a quick glance with raised eyebrows as they bent slightly to pass through the low door. The inside of the cottage was warm and bright, and a fire was crackling in the fireplace. A woman stood up from her chair by the fire and came to stand beside Wallace, a look of fear on her elegant face. She had thick black hair which was done up in an old-fashioned style, and she looked to Clive to be older than Wallace, closer, actually, to his own age. She stood heavily, and it became obvious that she was very pregnant.

"This is my wife, Amelie," Wallace said, smiling at her as he put his arm around her.

"Your wife?" Clive said, stunned.

Henrietta, on the other hand, instantly held out her hand to the woman. "I'm very pleased to meet you, Mrs. Howard," she said warmly.

The woman took her hand and smiled gratefully. "You muzt be 'enrietta," she said with a thick French accent. "And you muzt be Clive," she said, turning to him now. "Wallaze 'az zaid much of you both. We've been expecting you, 'aven't we, Wallaze?" she asked, looking up at him.

Wallace shrugged.

"Your home is lovely," Henrietta said to her. "So warm and inviting."

The woman smiled. "You are very welcome 'ere, are zay not, Wallaze?" she said. "Pleeze, zite down." She gestured toward a rattan bench to the left of the fireplace. "Would you like tea?"

"Thank you," Henrietta said graciously as she sat down. "That would be lovely."

Clive followed as if in a daze. How could Henrietta be so nonchalant? She was acting as if what they had found was perfectly normal! He should be questioning Wallace, not sitting down to tea!

"Wallace! What is the meaning of this!" Clive demanded, trying to exercise some control over the situation.

"Just what it seems, Clive," Wallace said defensively. "I'm married. Several things should be adding up now, I should imagine."

Linley, sensing the tension in the air, began to cry.

"'ere," Amelie said, reaching for him as he leaned toward her from Wallace's arms. "'eez tired. I'll put 'im to bed now. Zat way you can talk. I'm sure you 'ave much to zay." She gave them a smile as she rubbed Linley's fine blond curls at the back of his head, trying to soothe him. "*Dodo, l'enfant do, l'enfant dormira bien vite,*" she sang to him softly as she disappeared up a few tiny steps to a room beyond.

Wallace watched them go and then turned back to Clive with a look of grim resolve as if mentally preparing for a grueling battle.

"So this is the alibi," Clive said first.

"Yes, I was here that night, as I try to be most nights, especially with the baby due so soon."

"Oh, Wallace," Henrietta said compassionately. "It must be terrible for you, for you both."

"But why?" Clive asked, mystified and ignoring Henrietta's comment. "Why the secrecy? You could quite easily have been hanged for murder. You do realize that, don't you?"

"Yes, I bloody well know that, Clive. I had it in hand."

"Is that so? What was your plan, then?"

Wallace let out a sigh. "We were going to leave the country as soon as you buggered off to London."

"With your wife due any time?" Clive asked incredulously.

"I didn't say it was the best idea! Just the only thing I could think of," Wallace said, irritated, his voice rising. "What would you have me do?"

"I can think of several things, actually . . ."

"It's not that easy, Clive!" Wallace shouted, but then, conscious of the baby in the next room, he lowered his voice to a hoarse whisper. "It's all right for you! You can marry whom you want," he said, looking over at Henrietta, "*be* what you want, but not the likes of me! This lot should never have fallen to me; it was always meant for Linley, but the poor bastard had to go get himself killed."

"I understand that, Wallace, more than you know, actually, but how long did you think you could suspend your father's disappointment? Surely he has to find out sometime. And I would think the knowledge that he has a grandson—an heir—and possibly another on the way would be of particular interest to him."

"Even if their mother is French and poor?" he said bitterly. "If you think that doesn't matter to him, then you've judged him very wrongly."

"What's done is done . . ." Clive began, but then he paused to consider something. "Was it legal?" he asked skeptically.

Wallace shot him a look of deep offense. "Of course it was bloody legal! It was in a church, too, in case that's your next question. St. Ignace in Reims," Wallace said disgustedly and looked away at the fire.

"Tell us about her," Henrietta suggested tacitly. "She's so elegant, so beautiful," she went on, clearly trying to draw him out. "She obviously loves you very much. I can tell by the way she looks at you."

Privately, Henrietta was of the opinion that Amelie must indeed love Wallace very much in order to have agreed to be hidden away in secret in the English countryside while her husband lived at the manor house, dancing with his mother's young female houseguests and becoming the subject of many a mama's matrimonial aspirations. She was pretty sure she wouldn't have been so conciliatory.

Wallace glanced at her and gave her a grateful smile, letting out a deep breath. "She was a nurse at Rouen, where I was sent from the front to convalesce. I was there for about two months, long enough to fall in love with her, by wartime standards, anyway." He looked down at his hands, balled up in his lap. "I used to lie there and count the minutes until she would come on duty each day. It was agony if she had leave or was off for the weekend. It was all I lived for for a while." He looked up at Henrietta again before going on, eagerly now, as if glad to finally tell someone the story.

"Her smile in the morning as she did her rounds, her laughter and her . . . her kindness as she helped me learn to walk again became everything to me. And then I discovered, eventually, to my despair, that she was married to a French private who had been taken prisoner early on. From the little I could get out of her, I suspected it had been a hasty marriage before he had gone off to war." Wallace shifted his attention to Clive now. "I was utterly shattered by this, but I couldn't help being in love with her. I let myself believe she shared my love, but I couldn't act on it, and neither did she." He paused, gripping his hands tightly now. "In truth I had dreams about stealing her away, but I had too much honor back then to steal a man's wife after what we had all been through at the front. I have to confess, though," he said quietly, "I hoped he would die. God knows I hated myself for thinking that," he said bitterly and exhaled, deep in thought. When he spoke again, his face was grim.

"I was eventually sent back to England, though I think she prolonged my convalescence as long as she was able. I asked if I could write to her, if only to relate my progress with my leg. She agreed, and we wrote back and forth a few times until her letters stopped coming. I told myself that it was for the best, really, and tried to forget her, which I proved miserable at." He was silent, then, and sat absently rubbing his bum leg through his thick trousers.

"And then?" Henrietta asked, prompting him.

Wallace looked up at her and, after seeming to consider it, decided to continue. "Then, about two years ago, I received another letter from her, telling me that Jules, her husband, had passed away. That he had indeed been taken prisoner and gassed. He was an invalid after that, and she spent years nursing him before he died, poor sod. She wrote to me, assuming I had married and had a big brood of children around me by this point, to wish me well and to tell me, for what it was worth, how much she had loved me. *For what it was worth,*" Wallace repeated, shaking his head faintly.

He glanced at Clive, who was listening intently, and then back at Henrietta. "I left immediately and found her living in a small house near her parents outside of Reims. We married there, and the month I spent with her was one of the very best of my life," he said with a smile. "Eventually, however, reality set in, and I knew I had to return to England. Amelie begged me to take her with me, and I'm ashamed to say I had not the fortitude. I wanted to break it to Mother and Father gently, to ease them into the idea, as ridiculous as that sounds. God knows what nonsense was going through my mind! I knew of my father's despair over the estate and my mother's schemes to marry me to a rich heiress, and it was all I could do to face them, much less present them with their new, penniless daughter-in-law."

"But surely they would have come around eventually," Clive said, giving Henrietta a quick, knowing look, to which she smiled.

"Yes. I suppose. But I'm a coward at heart, Clive," Wallace said despondently. "I'm not like you . . . or Linley, for that matter. I can face a line of Huns firing artillery at me, but I can't seem to stand up to my own father. I've tried to get him to let go of the estate, for example, to turn it into something useful—like a school or a home for shell-shocked soldiers. Amelie and I have so many ideas . . . I don't bloody give a damn about being a lord or sitting in parliament or having bloody Stevens scurrying about serving me biscuits and tea. It's too much to be borne, really!" he said, flinging himself backward.

Clive raised an eyebrow, a reluctant smile forming as well. He was about to comment, but Henrietta interrupted.

"How is it that she came to live here in this place, then, if you had left her in France?" she asked. "Was it the baby?" she guessed.

Wallace, his face looking pained now, nodded. "She wrote to say she was with child, so I brought her here. I meant to tell them . . . honestly, I did. It just . . . it just never seemed the right time."

Amelie conveniently appeared then, pulling the door softly shut behind her as she tiptoed down the couple of steps and sat down beside Wallace, taking his hand in hers. "Zo 'e 'as told you zee story, zen?" she said with a smile.

"*La partie importante*," (The important part) Clive began in perfect French. "*Je dois présenter mes excuses pour mon comportement plus tôt, Mme Howard. Vous avez mes félicitations sincères. Je vous souhaite et Wallace serez très heureux ensemble. Vraiment.*" (I must apologize for my behavior earlier, Mrs. Howard. You have my earnest congratulations. I hope you and Wallace will be very happy together. Truly.)

At the sound of his words, Amelie's face lit up. "*Tu parle français!*" she said with a smile. "*Amélie, s'il vous plaît. Et merci pour vos bons voeux. Mais je dois le mien offrir ainsi. Votre femme est très belle.*" (Amelie, please. And thank you for your good wishes. But I must offer mine as well. Your wife is very beautiful.)

"*Oui, merci*," Clive said, his eyes grateful. He turned to Henrietta, who was watching him in amazement at his ability to speak French. "She says you are very beautiful," Clive repeated to her.

Henrietta continued to stare at him, wondering what else she didn't know about her husband and felt a new surge of attraction for him as the French rolled off his lips.

"All those years at prep school, darling," he said, his mouth twitching. "They had to amount to something. Came in handy in the war, I suppose," he said, giving Wallace the slightest wink.

"'ave you not 'ad tea yet?" Amelie asked, looking around. "Wallaze!" she said, standing up again to prepare it. "*Excusez-moi*," she said to Clive and Henrietta. "Eet will juzt be a moment."

"Oh, let's forgo the blasted tea!" Wallace said, looking back at her as she went to the kitchen. "I'll open some wine. Would you like wine?" he asked, turning to Henrietta and Clive.

Clive nodded eagerly, obviously preferring that, and Henrietta followed suit, though she had actually been very much in the mood for tea, chilled from their sojourn in the car. The fire had gone a long way to warming her, however, and she felt she could rise to the challenge of something stronger.

"I'll get it," Wallace said, standing up. Amelie, her large belly preceding her, brought out four wine glasses from the cupboard, Henrietta watching. From the moment they had entered, she had been reminded of Helen's cottage and suddenly missed home very much. She wished, as she had done many times before, that this simple existence could be her life with Clive. She felt immediately guilty, however, that she was ungrateful for all that had come, and would come, to be hers, and she supposed that Amelie and Wallace's days as idyllic peasants were as numbered as hers and Clive's. Still, Wallace's mention of his plan to do something useful with his eventual estate struck her, and she resolved to bring it up later with Clive. No matter what Wallace's faults or politics were, she decided, she admired his concern for the average man.

"Let me come with you," Clive said, standing up and following Wallace into the kitchen as Amelie sat down next to Henrietta.

In the little kitchen, Clive watched as Wallace opened a corner cabinet and pulled out a bottle of 1897 Saint-Emilion, holding it up for Clive's approval.

Clive whistled. "Doesn't quite go with the setting, old boy. I was expecting elderberry or some such nonsense."

"Yes, yes, I know. I'm full of contradiction. I pilfer it from the cellars at Linley, if you must know," he said with a wry smile. "Add it to my list of sins. But I figure it's mine anyway, or will be, plus it keeps bloody Stevens on his toes. Makes it impossible for him to keep an accurate inventory. He suspects a thief, of course. Currently he suspects Compton, I'm afraid, so I'll soon have to set him straight. That or make him suspect it's someone else."

"Does Compton know? The truth, I mean, about you?" Clive asked quietly, wondering if a lie had slipped past him.

"Not exactly," Wallace said, exhaling. "He obviously knows I go off. He's covering for me now. You don't honestly think I'd lock myself in my room for days like some spoiled twit, do you?"

Clive shrugged.

"He doesn't know where I go, however. So whatever he told you is probably true, as far as he knows. I didn't want any of the servants to know, to have to keep my secret. I'm a scoundrel, to be sure, but not such a one as would add to the burdens they already labor under, poor devils. They don't need me to compromise their situation."

"You're not a scoundrel," Clive said. "A fool, maybe." He smiled here, and Wallace laughed.

"Perhaps. I've made a right mess of it, Clive," he said more seriously now. "What am I to do?"

"I think you know."

Wallace sighed. "Yes, I suppose I do."

"We'll come back for you in the morning. It's too late now, and you won't all fit in that contraption, anyway," he said, referring to the motorbike. "Where'd you get a thing like that, by the way?"

"It's a long story," Wallace said with a smile as he pulled on the cork with a rudimentary corkscrew. He let out a deep breath. "I should have done this long ago. Now that I've decided, however, or, rather, now that it's been decided *for* me . . ." he said, looking up at Clive ruefully, "I'm eager to get it over with. It will be better for Amelie, anyway, though, on my honor, I thought I was saving her from the volley of unpleasantness that's sure to unfold tomorrow. However, maybe I've done her a disservice, prolonging the inevitable. But we've been happy here." He paused, ruminating. "Oh, I'm not sure what to think anymore," he said wearily, rubbing his eyes with one hand. "Doubtless you think I'm an odd duck, tucking my wife and child away for almost a year."

"Not as odd as you might imagine," Clive said quietly. They were quiet then for a moment, each in his own thoughts, before Clive continued. "You'll have to face the inspector as well, you know."

"Yes, yes," Wallace said, waving his hand as if swatting away a fly. "But first my father. The inspector's questions will be easy after his. *Bloody damn fool, what have you done now?*" Wallace boomed out, imitating Lord Linley.

It struck Clive as peculiar that, unlike Wallace, he did not see Lord

Linley as a formidable character in any way. To him he was a blustering old gent who liked to blow off steam, but who was essentially harmless. It made it difficult to understand Wallace's trepidation around him, but he supposed a dynamic existed between fathers and sons known only to them. "He does love you, I'm sure of it," Clive said, feeling a twinge of regret for all the distress he had caused his own father.

Wallace shrugged, and Clive could not help but wonder if Wallace was really willing to give up the whole of the estate for a cause, but then suddenly realized he had come close to doing something very similar for much less noble reasons.

"Tell me," Clive said, looking over at him, "*are* you a socialist?"

Wallace looked at him for several moments before answering. "Would it matter if I was?"

Clive considered the question. "I suppose not."

Wallace let out a deep breath. "I *am* a socialist, in a way. But not really the militant I portend to be. I'm more of a Fabian, really."

Clive raised his eyebrows. "A Fabian? They still around? I thought they were all for imperialism and all that. Hardly what you eschew these days."

"The Victorian Fabians were all about imperialism, of course, but Fabian thought has evolved, especially after the war. We want a peaceful, gradual shift in society to one that is fairer for all. Free education, a fair wage, housing and medicine for the poor. Surely we can't go on this way as a society, Clive."

"I suppose not," Clive answered, not really sure what the alternative would be, however.

"How can you go back and live in the splendid palace that is Highbury when there are bread lines in your own city?"

"I don't know, Wallace," Clive said, irritably. "I've already been through this. I'm trying to see my way clear."

"For me, anyway, I can't be master of *Castle* Linley. How outrageous and nauseating! When father dies, I'm going to turn it into a school for underprivileged boys, raise up a new generation of thought based on Cole and Laski and Tawney.

"The Labor party will love you," Clive couldn't help but say with a smile.

"Joke if you want, Clive. It's not going to change anything."

"Well, perhaps you have the right of it." Clive watched him for a few moments. "Was Amelie part of your rebellion?" he asked thoughtfully.

"No," Wallace said tiredly. "I know it seems that way, but I actually do love her. With all my heart. And Linley, of course."

"So you were just going to run away with them with a murder charge on your head rather than reveal the truth?" Clive looked at him disbelievingly.

"I told you—I wasn't thinking clearly. And I'm a coward when it comes to my father. I should just tell him my plans for the estate now instead of waiting for him to die. No, I've been wrong, Clive. I see that."

"Shall we?" Clive said, nodding toward the front room, where the women were waiting.

"Quite right, old boy," Wallace drawled as he picked up the bottle of wine. "I apologize about our limited ability to accommodate you for the night," he said as he moved past him.

"Not at all. We are, as it happens, booked in tonight at the Palace, speaking of privilege. Shame to waste it," he said, winking at Wallace.

"Ah, young love," Wallace said with a teasing smile, as if he were Clive's elder and not the reverse. "Wait till you get a little nipper running about."

Clive smiled, suddenly conscious of how relieved he was that Wallace was innocent—of the murder of Earnest Jacobs, at least. He had been deceptive, true, but regarding a whole different matter, not something underhand as he, and everyone else, had been given to suspect. It brought him more satisfaction than he was expecting, perhaps because Wallace and Linley were the closest thing he had ever had to brothers, and now he only had Wallace left. As the two of them moved toward the door that separated them from the ladies beyond, Clive spoke again. "I'm sorry for the subterfuge, Wallace. For trailing about after you."

"Don't apologize," Wallace said, laying a hand on Clive's shoulder. "I was an arse. I should have trusted you. Sometimes it's, well . . . it's hard."

"Yes, I know," Clive said, and they went in, then, to find the ladies deep in conversation, Clive having saved Wallace, if not from the socialists, as he had been wont to imagine, but from a very different sort of fate.

Chapter 23

It was cloudy and overcast and bitterly cold, with even a few stray flakes of snow making a sporadic appearance, heralds perhaps of a bigger storm to come, when Clive drove the Bentley up to the entrance of Castle Linley. Wallace was seated in the front next to Clive, while Henrietta and Amelie, with Linley on her lap, shared the tiny back seat. Henrietta could tell by the way Amelie kept brushing Linley's fine hair into place that she was nervous. Henrietta gave her hand a comforting squeeze. Amelie hesitantly returned the gesture, but with no accompanying smile, her face instead frozen. Clive had telephoned ahead to Stevens, explaining that they were returning from Buxton earlier than planned and that they would be attended by Mister Wallace and two guests, should Lord and Lady Linley wish to be on hand to receive them.

"Might I ask their names, sir, so that I might inform his lordship?" Stevens's dull nasally voice crackled over the telephone.

"It's a surprise, Stevens," Clive had said from the telephone at the front desk of the Palace Hotel, to which the elderly butler had responded with a perfunctory, if not slightly disappointed, "Very good, sir."

If Stevens *was* disappointed when at first only Mr. Wallace stepped out of the Bentley, his face did not reveal it, an indication of his extreme correctness, but Clive thought he saw perhaps a flicker of surprise when a woman holding a child then stepped out from the back after a footman opened the door for her. Doubtless in all of his years of experience, Stevens could have probably predicted what was coming next, but he, of course, remained silent as the little group climbed the stone steps and huddled in the front hall.

Clive had asked Wallace the night before if he wanted him to be present while he faced his father, but Wallace, though he said he would have appreciated the moral support, replied that no, he would present his wife and child privately. It was not to be, however, because before Stevens could even lead them through to the drawing room, Lord and Lady Linley had uncharacteristically come out in their haste to see Wallace, his disappearance yesterday only coming to light just this morning, when it was discovered that he had not slept in his bed—again.

"Wallace!" Lord Linley burst out. "Where the devil have you been? What is the meaning of this, sir? I *will* have an explanation, and I'll have it now!" he sputtered.

"You are right, Father, forgive me. I owe you an explanation . . ."

"Indeed! God knows we've been worried sick! That blast inspector was back here again this morning. We *will* know the meaning of these disappearances. And we will know them now!"

"Yes, Father, we can talk about that later," he said, moving toward Amelie, and only now did Lord and Lady Linley seem to notice her presence, so intent had they been on addressing Wallace.

"Who is this, Wallace?" Lady Linley asked querulously.

"Might we not attend each other in the drawing room?" Wallace asked.

"Certainly not!" Lord Linley boomed. "Explain yourself, sir!"

"Very well," Wallace grimaced. "Have it your way." He moved to stand very close to Amelie, then, and drew himself up as if at attention. "Father, Mother . . ." he paused, bracing himself, "this is my wife, Amelie. And this is my son, Linley Wallace Gustave Howard," he said clearly, though Clive detected a slight tremor in his voice.

No one said anything for what seemed like several minutes, and Henrietta, standing with Clive near the grand staircase, took his hand.

Lord Linley's face was one of extreme consternation as he finally blustered out, "Your what?" Not waiting for a response, he went on, "This cannot be true! Give me your word, as a gentleman," he hissed. "Are you truly married, sir?"

"I give you my word, Father. She is my wife. We met during the war. She's French; she was my nurse. I . . ."

"Confound it, man! You're married?" Lord Linley boomed, causing Henrietta and Amelie both to jump. Linley began to cry.

"For shame, Montague!" Lady Linley said, having finally found her voice. "Now look what you've done!" She took a step toward the child that Amelie was shushing, and Henrietta could see that the older woman had tears in her eyes. She reached out a hand that was beginning to be gnarled with arthritis. "Did you say that his name is Linley?" she asked Amelie, almost timidly. Amelie, a tentative smile creeping up, nodded and turned so that Lady Linley might have a better view of him.

"Oh, Montague! He looks just exactly like Wallace, though there's a touch of . . . Oh, my dear!" she said, resting her arm on Amelie. "You must have had a very long journey. Have you come all the way from France? Come in, come in. We must get you out of this wet. Stevens!"

"Yes, my lady," said Stevens from where he stood at attention in the corner.

"Bring some tea immediately! And some milk for Master Linley!" At the sound of those words on her lips, however, those which she perhaps never thought to utter ever again, Lady Linley suddenly lost her composure and began to cry. Wallace immediately went to her and awkwardly embraced her.

"I'm sorry, Mother. I should have told you before now. I . . ."

Lady Linley allowed herself to be held by him for just a moment before pulling back, a forced smile on her face as she wiped her eyes and patted his hand, which was resting on her arm. "Forgive me. I'm quite recovered now. I'm sure you had your reasons for . . . for not telling us . . ." she said as she shot Lord Linley a dagger.

Lord Linley's face was still flushed red despite the touching outburst that they had all just witnessed, having not been affected in the least by its sentiment. "Wallace," he said in a defeated tone now, "how could you do this? We are undone," he said quietly. "There's nothing more for it. We are utterly ruined." He let out a long, anguished groan. "I suppose this is my fault, though, in more ways than one; I see that now. Come along; let's go into the drawing room. You might as well come too, Clive. I asked you to find out what was going on, and so you have," he said with a sigh.

"No, your lordship," Clive said with a tilt of his head as he gave Wallace and Amelie a look of encouragement. "I think it best if you are alone just at present. And at any rate, I have an important telephone call of my own to make, if I might use your study."

"Yes, yes," Lord Linley waved absently. "Of course you may," he said wearily, and, giving Amelie and the child one more disparaging glance, he turned and walked dejectedly off toward the drawing room, clearly a man defeated.

Clive whispered something to Henrietta, then, who smiled and patted his hand before she turned to go upstairs.

Eagerly, Clive made his way to Lord Linley's study to telephone Inspector Hartle at the station, wanting to quickly explain Wallace's secret and provide his alibi. When Hartle did come on the line, however, Clive's information proved a bit too late, the inspector himself explaining that his sergeant had finally gotten his hands on Rory Fielding's brother-in-law—Briggs, the bookie—who confirmed that Joe O'Brien had not won in a long, long time. Lost, in fact, and heavily. Confirmed that he had paid off a substantial debt but wouldn't say how he'd come by the money. The woman he was living with also confirmed that he had gone to London, said on business, not much else. Hartle himself had then gone to question Mrs. O'Brien, Terrance O'Brien's mother, to check his alibi. Again, Hartle and his constables were put off, the housekeeper saying that Mrs. O'Brien was indisposed at the moment, but Hartle persisted and found Mrs. O'Brien unable to speak at all. The housekeeper confessed that her mistress had been this way for weeks, just as Rory Fielding had said. The housekeeper recalled that Terry came home late the night in question, around midnight. Told her to go home, she reported, which was unusual.

"Did she notice if he had a black case on him?" Clive couldn't help but ask, though it was the obvious question.

"Spot on. She did indeed remember. Thought it peculiar, she said, as she'd never seen him with something 'half so nice,' I think is how she put it."

"But it's gone now, right? Nowhere to be found?"

"Indeed. Oddly enough, O'Brien has made his way to London as well. The housekeeper said that he paid her a tidy sum in advance to stay with his mother until he returned."

"Now what?"

"We've informed the Yard. All we can do, really. Might send my sergeant back to Joe O'Brien's woman to see if she remembers anything about where he said he was going. Besides that, it's a waiting game. You'd know all about that, I would imagine."

"Too much, as a matter of fact," Clive answered.

There was an awkward silence on the line.

"Thanks for your help, Howard," the inspector finally said.

"Would you keep me informed of any developments?" Clive asked.

Hartle assured him that he would, as a courtesy, mind, and rang off then. Clive could not help feeling deflated, though he wasn't sure why. The case was all but solved; it was really just a matter of apprehending O'Brien. Slowly he switched off the desk lamp and left the now darkened room.

Several lines of thought occupied Clive's mind as he slowly made his way up the stairs to his and Henrietta's room. As he entered, he looked for Henrietta so that he could relate the news of the case and he was surprised to see her sitting on the edge of the chaise lounge at the foot of the bed, looking very ashen indeed. She was holding a letter, which she looked up from now as he came in.

"Oh, Clive!" she said, her voice tremulous.

"What is it?" he asked, suddenly alarmed.

"It's a letter from Elsie . . . she . . . here, I'll read it."

Dearest Henrietta,

By the time you read this, dear sister, I will be married to Lieutenant Barnes-Smith. He proposed to me after an incident that I will perhaps share with you when we are alone together, and, after careful thought, I accepted him. Please don't think ill of me, Henrietta. It is for the best; believe me. You might think I have cruelly used Stanley, but don't worry, I have spoken to him, and I believe we quite understand each other. It seems he is quite attached to your friend, Rose, and may be even on the brink of his own engagement there. So you see, it isn't exactly as though I was throwing him over, is it? In fact, I rather think it was the other way around, or perhaps it was at least mutual. I will always remember him and our times together with fondness, but that is all over now, as it should be. (Goodness! How odd that so much of this letter is so far filled with Stanley, when it ought to be mostly of Harrison!)

Regarding the lieutenant, he fears what Grandfather Exley will say when he finds out we have engaged ourselves to each other and that he will not allow us to marry, and I daresay Harrison is probably right in this. We have decided, then, that the best course would be to elope, and I leave in a couple of hours to go with him. Ma does not know, of course, nor does anyone, really. It must be very secret, Harrison says, and then everyone will surely come round eventually, and we will then go to Grandfather to see what can be done for us. I am not at all convinced of this scheme, but Harrison says Grandfather will no doubt soften over time. So you see, if you are reading this now, I will have already been Mrs. Barnes-Smith for well over a week at least.

Please write and tell me you will be happy for me and wish me joy. I only wish I could have had a real wedding so that you could stand beside me as my bridesmaid as I once did for you. Still, we can't have everything, can we? I hope Ma will not be too angry, but she usually is anyway, so it doesn't much matter. She will not notice my absence for a very long time, I daresay. I have told the servants I am to be at Uncle John and Aunt Agatha's for an extended visit, so I will not be discovered for some time, I expect.

Once we are married (does that not seem odd, Hen?), we are to live for a time with the major. You can write to me there, if you wish. Oh, please don't be angry, Hen! You'll understand when I tell you the whole story, I hope. I pray you are keeping well. Give my love to Clive.

Your loving sister,
Elsie

"Oh, Clive," Henrietta said as Clive, sitting beside her now on the chaise lounge, put his arm around her. "What are we going to do?"

"I don't know, darling. It doesn't sound like there's much we can do," he sighed. "Is this what Elsie's other letter was about? I forgot to ask you about it. I'm sorry," he said sincerely.

"It's all right," Henrietta said absently. "There's nothing you could have done, anyway. I . . . I just didn't expect this. That she would do something so drastic."

"Yes, this is a fine mess," Clive muttered, letting out a deep breath. "I always did think Harry was an ass. He's obviously a mercenary out for what he hopes will be a big Exley dowry. And yet he doesn't seem to realize how ruthless Exley is, so he's a fool as well. If old Exley had no qualms about cutting your mother off, I shouldn't imagine he'd think twice about cutting off his granddaughter. I always knew Harrison was bad news; I should have said so from the beginning when I first suspected his motives at the engagement party," he said, annoyed. "I thought he perhaps sought a dalliance, but I never suspected he would try to marry her. Although, I'm not sure which is worse . . ."

Henrietta thought back to how the lieutenant had been very attentive to Elsie and how thrilled Elsie had been. It seemed so long ago. "No, it's my fault," Henrietta insisted. "I've been so stupidly selfish! So utterly blind!"

"That's not true, darling. If anyone's to blame, it's me. I never should have had the major in the wedding at all," Clive went on. "None of this would have happened then," he said, running his hand through his hair, disturbed. "I should have lowered my pride or stood up to mother and had the Chief or Jones . . . even Clancy."

"Oh, Clive, what does it matter? How could she do this?" Henrietta said, distraught. "I'm sure she doesn't love him . . . I wrote to Julia asking for her help . . ."

"You did?" he asked, clearly moved that she had implored his sister's help.

"Yes," Henrietta mused, looking back at the letter without really reading the words. "I guess she didn't get it in time, or perhaps she tried and failed."

"Perhaps I should have written Father . . ." Clive suggested.

"She mentions an incident . . ." Henrietta said anxiously, her eyes focusing on the words again. "You don't think . . ."

Clive didn't answer, but his eyes were very troubled when she looked back at him. "I wouldn't put it past him," he said quietly.

Henrietta's eyes filled with tears.

"Bastard," Clive muttered as he took her hand.

They were both startled then by a sharp knock at the door. "Come in," Clive said loudly, clearing his throat and standing up now.

The door opened to reveal the immovable Stevens standing in the threshold, holding the silver mail salver. "Excuse me, sir," he said emotionlessly, "But a telegram has just arrived."

"Oh, Elsie!" Henrietta whispered, wondering what worse news it could possibly be.

"Thank you, Stevens," Clive said grimly, reaching for it. He did not open it immediately but waited for Stevens to leave.

"May I get you anything else, sir?" Stevens said, an uncharacteristic trace of hope in his voice.

"No, Stevens, that will be all," Clive said, trying to keep the irritation from his voice as he patiently waited for him to withdraw.

"Very good, sir," Stevens said evenly, bowing with what seemed exaggerated slowness and then finally closing the door behind him.

Clive was in the process of handing the envelope to Henrietta when he noticed that it was actually addressed to him. "It's for me," Clive said, puzzled, as he reread the front of it.

Henrietta accordingly lowered her outstretched arm and watched as Clive ripped open the envelope and allowed his eyes to quickly travel over the words. Immediately upon doing so, his face contorted as if in pain.

"Clive, darling, what is it?" Henrietta said, rising.

"It's father," he said thickly. "He's . . . he's dead."

"Oh, Clive!" Henrietta cried and went to him, dropping Elsie's letter on the floor as she raced to wrap her arms around him. "Oh, darling, let me see," she said, peering at the telegram in his hand, and she read for herself the fateful words.

"My God! How could this have happened?" Clive asked, staring wildly at her as if in shock. "He wasn't even ill . . . I . . . we'll have to leave immediately, I'm afraid."

"Of course. Yes, of course we will . . ."

"I'd better go tell them below . . . No, I should first see if I can make a transatlantic call. Oh, God . . . Henrietta . . ." he said, gripping her now a bit unsteadily. "My poor mother . . . What am I going to do?" he said, distraught.

"You mean, what are *we* going to do," she said, holding him tight.

—

Days later, back on the *Queen Mary*, Clive again related to Henrietta what he had managed to extract from his mother on the telephone before they had hurriedly departed Castle Linley. He seemed to want to tell the pitifully short tale over and over. It had been difficult to understand Antonia through her tears and the bad connection, but Clive had ascertained that it had been a sort of freak accident. Alcott had apparently slipped and fallen in front of a morning train and had been killed instantly. It was a terrible shock for everyone, and Antonia begged Clive to return immediately, the wheels of which he had of course already put into motion. They had frantically packed, with the help of the servants, of course, Lord Linley being especially distressed at the news of his brother's death coming so inconveniently on the heels of his introduction to his grandson and heir. He could barely stand upright for days and had to say his goodbyes from his bed. He had at first insisted on accompanying them for Alcott's funeral, which everyone else around him saw as ludicrous, given his current state, and only when the doctor had been procured and had likewise advised against a sea journey at this time did he sadly concede. Wallace had wanted to come as well, but Clive insisted he stay with Amelie and the new baby that was due any moment. Wallace had clasped him tight before he left, promising to write and wishing him God speed, and thanking him, oddly, for bringing him back to his own father, at which point Clive had very nearly broken down.

Clive and Henrietta stood now, bracing themselves against the icy wind off the North Sea, which buffeted them fiercely and caused them to grasp the rails tightly. It was hardly a day to stroll on deck, but Clive had wanted some air and Henrietta had worriedly followed him. She had no idea how long they had been standing there, but her cheeks and her fingers were beginning to grow numb despite the leather gloves she had managed to grab on her way out of the cabin. Clive was staring absently out at the huge whitecaps, and, as she followed his gaze, her mind drifted between a multitude of sad themes. She was mostly preoccupied with thoughts of the upcoming funeral and Clive's utter loss, of course, but she likewise privately

despaired about Elsie and her hasty, ill-advised marriage to one
whom Henrietta felt sure was a scoundrel. She vacillated between
blaming herself and then blaming Elsie for being so terribly foolish.
What on earth had prompted her to take such a step? She prayed he
was not brutal to her, at least, her mind straying to Julia's sad woes
as well as her mother's, which brought to mind a new thought about
what Elsie's elopement would mean for Ma and the kids. And she
could not help at times wonder what would happen to Stan, unwittingly infatuated (surely not in love with?) with a lesbian.

With a heavy sigh, Henrietta realized that they were returning to
all of her same old problems. None of them had gone away in their
absence, but, rather, they had seemed to have gotten decidedly worse.
And now Alcott's death presented a whole new, more devastating set
of issues. But then again, Henrietta mused, was death worse than
a hasty, unfortunate marriage? Wasn't that merely a different sort
of death? And as she saw Elsie's sweet face in her mind's eye now,
Henrietta felt in danger of crying again. Forcing herself not to give in
to her emotions, she attempted to console herself by reasoning that
haste in marriage did not necessarily spell disaster, thinking of her
own hasty but happy marriage to Clive. Surely it was a lack of love
that made a marriage unfortunate? Her mind went to Captain Foley,
then, who had proclaimed a mere fondness for his affianced, though
he seemed happy enough to proceed. Oh! she exclaimed to herself, if
only she could stop thinking about it all!

She looked at Clive now almost as a way of distracting herself, but
he was still staring out at the sea. And, as usual, as if he had been just
reading her mind, he turned to look at her and suddenly spoke. "You
were right. It was a woman."

"What?" she asked, surprised.

"Wallace's mystery."

"Oh, that. Well. I hope they're okay. I wonder if the baby has come
yet."

Clive did not respond but looked out at the sea again.

"I gave Foley a thousand pounds," he said over the roar of the wind.

Henrietta looked at him again in surprise. This is certainly not what she had imagined he would say at this moment.

He told her then about Foley and his request for money and its purpose. Henrietta was not sure what to be more stunned by, Bertram Foley's exploits or his audacity in asking Clive for help.

"So . . . you gave it to him?" Henrietta asked tentatively.

"I did. Yes."

"Why didn't you tell me before now?" she asked, her own feelings of hurt hovering dangerously near.

"I don't know," he said emotionlessly. "Forgive me."

It was Henrietta's turn now to stare out at the icy waves.

"You realize, don't you," he said softly, "that nothing will ever be the same now. It's the end of just being Clive and Henrietta, the end of our dreams of something different . . ."

"No, it's not," she said, putting her hand on top of his on the railing. "It's just the beginning. I promise . . . wait and see."

Clive looked at her, his eyes brimming with tears, the first tears she had seen since they received the horrible, sad news.

Clive roughly clutched her to him. His father's words regarding Henrietta in his final letter came back to him and filled him with such a feeling of longing and regret that he felt he might die, too.

"Oh, Henrietta, I love you so much," he whispered into her hair as he held her to him and daringly allowed his heart to hope that she might, after all, be right.

Acknowledgments

Thanks to all who helped to put together this third volume in what is turning out to be a—somewhat accidentally—longish series. The list of people who labor to bring a book into the world is immense, and there are many who work behind the scenes on my, or rather, Henrietta and Clive's behalf. To all of you, I offer my genuine gratitude and praise. You are all wonderful experts in your field.

There are a few people, in particular, however, whom I would like to thank especially. The first, of course, would be my publisher, Brooke Warner, of She Writes Press, who continues to lead forth her tribe of authors with fierce vision and decided grace. You are a trailblazer extraordinaire! Thank you for what has become a lovely partnership.

Second, of course, is the very talented, Lauren Wise, who shepherds my books from tattered manuscript all the way through to the lovely copy you now hold—and beyond, actually! Thank you, Lauren, for all the support and encouragement you give and for answering frazzled emails with such patience.

Another big thank you goes out to Crystal Patriarche and her dedicated team at BookSparks, who help to get my books into the wider world. You are a very talented and savvy group of publicists, and I am honored to work alongside of you!

I'd also like to take a moment to thank Yolanda Facio, who manages my website and my subscriber lists, posts my blog and generally answers any social media issues I might have. She is a real time-saver, not to mention a font of great ideas, and I am grateful to also call her, I hope, a friend.

And then, of course, we have the usual suspects, my family and friends who pose as beta readers and comb through various versions of the book looking for errors or plot points that don't make sense. My only regret in using their generous services is that they—the ones whose opinions mean the very most to me—are stuck reading the crappy versions of what eventually becomes, dare I say, a polished work. Alas. So I will take this space to especially thank: Marcy, Liz, Amy, Margaret, Otto, Susan, Wally, Carmi, Kari, and Rebecca for your willingness to wade through the muck. I hope that being the first to "find out what happens next" is worth the sloppiness in which it's uncovered. Also, I'd like to thank my newest recruit, Paul Cox, for your careful reading of my ARC!

Lastly, I again thank you, Phil, for helping me to succeed in a thousand little ways, of which perhaps only you are aware. I know you didn't sign on for the huge process this book-writing thing has become, but I want you to know, I feel it deeply. Thank you, with all my heart.

About the Author

Michelle Cox holds a B.A. in English literature from Mundelein College, Chicago, and is the author of the award-winning Henrietta and Inspector Howard series, as well as the weekly "Novel Notes of Local Lore," a blog dedicated to Chicago's forgotten residents.

Cox lives in the Chicago suburbs with her husband and three children and is currently hard at work on Book 4 of the series. In her vast free time, she also sits on the Board of the prestigious Society of Midland Authors and is a reviewer for the New York Journal of Books.

SELECTED TITLES FROM SHE WRITES PRESS

She Writes Press is an independent publishing company
founded to serve women writers everywhere.
Visit us at www.shewritespress.com.

A Girl Like You by Michelle Cox
$16.95, 978-1-63152-016-7
When the floor matron at the dance hall where Henrietta works as a
taxi dancer turns up dead, aloof Inspector Clive Howard appears on the
scene—and convinces Henrietta to go undercover for him, plunging her
into Chicago's gritty underworld.

A Ring of Truth by Michelle Cox
$16.95, 978-1-63152-196-6
The next exciting installment of the Henrietta and Inspector Clive series,
in which Clive reveals that he is actually the heir of the Howard estate
and fortune, Henrietta discovers she may not be who she thought she
was—and both must decide if they are really meant for each other.

The Great Bravura by Jill Dearman
$16.95, 978-1-63152-989-4
Who killed Susie—or did she actually disappear? The Great Bravura, a
dashing lesbian magician living in a fantastical and noirish 1947 New
York City, must solve this mystery—before she goes to the electric chair.

After Midnight by Diane Shute-Sepahpour
$16.95, 978-1-63152-913-9
When horse breeder Alix is forced to temporarily swap places with her
estranged twin sister—the wife of an English lord—her forgotten past
begins to resurface.

In the Shadow of Lies: A Mystery Novel by M. A. Adler
$16.95, 978-1-938314-82-7
As World War II comes to a close, homicide detective Oliver Wright
returns home—only to find himself caught up in the investigation of a
complicated murder case rife with racial tensions.

Just the Facts by Ellen Sherman
$16.95, 978-1-63152-993-1
The seventies come alive in this poignant and humorous story of a fearful rookie reporter at a small-town newspaper who uncovers a big-time
scandal.